Praise for the works of Terry Wolverton

Season of Eclipse

With more twists and turns than a coiled snake, *Season of Eclipse* is also a deep examination of who we are and what happens to us when we can't be the person we thought we were. Both make this thriller hard to put down.

-J.M. Redmann, the Micky Knight mystery series

Plucked out of her own life and plunged into witness-protection-program obscurity, Marielle Wing has the guts to activate her ire and her creative imagination to try to win back her name, all while discovering some rough truths about the life she left behind. She does this with the aid of one of the most deliciously irksome young women ever to appear on the page: Tuna, who might bring Marielle to new life if she doesn't kill her first. Terry Wolverton's *Season of Eclipse* is a fun and subversively serious novel about finding yourself while losing yourself, in spite of yourself.

-David Groff, author of *Live in Suspense*

Terry Wolverton's *Season of Eclipse* is a wild ride of a thriller, with a protagonist who's as lovable as she is flawed. Marielle Wing witnesses a bombing and then is forced to go into hiding, with several ensuing changes of location and identity. Who is a friend and who is a foe? We don't know until the exciting conclusion. Rooting for them all the way, we follow Marielle and her cat, Dude, through a maze of danger and conspiracy. Don't begin reading this book in the evening unless you plan to stay up all night!

-Alice Bloch, *Mother/Daughter Banquet*

A page-turning thriller from award-winning author Terry Wolverton. A terrorist event changes novelist Marielle's life and outlook forever as she finds wisdom and help in unexpected places.

-Katherine Rupley, author, *Antarctica*

Season of Eclipse is a thrill ride through the trust-no-one aftermath of a terrorist attack, and a meditation on the nature of self. Reading this novel is at once a shot of adrenaline and a deep, cleansing breath.

-Cheryl E. Klein, author, *Crybaby: Infertility, Illness, and Other Things That Were Not the End of the World*

Who is Marielle Wing, and how does she stay ahead of an enemy that knows her every move and mistake? And as fragile relationships hang in the balance and close alliances shift, Marielle must test the limits of what she's capable of to find the truth. This thrilling novel is one that you can't wait to find out what happens next, and yet, also want to read slowly and savor the delicious sentences. Will Marielle survive?

-Kathleen Brady, author, *Language of Light*

Marielle Wing's journey reminds us that in a world where the worst of humanity is perpetually on display, the best is just as possible. A single act of violence can send your life spinning out of control. Strangers may take you in and bind your wounds, help make you whole again.

-Bronwyn Mauldin, author, *Love Songs of the Revolution*

Imagine everything about who you are is erased overnight? Your name, home, career, friends, family – poof! Gone! This is exactly what happens to novelist and protagonist Marielle Wing after she witnesses a bombing at JFK airport and snaps a photo of one of the fleeing suspects. In short order, she is whisked by Homeland Security into Witness Protection against her will. Her obituary in the New York Times seals her fate. A suspenseful, moody, sharply layered story, Wolverton's thrilling *Season of Eclipse* is also a meditation on identity and breathtaking transformation

-Elise D'Haene, author, *Licking Our Wounds*

Stealing Angel

Stealing Angel reads like a book of prayer, putting the reader in touch with struggles and questions each may have had in their own lives. The basic message that letting go is the key to inner peace permeates the story—and through this fascinating story, personal lessons may be learned. There are no lulls in the excitement either. Page after page is filled with movement.

-Anna Furtado, *Just About Write*

Stealing Angel is a very different novel. Maggie Seaver is estranged from her lover, Yoli, a singer whose career is just beginning to take off. When Maggie discovers that their daughter, Angel, is being abused by her caretaker, she sees no option other than taking Angel and leaving the country. What follows is the story of their hasty flight down the coast of Baja California. ...She's given her readers a memorable and thought-provoking read.

-R Lynne, *Just About Write*

The Labrys Reunion

There's a murder at the heart of this novel about the fundamental necessity of fierce feminist art, but the story is no whodunit. In the guise of entertainment—and this is an evocative read—Wolverton digs into the confounding question of how feminist ideals that fueled both art and life in years past might yet hold sway as creative women move into their middle and elder years...There's a whiff of nostalgia to Wolverton's story, but its emotional assessment of an era and its hope that feminist art still matters are inspirational.

-Syndicated , Book Marks by Richard LaBonte

These are the perfect tiny snapshots and vignettes that make this book worthwhile and wonderful… As always, the women argue all through the novel, validating and not-validating each other. As feminists always have. Don't miss this one, particularly all you feminists over 40. Certainly, one of these carefully-and-lovingly-drawn heroines is you.

-Daisy's Dead Air

SEASON of ECLIPSE

TERRY WOLVERTON

Other books by Terry Wolverton

Spinsters Ink
Stealing Angel
Labrys Reunion

SEASON of ECLIPSE

TERRY WOLVERTON

2024

Bella Books, Inc.
P.O. Box 10543
Tallahassee, FL 32302

Printed in the United States of America on acid-free paper.

First Edition - 2024

Editor: Katherine V. Forrest
Cover Designer: Melodie Pond
Author Photo Credit: Mary-Linn Hughes

ISBN: 978-1-64247-514-2

PUBLISHER'S NOTE

Acknowledgments

My heartfelt gratitude goes to:

My spouse, Yvonne M. Estrada, who remained enthusiastic over the reading of multiple drafts;

Gary Phillips, who provided generous and astute feedback about how to make the book more thrilling;

Katherine V. Forrest, not just an editor par excellence but also a champion of this book when I most needed it;

David Groff, who provided munificent and invaluable support;

Members of my workshops at Writers At Work, who read various chapters and offered important feedback;

Mary-Linn Hughes, my cherished art buddy;

Michele Karlsberg for helping me to let the world know about this book; and

Bella Books for giving it a home.

CHAPTER ONE

The security line in the American Airlines terminal at JFK snaked around several times. The airport was crowded with people taking advantage of the three-day weekend—President's Day, whatever that meant. Most people could no longer tell you *which* presidents the day was intended to honor. Marielle had gotten to the airport in plenty of time, but she hated waiting in any circumstance, and it was making her cranky.

But everything was irritating her today: In the cab on her way to the airport she'd taken a call from her attorney, Reza; the option on her last novel, *The Time Before the Last Time*, had lapsed and the film company was not going to renew. The PEN America event that had brought her from temperate Los Angeles to New York in the dead of winter had been a listless affair, even though she'd been the keynote speaker; all anyone in her industry could talk about was the death of publishing. Even as she'd gamely delivered her prepared address about "the freedom of speech," she couldn't help but wonder, what good was speech if no one was listening anymore? Then, at the dinner, she'd been stuck sitting next to the man who won the Pulitzer for fiction last year, *her* Pulitzer—the first time she'd been nominated, and she deserved to win. But she hadn't won, and the dance of appearing to be gracious while the winner appeared to be humble had sparked her umbrage anew.

New York in February had never been her idea of a good time, and she was fuming about the frigid, slippery streets and the overheated rooms and the bristly competitiveness that charged the atmosphere whenever writers gathered. Her temples pounded with a hangover from the previous night; the other thing guaranteed when writers convene was that there would be a lot of drinking.

And she was grumpy too about having succumbed to the charms of a young journalist she'd met in the elevator of her hotel. Araceli? She thought that was it. She'd been flattered to receive the attention of a woman two decades younger than she was. Several mojitos at the reception following her speech had helped convince her that the young woman's declaration that Mariel was her "role model" was not a red flag. Or maybe she *had* known but didn't care; she'd been lonely for a long time.

She'd been too intoxicated to remember much about the sex itself. And afterward, all the young woman really seemed to want from her was to agree to blurb her first novel, coming out next spring.

But worse than all these things, Marielle was currently stuck on chapter seven of the first draft of a new novel.

For Marielle Wing, the blank page was her enemy, its slick white face always taunting her to prove herself anew, a void sneering that no words would come, ever. That her true nature was emptiness.

Despite nine published novels, each garnering praise, or prizes or both, Marielle still found it punishing to eke out a first draft. She hated the not knowing, the clumsy stage of having to wander and flail, the struggle to bring a world into being.

She'd never had children. Though many lesbians did, she'd never wanted to; *this* barrenness she embraced, but she'd frequently likened the first draft process to labor—excruciating, protracted, and bloody. It was in subsequent drafts that she became a sculptor of language and ideas, an architect of plot, a weaver of character and theme.

She was trying to pinpoint the real problem of chapter seven at the same time she was checking messages on her iPhone. The security line seemed not to have moved the entire time she'd been standing there. She was only half paying attention when suddenly her body was shoved hard and propelled forward; there was a sound so loud she felt it on her skin, repeating again, again, again. The word "bomb" slowly crawled into her consciousness. Then, fire and smoke and screaming. Some people dropped to the ground; others scrambled.

Once she had a word for it, Marielle grew calm. She had always been someone who became unnaturally composed in a crisis. During the Northridge earthquake in '94, her then-partner, Liana, had become unhinged as the pitching of the house had jolted them awake at 4:17 a.m. Marielle had wrapped her body around Liana's wiry frame, rolled them off the bed and onto the floor, whispering, "It's okay, it's okay," until the shaking stopped. Now, even with her ears ringing from the blasts, even as chaos surrounded her, her senses were heightened, not dulled. She dropped into a crouch and began to scan the scene. Her writer's instinct took over.

That was how she happened to notice the two men who came running in her direction. Despite the pandemonium the two ran in the opposite direction of the panicked scrimmage to exit the terminal. They ran right past her and she observed details: the orange sweatshirt and gray athletic pants worn by one, the gold cross that flapped against his chest as he sprinted, the scar that had taken part of the other man's eyebrow, and the words he yelled at his companion: "Go to Magda," it sounded like, his accented voice cutting through the roar of sound that filled the terminal.

Marielle, without planning it, without even fully realizing what she was doing, lifted the iPhone still clutched in her hand and snapped a photo. It was reflexive, a habit; the phone was set on camera because she often took a picture when she saw something she might want to describe later in a piece of writing. The taller of the two men, the one in orange, saw her do it; for a second their eyes locked as he passed her. Then they were gone.

There was something else, too, a white man with short cropped gray hair and an impressive case of rosacea. Where had he come from? He wasn't freaking out like everyone else, but surveying the terminal, scanning in all directions. He wore a uniform—NYPD, she supposed, but maybe TSA—but wasn't running or yelling or giving directions. He was watching the scene; he was watching her watching. Without thinking any further about it, she snapped a photo of him too.

He sprinted over to her. Wrested the phone out of her hand.

"That's mine!" she protested, as she snatched at empty air.

"It's evidence now," she thought she heard him say. Her ears were ringing and the air was filled with shouts and crying, yet she heard his words. The glare of his blue eyes pierced her. Even his tone seemed to slice through her, so cold and sharp, maybe a hint of an accent—German? Russian? He was already moving away.

"But how will I get it back?" she called after him.

"We'll find you," the man called over his shoulder as he disappeared into the crowd.

By this time the authorities were starting to mobilize. They began a not very well orchestrated effort to secure and evacuate the terminal. Airport police and men and women in TSA uniforms attempted to herd highly agitated passengers out into the frosty dusk. NYPD officers arrived to provide reinforcement. Some in the crowd were argumentative, and ordinarily she might have been one of them, but Marielle numbly followed the officers' shouted commands.

Everyone was made to line up on the sidewalk outside the terminal. No one would be allowed into or out of the airport until a thorough search of Terminal 8 had taken place. Children cried from cold or hunger or boredom; every few minutes an adult launched into a squabble or tried to plead his case with one of the officers, or threaten a lawsuit against the City of New York, but to no avail. Whether their tickets were first class or coach, they'd all become refugees, without a destination, without shelter.

Marielle tried at first to make a study of her fellow exiles; work was always her panacea in any circumstance. She observed the woman in the cashmere coat who expressed outrage to anyone who would listen; the stocky African American man who kept muttering, "This is *bull*shit!" but after an hour the plummeting temperature overwhelmed her and she retreated into herself. The wait lasted over three hours, after which time the authorities determined there were no other bombs in the terminal and everyone might as well try to proceed to their destinations via other airlines.

At an agonizing pace, they were boarded onto shuttles and driven to other terminals. One by one, overworked ticket agents tried to find seats on other flights. The security processing took another two hours. At last she dragged her thoroughly chilled body to the gate and boarded an aircraft bound for Los Angeles.

Her flight home was nerve-wracking but uneventful; like her fellow passengers, her anxiety competed with sheer exhaustion to produce a jittery numbness that pervaded the cabin. She was certain a lot of alcohol got consumed on that westbound flight. She'd downed a number of small bottles of white rum herself, along with as much hot tea as she could persuade the attendants to bring her. She often used her time on airplanes to write—the anonymity of travel providing a comfortable ambience for creativity—but there was no possibility of that tonight.

Desperate to contain her agitation, Marielle quietly fretted about the loss of her phone and the inconvenience it would mean to her—the need to call the phone company, re-create her contact list, get a new phone and a new number and notify everyone. She conjectured that the officer must have seen her snap the young men's photo; if they'd had something to do with the bombing, it might well be evidence. She'd been stupid to take that picture; it was not like she was some citizen journalist.

Marielle was grateful to slip into her own bed that night, to curl up next to her cat, Dude, who was happy to have her home and showed it by licking her neck. Still, she couldn't fall asleep until she'd watched the CNN report on the incident, as though what she'd witnessed would be more real once reflected by the media. They'd gotten hold of some shadowy video shot on someone else's cell phone; that person must have been in another part of the terminal, because what the video showed was mostly smoke. They also broadcast the standard commentary from officials: "No one has yet claimed responsibility for the bombing. This incident is still under investigation and we are not releasing any information at this time," plus a few incoherent interviews with terrified passengers who huddled, shivering, outside the terminal. One couple was to have left that night on their honeymoon. There was a shot of a child's stuffed rabbit abandoned on the curb. The banality of these images could be made to substitute for the images stored in her memory; she could almost pretend it had happened to someone else. This allowed her to drift into a deep sleep, and if she dreamed that night, she did not remember when she woke.

The next morning the city of New York was placed on a heightened security alert; a car found abandoned in the airport parking lot contained suitcases with homemade bombs that were believed to be the same as those that were exploded in the terminal. Officials didn't know if that meant there were other intended targets. Those bags were being examined along with evidence gathered from the site.

Marielle was relieved to be back in L.A. She ran for an extra half hour on her treadmill to disperse the adrenaline from the night before, then took a long shower—water conservation be damned. She read the account of the bombing in *The Los Angeles Times*, drinking coffee in her garden and feeling smug as she often did at living in a city where the temperature can reach eighty degrees in February. She was shaken all over again to read about the loss of life—two ticket agents, a baggage handler, and at least one passenger, several others in critical condition. Still, with the trees full of songbirds, the danger felt comfortably far away.

Although Marielle Wing could always find something not to her liking, she also had faith she'd been born to live a charmed life. While she'd gone through her share of difficulties—the loss of her parents while she was still in college; the messy, expensive breakup with Liana—she took for granted she was endowed with a certain specialness that brought with it her success as a writer, her physical beauty, and a life of relative financial comfort. Although the events of the previous night had been harrowing, she felt a stir of satisfaction that she'd escaped back into her routine.

An unnamed source at Homeland Security, she read, *stated that they'd been following the activities of a group of young Muslim males in New Jersey who were believed to have traveled to Pakistan to receive training in a terrorist camp.* She put the paper down and stared at the wall that rimmed her yard; it was glowing with magenta bougainvillea.

She thought about the two men she'd seen running. They'd looked like boys; they wouldn't have seemed out of place on a basketball court or plugged into an MP3 player on the subway. Then she shook off the memory, refolded the newspaper, and turned her attention to the stack of mail that had accumulated during her absence. There was an invitation to a reading and book signing by a colleague who'd been nominated the same year she'd won the National Book Award—it would be ungracious not to go—and a letter from Squaw Valley asking her to be a visiting faculty at an upcoming fiction conference. She would decide about this later.

Marielle's renown as a writer had not come from being a lesbian. She had neither hidden her personal life nor embraced it as a cause, and addressing the mainstream in her work had been a conscious decision. Early on, an agent had told her, "If you want a wide audience of heterosexuals to read your work, you need to write about heterosexuals." She had taken that advice to heart. Her protagonists were strong, powerful women whose romantic attachments were with men.

Marielle propped her feet up on a patio chair and turned her face to the sun as she began to obsess once more about what to do with chapter seven of her newest novel, *Weeping Minerva*. She'd begun to worry that the action—involving a woman who attends the funerals of people she does not know—was proceeding a little too smoothly, dare she say predictably? She needed something to disrupt the narrative flow, catch the reader by surprise, amp up the stakes. She was mulling over the possibility of killing off someone close to her heroine when her cordless telephone—her landline—jangled beside her. She picked it up with a curt, "Yes?" There was nothing but static on the other end. "Hello?" she repeated, annoyed at the interruption, then hung up. A salesman? She was on the "Do Not Call" list, but people still called. She returned to considering which character she might be willing to lose. After a moment she opened her laptop and began to peck at her keyboard, listless and uncertain at first, but then with increasing momentum as the scene appeared before her.

About thirty minutes later, her doorbell rang. Ordinarily, she would ignore this while in the midst of writing but she had the strangest intuition that whoever was at her door was somehow connected to the phone call. Contemplating this, instead of simply stepping through the garden gate, she took the long way through the house, through the study, the dining room, then the living room. By the time she opened the front door, no one was there. Except for a gardening crew a few houses down, there was no one to be seen up and down the street. She couldn't recall hearing a car, but her home's thick stucco walls did filter out a lot of noise, one of the many things she loved about the house. Still, it seemed strange to find no sign of whoever had rung the bell; this was scarcely the kind of neighborhood where kids would play a prank like that. But she was also relieved not to have to interact with anyone. Might she have just imagined she heard the bell? Marielle shrugged, prepared to return to her reverie in the garden.

It was only by happenstance that she looked down and was startled to see her iPhone lying face down on the welcome mat. For a moment, she felt disoriented—had it dropped from her purse when she'd come in last night? Of course it hadn't. It had been confiscated by an officer after a terrorist bombing in Terminal 8.

"We'll find you," she remembered him saying, and she guessed it was possible with technology these days, though she hadn't expected it to happen so quickly. New York was three hours ahead, but someone must have gotten on a pretty early flight to have it on her doorstep by noon. Why would they go to all the trouble?

Still, she felt relieved as she stooped to pick it up—she would now be spared the inconvenience of replacing it. How familiar its curved shape felt in her hand. Its reappearance somehow neutralized the trauma of the night before, her sense of order restored. She was about to turn it on—not because there was anyone she needed to call, perhaps just wanting to assure herself it still worked—when a black sedan sped up the narrow street and careened into her driveway. A slender African American man in a charcoal suit dashed from the passenger door and yelled, "Marielle Wing, don't touch that!"

She ignored him. Since adolescence, she'd bristled at any direction given to her by a man and often acted contrarily just for spite. This tendency had been nearly disastrous with traffic cops and was one reason she always worked with women editors. *And* chose relationships with women. Her finger hovered above the Sleep/Wake button, ready to do just what she'd been ordered not to do.

That was the moment he tackled her, pushing her body into the hedge and throwing the iPhone with as much force as he could. It exploded in the middle of the street with an astonishing burst of flame and a powerful boom that set off a chorus of car alarms. The gardeners up the street dove for cover.

The man leaped to his feet as soon as the explosion stopped; he quickly dialed a number into his phone and repeated her address. She slid from the hedge down onto the flagstone and remained slumped there, ears ringing and limbs shaking. The cacophony of car alarms seared every nerve. She had experienced her second bombing in less than twenty-four hours, and even though she'd been unharmed in both, her skin felt brittle and porous, useless to protect her now.

When at last she could concentrate, she focused her attention on the man who'd arrived just in time to keep her from blowing herself to smithereens. He was a better dresser than she would have predicted had she been inventing his character—his canary-yellow silk tie was actually sharp—but he had dark, expressionless eyes and a nervous energy that he seemed to be devoting considerable effort to containing. He appeared quite tall until she realized she was sprawled on the pavement looking up at him.

"Ms. Wing?" He extended a hand and attempted to pull her to her feet. Her knees were reluctant, though; they buckled, threatening to send him toppling, and she had to settle for sitting on the step that led to her front door. Maybe half the car alarms had ceased of their own accord; the rest might continue until the owners of the vehicles returned.

The man with the yellow tie was saying something to her, but she couldn't hear. She stared intently at his lips and eventually understood that he was introducing himself as, "Donald Watkins, Homeland Security." She gestured wildly with her fingertips to her ears. He nodded and moved so close that she could feel his breath in her ear. "I'm afraid I'm going to have to ask you to come with me."

She pulled back to look at him quizzically and saw that his face was unsmiling, as if she had done something wrong.

Just then, the bomb squad van arrived, siren wailing and further abrading her nervous system. Two squad cars raced up and parked at either end of her street, closing it off, while a truck sped toward the middle of the block, stopping directly in front of the smoking char that had been her iPhone. One team turned its attention to examining the remains of the detonation, no doubt to gather clues about the method of bomb-making and perhaps, by extension, the bomber. Another team pushed past her and entered the front door.

"What are they doing?" she yelled.

"They have to search the premises," he responded.

"They can't," she protested. "Do you have a warrant?"

"Don't need one. It's a matter of national security." He repeated, "You're going to have to come with me."

Despite the sound that still shattered her ability to think, she insisted on verifying his credentials, more to assert her right to do so than because she disbelieved him. He patiently produced government identification.

"I need my purse. And my shoes." She did need these things, but also she was stalling. She didn't want to leave her house unguarded against these officers. She didn't want to leave Dude.

Uninvited, Donald Watkins followed her inside the house, which the police were ransacking like a marauding army. Then she understood she did have to leave; if she stayed and watched, she'd be unable to keep from getting in one of these guys' faces and would probably end up in handcuffs or worse.

The Homeland Security agent tried to hurry her, but she insisted, "I have to get my purse." She darted into the next room before he could protest and made her way out to the garden, where she retrieved her laptop. As it happened she'd been using her huge purse—big enough to fit a laptop—in New York, so all she had to do was slip the computer inside and she was ready to go.

She wanted to take the time to locate Dude, but she imagined that after the explosion, he'd been hiding in the laundry basket in her bedroom closet, the place to which he always retreated when he was disturbed. She decided to leave him in peace, although she circled through the kitchen to make sure he had crunchies in his dish.

Returning to the living room where Donald Watkins was pacing, she announced with far more composure than she actually felt, "I want my attorney to be with me during the interview."

"You don't need an attorney. You're not a suspect here," Watkins countered.

The reflexive habit of a lifetime of defying male authority gave her the courage to say, "Nevertheless, I'm calling her. Where should I tell her to meet us?"

* * *

One might not suppose that a lawyer specializing in intellectual property would be of much help in such a circumstance. But Reza Caldicott was not only a negotiator of contracts and deals, she was also an expert on the First Amendment and served on the Board of the ACLU. From the moment she arrived at the squat, frigid building in a remote area south of LAX, Reza was like a bulldog with Donald Watkins.

"Are you charging my client with something? If you're not charging her, you can't hold her. I insist on time alone to confer with my client." What Reza lacked in height—barely five feet in heels—she more than made up for in belligerence. It was part of the image she carefully cultivated that she always dressed in a tailored suit of bright confrontational red.

Donald Watkins coolly informed her that her client was not a suspect, but a witness in a terrorism case and, under new laws enacted since 9/11, she was not even entitled to counsel, but he was allowing Reza to sit in on the proceedings as a courtesy; "One," he added, "that could be revoked at any time."

Reza was unfazed. "Courtesy, my ass," she bellowed. "You know that Ms. Wing has a public profile. You're just hoping to avoid a stink in the press."

Marielle suppressed a grimace. For all the recognition a writer might gain, in this country no man or woman of letters would ever attain the status of a rock star or a sports legend. They could lock her up and throw away the key and no one prominent, outside of a few PEN members, would even notice.

Donald Watkins must have known this too. He made no more effort to rebut Reza's protests, but went right to his point. "Yesterday afternoon there was a bombing at the American Airlines ticket counter at Kennedy Airport. Four people were killed; several other passengers were injured, including some children. We have reason to suspect that this is the work of a terrorist sleeper cell based in Hoboken."

He continued, "We have surveillance video that shows two suspects fleeing the scene. The same video shows Ms. Wing positioned directly in the path of their escape with a clear, direct view of their faces. We need to take your statement, Ms. Wing, work with our specialist on facial recognition, and it is likely we will need you to testify against them once these suspects are apprehended."

"She couldn't have seen anything," Reza broke in. "The noise, the smoke, the confusion. She was on her belly, trying to protect herself." Clearly the attorney was adlibbing.

"Is that what the video will show?" Donald Watkins asked, waving a hand in the direction of his computer monitor.

"Not exactly," Marielle admitted. She was preoccupied with the chilled temperature of the room. It was February, after all; how much air-conditioning did anyone need? What she really wanted in that moment was a drink, something to settle her nerves. In the aftermath of this second bombing, it was hard for her to give her full attention.

"Why are you so sure that video shows Ms. Wing?" Reza gamely tried again.

"When we saw on the security tapes that an unidentified suspect had confiscated the cell phone of a witness, had come into direct contact with her, we put considerable effort into finding her before they did." His look appraised Marielle. "Your 'public profile' did help us to identify you."

"What do you mean, 'an unidentified suspect'?" Marielle was trying to follow the conversation, but it wasn't making any sense. "He was dressed in a uniform. He said it was 'evidence.'" *He said, we'll find you*, she did not add.

"We've been going over the video from the scene since it happened. The man we saw take your phone could not be identified as any of the officers on-scene. We have to conclude that he had a role in the incident."

Nausea swept through Marielle. It took all her will to keep the bile from spewing onto the tidy wooden desk before her.

"You were almost too late," Reza argued.

"They had the phone. They knew who and where Marielle was a whole lot sooner than we did." Donald's tone was not apologetic.

"Surely you have other witnesses," Reza began again. "The terminal was full of people."

"Obviously I can't disclose any other details of our case," responded Donald Watkins, "but I will say that on this video Ms. Wing demonstrates a remarkable presence of mind and a singular focus. We believe she has critical details to offer us and that she will make a convincing witness at trial."

"At trial!" The color in Reza's cheeks flared to match her scarlet suit. "My client is certainly not going to testify at trial. These people have already tried to blow her up this morning. You can't put her in that kind of danger."

Donald Watkins didn't miss a beat. "That's why we're prepared to enter your client into the Witness Security Program this afternoon."

"Enter *what? When?*" Marielle had been watching the conversation like a tennis match as if it didn't involve her, but this proposal startled her into speech. Her fingers were so cold she was sitting on her hands to try to warm them.

"That's outrageous," Reza protested, "Marielle Wing is a much-honored author with a public career. She can't just change her identity and go into hiding."

"She doesn't have a choice," Donald Watkins said curtly, cutting to the chase. "This is a terrorism investigation; we are going to find and convict the perpetrators. The government can and will compel her testimony. If she refuses to cooperate, she will be sent to prison." He paused before adding, "We can't guarantee her safety there."

Prison? Had she done something wrong? This episode was devolving from surreal into nightmare. Surely at any moment she would awaken. Without registering it, she'd begun to shiver.

"We will take Ms. Wing's complete statement. Then we are prepared to put her on a plane to another state this afternoon and begin the process of obtaining a new identity for her." Why was he talking about her as if she weren't sitting there? In a few weeks, he continued, they would discreetly pack up the contents of her home and have it delivered to her new location. Over time they would transfer her assets to an account in her new name and provide an income for her until she found the means of supporting herself.

Until that time, they would post round-the-clock security at the house in case the suspects or their cohorts were inclined to return. "Once we have apprehended our suspects, including others who may have been involved in the planning, execution, and funding of these acts, Ms. Wing will be called to testify before a grand jury to obtain our indictments. When the suspects' cases go to trial, she will be called to testify again."

"But once that's over," Marielle reasoned, "I can resume my life." It could be an adventure, like being undercover for a time. It could provide a tremendous boost to the sales of her books once it all was revealed. She could even write a nonfiction account of the experience. She would be on talk shows, maybe Stephen Colbert.

Reza looked at her with pity, shaking her head. Marielle didn't understand.

"There is no 'after,'" Donald Watkins explained, finally focusing directly on her. "You will never be able to live as Marielle Wing again."

"What about my career? Will I have to start publishing under some new name?" It could be a chance to break out of what she was known for, she thought desperately, try something new.

"It's too risky." Donald Watkins shook his head. "You no doubt have a recognizable style, perhaps certain kinds of themes or content you deal with. These terrorists will be looking for you. They will want to keep you from testifying and after your testimony they will want to make an example of you. They will want revenge. They will declare a fatwa on you."

Marielle had lived her life believing the normal rules did not apply to her. She decided, *He's just saying that because he doesn't know how long the trial will take. He can't stop me from living my life.*

"So how much time do I have to prepare?" Marielle asked. "I need to let my editor know because I've got a manuscript due in April..."

This time Reza placed her hand on top of Marielle's to still her words, a gesture so uncharacteristically tender that she did in fact stop talking.

"You have no time," Donald Watkins replied. "They had your phone; they know your name; they found your address in less than twenty-four hours. They also know the names of every single person whose number you stored in your phone. Whoever you tell, whoever you see from this point on, you put at tremendous risk. Do you think these people would hesitate to abduct anyone you care about as a way to get to you?"

He continued, "And you jeopardize yourself as well. Which of your friends do you really think would endure torture to protect you?" he asked rhetorically. "This has to be seamless, leakproof. Even your attorney is here against my better judgment."

"Have I gotten you in trouble?" Marielle turned to Reza.

"I deal with risk all the time." Reza dismissed this breezily, although intellectual property was rarely life-threatening.

Donald Watkins appeared to be about to deliver his opinion, but Reza intercepted him with a warning glance.

"What about my clothes? My books? What about my cat?" Marielle could hear that her voice was losing its cool detachment. Was it possible that she was really being asked to slither out of her identity like a used-up skin?

"If Marielle were married or had children or living parents, you would have to go to the trouble and expense to relocate them as well. Let me at least go and pick up her cat," Reza insisted.

Perhaps Marielle had never felt her solitary state—so necessary for a writer, she'd always rationalized—as acutely as she felt it now. No spouse, no children, no living family. Not even a steady girlfriend. She would go into exile with no one but her cat.

In truth, she and Dude, her large, orange, neutered tomcat, were not all that close. He'd been named by Liana. After their breakup, Marielle had wanted to rename him, but the cat was undeniably Dude.

He liked to stretch his body against her hip when she was lying in bed, he would jump up onto her lap sometimes when she was at the computer, but he was just as willing to sink his teeth into her in response to some unfathomable displeasure. Still, the idea of never seeing him again—perhaps the only concrete notion she was able to hold onto as her entire life was sinking into oblivion—brought Marielle to near hysteria.

"You're taking a terrible chance," Donald Watkins objected. "You could be seen; you could be followed…"

"I could be struck by lightning," Reza interrupted. "The Rapture could descend. For chrissakes, let her have her cat."

Marielle believed the only reason Watkins relented with a single reluctant nod was that he was ready to conclude this phase of the process. By saying yes he could be rid of Reza and get on with interrogating—he would call it "interviewing"—her.

Before the attorney left the office, she took both of Marielle's hands in hers and squeezed them.

"When will I see you again?" Marielle asked, gazing at her.

Reza shook her head. "I don't know. I'm sorry," she said, "I'll do everything I can, but our options are limited here." She left in a swish of red.

Later in the afternoon, after being asked the same questions in a dozen different ways by Donald Watkins and two other men with the same gray aura, just as Marielle had been loaded into the back seat of a car with tinted windows and bulletproof sides, a small man in a tan suit thrust into her hands a cat-carrying case and a large tote bag. Dude greeted her with yowling complaint; he'd never liked being in a car.

In addition to hardbound copies of all nine of her published novels, Reza had packed the bag with a few foil pouches of cat food, some water and a small dish, and a bottle of cat tranquilizers. Marielle was briefly tempted to swallow these herself. It was only later that she would find, folded up inside the pill bottle, Reza's card with a scrawled message: "This is a secure phone. Call me at this number when you are alone." Reading this, Marielle felt relief wash over the numbness into which she'd lapsed.

Late that night Marielle's private plane landed at a small military airport in what she would later learn was southeastern Michigan. She knew she was no longer in California as she gazed across the gray tarmac, a landscape made almost lunar by the cold gleam of halogen lights, rimmed by clumps of frozen snow, dirty with smog and car exhaust. The temperature was south of freezing; it seemed she had been cold for as long as she could remember. One of the men in charge of guarding her handed her his overcoat.

A car drove her to a rundown Sheraton, where she and Dude were installed in a charmless room at the end of the hall on the fourth floor. She was introduced to Deputy Eric Orellano, a burly Latino who was staying in the room next door. This was ostensibly for Marielle's protection, but also, she knew, to keep an eye on her.

That first day, there was no need; she ordered a bottle of white rum from room service, slept most of the day, and spent the rest of it in a kind of stupor. Dude, coming off the tranquilizers, was equally subdued. When the deputy knocked to ask if he could bring her any food from the coffee shop downstairs, she'd waved him away.

The second day she awakened early and famished; she called room service for a big breakfast and called the front desk for *The New York Times*. They claimed not to have it but she told them there'd be a big tip if they produced it within the hour. It showed up at the same time as her coffee and eggs, and she proffered a twenty-dollar bill as promised.

Without bothering to look at the front page, she turned directly to the Arts and Leisure page and could not believe her eyes.

BOOKS
Marielle Wing, 51, National Book Award Winner and Celebrated Novelist, Found Dead

She leaped from her seat, burst into the hallway and started pounding her fist against the deputy's door. He looked disheveled when he opened it; clearly she'd woken him up.

"What have you done?" She shoved the headline in his face.

"Calm down, ma'am." Deputy Orellano clearly had no idea what she was talking about.

"Let me talk to Donald Watkins."

"Who?"

"Don't pull this shit with me! I am not in the mood," she bellowed, so angry her vision was red. "Watkins, the Homeland Security agent who's responsible for me being here."

"Ma'am, please keep your voice down."

"If you don't get Watkins on the phone to me right now, I'll wake this whole goddamn building."

"Go back to your room, ma'am. I'll have someone call you as soon as I can."

"Don't fucking call me ma'am," she raged, and slammed the door to her room behind her. A few minutes later, the phone in her room rang. Without waiting for the caller to identify himself, she answered, "When were you going to tell me, you bastard?"

"I didn't know you were such an early riser. I was planning to talk to you this morning."

She was staring out the window at a bleak suburban landscape. Snow flurries had been falling since she'd awakened, but seemed to melt on the gray cement below. "You have no right to kill me. I've been cooperative. I haven't done anything wrong. You can't just decide I'm dead and notify me later."

"It's for your protection," he insisted. "I don't want them looking for you."

"If I'd known this was what you had in mind I would have taken my chances in jail." Then she hung up.

She went back to bed that day, even though Dude paced the room, howling. She wasn't asleep and she wasn't awake. She was dead. When Deputy Orellano knocked in the late afternoon and said he had her paperwork, she told him to just slip it under the door.

In a manila envelope was a birth certificate. Lorraine Kaminsky, born May 1, the same year as Marielle. *They could have shaved off a few years*, she thought. And did they have to make her a Taurus? Lorraine had been born to Herbert and Loretta Kaminsky in Highland Park, Michigan.

She took the paper in her hands and held it up to the light; it looked just like the real thing. Just a sheet of parchment; she could rip it in half, yet it had the power to take away everything she'd ever been and done.

CHAPTER TWO

In the middle of the night she got up and opened her laptop. The computer screen before her gleamed white and blank as the moon. The unlit room devoured its light. Dude crawled into her lap, placed his head under her left armpit.

Stiffly, her fingers recalled the once-familiar motion of keystrokes and she began typing the words: **My name is Lorraine Kaminsky**.

As soon as she read what the letters spelled out, she slammed shut the lid of the laptop, plunging the room into darkness and sending Dude to the floor. *Everything is a lie*.

She had once found it so gratifying to spin a fiction. Those were the days when she could get up from her desk, turn off the make-believe world she was architecting inside the computer, and return to what she'd rather cavalierly referred to as "real life."

But now she lived inside a make-believe world, and those computer realms were declared off-limits, and real life and the woman who once took it for granted were officially deceased.

Each lie fell like a stone on her chest. They piled up until one day she would be buried, sternum crushed, her crypt constructed by falsehoods. Would they even use her real name on her grave marker? They would not.

Don't feel sorry for yourself. That's what Deputy Orellano of the U.S. Marshals had advised when he'd checked on her earlier in the evening. *At least you're alive.* His eyes were chocolate pools of sincerity as he mouthed the words. She'd snarled back that no, she was dead; it was in all the papers.

She wasn't supposed to be *dead*, only vanished. Living under an assumed name until such time as she could resurface, draped in a mantle of intrigue and heroism, the subject of talk show interviews and magazine cover stories. Perhaps they'd even want to make a movie of her life.

She wished they'd used a better picture in the obituary. The one from her last novel—the one that had won the National Book Award and been a finalist for the Pulitzer—was so much more flattering. But of course she'd had no choice about it. At least *The New York Times* got Edison Guy to write it; he covered all the important deaths. She wondered why it wasn't more comforting, having her death considered important.

But she'd never agreed to be dead, although even as she thought this, she recognized the irony—how many of the dead had agreed to it? And it wasn't even a glamorous death, "dead of an aneurysm"—didn't that happen to old people? She would have written it in a more thrilling way; why couldn't they have said she'd died in the explosion, since she actually might have? And come to think of it, had there been any news coverage of that explosion in front of her house? No, Donald would have made that go away.

Death was utterly final. She knew she'd be assuming another identity, but she'd firmly believed, no matter what Donald Watkins said, this would be a temporary matter. They'd talked briefly, that afternoon in Los Angeles—was it just two days ago—about whom she might become. Marielle had imagined a character both flamboyant and heroic—a woman hiding from terrorists yet continuing to do important work. Like Odette

Fournier, a young Frenchwoman working for the Resistance during the Nazi occupation in her novel *The Flat Earth*. *The Los Angeles Times* reviewer had written, "Although the reader expects the terrain to be familiar—another WWII book, we think—we are unprepared for the quirkiness and sheer audacity of its diction and of its heroine…This book has as much to say about our own time as about the period in which it is set."

No, she'd been told. You must invent yourself as someone who will never be noticed. You must keep under the radar. You must not stand out.

But she had always been exceptional, from the time she was a tiny girl, her head wreathed in a cloud of blond curls, always knowing the answer to any question. From the honors she'd gotten in school to the National Book Award, she did not know how not to stand out.

So she'd asked if she might adopt the name of one of her characters, even a minor character like Trixie Grenoble from *The Disappearing Moon*. Just a wink in the direction of who she had been, what she had done. Something the biographers might catch, decades in the future. No, she was told again. It was too risky. You cannot leave any clues that will help the people who are after you to find you.

No one, they'd all told her—Donald Watkins and Eric Orellano and the handful of others who had knowledge of what really had become of her—*no one who has followed the security rules of the program has gotten killed*. Those who hadn't followed those rules—some of them died hideous deaths.

"We used to think the Mafia was brutal," Donald Watkins had told her gravely as she'd sat in his high-security office with the shades drawn. The whole building seemed to emit a low, ominous hum. "Some of these terrorist groups," he'd said, "will dismember your body part by part without bothering to kill you first and post a video of the process on the Internet."

Really? she'd been tempted to ask; *they really do that in Hoboken?*

And while such threats did give one pause, she'd also wanted to respond: but what does it mean to be *alive*? Surely it's more than a continuation of biological processes? And what is the value of being alive if one cannot pursue one's work, enjoy one's friends, reap the benefits of a life carefully constructed over decades?

So, Lorraine Kaminsky, whoever she might be, was alive, but her life (and therefore her death, whenever that might occur) was not important. She suspected Donald Watkins had enjoyed the abrupt extermination of her public life, her artistic career, the taking down of a powerful woman. At any rate, he had not seemed sorry.

Lorraine Kaminsky was alive, but Marielle had taken over her skin. In California, certain metaphysical types believed in spirits known as "walk-ins," that take over the body of another. The question was—had *she* taken over Lorraine's body or had Lorraine taken over *hers*? Which was the original, and which the fake?

Lorraine Kaminsky was a character she would invent, just as she had conjured hundreds of characters in her life as a writer. It had always been hard for her to write quiet characters, to sustain reader interest in them. But after critiques of her early work, she'd learned to apply a more subtle hand. This character might prove the greatest challenge yet to her powers of invention.

The difference was she had to actually live this character's life. Her quiet, unremarkable life. And utterly relinquish her own.

* * *

By the third day of exile from her former life, she had a new plan. How much more dramatic will it be, she told herself, when Marielle Wing *comes back* from the dead? She watched the scene unfold in the same way she'd visualize scenes from her novels: she walks into her agent's office; no, better her publisher's; better still, she walks into the dinner where the Pulitzer Prizes are being announced. She looks magnificent, everyone is stunned, they missed her so much, and then she holds them enthralled as she tells them her harrowing tale. No, she revised. Better to show up on *Good Morning America* or *Today*; people are more likely to believe what they see on TV.

She revised this scene in her mind—changing what she would wear, what she would say, who would be in the room, how they would look at her—over and over for the two weeks she stayed at the Sheraton. Without transportation in the suburbs of Detroit in late February, her only entertainment was to trudge across the eight-lane highway to the mammoth shopping mall and its adjacent multiplex. Deputy Orellano was reluctant to let her leave her room at the hotel, but she'd insisted, "Even prisoners get to exercise." Besides, she needed a wardrobe appropriate to the weather.

They argued back and forth about the risk of her being recognized until she dispatched him to the local drugstore for scissors and a bottle of L'Oréal. Only when the natural blond, of which she'd always been so proud—scarcely a trace of gray—was chestnut brown, and her signature tresses were clipped to a soccer-mom bowl shape around her head would he agree to release her from confinement. He added a pair of wire-rimmed aviator glasses, *sans* prescription, that might have been fashionable in the 1970s. Staring at her image under the cold light of the Sheraton bathroom, she could not escape the conclusion that she now looked like a lesbian, the kind of lesbian she had been so determined to never identify with. But so many of the women she observed in this suburb of Detroit looked just like this. Surely, they couldn't *all* be lesbians?

And was Lorraine Kaminsky a lesbian? Who did she yearn for? What did she like to do in bed? Since she couldn't imagine having *any* kind of close-up interaction with *anyone* in the future, she didn't know how to answer these questions.

"Eventually"—Deputy Orellano's voice pulled her back to the present moment—"the government will likely have you undergo plastic surgery." But because her identity would be changed again after the trial, they weren't going to put her through the procedure at this time. Marielle had always imagined she'd have a little work done at some point, her eyes, certainly, but she was alarmed at the idea of becoming unrecognizable to herself. She'd try to figure out a way to dissuade them.

The deputy also warned she could not use her credit cards or ATM; although they had been cancelled, there mustn't be even an attempt that could be traced back to her.

"Then get me some goddamned cash," she snapped.

Within the hour she was wandering through Twelve Oaks Mall—in Michigan they seemed to like to put the names of trees in their malls, no doubt to commemorate those that were cut down to make room for the sprawl of Detroit's burgeoning suburbs. The mall became her refuge from the beige walls of the Sheraton.

Day after day, she studied what passed for fashion in this part of the world and tried to discern the styles Lorraine Kaminsky would wear. She had a manicure one day, a pedicure the next. She browsed the mediocre selections in the chain bookstore—only one of her titles—and saw every movie at the eight-plex across the street, sometimes two or three a day. Deputy Orellano was always in tow; though he kept a respectful distance, he never let her out of his sight.

She tried to persuade herself to use the time as an unplanned writing retreat, to use this opportunity to finish *Weeping Minerva*. But the bleak fact that it couldn't be published, that she wouldn't be able to read the reviews or give interviews or check in on the sales figures sapped her motivation. She never would have believed she could become disinterested in her own work, but when she opened the computer she found herself staring into space, her mind empty and fitful. She'd type a line and delete it, retype it and delete it again.

The news reports about the bombing investigation seemed designed to conceal more than reveal. They now knew the airport bombs had been detonated by a cell phone signal; they believed that the plot had called for even more bombs, but something must have gone awry. The same facts were regurgitated in only slightly different language, the president offered the same condolences to the victims and expressed the same resolve to bring the perpetrators to justice. The same experts were quoted or referenced. The spokespeople knew only what their superiors—people who would remain unknown and unseen by the public—wanted them to know.

She'd seen a brief story a day earlier on the local news stating that some suspects in the JFK bombing had been apprehended. She wondered whether this included one or both of the men she'd spotted fleeing the terminal, or the "officer" who'd confiscated her iPhone. In a terrorism case, at least since 9/11, few details were ever released to the public and only those items deemed to have propaganda value ever found their way into circulation.

Dude was every bit as unhappy and claustrophobic as she. He was accustomed to roaming the quarter acre of her yard in the Hollywood Hills and was not happy about relieving himself in a litter box in the bathtub of the Sheraton. He clawed the polyester bedspread and several times a day would launch into a long and vigorous complaint about the terms of his confinement. "Tell me about it," she'd say in response.

Still she was glad to have him. In Los Angeles, being unmarried and childless was not an exceptional thing; between the hours she spent writing and the socializing required to effectively market her work, she had no time to be lonely. Now, without those outlets to occupy her mind, she felt pathetic. Even hardened criminals, she imagined, had someone to bring into witness protection with them; she'd read about one Mafia boss who'd brought both his wife *and* his mistress into the program.

On the thirteenth day Deputy Orellano knocked at her door in the early morning. "Miss Kaminsky?" No matter how many times she told him, he could not call her "Ms." "I just got word that you'll be flying to New York first thing tomorrow morning. You're gonna testify for the grand jury."

"About goddamn time!" she said, desperate for diversion, but she had no idea whether this was fast or slow in terms of this kind of crime.

"Your information proved very helpful," the deputy responded, in what she imagined was a breach of department policy. This was a mixed blessing; glad as she was to hear that the bombers were not still running around, she would have preferred it if someone else's information had helped lead to their arrest.

"Will I be coming back here or will Dude be coming with me?" she asked.

He had to call his superior for the answer; it was decided that Dude should remain at the Sheraton in Deputy Orellano's care. She could tell he wasn't thrilled to be assigned to feline babysitting, but she imagined he'd had to do worse in the line of duty.

She convinced him that she needed to buy something new to appear in court; thus far she'd purchased only a down parka, a pair of flannel pajamas, some casual wool pants and two turtleneck sweaters. "I can't appear before the Grand Jury looking like I'm off on a ski weekend." By this time the deputy was used to her restlessness, and knew she would not let up until he assented.

While in one of the big department stores that anchored each of the mall's four spokes, she took the opportunity to use the ladies' room, which she had scouted out the day before; it still had pay phones in a little anteroom off the main lavatory. This was the first opportunity she'd had—other than in her motel room where her phone was undoubtedly monitored—to be away from the deputy's watchful eye. Using the coins she'd been accumulating for just this occasion, she called the number on the card Reza had hidden in Dude's pill bottle.

Reza answered on the second ring and said, "Marielle?" Marielle was surprised that she was the only person who had the number; she wondered if that was what Reza had meant by a "secure phone." "Are you okay?"

"They're flying me to New York tomorrow. I guess I'm going to testify before the grand jury in the afternoon."

"There's nothing to worry about," Reza assured her. "The defendants won't be there, nor will their attorneys. Just the U.S. Attorney, the court reporter, and the grand jury members."

She wasn't really paying attention. Reza had called her "Marielle," and she was shocked at the depth of the relief that ran through her nervous system. Ever since the night of the bombing at JFK, she'd been bearing up in her usual fashion, what Liana used to call "granite-jawed." Her ex had always complained that Marielle saved up all her feelings for her work, and she supposed Liana had been right. Now she no longer had her work, but she hadn't indulged in a lot of emotionalism either, until that moment. As her mother used to say, "No use crying over spilt milk."

But there, huddled over a pay phone in the women's bathroom of this department store, her eyes began to flood.

"Oh, Reza..." It came out like a sob.

"Are you all right? Are they treating you well?" the attorney asked. Reza sounded ready to fight if Marielle answered negatively.

"Reza, they declared me dead! They disappeared me!"

"I know. I was stunned. Well, everyone was stunned, but I knew...I couldn't believe the government would go that far."

"They said it was for my protection."

"That's how those bastards think. They kill you off in order to protect you."

Ordinarily Marielle might have joined in the government bashing but she was in no mood for politics. "Will there be a memorial?" she couldn't stop herself from asking.

"There was one in L.A. last night at the downtown library, in that beautiful auditorium. Your friend Francesca Starris organized it. The place was packed. And there's another one in New York next week."

Francesca. The mention of the name made her chest ache. A flame-haired painter, Fresh had been Marielle's first love. They'd met in their early twenties, shortly after each had arrived in Los Angeles. Those were the years when it seemed as if every creative woman knew every other creative woman in town. The two would drink Blue Moons in a bar in Little Tokyo and promise each other they'd both become famous. They'd be a famous couple, like Simone de Beauvoir and Jean-Paul Sartre. Except they'd be two women.

She no longer quite remembered why she had thought Liana would be a better choice of partner for her. Maybe she'd been jealous of Francesca's success in the art world, which came more quickly than Marielle's. Perhaps her characteristic restlessness made her think the grass would be greener. Maybe she and Fresh were too much alike. Whatever the reason, it was quite possibly the worst decision she had ever made. Although Francesca had remained her close friend all these years, she would never consider rekindling their romantic relationship, although Marielle had suggested it more than once.

Fresh must be devastated with grief, but of course she would be the one to step forward to organize a tribute. Marielle had wanted to find some way to tell her what was really going on, but Donald's warnings about safety held her back.

An automated operator cut in on the call, demanding she feed more coins into the machine. As she fumbled with quarters in the pocket of her parka, she asked, "Did Caroline come?" Caroline Kilhane was her editor at Knopf.

"Marielle, *everyone* was there, and everyone is completely distraught. I thought Dudley Harris—who *asked* to speak, by the way—was going to have a stroke before he finished his remarks." Dudley was a fellow author who'd savaged Marielle's last book in the pages of the *Washington Post*. He was the president of the Los Angeles chapter of PEN, and thus was ubiquitous at literary events around town. She had a fleeting moment of satisfaction at the notion of him having to say nice things about her in public.

Reza continued, "And Liana, of course, was there. She actually had the nerve to come up and ask me if I knew the contents of your will!" Reza had only met Liana a few times before, or this would not have surprised her.

Liana always used to tell Marielle she was a "bad lesbian." "Why don't you ever write lesbian characters? Why don't you march in the Pride parade?" It was one of so many points of contention between them. "Why do you stay in the closet?"

Marielle did not consider herself in the closet. She hadn't taken pains to hide her relationships with women; she just didn't feel the need to make pronouncements about it. In her mind, her sexual identity did not define her. And, as far as that went, Liana was more than happy to benefit from the financial success of Marielle's work.

The mechanical voice broke in again. "Deposit twenty-five cents for the next two minutes."

"Marielle, I'm due in court," Reza begged off. "Will you call me later?"

"The next time I can elude my bodyguard. Probably not till I get back from the grand jury."

"Don't worry about that," the lawyer said again. "They're going to do whatever they have to do to keep you safe."

"Reza…" She wasn't ready to let her go.

"What?" The attorney sounded just slightly impatient.

"Can we undo this?"

"What do you mean? Can I get you out of witness protection?"

"No, well, not now. I mean, can we undo—the death thing? Once the trial is all over with?"

Reza chuckled. "Marielle, I'm a good lawyer, but no one's ever asked me to bring them back from the dead!"

"Does that mean you can't?"

There was a pause on the end of the line, as if Reza were considering it. Or as if she were choosing her words carefully. "I think we could make a strong argument that your civil rights have been violated." But her tone signaled she would be no more committal than that. "Now, don't be afraid about the grand jury. We'll talk later." With that, the attorney clicked off.

Though she'd been a little nervous about her testimony, it hadn't occurred to Marielle to be worried. As a matter of fact, she was looking forward to a little dramatic relief from the monotony of the Sheraton and the mall.

But life, she knew, is rarely as compelling as fiction. Although she traveled in an armored vehicle from the airport in Newark to the federal courthouse in Lower Manhattan, and although four armed marshals escorted her in through a special entrance underneath the building to the shabby room in which the grand jury was convened, on the day after talking to Reza all she could focus on was missing all the people she had left behind. Even Liana, though by the time the domestic partnership had been dissolved, she would have sworn *that* would be impossible. It felt as if *they'd* died, everyone she'd ever known or cared about, and she was left alone.

Marielle went through the ritual of testifying on a kind of autopilot. Donald Watkins was not in the grand jury room, and in her newly aroused state of nostalgia, she missed him too, with his yellow tie and his by-the-book attitude. In her re-creation of him, he smelled of Armani Code.

As she'd been instructed, she was sworn in under her new name, and promised to tell the truth, the whole truth, but of course that was a lie. The congregation of grand jurors—nineteen were present that late afternoon—was unremarkable, the kind of people you'd sit next to in a restaurant or pass by in the drugstore and never notice. If any of them knew who she was, who she'd been, it didn't appear to register. Writers rarely have that kind of face recognition; people don't walk up in the supermarket and ask for an autograph. And she really did look different without her golden hair.

The U.S. Attorney asked Lorraine the same questions over and over again that Marielle had answered several times in Donald Watkins's office two weeks earlier. *What time had she arrived at the airport?* To this question she answered truthfully. *What had she been doing in New York?* To this question she provided the response she'd been coached to provide: she was in New York to see some plays over the long weekend. *What was she doing when she heard the explosion? What did she do then? What did she see?* It was oddly dislocating—what could Lorraine know of these events? Had Lorraine ever been to New York City in her life? Yes, on a senior trip when she was in high school; she saw *The Fantasticks* and had lunch at Sardi's.

Still, Lorraine dutifully repeated the story of what had happened to Marielle at the airport, blurring the lines between one existence and the next. The more she spoke, the more it felt to her like a scene she had written and rewritten, refining the details, embellishing or diminishing certain aspects as the work matured, rather than an event through which she'd lived.

The forewoman of the jury, who wore blue cat-eye glasses and looked like someone you'd see haunting the sale racks at Bloomingdale's, followed up with a few questions that were utterly redundant to the ones Lorraine had been answering for the last half hour. Had the forewoman not been listening when Lorraine responded to the U.S. Attorney or did she just feel it incumbent on her position to speak?

The other grand jury members were then given the opportunity to ask questions too, but no one did. Perhaps it was the after-lunch lull, but was she so unimportant, she wondered. Did they realize she had given up her entire life to be here? The forewoman thanked her; the U.S. Attorney escorted her out, and then she was hustled back to the basement, back to the armored car, and before she knew it, whisked out of town once more. She watched wistfully as the Manhattan skyline receded in the back window of the car. *Except for testifying, at the Grand Jury and at the trial, when you'll be in protective custody*, Donald Watkins had told her on the last day of Marielle Wing's life, *you'd do well to consider your trip to Manhattan your last.*

The next day Lorraine was back in Michigan, ensconced in a townhouse in Novi, albeit without furniture. Two weeks later, mid-March, her furnishings from the house in California were delivered; they looked abysmally out of place in the bland surroundings. Dude however was happy to have his favorite stuffed chair back, the one with the mustard-colored upholstery that showed off his orange fur to great advantage.

That same week, the marshal found her a job substitute teaching at Novi High School. The previous English teacher had died of cancer, a sudden invasion of her brain that spread so fast she was dead a month after diagnosis. The school needed someone who could complete the semester.

Although the idea of having someplace to go every day was appealing after weeks of idleness, she'd balked initially. "You couldn't find me a job at a university?" she'd complained on the phone to Donald Watkins.

"It's too risky. The potential for exposure would be too great. And doesn't a university career demand you publish or perish?" he'd said. "In your case, if you do publish, you might well perish."

"You're a barrel of laughs, Donald," she'd said before hanging up on him.

When she arrived at Novi High that first day, she was greeted by the principal, who told her how fortunate she was that she'd be teaching Advanced Placement classes. Marielle had been tempted to correct him; *they* were the fortunate ones, but Lorraine would never say, nor probably even think such a thought, so she'd simply smiled and nodded.

The now-deceased English teacher had left elaborate lesson plans so dull they made her eyes cross; she couldn't imagine having to implement them. Instead she gave her classes writing assignments: *Imagine you've witnessed a traumatic event; describe the event and how it changes your life. Imagine you have the opportunity to become someone else, someone invented; describe that character.* After a few days she realized that the students and the administration expected her to actually read everything the students produced, and this she could not abide, no matter how much white rum she drank. This led her back to the lesson plans, which required little of her.

Teacher of the Year she was not going to be. And it didn't matter, because after this semester, Lorraine Kaminsky was never going to teach again. It was slightly unsettling to realize that what she had assumed was a natural tendency to excel at whatever she did was more tied to reward and recognition than she'd ever realized.

She returned each evening to try to sort through the chaos of Marielle's former life. Once she determined that her writing files had arrived intact, she was in no hurry to unpack the rest of the boxes—clothes and jewelry that Lorraine would never wear, books that no longer inspired her to write, some of Francesca's earlier paintings that broke her heart to look at.

It wasn't until mid-April that she realized her photo albums were missing. Pictures of Marielle as a little girl with her parents. Pictures of her with Francesca. She and Liana exchanging vows they were destined to break. Miscellaneous author photos of her. Snapshots of friends and colleagues. Travel photos.

When questioned, Donald suggested they must have gotten lost somehow. And a few days later, another box was delivered by an apologetic deputy, her albums appearing intact. She didn't believe Watkins's explanation. Why had they wanted her pictures?

It was May now, and the threat of snow in southeastern Michigan was finally past. The garden beds that decorated the townhouse complex were full of blooms, and green was beginning to replace gray as the predominant color. Soon school would draw to a close for the year; the students who populated her classroom were already dreamy-eyed and inattentive, ready to escape the cramped desks and confining walls of their classrooms.

She knew how they felt. The trial was currently scheduled to begin in September, but she'd been warned that the defendants' attorneys were likely to file motion after motion to delay.

It hardly mattered. Once she had testified, Lorraine Kaminsky would also cease to exist and she supposed that whoever rose in her place would no longer reside in Michigan. But where then—Idaho, Wyoming, Arkansas? Why not Hawaii? The Bahamas? Why not the south of France?

Whatever Donald had in mind for her, she had her own plans. Reza had promised to set up the *Today* appearance and file the lawsuit the morning after the verdict was announced. Marielle Wing would return with a vengeance.

But that would be months away. Maybe more than a year. Today was Sunday. In her old life, Marielle would be meeting someone for brunch or walking in the Hollywood Hills that barricaded the city from the San Fernando Valley. She would be half-present in whatever she was doing, the more engaged part of her mind puzzling over how to resolve chapter seven of *Weeping Minerva*. She would spend the afternoon, as she liked to spend every afternoon, at her desk with the computer, her unabridged dictionary, her thesaurus, and a dozen half-used legal pads strewn about her.

In the last two months she'd made desultory attempts to work on the novel, despite having been warned not to. She'd power up her laptop, stare for a while at the blank screen. She couldn't seem to reimagine herself back into the world of the book, as if the borders had closed. She might try retyping a page or two from one of her published works, trying to prime the pump, but the characters seemed contrived, and the prose tortured. Had she been deluding herself all these years?

Marielle used to scoff when anyone talked about "writer's block"; she'd never experienced it and didn't believe in it. *A pitiful excuse for lack of discipline*, she used to opine, when the inevitable question came up at a conference or a reading. But now something had sapped her discipline and it felt beyond her control. Most days she didn't even open her computer.

Today she had papers to grade, although she couldn't bring herself to care about what these semiliterate adolescents had or had not gleaned from *Hamlet*. She could drive out into what remained of the vanishing countryside and walk, but she found herself beset by an irrational fear of being alone in a deserted location. And she'd imposed the rule of no alcohol before two p.m. So instead she picked at an execrable bagel and drank her third cup of coffee as she contemplated reading *The New York Times*.

In the ten weeks since the Grand Jury, she'd gone back and forth about reading the *Times*. Sometimes it felt like her only link to a life where people talked about things other than raising their children, sports, what the minister had said at church, and what was on sale that week at Meijer's. Sometimes it was an intolerable reminder of the life she no longer had. Some days she'd find a small article about the progress of the case against the JFK bombers, though she never trusted it. Some days she would read only a section she didn't care about—the real estate news, or the business page. Some days she'd skim the front page, maybe do the crossword, but scrupulously avoid Arts and Leisure, where life went on so easily without her.

Today, though, she allowed herself a lazy scan of that section, shooing Dude from where he'd sprawled his big orange body across the newsprint, till her eye fell across an astonishing headline:

BOOKS
Marielle Wing's Final Novel to Be Published Posthumously

Fans of the work of National Book Award winner Marielle Wing, who died suddenly of an aneurism in February of this year, will have one more opportunity to visit the worlds she so vividly evoked, a spokesperson at Alfred A. Knopf, Inc. announced yesterday. Caroline Kilhane, Wing's longtime editor, has worked from early drafts to complete what the celebrated author was finishing at the time of her death, a novel titled *Memory's Trail.*

Before she could read further, her telephone shrieked at her. Not her regular line; it was the phone installed by the U.S. Marshals, to be used only to conduct business related to the Witness Security Program.

"Are you crazy?" Donald Watkin's normally unflappable demeanor was agitated.

"Are you calling about what's in the *Times*?"

"Is there something else I should be calling about?" He didn't usually go in for sarcasm either. "Lorraine, I thought I made it clear to you that you had to suspend all activities related to your career."

"You did make it clear and, devastating as it's been, I've followed your instructions. Donald, I never gave my editor one word of what I was working on."

"Then how did she get hold of it?"

"Donald, she didn't. I brought my computer with me; there were no printed copies; and my handwritten notes were delivered along with the other contents of my files when you closed up the house in Hollywood."

Dropping any appearance of patience, he said, "I'll ask you again, Lorraine. How did Knopf get a copy of your book to publish?"

"That's what I'm trying to tell you. They didn't. That's not even the title of the book I was working on. Whatever Knopf has or thinks they have, the book isn't mine."

"Then what's going on?"

Her first thought was that either Caroline had lost her mind or she'd lost hers. Was it possible she'd given the editor something years ago that she'd forgotten about? Or that Caroline was confused about a manuscript she'd received and mistakenly thought was Marielle's? Neither scenario seemed plausible.

"I can't understand why some rival would go to the trouble of writing a book and then publish it under my name," she told Donald. "Even if it were a lousy book that might ruin my reputation—what point would there be now that I'm dead? And even if the publisher were cynically willing to capitalize on my untimely demise to make a quick buck, surely my editor wouldn't participate in that kind of scheme, would she? I should just pick up the phone and call Caroline to find out what's going on."

But Donald Watkins had a different take on the situation. "They're trying to flush you out," he said gravely. "This organization suspects or, God help us, knows that Marielle Wing is not dead. You don't have a child or living relatives to threaten, so this is the way they mean to get you to surface."

She was staring out the kitchen window of her townhouse. As happened all too frequently in Michigan, the bright morning had grown overcast, clouds promising rain this afternoon. A chill traveled her spine and she reached for a sweater she'd left draped on the back of a chair in the dining nook.

"How would they suspect that?" she asked him. They never talked about who *they* were.

"Worst case, they might have gotten to someone on the Grand Jury," he speculated. "Or someone in the prosecutor's office…"

"My God," she interrupted, "are you telling me *now* this process isn't secure?"

"What's more likely," he continued, "is they don't know anything for certain; they're fishing. If they actually had information, they wouldn't employ such a roundabout way of getting to you."

She didn't like the sound of any of it, nor the sour liquid beginning to flood her intestines. She had a fleeting memory of Marielle, who'd felt at home walking in any neighborhood of Los Angeles or New York at any time of day or night. She'd been fearless; even the airport video had confirmed that. Lorraine, on the other hand, was a woman who jumped whenever the house creaked, who avoided parking garages, especially after dark, and denied herself the pleasure of solitary country walks. Lorraine was always looking over her shoulder.

"So what am I supposed to do?" she snarled.

"Nothing, Lorraine. Nothing at all. You need to sit tight and not react to this."

She could feel her temper starting to boil. "You mean," she began with such ferocity that Dude jumped from his perch on the dining room table and bolted into the bedroom, "I'm supposed to sit back and allow these people, whoever they are, to not only kill me but now to undermine my life's work?"

This was not in her plan. She didn't want to have to go on Stephen Colbert and say, "Marielle Wing is alive and, by the way, I didn't write that stupid book!"

She heard Donald's brief sigh of frustration. "Lorraine, I'm not going to pretend this is easy or fair."

Early on in the process he'd told her that the Witness Security Program was never designed to accommodate someone like her. The program had been launched in 1970 to assist the government in prosecuting mob bosses. The witnesses tended mostly to be criminals themselves, or their wives or girlfriends. In exchange for testimony against higher-ups, they'd get the protection of the program. "For most people," he'd said at the time, "it's a stay-outta-jail card."

Still, he continued now, "In the 9/11 attacks, almost three thousand people left behind family, friends, coworkers who've suffered those losses. What you're being asked to do is to help us to prevent a reoccurrence of that awful day, and I won't apologize for asking you to do it."

"Spare me," she told him. "I've been cooperative, not that I've had much choice. But don't wave the flag in my face and ask me to feel good about my sacrifice."

"Frankly, how you feel about it is beyond the scope of my concern," he snapped. "My job is to keep you alive."

"At least until the trial." She couldn't help but poke at him. He was, after all, as stuck with her as she was with him.

"Until you die of natural causes at a hundred and two," he corrected. Then he returned to the business at hand. "We're going to find out what's going on with this book. Someone from our office will contact the publisher…"

"Get a reporter to do it!" she suggested. "See if you can get your hands on an advance copy of the galleys. I want to see what's being peddled under my name—I mean, under Marielle's name."

"That's the last thing I want to see happen. Lorraine, the further away from this whole situation you stay, the safer you'll be."

"But, Donald, leaving aside the issue of my deeply wounded ego, isn't it possible that the text might provide some clue to who they are and what they want?"

Donald Watkins seemed not to have a comeback for this, so she pressed her advantage.

"And who better to be able to interpret that text than the writer whose work it is supposed to imitate?"

He'd also once said that most of the witnesses in the program were not as smart as she was. He'd said it in a way that suggested the dumb ones were easier to deal with.

"I don't want some journalist digging around this story," he grumbled, but she knew she'd persuaded him.

"I'm sure the government has some shill they can put on this," she teased him. "Pull him off the White House briefings and let him pose as a book reviewer."

As usual, he avoided her attempt to provoke him into a political argument. "Do you suppose Marielle's attorney might help us out with this?" he asked. This surprised her.

"I don't know. You made it pretty clear you didn't want her involvement." She knew Reza would jump at the chance to do reconnaissance, but she couldn't resist a dig. Of course, she couldn't let him know she'd been in touch with her either.

"She might contact your editor, representing your estate or your interests, and not arouse suspicion." He was thinking out loud. "But wait, how could they have even contracted this without her approval? Didn't she handle all Marielle's business dealings? And she's the one person outside the government who knows you're still alive. She could be the source of the information leak."

"Not possible." She pushed away the stab of fear that accompanied this idea. "Not Reza. I'd stake my life on that."

"Ms. Kaminsky, you have in fact done just that." Donald Watkins was silent a moment; he seemed to be weighing a decision. "I'll go ahead and set up a phone call with your lawyer to talk about this book business. It will be interesting to hear what she has to say. In the meantime, Lorraine, don't do anything, and I mean, *not anything*, about this matter until we've talked again."

CHAPTER THREE

Of course, the first thing she wanted to do was call Reza, to alert her to Donald Watkins's impending call and find out what she knew about this book and what she thought they should do. Since the grand jury, Lorraine had talked to her about every two weeks. She would have liked to do it more often but it seemed judicious to limit herself; she didn't want to risk Reza telling her she was becoming a nuisance. She found it supremely comforting to talk to someone who knew who she really was, or at least who she used to be.

But she found herself caught up short by Donald's question: *How could they have contracted this without Reza's involvement?* This was another thing she was hoping to find out.

She never called Reza from her home phone. Although the Feds wouldn't admit it, she was sure it was being monitored. Sometimes she half believed federal marshals were following her as well, but she tried to dismiss this as a paranoid fantasy. She had a lot of paranoid fantasies these days, but then, as they used to say in the seventies, just because you're paranoid doesn't mean they're not out to get you.

Some of the kids at school had prepaid cell phones; it was their parents' attempt to budget their monthly charges. She'd thought of pulling a student aside after class and asking where she could get a prepaid cell, but she didn't want them involved in her business. If she asked one of the other teachers, he might say, "Oh, it's cheaper to just get a plan through one of the regular providers. I got a great deal from T-Mobile." Lorraine wondered where drug dealers bought their untraceable phones, but she only knew about this from TV, so it might have been urban legend. The Witness Security Program was making her think like a criminal, but not necessarily a successful one.

But the truth was, she didn't want another cell phone, prepaid or otherwise. She could still feel the wrench in her wrist when the phone was snatched from Marielle's hand. She could still summon the charred scent left from the explosion in front of her home. Whenever this sensation returned, she'd find her hands shaking as if they didn't belong to her.

These thoughts preoccupied her as she went through the motions of leaving her townhouse—pulling on her raincoat, gathering purse and keys. Her sunglasses, too, despite the rain. In L.A. one might wear sunglasses at any time, even at night, but here people found it odd to wear them absent a bright solar glare. Still, she told herself she was more disguised, less recognizable with her eyes shielded from scrutiny. And, too, she didn't really want to pass as a Midwesterner.

When people at school or other homeowners in the complex asked where she was from, she told them, "New York." This explained the "otherness" of her appearance and demeanor, but deflected them from otherwise thinking, "California." Depending on the kind of person they were, they either expressed their distaste, like the older couple whose townhouse adjoined hers—"You couldn't pay me to live in New York"—or looked at her with a sad envy, like the young woman who answered the phone in the office at school—"I bet you really miss it."

Either way, Lorraine would always smile and say, "Michigan is really green," a neutral enough statement, which seemed to be an appreciation they expected for their state.

There was a carport off the kitchen leading to her garage, so it wasn't until she pulled out of the driveway that she realized the sky was hailing sharp pebbles of ice bouncing off the windshield. Only a few cars were on the road—one would be crazy to be out in this if one didn't have to be. *This is what it's come to*, she told herself, *my life reduced to cheap thrills in inclement weather.*

Her car fishtailed as she pulled out onto Haggerty Road. She was driving an American car, a dark-blue Buick LeSabre. Deputy Orellano had assured her this choice would help her to better blend in with her new environment. "Not too many foreign cars in this part of the country," was what he'd said, trying to discourage her from investing in a Z4. "People tend to look on you with suspicion if you don't support the local industry." She hadn't bothered to tell him that most "American" cars aren't manufactured anywhere near Michigan anymore. Whenever she drove this boat, clunky and inelegant, she profoundly missed her silver BMW, its tight suspension, its sharp handling.

Despite the treacherous conditions, her mind was not on her driving. She kept being pulled back to the blurb in *The New York Times*: "Wing's longtime editor has worked from early drafts to complete what the celebrated author was finishing at the time of her death, a novel titled *Memory's Trail*." What the hell was Caroline thinking? Surely she knew what Marielle had been working on; they'd had three lunches to talk about *Weeping Minerva*, and how it would need to be positioned differently than her previous books.

And had Caroline negotiated a deal with Reza that Reza didn't tell Lorraine about? It was beyond comprehension because surely Reza would know that Lorraine would find out.

More importantly, from where and from whom had this book come, and why? She had to get her hands on a copy of the manuscript.

She was so preoccupied with these thoughts she nearly missed the entrance to the mall.

She supposed it was irrational to keep coming all the way to the mall to use the pay phone. She could use any pay phone, not that those were plentiful anymore, given the ubiquity of cell phones. She could go to one of the hotels; even the Sheraton, where she'd begun her sojourn in Michigan, had a bank of them on the ground floor. Or the occasional gas station still sported one of the classic glass booths on a corner of its lot. But, as in the days when Deputy Orellano was her constant companion, she continued to believe that the pay phone in the ladies' room of the department store offered her a unique kind of privacy. Just in case the Feds were still following. Although they might have wised up and assigned a female deputy to her case, she doubted it.

Ordinarily, the mall would be packed on a rainy Sunday, but perhaps too many people had been fooled by the morning sunshine and planned a day out-of-doors; they couldn't switch gears back into purchasing mode. Then too, Mother's Day had passed and, while retailers were valiantly trying to push the Dads and Grads theme, these tended not to be major shopping holidays.

She found a parking place easily, taking pains, as had become her custom, to park near one of the other flagship department stores rather than near her actual destination. She told herself it provided the excuse for a walk; the weather, her job, and her general malaise were conspiring against the trim figure she'd always maintained with a rigorous schedule of workouts. Arturo, her former trainer, used to scold, "Size four is too large for a woman of your frame! Now, give me another hundred sit-ups a day and we will have you back in size two in no time!" But all the women in the Midwest seemed to have more pillowed bodies than those of professional women in Los Angeles or New York. The mall was full of stores stocking plus sizes.

She made her way past all the familiar retail chains, inhaling the familiar mall smell of chemical air, scented candles, and the heavy grease of the food court. Past mothers struggling with baby carriages, overly made-up teen girls in packs, a few dads dragging behind their families as if tethered but longing for escape. She entered "her" department store, took the escalator to the third floor, and expertly navigated the housewares until she found the restroom. Mercifully, it was empty. Mercifully, it was clean, and the noise from the store was muted by the white tile.

She'd taken to hoarding quarters for these phone calls, which gave her purse an unnatural heft. "What do you keep in here, bricks?" asked one of the other teachers who'd needed to move her purse to warm his coffee in the microwave.

"Brass knuckles," she'd responded, although this suburban school was no Blackboard Jungle. The teachers at Novi High liked to pretend they were embattled, when really the enemy was an oppressive workload, boredom, and stupidity.

At the pay phone she lined up coins in little stacks—quarters, nickels, dimes. Depending on how much time Reza had available, Lorraine could go through a tidy sum in just one call. She inserted the fifty cents it cost to get started, then dialed Reza's number, which by now she'd memorized.

The phone rang four times, and she was almost ready to hang up when she heard, "Marielle," in a breathless tone.

"Did I get you at a bad time?" Reza had always answered quickly, in just a couple of rings. But Lorraine had never called her on a Sunday before.

"No, no, are you all right?"

"I don't know, Reza. Have you read *The New York Times* yet today? It seems Caroline is finishing a book I was supposedly working on when I died, only I've never heard of this book. How could that be?"

A woman laden with packages as well as her young son had come into the restroom. She took him into a stall, awkwardly maneuvering an armload of shopping bags into the narrow space. Lorraine dropped her decibel level, which had risen with her upset. "And how can a contract have been negotiated without my lawyer being involved? Reza, what the hell is going on?"

"I was as shocked as you are," Reza told her, although she didn't sound shocked, she sounded nervous. "I tried calling Caroline at home as soon as I read it, but she might be away for the weekend. I'll talk to her first thing tomorrow morning."

"Reza, I don't understand! Where could this book have come from? Why would someone want to publish 'posthumously' under my name? And why would Caroline go along with it?"

"These are all good questions, Marielle. I'm going to work to get answers for them. I just don't have them now." Something in her voice seemed different; Lorraine couldn't put her finger on it. Ordinarily Reza would be speculating causes and motives, brainstorming solutions.

"Are you sure I didn't interrupt something? You sound... funny."

"No, no, it's fine," she said, but it wasn't. Her voice was artificially light, and Lorraine wasn't fooled by it. In her old life Marielle would have said, "Reza, I'm coming over right now and I'm not leaving until we get to the bottom of this." People couldn't hide from you face-to-face the way they could over the telephone. But that option was not available now. She supposed she could fire her, or threaten to, but how does a dead woman obtain new legal representation? She had no choice but continue on.

"Reza, Donald Watkins is also going to call you about this. He wants your help in getting to the bottom of it."

She expected her lawyer to make a crack about his needing her help now, but all she said was, "Okay, fine."

"And, Reza, I want you to get me a copy of the manuscript. Tell Caroline you need it for something and send it to me."

Reza paused, almost as if consulting with someone, her hand over the mouthpiece. Then she said, "I'll need an address to send it to, and a name."

This felt odd. Reza had taken pains never to ask where Marielle was or what she was calling herself these days. But of course, she'd never asked Reza to send her anything before. She had the instinct to tell her to send it to Donald but since he didn't want Lorraine involved, she had no faith that he'd really forward it. It came down to who she trusted more, and even though Reza was behaving strangely, she'd been Marielle's attorney for more than twenty years.

The mother was trying to back her way out of the stall; by this time her boy was crying, that kind of out of control wailing that made Lorraine wonder why even more children weren't abused. The mother was patient with him, more so than Lorraine would have been, or else she was just numb to it. Lorraine waited for them to exit the restroom before she spoke again.

"Got a pen?" she asked Reza once the commotion was over, and then, taking a deep breath, gave her the address of the townhouse, along with her new name. "Can I call you in a day or two and find out what you've learned?"

"Of course," Reza replied, then hung up without saying goodbye.

Lorraine hung up the phone feeling unsettled; usually talking to Reza lifted her spirits, but this time things felt even murkier. The thought occurred to her—*she's hiding something*—but it was too unthinkable that her only ally might be being less than forthright. She told herself, "Maybe she has a new boyfriend. Maybe they were having a fight. Or having sex. It was probably just a bad time."

Still, she was rattled enough to contemplate something she'd forced herself not to think about until that moment. She wanted to write to Francesca.

She'd argued herself out of this before: It would be dangerous to Fresh, it would be dangerous to herself, nothing could come of it. But standing in the middle of this mall on a rainy Sunday in May, questioning whether her editor was trying to exploit her reputation for a quick buck, whether her attorney was lying to her, and whether those assigned to protect her even understood what was most important to her to protect, it suddenly became unbearable that the only person she could truly say she loved thought she was dead. If there was anyone who would fight for her and for her work, it was Francesca.

She should have made Francesca her literary executor instead of Reza. They'd talked about it, maybe a decade earlier, after Francesca had her cancer scare. They'd been at Rita Flora, the now defunct Los Angeles café that was also a flower shop, picking at salads and talking about how to ensure their work would live on after death.

Marielle had proposed, "Let's do that for each other."

Francesca said she'd be honored, then reversed herself, saying, "But, honey, I don't know enough about the literary world to manage your work in the way it needs and deserves. Reza can do that better than me. Besides," she added, "I don't want to live in a world without you in it. We have to die at the same time, then other people can worry about both our legacies." They'd raised their glasses to toast.

It was this kind of statement that filled Marielle with an irrational hope that Fresh would someday change her mind about becoming lovers again. Francesca probably felt like Marielle had abandoned her. She had to let her know she hadn't.

She took the escalator down one flight, walking to one of the other four arms of the mall where there was a card shop. She'd never liked sending a premade card, a sentiment fashioned by someone else, but now that impersonal quality suited her purpose, to stay below the radar. She browsed the racks for a long time, looking for something that would appear innocuous to others but be clear to Francesca.

At last, she found it: a card with no message, illustrated with a drawing of a green-and-purple artichoke. Her favorite food in the whole world was artichokes; and needless to say, they were not easy to lay hands on in the supermarkets of the Midwest. She and Francesca used to buy them by the armload at the Farmers' Market in Hollywood and bring them home and steam up a half dozen with white wine and herbs, then spend the evening eating every one of them, each leaf drenched in butter. They'd have to fast on lemon water the whole next day to atone. It was their great vice.

She bought the card. The store was empty, and the saleswoman, who wore her gray hair in a French twist, looked slightly bored as she handed her the change. "Excuse me," Lorraine said. "I wonder if I might ask you a favor."

The saleswoman looked willing though noncommittal, so Lorraine continued, "I hurt my wrist playing tennis yesterday and I'm having trouble writing. I need to send a birthday card to my friend. I wonder if you'd be willing to write a message inside and address it for me?"

The saleswoman perked up a little; she looked like someone who might take pride in her handwriting. "I don't mind, if the message isn't too long." She picked up an expensive fountain pen that she kept tucked behind the register.

"It isn't." Lorraine spread the card open before her on the counter and dictated: "My darling Fresh…"

"F-r-e-s-h?" the saleswoman asked.

"It's a nickname." No one called Francesca that but Marielle. Then she continued, "Things are not as they seem."

This was a stock phrase between Francesca and Marielle. They'd use it whenever they'd been disappointed—by a publisher, a gallery, a reviewer, a date, or their own artistic output. They used it to reassure one another that things would get better. When Marielle hadn't won the Pulitzer, Francesca sent her a telegram: "Things are not as they seem."

"What else?" the scribe wanted to know.

"That's it."

"Don't you want to say, 'Happy Birthday'?"

"No need. She'll understand."

"No signature?"

"Just add 'Shhh.'" Lorraine put her finger to her lips to illustrate. This was their code for keeping secrets. She was counting on Francesca to know not to tell anyone she'd received this.

The saleswoman looked up as if expecting more.

"That's all I need, except the address."

Lorraine took the card and put it in the envelope, making it look like an effort with her injured wrist, then presented the front of the envelope to the saleswoman for addressing. She dictated the address, which she knew by heart, including the plus-four numbers of the zip code. That way, just in case anyone was monitoring Francesca's mail—though why would they—Marielle's handwriting would appear nowhere on it.

"Do you need a return address?" the saleswoman wondered.

If only she could include a return address. If only she could say, "Come find me." Instead, Lorraine said, "No, thank you."

She tucked the card into a pocket of her purse. She felt almost giddy with excitement, as though she were playing an elaborate prank on her friend, something they would laugh about later.

"Thank you so much," she told the saleswoman. "You've helped me more than you know." She couldn't wait to put the card into the mailbox. She had a packet of stamps in her wallet because Donald had instructed her to pay all of her bills by check instead of online. "In your situation, you don't need to risk identity theft," he'd told her. It occurred to her that that was exactly what had happened with this fake book, *Memory's Trail*—someone had stolen her identity. Even though Marielle Wing was supposed to be dead, she felt it as a great affront. Would she even care if someone were to steal Lorraine's?

The mall had a mailbox tucked in another one of its corners, and she walked there, eager to have her task accomplished. It dawned on her that the envelope would have a postmark from Novi, Michigan. She wished she had someone to send it to in Kansas, who could send it to someone in Alaska, who could send it to Francesca. She'd have to count on Francesca's discretion. She let the envelope slip from her hand into the dark mouth of the blue mailbox.

There was nothing she wanted at the mall, which felt oppressive in its relentless hawking of unnecessary items, but she didn't feel ready to go back to the townhouse either, to face the banality of student papers or the reproach of her neglected novel. Nor did she feel like sitting through a bad movie.

Lorraine had an Internet connection, of course. You couldn't teach high school in the 21st century without the ability to email your students, search to determine whether or not they'd plagiarized their papers, and bring in additional media—interviews, videos, apps—to help students glean whatever understanding they could of the text you were teaching. Books were no longer enough, apparently, in the Digital Age and if Marielle Wing had resisted this notion, Lorraine Kaminsky could not disavow it after working with these teenagers.

But Donald had warned her many times that Lorraine needed to keep a low profile and not attempt to transact any business that might associate her with Marielle. "The Internet is more porous than most people would ever imagine," he'd cautioned.

Thus far, she'd been good. She'd never been a big one for social media; she'd had an assistant create posts for Facebook and Twitter. Although the marketing people at Knopf put pressure on her, she'd resisted doing a blog; she did not believe that generating free content would induce anyone to buy her books. Lorraine's observations of her students seemed to bear this out; they didn't understand why they should ever have to pay for music, movies, or books.

But being good hadn't gotten her anywhere, had it? Marielle was dead, Reza and Caroline were up to something and someone was circulating a phony book under her name. So Lorraine decided to go to the library to use one of their publicly available computers, which, she reasoned, should provide a pretty good assurance of anonymity.

The Novi Public Library was part of a cluster of city buildings located off of Ten Mile Road. This included the high school where Lorraine taught, as well as City Hall and the Police Station. The library was right next door to the high school, although today was the first time she had been there.

Just outside the main door was a bronze statue of three children sitting on a park bench, reading over one another's shoulders. Once inside, Lorraine was directed to the escalator to the second level.

A librarian sat at the information area. He was a slender African American man with wire-rimmed glasses, who explained that she could use her library card or pay a dollar for a guest pass. The latter option would require no disclosure of information, and that's what she chose. She could also select between several hexagonal tables with six workstations at each or the glass-enclosed computer lab, which was quieter. She opted for the lab. Then he added, "We're supposed to enforce a thirty-minute limit, and during after-school hours on weekdays we really need to. But it's been slow all day, so take all the time you need."

He didn't ask her name, and neither did the Acer computer. She had always used Macs—Francesca's influence—and she struggled a bit to figure out the basic operations of the PC she sat before, but once she'd logged on with the library's passcode, she could navigate seamlessly onto Google Chrome, and was presented with the opportunity to search.

Only one other library patron sat at the opposite end of the row of computers, a middle-aged man dressed in dark pants and a short-sleeved shirt. She invented fictions to explain him: his computer had crashed, and he had a big job to finish for his company by tomorrow morning. Or, he was having an online affair, and couldn't risk using his computer at home. This was a lifelong habit, making up stories about people she observed, one of the few such habits that had transferred from Marielle to Lorraine.

The first site she went to was Amazon, to check the sales stats on Marielle's books. She was gratified to see that her sales figures and rankings had risen considerably after her death, but the big bump that occurred in February and March had dipped in April and was flatlining in May. Wait until everyone found out she wasn't dead after all! Then she wondered glumly what the figures might be for this imposter book, and caught herself grinding her teeth.

As long as she was breaking the rules today, she went next to Facebook, where she skimmed the posts her friends and readers had left over the past few months. She'd never given any thought to what happened to a Facebook page after its owner had departed this mortal coil, but she was stunned to see that people used it as a way to continue to feel connected to the deceased. "I've spent the week rereading all your books," one fan wrote, "I can't believe there won't be any more." Maybe there was a way to work this into *Weeping Minerva*?

It was the first time she'd felt anything like inspiration about her novel in months, and she was tempted to rush right home and work on it, but she recalled that she was here on a mission of sorts, and she wanted to see what she could find out about her situation.

But where to begin? She wanted to know who these terrorists were that lived in New Jersey and bombed American Airlines and manufactured ersatz literary fiction as a strategy in their cause. Assuming, of course, that Donald's theory was correct.

She began with a Google search of "domestic terrorism." There were 36,100,000 entries, from print and broadcast stories to government reports to blogs. While the president had kept the media focused on international threats, especially from Muslim groups, in fact there had been an increase both in the number of hate groups, the number of plots discovered, and the number of actual incidents of terrorism in the US by its own citizens. The causes were numerous—white supremacy, hatred of the government, antiabortion, ecology and animal liberation, and nationalist movements by people of color—but more and more people were stockpiling and using weaponry to fight for them.

It was a little sobering, but also fascinating to contemplate this mindset of individuals ready to kill and die for their beliefs. Especially when their beliefs seemed so crazy to Lorraine. She'd love to write that novel, about a character who enacts a terrorist plot. Or maybe, when the trial was all over, the young men who bombed JFK (assuming they were convicted) would let her write their story. It could be like Truman Capote's *In Cold Blood*. Wouldn't that garner some press—"Wing spent ten months in the witness protection program to ensure her safety to testify against them; now she has the exclusive rights to their life story."

There were articles about the bombing at JFK, but there was maddeningly little information in these stories, which seemed to focus primarily on how effective the government had been at apprehending the suspects and the promise of a speedy trial. Over and over, the "unnamed source at Homeland Security" alluded to "a sleeper cell based in New Jersey" as the most likely source of this attack. Who were they, though? What was their cause? And why American Airlines?

She Googled "sleeper cell." Nearly nine million listings, but an overwhelming number of them had to do with a TV series of this name on Showtime, about a terrorist plot against Los Angeles. Reading through a portion of them made her restless; in the past Marielle had had an endless capacity for research, but perhaps that was the difference between having an assistant and not. For years she'd been blessed with a steady parade of graduate students, different ones for each book, happy to earn ten or twelve dollars an hour to conduct preliminary research and bring her the nuggets of gold. How did they have the patience to wade through all of this to find those nuggets?

Remembering the command "Go to Magda" one of the men had shouted to the other as the two sprinted through JFK, she Googled "Magda." There were more than sixteen million listings, including a music group by that name promoting their album, an international DJ, a belly dancer, the Museums and Galleries Disability Association, and the Montana Art Gallery Directors' Association. Famous Magdas included Magda Goebbels (wife of Joseph) and Magda Gabor, sister of Zsa Zsa and Eva. This seemed for the moment like a dead end.

Then she tried "American Airlines." She browsed their corporate web page. On first glance, they didn't seem to own other businesses that would set off alarm bells; there didn't seem to be pending lawsuits of any extraordinary nature. Maybe it wasn't a political cause, but a personal vendetta. A disgruntled employee or a distraught person whose loved one died in a plane crash. The thought gave her pause; if everyone with a grudge started bombing the objects of their grievance, then civilization was truly done for. But if it was just a couple of guys with an axe to grind, how could they have tracked her down the next day? How would they have had the infrastructure to be a threat to her once they were in custody or after she testified? She couldn't make sense of it.

"Closing time in ten minutes," the librarian whispered over her shoulder. With a start she saw it was almost five p.m. The Internet devoured time. And she was no closer to knowing anything than she was before she'd sat down.

Before she left the computer, though, she couldn't resist googling "Marielle Wing." There were 33,000 entries. The older ones she'd seen before, of course, but the first few pages were mostly obituaries, some from around the world. It was gratifying that newspapers in Russia and Japan, as well as

Western Europe, had found her passing newsworthy. There was the story from today's *Times*, and she felt all over again that wave of violation as she reread it. How dare someone, anyone, presume to be Marielle Wing, to write like Marielle Wing?

She was preparing to sign off in a huff, but there was another entry that captured her attention: MARIELLE WING LIVES was how it began. Involuntarily, she looked over her shoulder; she had the creepy feeling she was being watched. But the middle-aged man she'd seen earlier had gone, and the librarian was busy shooing patrons out into the drizzle.

The URL was frederikslastblog.com and when she went to it, the text seemed to be unrelated. The writer was talking about music, or at least she presumed that Dreaded Parsnips and Dinner for Days were bands, and then about the travails of love replete with all the tortured metaphors of adolescent angst. Then out of nowhere: MARIELLE WING LIVES, a non-sequitur dropped into the text. And then a return to lamentations over one "chocolate eyed Sarita." She read on and on, but nothing ever linked back to this phrase.

Her response was a study in ambivalence: On the one hand it was terrifying to see her secret revealed in public. On the other hand she wanted to leap with joy at the confirmation of the fact—*it's true, I do live!*

She needed to approach this logically. She tried to figure out if the blogger was referencing something particular in her writing. Maybe in his heartbreak, he'd found something meaningful in her work, and thus Marielle remained alive for him.

Or maybe it was some bizarre code. A message, intended for some unknown other.

Of course, she was going to have to tell Donald about it, which was likely to make trouble for this already troubled young man. She assumed it was a man, a young man, but that was the thing about the Internet. It could be anyone.

Then, too, if she told Donald, he'd want to know why she was searching the Internet. It wasn't his business, that's what she'd want to say, but she would tell him she was trying to track down the source of a student's term paper that sounded a little too familiar to her.

Lorraine sighed as the overhead lights began to go out. It was time to go home. This had been a day without comfort, without respite—not *The New York Times* or talking with Reza or trying to research her fate. A day without solace, as so many had been since she'd passed away.

CHAPTER FOUR

June now. School was out and the hours dragged as Lorraine waited for the mail each day, hoping the manuscript would come as Reza had promised. She'd tried a couple of times to call Reza but had gotten no answer; this had happened several times before so she didn't think much about it. She'd left brief messages but of course, Reza couldn't call her back. She supposed the attorney was busy—the ACLU was filing lawsuits right and left—and she didn't want to seem like a pest.

It was as if she were suspended in amber; she didn't know what to do with her time. Some days she tried to work on *Weeping Minerva*, but her protagonist's dilemma now seemed trivial and contrived compared to this world where airports were bombed and citizens were forced to disappear. She couldn't get herself interested any longer in the psychological, and *Weeping Minerva* had certainly been intended as a psychological novel. *Had been intended.* Had it crept into the past perfect tense without her realizing it? She had never in her long career abandoned a novel without finishing it, even those she knew she would never want to publish.

But Lorraine couldn't read even fiction anymore; stories—whether good or bad—seemed to taunt her, so instead she was gorging herself on nonfiction books that documented the desperate state of the human condition and confirmed the sense of hopelessness she felt. She read late into the night and woke up listless and headachy each morning. Although that could also be because she was drinking more than she should. She knew it wasn't a good sign when she found herself pouring a glass of white rum at noon.

Not since Marielle's parents died had she had a steady practice of drinking during the daytime. She'd just been twenty, in the middle of finals in her junior year of college. Two state policemen had walked into her classroom while she was in the middle of taking her exam for History of Middle English Literature. As the other students barely gaped at her before bending their heads back over the papers in front of them, she followed the officers into the hallway. Without making eye contact, one informed her that her Dad's Volvo had been struck broadside by a hit-and-run driver just outside of Santa Rosa. Her mother had died on impact. Her father might have survived, the officer told his polished shoes, except he'd had a heart attack while the paramedics were transporting him to the hospital.

She'd nodded, her head filled with Langland and Chaucer and the Pearl Poet. "I think they would have wanted to go together," she'd said.

The officers looked at her oddly. "We're here to drive you to the morgue so you can start making arrangements."

"I need to finish my exam," she replied. "It's the final. I'll come later this afternoon." And that's what she had done. Liana always used that story as an example of what a cold-hearted bitch she was, usually when she wanted Marielle to buy her something and she'd said no. But when she'd told the story to Francesca, her friend had said gently, "You were in shock and just trying to keep everything as normal in your world as you could."

After that day, she'd spent the next three seasons drinking white rum in the afternoons. She'd take her classes in the morning, study late into the night, but it was in the afternoons that she felt most acutely alone. As she did now.

Some days she half-heartedly tried to work out to an exercise video she'd bought at the mall, some Zumba routine, but she found it so banal she never made it all the way through. And she couldn't really see why she had to be in shape now. All her life she'd been disciplined, but that rigorous focus seemed to be draining away. She hadn't once been bored since she left her parents' home at age seventeen to enter college. She used to say to anyone who would listen that she didn't believe in boredom, but now she had to admit she was bored.

She hadn't heard from Francesca, and of course she couldn't expect to. Her friend had no way to reach her, and that was for the best. Lorraine wanted to keep Francesca safe, but still, it comforted her that her best friend knew she was alive. At least, she hoped Francesca knew. Lorraine couldn't really know what her friend knew, or what she thought, because she was supposed to be dead, and the dead didn't get to influence things anymore. Once Marielle returned to life, the two of them would laugh and laugh about these matters. Once she stopped being dead.

Seemingly, the dead can be employed, so Lorraine thought about getting a job for the summer, but opportunities were not exactly abundant in the pinched economy of Southeastern Michigan, and she couldn't envision herself dispensing burgers at a fast-food joint or answering phones in an office. Besides, what would she do for a resumé? Aside from less than four months teaching English at Novi High, what had Lorraine Kaminsky done with her life? For amusement, she spent an hour inventing a faux resumé for Lorraine: she'd been a stripper at a topless bar before becoming a dental hygienist, she'd spent seven years teaching Sunday school, she was a wife and homemaker before returning to school to get a degree in nuclear physics. She tried to share this with Donald, but couldn't even get a chuckle out of him.

"Hey, I'm putting you down as a character reference," she warned him.

Improbably, she found herself looking forward to her calls to Donald. It wasn't that he'd instructed her to check in with him at any regular interval, but he'd had the special phone line installed in her townhouse and said she could call him if she ever needed to. Since Donald was the only person, besides Reza, who knew the truth about her life, when she spoke to him, she did not have to pretend to be someone else. Plus, it was fun to try to rile him up, fun because it wasn't easy to do but she was learning over time how to get a rise out of him. He never really played along, but sometimes his response seemed an appreciation of her, as close as she could get to affection these days. Like a schoolgirl with a crush, she would have called him every day if she'd thought she could get away with it.

In her second week of summer "vacation" (Marielle Wing never took vacations; she took research trips for her novels; she traveled to make presentations or accept awards; she rejected idleness) Lorraine walked back into the library and asked whether they needed any volunteers. She had a romantic vision of spending long afternoons in the cool quietude of the stacks, shelving books, inhaling the scent of old paper and binding glue, fingering soft cloth spines. Instead, the librarian with a large birthmark on her right cheek responded, "If you can read pretty good, we need someone to read to blind people."

"Read what?" Lorraine wanted to know. She'd never personally known any blind people, and she wasn't sure what they'd be interested in.

The librarian seemed taken aback by the question. "Whatever they want—the newspaper, magazines, books and stories, I guess."

This changed the romantic ideal. She'd been envisioning solitude, but after two weeks home with no company but Dude's, perhaps this was an answer to her malaise. *It's risky*, she heard Donald say. She carried his voice in her head now.

No chance of a blind person recognizing me, was what she said back to him in her mind, and to the librarian she said she'd be willing to try it.

The next day she arrived at the address the librarian had written down for her on a yellow Post-it. It was some miles east on Grand River Avenue and, rather than being one of the ubiquitous town home complexes that blighted the suburbs, it was an old Victorian farmhouse. She wouldn't have been surprised to find it ramshackle, but instead it sported a new coat of pale peach paint with contrasting trim in dove gray and a mess of lavender petunias in window boxes surrounding the house. The owner must not have been from this region, where home décor ran toward the traditional rather than the distinctive.

She rang the doorbell and waited, then rang again. She heard brisk footsteps; the door was opened by an immaculately groomed gentleman who looked to be in his early sixties.

"I'm looking for Garland Macpherson." Lorraine spoke a little too loudly.

"And you've found him." He smiled and seemed to gaze at her. His hair was silver, perfectly cut; he wore a pressed blue linen shirt and well-creased khakis. His sockless feet were slid into navy topsiders. Even his fingernails were perfectly manicured.

"I'm sorry," she said, confused. "The library gave me your name and address and said to come about reading to…" She'd been going to say *reading to blind people*, but stopped herself. "… to you," she finished lamely.

"I'm not completely blind," he informed her, as if he'd heard her thoughts. "But I can no longer read letters on a page. The characters tend to swim around like sperm looking to fertilize an egg!" He laughed a little breathlessly, and it occurred to her that Garland was a gay man. Perhaps he had a boyfriend or a paid assistant to keep him looking so well turned out.

"You are…?" he continued.

"Lorraine," she told him. "Lorraine Kaminsky." She hated lying to him. She wanted Garland to know that *Marielle Wing* was at his door to read to him; for some reason, she expected he would appreciate that fact.

He offered his hand; the skin was soft, not clammy. "Well, Lorraine, come in. Do you mind my asking what interests you about reading to me?"

At first she bristled. It had been decades since she'd been on a job interview, or in any situation where she had to justify what she wanted to do. Then she reminded herself that she was here as Lorraine, and needed to act the part. "I'm an avid reader myself," she told him. "And I teach English at Novi High. I got a little bored on summer break, and thought it would be nice to help others."

He laughed. "You're the first teacher I ever heard say they were bored on summer break!"

Was her story implausible? Donald was always encouraging her to give as few details as possible, fearing she might get tangled up in her lies. He didn't understand that keeping a story straight in her head was her stock in trade. And anything can be plausible if rendered well, she reminded herself; all writers know this. So she said, without apology, "I've always liked to keep busy."

This seemed to satisfy him. He led the way across polished oak floors, the original wood restored exquisitely, into a den area that featured shelves of books on every wall save where there were windows and doors. In the center of the room were two overstuffed loveseats facing each other across a glass coffee table.

Garland Macpherson seemed to have no further interest in chitchat. Her interview concluded, now it was time for the audition. He walked to a shelf and chose a book as deliberately as if he were reading the spine. "Please, sit down," he bid her, and gestured toward the loveseat facing the windows. Then he handed her the book he'd pulled from the shelf and sat across from her. The book was *Raise High the Roof Beam, Carpenters and Seymour: An Introduction* by J. D. Salinger. Hardbound, it was a first edition.

"Have you read it?" he asked.

"Of course," she said, "but a long time ago. Have you?"

"Oh, yes." He smiled again. "I've read every book in this library, most of them more than once."

Although she was surprised that he would want to hear books with which he was already familiar rather than encounter new titles, or simply order audiobooks online, she felt it wasn't her job to question his literary tastes nor the service he'd requested she provide him.

"So you're an avid reader," she said. "It must be hard to have to give up something that you love so much." Her voice was thick with self-pity at her own forced renunciation.

"There is always more to enjoy about this world," he said simply. She felt slightly rebuked, as if he'd guessed her own inability to find those things.

"I told the librarian I would go for an hour at a time."

He agreed this was a good increment of time. "Although, if we're right in the middle of something, you won't just stop and leave me hanging, will you?"

She assured him she would not, even though, since he'd already read the books, it wasn't as if he'd be left in suspense about the eventual outcome.

With that, she opened the book and begin to read aloud.

After a couple of pages, he stopped her. "You're an amazing reader! You're good enough to record books on tape."

I have, she longed to tell him. Then she felt nervous; what if he recognized her voice? *Too late.*

"Thank you." She summoned Lorraine's sense of modesty. *She* was the type to be uncomfortable with compliments.

* * *

Each day she haunted the mailbox looking for the manuscript of *Memory's Trail*; each day she was disappointed. Events were taking place somewhere far away that had considerable bearing on her, at least on who she used to be, but she couldn't affect them. *That's what it's like to be dead.*

She visited Garland three afternoons per week, and found those days easier to bear than the days when she didn't visit. After the first session, her time with him expanded, first to two hours, then to three. She read as long as her voice would hold out. They'd finished the Salinger and were nearly through with Toni Morrison's *Song of Solomon*, which she'd always considered the author's best, despite the wider attention paid to *Beloved*. She'd figured out that his books were alphabetized by author and that he'd memorized the exact placement of each one on the shelves.

She couldn't yet discern what moved him to choose one book over another, but she was grateful he had a taste for literature and not for pulp. Although she found his choices a bit predictable, she also found it soothing to immerse herself in the diction of great works; something about actually giving voice to this language seemed to be changing her in ways she couldn't quite name.

Each time she saw him, Garland was immaculately appointed and his house was spotless. Always there were fresh flowers on the fireplace mantel in the living room, and at the center of the dining room table. If he had a companion, Lorraine had yet to meet him, though it seemed impossible that even a partially sighted person could keep up this presentation all by himself.

It was an oddly intimate activity, reading to someone, even though Garland and she seldom talked beyond the pleasantries of her comings and goings. Reading aloud to someone involved entering into a world together, where the sighted person usually traveled alone. She could see on his face the moments of puzzlement, the expressions of satisfaction with a turn of phrase or a twist of plot. She heard his sighs when events turned dark or when a particularly profound insight had been offered. She imagined he must know similar things about her own responses to the text. In an odd way, she felt closer to him than to anyone else in her life now.

It was on a day when she wasn't reading to Garland, after more than five weeks of checking her mailbox several time a day, that Reza proved true to her word. Lorraine found her mailbox stuffed with a thick envelope with no return address. Although she might have been concerned about being observed, she couldn't even wait to go back into her house before she tore it open and pulled out the manuscript of *Memory's Trail.*

Instead of relief, she felt a stab of annoyance. Such an insipid title to be posted above Marielle's name!

The weight of its pages in her hands was almost unbearable. As some women might long to cradle a baby, such was her longing to hold once more a finished manuscript of her own. She remembered the sense of pleasure at the accomplishment, the fullness of holding a world of her own creation. But this stack of papers carried no such joy; its energy was toxic, malevolent. Her urgency to read it was matched with an equal impulse to light it on fire. Walking into the townhome, she dropped the manuscript onto the kitchen counter and returned to the mailing envelope, eager to see what Reza had to say.

But inside the plain manila envelope there was no note from Reza. Lorraine told herself that her attorney was merely trying to be cautious. But she still didn't know the answers to any of her questions, and she needed to. So before reading a word of the text she'd waited so impatiently to receive, she grabbed her purse and left the house again, setting out for the mall. She drove a little recklessly, speeding, tailgating, changing lanes in her haste to get there. Once more she enacted her elaborate and now ritualized subterfuge of seeking out the pay phone in the ladies' room of the department store, setting up stacks of coins on top of the phone, punching in the number more familiar to her than her own. She held her breath and waited to hear Reza's brusque voice say, "Marielle?"

This time, though, an electronic voice announced, "We're sorry, the number you have dialed is no longer in service." She tried again, thinking she must have misdialed, and again, each time a little more panicked. On the seventh try, she fished into her purse for the card Reza had given her, in case something had happened to her memory. No, she'd made no mistake, and the electronic voice was quite adamant; there was no more secure phone on which to call Reza.

Lorraine slumped against the wall of the restroom and felt her knees give way. Her body slid involuntarily to the floor. She tried to rationalize this event, to calm the too-rapid beating in her chest.

Was Reza taking her precautions too far? Had Donald somehow found out they were in contact and ordered her to stop?

Then fear swept through her nervous system. Had someone else found Reza out? Had she been threatened? Was she all right?

Lorraine forced herself to stand and reinsert coins into the phone. She started punching in the numbers of Reza's law office, but stopped when she remembered that Altovese, her receptionist, would surely recognize her voice. Maybe she could call at night and leave Reza a voicemail. Though she'd have to find another payphone; the mall wasn't open late.

Her only recourse was to go home and call Donald. Which she did, fretting every mile of the trip back. She'd taken to pestering him about every three days since school let out, but, as he had each time before, he refused to tell her whether he'd talked to Reza or not.

"Just tell me if she's okay, Donald." *Why wouldn't she be*, Lorraine heard him think, and so she added, "I had a dream about her, and I'm worried."

His laugh was condescending and Lorraine wanted to punch him. "I didn't think you were the superstitious type."

You have no idea what type I am. Her breath sighed into the receiver.

"Lorraine, it's only a dream. Now, just relax and let me do my job."

She hated when he called her Lorraine. He refused to call her Marielle, he said, because she had to get used to the fact that Marielle's life was over. Wouldn't he be surprised when she reappeared one day?

She switched tactics. "Well, have you gotten a copy of the manuscript yet?"

For weeks he'd rebuffed every request she'd made of him to tell her his theories about this book. "If and when I do, I'm not going to tell you. Your imagination is too active, Lorraine. You need to just stay out of this."

"I'm going to assume you do have it," she told him. "So I'm going to ask you again to send me a copy. I'm entitled to see what's going out under my name." She didn't let on that she already had a copy. A copy Reza had sent her. And now the attorney had disappeared.

"Lorraine, this has nothing to do with you."

"Well, what about the blogger? The one who posted MARIELLE WING LIVES? Have you talked to him yet?" She knew he had, but he wouldn't tell her what he'd found out.

"Stay off the Internet, Lorraine. We have a terrorism case to prosecute, and believe it or not, it isn't all about you."

"This paternalism is only going to backfire," she told him. "Do you really think I'm going to just sit back and trust that Daddy is going to take care of me? As a high school teacher, let me tell you, kids who aren't allowed any agency act out."

"If you act out, you may be killed," he said simply. "It's my job to try to prevent that from happening."

According to you, I'm already dead, she wanted to scream at him. "Goodbye, Donald. Thanks for another informative chat." She hung up. She'd kept her dignity, barely.

She didn't know what else to do to find out about Reza. Worry was a dull whine in the back of her brain as she poured herself a tumbler of white rum and ice, curled up beside Dude on the couch, and turned to the pages of *Memory's Trail* to look for clues. Perhaps Reza had scribbled some message on one of the inner pages.

Ingrid Warren had always believed in human dignity.

"What a terrible opening sentence," she protested to her orange cat, who raised his head to let her know that her complaint had been duly noted. Then he drifted back into his midday slumber.

Ingrid was not old enough to have been active in the progressive struggles of the 1970s—the movements of women, cultural minorities, gays and lesbians—although she'd been a precocious child who read the newspaper and was thus aware of them.

I've never used the term "cultural minority" in my life. If I wrote like this, I would *change my name and leave town. How do they imagine they're going to pass off this turgid prose as mine? No one will be fooled. What's Caroline thinking?* It was all she could do not to pick up the phone right that minute and call Caroline to find out. That must be exactly what Donald was afraid of, why he didn't want her to get her hands on this manuscript.

He was right to worry. She'd be damned if she would just sit by while this fraud was perpetrated on her readers. But if Caroline was somehow involved in this, it wouldn't do to blow her cover just yet. She needed to find out more about what her editor had in mind.

Even after the major success she'd achieved in her career, Ingrid continued to speak up for civil rights, individual rights, and freedom of speech. Although she'd never progressed beyond liberal thinking or taken truly radical positions, she continued to be a stalwart liberal long after it became unfashionable, supporting the ACLU and Amnesty International and the Southern Poverty Law Center and People for the American Way. She frequently spoke at fundraising dinners and at conferences and lent her name to various campaigns. Because of her beauty, still vibrant into her fifties, even more than because of her stature, she lent cachet to the causes she endorsed.

Where was the writing professor to tell this writer to *show, don't tell*? And in what career had the character achieved "major success" and "stature"? Because Marielle was meticulous about her craft as a writer, she could never bring herself to suffer sloppy technique in her reading material.

Ingrid Warren had always believed in human dignity. This notion gave her comfort, allowed her to congratulate herself for being a good person.

The repetition was a cheap rhetorical strategy, favored by preachers and snake oil salesmen and bad poets. Marielle had never resorted to it in her work.

And so when the government asked her to betray this principle, it was startling how readily she agreed. Later she might ask herself: was her system of belief so shallow, was her fear of the loss of comfort so great that she would so easily agree to do the bidding of those whom she had considered adversaries?

This is what Ingrid did when she agreed to testify against those who'd committed their lives to resisting the growing fascism of the State.

With this last sentence, she nearly choked on her drink. She coughed so much that Dude jumped down from the couch.

This action cost her. It cost her writing career and it cost her fame and it cost her her belief that she was a good person. Ultimately, it would cost her life.

Lorraine snatched up the envelope. Her address was scrawled in handwriting she didn't recognize. Who'd sent this to her? Surely Reza wouldn't participate in a scheme to threaten her life. Would she? What kind of pressure would she have had to be under in order to do that? And was it possible that Caroline was in on it too?

But if it wasn't Reza who'd sent it, who else had Lorraine's address?

She wanted to call Donald back. She wanted to come clean about her calls to Reza since she'd been in witness protection, how she'd given the attorney her address, how the manuscript had come to her, how it seemed to be not *by* but *about* her.

But it didn't make sense. If the group that bombed the airport was a domestic terrorist group dedicated to "resisting the growing fascism of the State," how could they have enough power and organization to infiltrate Knopf, one of the most respected literary publishers, an imprint of Random House, owned by Bertelsmann AG, one of the largest media empires in the world?

How would they have been able to create a network of trickery that included not only her publisher but also her lawyer and *The New York Times*? Who would have the power to pull that off? And then, like a blow to the chest came the thought: the government. The same government that had declared her dead.

She was inexplicably cold now, her teeth chattering against the glass rim as she tried to calm herself with another swig of rum. A theory began to spin in her brain and no amount of alcohol could dull its insistence.

If the government were behind this fake book, if they'd gone to the trouble to enlist Reza and Caroline and *The New York Times*, why would they do that? Could Reza have told Donald about Lorraine's plan to reemerge as Marielle after the trial? If they wanted her out of the way for good, why not just kill her? Why go to all the trouble of creating the fiction of Lorraine Kaminsky and putting her in witness protection? Maybe they did need her to testify. Maybe after the trial, that's when they'd kill her.

She'd resisted these kinds of conspiracies in the past. All the theories about 9/11 and the assassinations of the 1960s. It wasn't that she found them impossible to imagine. It was more a matter of feeling *who can live like that, mistrusting every bit of information we receive, always being in the shadow of some omnipotent power structure?* And if the theories were true, what could she do about it? She didn't like feeling helpless, and so she'd chosen to eschew—more or less—the most dire of the conspiracy theories that had floated through the zeitgeist.

But she wondered now, what was the best way to help herself? She'd tried to take control by keeping in touch with Reza, and now she didn't know what had happened to her attorney. She'd tried to take control by getting a copy of the manuscript, but all she felt now was more endangered. Should she trust Donald and follow his instructions, or was he working, wittingly or unwittingly, to bring about her actual death?

She took the manuscript, holding it out from her body as if it might detonate at any moment, and stuffed it in a kitchen drawer. She wasn't yet ready to read about the gruesome death the author had in mind for her. She drained the rum from the glass, but it was powerless to offset her anxiety.

She paced the bland beige carpet of the living room. Should she call Donald? Should she call Reza? Was there anyone else in the world to call?

More than anything, it was Francesca she wanted to talk to. Fresh had always been the person who'd helped her figure out what she couldn't understand. Her view was hardnosed, unsentimental, unfailingly calm. In the darkest situations, she'd always found something to make Marielle laugh. She longed to call Francesca, hear her deadpan response to this hysteria. Somehow she would know what to do. Lorraine couldn't risk her safety, though, not without knowing what had become of Reza.

Out of the blue, she thought of Garland Macpherson, of sitting across from him on that mauve loveseat as the afternoon light poured in through the windows. Watching his face crease with pleasure upon hearing something she'd just read. Watching his eyes pool with tears when he was moved.

It must be the need for human connection she felt. She knew almost nothing about him and he knew less about her, yet she sensed a kindred spirit in his love of words. Still, she couldn't involve him. She wouldn't.

Yet perhaps there was some way to elicit his opinion without revealing more than was safe for him to know.

CHAPTER FIVE

Armed with her newly inflamed paranoia, Lorraine went in search of another pay phone. It was a challenging task; she didn't want to be visible to unseen observers in case she was being watched by the Feds. That ruled out the glass boxes at gas stations. A hotel might afford more privacy, and convention hotels often had pay phones outside the meeting rooms, but a nice hotel was also going to have security cameras everywhere.

Then she remembered that the multiplex at the mall had a pay phone in the back near the restrooms. It wasn't ideal, but at least she'd have the advantage of being able to see anyone who might be looking at her. She paid the matinee admission for a movie she'd already seen. It was the middle of a summer afternoon and only a few elderly couples were at the movies. The ticket taker looked bored; the popcorn machine was silent.

She didn't bother with the subterfuge of finding a seat in the theater, but went immediately in the direction of the ladies' room. A woman with a walker struggled to enter the restroom door. Lorraine assisted her, then worried this might make her too memorable.

Once more she piled stacks of coins on top of the phone, and tried the number of Reza's secure phone again. This time it just rang and rang, no answer, but no message saying the number was not in service. That was weird. She counted ten rings, then twenty, then thirty; each ring sounded more ominous than the last.

Then she decided to risk calling Reza's law office. She was preparing to affect a Southern accent to disguise her voice, but the phone was answered not by Altovese, who had worked for Reza as long as Lorraine could remember, but by a man. "Law office." The voice was curt.

"Reza Caldicott, please." She was so surprised she forgot to use the accent.

"Ms. Caldicott no longer works here."

"Since when?" Could he hear her accelerated heartbeat through the phone line?

"About a month ago." He sounded put out to have to give her information.

"What happened? Is she ill?"

"Please hold," he snapped, and disappeared. She wondered if he was alerting the authorities, although she couldn't be the only person who'd called for Reza. She should just hang up, but she needed to know more. Nothing would have made Reza leave her firm voluntarily; she loved her clients and her colleagues and her work.

Before he returned, an operator's automated voice broke in, requesting that she deposit more coins. She dumped in several; she didn't want this receptionist to know she was calling long distance.

"Law office." The curt voice again, thinking he'd picked up a new line.

"I was asking about Reza Caldicott," she reminded him.

"I don't know the details."

"Why haven't her clients been informed?" Then she realized: Marielle wouldn't be informed because she was dead. The dead did not receive a courtesy call.

"An effort was made to contact *all* of her clients. If you'll give me your name, I'll transfer you to the attorney who's been assigned to you."

Maybe she could get more information out of someone higher up. "Devora Sloan," she said. It was the name of a character in *Fear of Elevators*, but she'd wager a thousand dollars he didn't know that.

She heard only the man's breathing as he searched the computer files.

"I'm not finding anyone by that name," he reported. He didn't sound the least bit sorry.

"Well, that's just great." She took the offensive. "My lawyer up and quits with no warning, and your firm can't even keep track of my files. To whom should I speak about this?"

The thing about nastiness was that it worked so well. "Let me transfer you to Darrell Odums; he's executive assistant to the senior partner." Suddenly the man sounded almost helpful.

She almost slipped and said, "Let me just speak to the senior partner," but she'd met Erik Snowden a number of times and she couldn't risk it. "Thank you."

While on hold, she fed more quarters into the pay phone to forestall an interruption. By the time Darrell Odums came on the line, he'd obviously been briefed. "Ms. Sloan," he began, "I want to apologize for the confusion. We've been busy playing catch-up since Ms. Caldicott announced her abrupt departure." He had no idea who she was but he'd obviously decided to fake it.

"What happened to her?"

"We don't really know." He wasn't supposed to give her information, but he was going to try to mollify her by doing so. His tone confided, "We just got a call from her one morning saying she wasn't going to return to work, that she was exhausted and needed to go away for some rest."

"That doesn't sound like R—uh, Ms. Caldicott. Are you sure the call came from her?"

He sounded perplexed. "Well, who else would it be?"

"I'm just saying, it's highly uncharacteristic behavior. Did anyone go to her house, see if she was all right?" Lorraine could hear she was sounding too agitated; she needed to calm down.

"I don't really know." He was taken aback. "I can ask Mr. Snowden when he returns."

She should shut up, or hang up, but she could do neither. "I think you should. What happened to Altovese?"

"I believe she gave notice the same day as Ms. Caldicott resigned."

Had Reza tipped her off, or was Altovese threatened too? Altovese wouldn't have quit; she was a single mother of a thirteen-year-old with Down's Syndrome. She needed her job.

Darrell Odums took back the reins of the conversation. "Now, Ms. Sloan, I know this must be quite a surprise, but our firm stands ready to continue serve you. How may I help you today?"

"You've already been helpful, Mr. Odums, but on the basis of this news, I'm going to need to reassess my options and call you back. May I ask for you directly when I do?"

"Of course, Ms. Sloan." She could hear relief in his voice that she'd given him additional time to find the missing file of Devora Sloan and avoid further embarrassment.

She replaced the receiver and tried to quell the anxiety building in her chest. After gathering up her remaining coins, she slipped through the nearest theater door—not the one for which she'd bought a ticket—to give herself time to think. On screen was an animated feature in which woodland animals were behaving like lowlife punks. Maybe half a dozen seats in the theater were occupied, none of them by children.

While a skunk in mirrored sunglasses attempted to seduce an opossum in a tube top, Lorraine tried to make sense of this latest information. It had been almost six weeks since she'd last talked to Reza and asked her about the manuscript claimed in *The New York Times* to have been written by Marielle. Six weeks since she'd sounded so evasive and nervous. Six weeks since Lorraine had provided her address.

Two weeks later she supposedly quit her job, the job to which she was completely devoted, with no notice whatsoever. And just today, the manuscript, well, *a manuscript*, had arrived in Lorraine's mailbox.

* * *

"Have you ever read the work of Marielle Wing?" Lorraine asked Garland the next afternoon. She was sitting with him in his study, as was their custom. She had browsed his bookshelves and found none of her titles. Was this because he was unfamiliar with them or because he admired them so much he'd given his copies as gifts?

His face took on the look of one who was sorting through an enormous mental reservoir of information. "Wing? Didn't she win one of the major prizes a few years back?"

She had to stop herself from saying, *yes, the National Book Award.* Instead she answered, "Did she?"

"I think so. I read one of her books—something about the Earth?"

"*The Flat Earth*," she said, struggling not to be snappish. This man had impeccable recall of the books in his library.

"Right," he said, and she could see him conjuring his memory of the read. "I have to say, I didn't see what all the fuss was about. It seemed to me she was holding back, making easy choices instead of riskier ones."

"Oh." She tried not to sound offended. She felt indignant, of course, but then another voice snaked in: *What if he's right?*

"I'm sorry if I offended you. You must be a fan of hers to have brought her up."

Would Lorraine Kaminsky be a fan of Marielle Wing? Garland found it plausible. But how could she engage him further if he held such a negative opinion? Still she pressed on. "You know, I read she died early this year, just suddenly, out of the blue."

If she'd been hoping for an expression of sympathy, it didn't come. "I can never decide whether that's the way I want to die, with no warning, or if I'd rather have more time to prepare, settle things." Garland was more interested in the topic of sudden death in general than in Marielle's particular untimely end.

Still she persisted, unable to stop. "I read that Knopf is releasing a book she was working on when she died; her editor completed it posthumously."

He shook his head. "They're not doing her any favors. No writer wants to have his work made public before it's ready. We'll never know what this book might have been, had Wing lived to finish it."

She shouldn't push it, but she did. "I got an advance copy. Once in a while I've done a little book reviewing, just for small publications, but it means I can request galleys. So I got this one, *Memory's Trail*. It's entirely different in style and approach; even her diction is different. It makes me wonder whether she wrote a word of it."

Garland raised his silver eyebrows. "Well, *that* would be a bit of a literary scandal, wouldn't it?"

"I was wondering if we might read it together, I mean, if I could read it to you, and you could tell me what you think."

He looked a little put out, as if he was thinking, *I asked for a volunteer who would read to me the books I suggested, not someone to force her reading agenda onto me*. She supposed she'd surprised him; it was out of character for Lorraine to be so forward.

Then he said, "I suppose that could be amusing. Although I won't claim to be an expert on Wing's oeuvre."

"I certainly don't claim to be an expert. It's just a hunch."

"What will we do if we decide it's a fraud?"

She hesitated. The "we" sounded so welcome to her. "I don't know. Try to figure out why, I guess."

Garland grinned. "Well, don't write it in your review, or Knopf may send some big, burly editors to rough you up!"

That should be the worst that happens, she thought, but forced a lighthearted laugh. "The places I review for are so tiny, I'm sure no one ever reads them." Then she picked up *Beloved* and read to the end in this sitting.

Before she left, she asked, "How about if I come back tomorrow instead of the next day?"

Again, the eyebrows aloft. "You are eager to introduce me to this book, aren't you? I'm afraid if you're bent on converting me, you may be setting yourself up for disappointment. I'm the kind of man who likes what I like. I've always been that way."

"No, it isn't that. Never mind, I'll just wait until my regular day."

"No, no. Please come tomorrow. I just hope I won't have to give up the time on Friday and then have to wait the whole weekend. I rather look forward to your visits."

"Of course. I'll come tomorrow and Friday both. I enjoy our time as well."

Although it was a long shot, she felt a sense of excitement. Perhaps Garland could help her, if not to find a way out of her situation, perhaps to figure out the conundrum of it. She didn't know how she'd talk to him about it, but she decided she would just take the first step and then see what occurred. That was not much different than the way she wrote novels, often a scene at a time, without a blueprint of what was going to come next. Somehow, one thing always led to something else.

* * *

It was starting to rain as she stood at his front door the next afternoon, clutching the manuscript of *Memory's Trail*. Waiting for Garland to answer the doorbell, she felt the pangs of futility. What could she possibly expect to get from him? At best, he would concur that it was not even a passable fraud, but so what? If he even cared enough to speculate on the reason for such deception, he'd cleave to the obvious: Greedy publisher wishing to exploit the memory of dead author. And at worst, he would resent her for hijacking his reading process and ask her not to come back.

The rain accelerated; she hoisted her umbrella and rang the bell again. However risky or flawed the strategy, she was grateful for this opportunity. When she'd tried to pick up the manuscript again the previous evening, she couldn't make herself read it, no matter how much rum she drank. How did one absorb a seventy-five-thousand-word death threat? If nothing else, Garland's companionship would at least allow her to find out the fate they had in mind for her, whomever "they" might be.

Garland answered the door with a look of confusion on his face. Unlike his customary state of high grooming, he looked disheveled, his clothes rumpled, his face stubbled. "Lorraine, I thought you weren't coming."

"But I told you yesterday…"

"I got a call this morning from the library. They told me you'd had a personal emergency and wouldn't be coming back."

"The library?" Aside from the first time they'd given her Garland's contact information, she'd never had another interaction with them. Then she realized: *It wasn't the library who called.* She'd never told Donald about her volunteer job, although he could have had her followed. And if the terrorists now knew her address from Reza, they could be following her too. Either way, she had to keep Garland out of it.

"Despite the confusion, I'm glad you're here." He looked genuinely happy. "I'm afraid I'm not ready for you, but come in, come in," he urged. "I can hear that it's starting to rain out there."

"Garland, I'm sorry about the mix-up. I don't want to bother you." Irrationally, she was even more disturbed by his appearance than by the phone call. This gentleman who'd had such pride in his grooming. Today he looked like what she'd imagined a blind person would, and she knew somehow she was responsible for that. She had to get away from there before something bad happened.

"It's no bother…"

"Really, Garland, I'll come back another time." She was already retreating toward the street, keeping an eye out for cars that might be stopped and watching.

"Tomorrow, then?" He looked hopeful.

"Surely, tomorrow," she promised, and genuinely regretted the lie.

* * *

She'd always taken a steely pride in being "a loner," more at home in the world of her head than in the company of others, independent, not "needy." But as she watched Garland close his door and realized that even the simplest interaction with another human might place that person in mortal danger, hunger for human contact threatened to overwhelm her.

The rain had picked up, and her LeSabre hydroplaned as she pulled out onto Grand River Avenue. She was speeding west, unable to aim in the direction of the townhouse, but where else was there? Visibility was not optimal, and the window defogger was slow to kick in. Thus it was a few minutes before she noticed the black van following too close behind her. Where had it come from? Had it been there since she'd left Garland's? Its headlights were not on—a stupid oversight on a day like today.

She pulled to the shoulder to let it pass, but it slowed too, and pulled to the right. She veered back into the left lane; the van followed. Was this just someone fucking with her? She slowed her pace, thinking that any prankster would grow impatient and pass her by. The van slowed too. When she tried speeding up, the vehicle moved closer to her rear bumper. Clearly, they meant to stick with her.

This is it, she understood suddenly, adrenaline flooding her body and sharpening every sense, although she couldn't quite bring herself to formulate what "it" was. She had an odd intuition that her existence—since the moment she'd heard the explosions in JFK and then, a day later, watched her cell phone detonate in the street in front of her own house—had been tunneling toward this moment.

If they wanted to kill me, she rationalized, *they could just fire through the back window. It would already be over.* Unless their visibility, too, was rain-impaired. A clattering on the window, like sharp stones, made her jump until she realized it was hail.

Are they just trying to scare me? Don't they realize I'm not testifying by choice?

Or is it the Feds? Don't they know they could just pay me to disappear? Like Ingrid Warren in Memory's Trail, *my principles are liberal, not radical. When it comes down to it, my beliefs are shallow; I'm not ready to die for them.*

In other circumstances, this would have been a disillusioning revelation. In that moment, though, she was simply trying to bargain, telepathically, with the unseen driver of the van. *I'll go away; I won't testify. I'll never tell. I'll never bring Marielle back to life.*

Why were there no other cars around? *You would never find a major road this deserted in California, no matter the weather.*

Self-defense classes advised women that if someone was following them in their car, they should drive to the nearest police station. She knew there was one by the high school, but she was miles from it now. Would driving to the mall provide the same deterrent? Somehow she suspected not.

Approaching Twelve Mile Road she made the abrupt decision to turn right; the LeSabre swerved dangerously, but remained upright and made the turn. So, unfortunately, did the van. So much for the stories about those behemoths tipping over. At least on Twelve Mile there were businesses—clusters of fast-food joints, open despite the rain. *Nobody's going to shoot me in a Subway or in Happy Sushi, are they?*

In case she'd been mistaken, she pulled into the parking lot of a 7-Eleven. So did her pursuers. Without stopping, she drove out again, and the van nimbly kept pace. The hail had stopped, but the rain was coming down harder than ever.

Although the suburbs of Detroit sprawled for miles, there would come a time when she'd enter more sparsely populated territory. Was that when they'd make their move, when there was no chance for witnesses?

She was struck by a certainty—she didn't want to die as Lorraine Kaminsky, terrified and cowering in a KFC. If this was her time to leave her earthly body, she wanted to go out as Marielle Wing.

This realization emboldened her, the way a shot of whiskey can give courage. She pulled off the road again, this time into the parking lot of a Farmer John's grocery. As if they were part of a tag team, the van did the same. She pulled the LeSabre directly in front of the double doors; they were already opening to take her in. If she'd dared, she would have driven the car inside. Not bothering to switch off the ignition, she flung open the car door and dove through the open portal. She skidded a bit on the polished floor, but remained upright. She gave an involuntary glance over her shoulder—her car door still swung wide, the map light illuminating the front seat. The van had pulled up just behind her car, but no one got out.

Outside the sky was dark with storm. It was a shock to adjust to the fluorescent lights that made everything inside gleam like shiny plastic. Outside, wind and rain sounded a frenetic rhythm, her own frantic heart its counterpoint. The grocery store, with its languid Muzak, seemed to move in slow motion. There were no other customers. One bored cashier looked at her as if she were a creature dredged from the sea. She was dripping all over the linoleum.

A man in dark pants and a white shirt moved to intercept her, deep furrows across his brow. At his age, most men had thickened, but he was skinny, too skinny, as if he'd spent his whole life smoking and worrying. "Manager" was embroidered on the breast pocket of his shirt. Like everyone she'd met in Michigan, he began by trying to convey an attitude of geniality. "Ma'am," he said, like he hated to bother her, "I'm sorry, but you can't leave your car like that."

Aware that she probably seemed crazy, she still tried, "Call the police! That van"—she gestured outside with a sweep of her hand—"it's following me." The speed of her words was more than double his.

She could read everything going through the man's mind—*bad enough the torrent outside and no shoppers inside and how was he supposed to make payroll this week, but now a hysterical woman is gonna get us cited by the fire marshal.* He made no move toward the telephone.

"Please," she tried again. "They're going to kill me."

She expected him to care because she was Marielle, but then she remembered she was Lorraine, and no one cared at all if she lived or died.

She could tell he thought she was nuts. Maybe she reminded him of his ex-wife.

"Ma'am..." This time the veneer of niceness was peeled away, revealing a weary annoyance underneath. "...just move your car."

She turned toward the door, just to see what the van was doing: just sitting there, behind her car.

The store manager made a move to take her arm, as if to usher her out the door, but she threw him off and broke into a run, her wet shoes slipping beneath her. She ran the wrong way past the checkout counter and deep into the frozen food aisle.

When she saw the manager following behind, she took off again, rounded the corner past the meat section. "Oh, for Pete's sake," she heard him say.

What could she do to get him to help her? She thought about starting to pull things off the shelves, littering the aisles with breakfast cereal and chocolate syrup. Shoplifting something in full view of the video monitors. Screaming obscenities at full volume. It was Lorraine and her soccer mom disguise that made her seem annoying rather than imperiled.

She ran back to the front of the store, grabbed the bored cashier, and pulled her so close to her body that she could smell the Herbal Essence shampoo in her hair. Through the pocket of her raincoat she poked a finger into the girl's ribs. "Empty that register," she ordered, "I've got a gun."

This was something Xaviera Temple had done in *Three Parts Grenadine*, considered one of Marielle's lesser works, but while Xaviera had needed a hostage, Lorraine wanted the police.

"Sta-an?" The girl in her grasp wanted the manager to do something. Tears were melting the Maybelline on her lashes.

The manager stopped in front of the register and scowled. "Goddamn it," he said. At last he walked behind the desk and picked up a phone.

In a very short time she heard a siren approaching.

Looking out the window, she saw the van pull out from behind her car and drive off in the direction from which it had come.

She released the young woman and held up both her hands. "I don't have a gun," she said. "I wasn't going to hurt you," she told the cashier. "Thank you," she said to the manager.

Stepping in front of the double doors that opened automatically, she jumped back into her vehicle. The front seat was awash with rain but the car was still running. Shifting into drive, she rounded the corner of the store and left the parking lot through a side exit onto another street. In her rearview she saw the police car pull into the lot and race up to the doors. She was pretty confident the manager would be unable to give much of a description of her vehicle.

Careful not to speed, she zigzagged her way out of the area. She drove a couple of miles, then realized she was shaking so hard she could scarcely steer.

She pulled over, turned off the ignition and sat for a moment, listening to the hammer of rain against the roof. She heard the hiss of her breath; saw it steam up the inside of the windshield. Her thoughts were no more profound than a fleeting memory of being a child in her father's car, drawing stick figures on the fogged up window.

Then she opened the heavy door of the LeSabre. Rain poured once more into the car, drenching her face, her hair. She stepped out into the downpour. Water soaked through the soles of her shoes, dripped down inside the collar of her coat. Her hair was plastered to her forehead, sunglass lenses streaming with rain.

It was another minute or so before she could unfreeze her limbs, coax her knees to bend, and return to the driver's seat of the LeSabre. She moved slowly, like a very old person, or someone recovering from a spinal injury. *Turn, step, step, grasp the door handle, pull*—she had to command her brain to execute each movement; nothing was automatic.

Once she was in the driver's seat, her fingers weren't cooperating either. Three times she tried to place the key in the ignition; three times her key ring clattered to the floor. Finally she gave up. She rested her head against the steering wheel and watched the water from her hair drip slowly onto the floor mat.

After a long time she picked up the keys; this time she slid one into the ignition and turned. Her reflexes seemed to be working again—she released the emergency brake, slid the gear into reverse, turned the wheel, then aimed forward—but now there was no conscious thought process guiding her.

A car horn sounded behind her. Her nerves leaped. It wasn't the van, just a driver impatient to get home. "Don't do things to draw attention to yourself," Donald Watkins had said to her more than once. To Marielle, who'd spent a lifetime drawing attention to herself.

That lifetime was over, she sternly reminded herself. This lifetime might be over sooner than she'd planned. And it wasn't the idea of death that bothered her most, but the thought of dying anonymously. Of dying as Lorraine Kaminsky.

Pathetic, she told herself. *You'd rather be a famous dead woman than a living nobody.* She tilted the rearview mirror and gazed into it; the face staring back was unrecognizable. She couldn't find a trace of Marielle. The mouth Liana had once described as "arrogant"—this had been during their courtship and she'd intended it as a compliment—was pinched with fear, the lips thin and trembling. Skin that had always glowed with the California sun looked pasty under the green tinge of rain. Her eyes had the look of someone who'd survived catastrophe, both vacant and haunted.

Looking at that face in the strip of mirror, she realized she had no idea where to go next. She longed to go home, but no longer knew where that was.

CHAPTER SIX

She didn't know how long she'd been sitting in the park or even how she'd gotten there. Presumably she'd driven there, because the LeSabre was parked across the street. She must have been sitting there for some time because she was soaked through. The rain had subsided, the sun was emerging just in time to set. Her watch said 3:24, but there was a haze of moisture under the crystal, so she had reason to doubt. It had been gift from Liana, another lifetime ago. By the angle of the sun, it must be more like six or seven.

The park was small, not even a square block, in a residential neighborhood. There was a scattering of old trees, maples mostly, their leaves a full, rich green, a couple of picnic tables beneath them, a swing set and a slide and a merry-go-round in one corner. A few iron benches, like the one on which she slumped.

Surrounding the park were older houses of brick, mostly two-story, framed by trees and pleasant gardens. She recognized nothing she saw before her. She felt only the dimmest curiosity about where she was. For a second she couldn't quite remember *who* she was. That was a very peaceful second. The air was warm enough that, wet as she was, she didn't feel cold. If someone told her she could live out the rest of her life never moving from this bench, it would have been fine with her.

She had never felt such torpor, as if to move or act would shatter her. She closed her eyes in order to slip deeper, to release whatever it was she'd been holding onto so hard.

"Are you all right?" A voice behind her—quiet, uninflected, male. Her buttocks levitated inches off the iron slats, so startled was she by this intrusion. She wheeled around, not sure what to expect. A few feet behind her bench, standing in a slanting ray of golden light, was an Asian man of slight stature with a shaved head. He was dressed in maroon-colored robes. He wore round rimless glasses. Beside him squatted the oldest Labrador she had ever seen, eyes rheumy, stance unsteady. The dog's yellow coat too was luminous in this shaft of waning sunlight.

"No need to be frightened," the man assured her, and this time she detected a slight accent. "I've been watching you for a while. I wanted to make sure you are all right."

If she could just say yes, he would go on his way. She wanted this encounter to be over. She wanted to sit there by herself until she disappeared into night. But she couldn't force the sound out of her mouth. Instead she stared dumbly, as if she didn't understand his language.

"Do you need any help?" he tried again. "The Zen Center is very near, less than a block."

Finally she found her tongue. "No, thank you. I'm all right." Her mouth felt as if it were stuffed with bees. Her words were scarcely audible, let alone convincing. She willed herself to stand then as if to demonstrate her ability to function and, nodding a polite goodbye, walked toward her car. Somehow her hands found her keys in the wet soup inside her purse. Somehow her legs allowed her to enter the car, sit in the seat, and put the key into the ignition, all under the scrutiny of the little monk and his ancient yellow dog. She didn't have a plan, didn't know where she would drive next, but she knew she couldn't bear to be observed like this.

She turned the ignition, pressed the gas, and nothing happened. She tried again. Nothing. She tried the lights, the radio, nothing.

The little monk approached the car. On his feet were black rubber thongs. The dog remained behind the bench, listing slightly to one side; no unnecessary steps for her. Still, she attended to his every move.

"Maybe you leave your lights on," he offered. "Maybe you need a jump." The term sounded incongruous coming out of his mouth.

"Maybe," she admitted, noticing that the headlights were in fact in the on position.

"You have cell phone?"

She shook her head. She wished he would go away. She didn't want help. She didn't want to spring into action. She didn't want to have to do a damn thing about her dead battery or her inert Buick. She wanted to return to her bench and allow the night to gather around her. She wanted to be devoured by mosquitoes until there was nothing left.

"You come with me. We have a phone at the temple. You have Triple A?"

Signing up for the Auto Club was something Lorraine hadn't gotten around to. That was out of character for Lorraine. Even Marielle used to have Triple A. She wondered, *is there roadside assistance for the dead?* This thought made her cackle, and the monk peered through the window with renewed concern.

Behind those round lenses, his eyes were dark water, and inside them she began to float. There was a little sliver of moon, partly obscured by cloud cover. The bobbing of the waves lulled her, like being rocked to sleep. The next time he said, "Come," she found herself climbing out of the car. He had to remind her to pull her keys from the ignition, although she thought: *Where's anyone going to go with it?*

They walked back into the park, where the old dog waited patiently. She found herself bending to pet her and the Labrador leaned her head into Lorraine's hand. The monk had to help lift the dog's hind legs before she began to walk. "Arthritis," he explained, and gently urged the dog forward.

Exiting the other side of the park, they made slow progress down the street, as with every few steps the Labrador's hindquarters collapsed beneath her, and she needed to be righted again for the next few steps. The monk had infinite patience as he whispered small encouragements to take the next step and the next.

Their destination—less than a block from the park, as the monk had promised—was another red brick house; on this one, though, the trim had been painted soft lavender. It glowed in the setting sun. Strings of prayer flags extended from the roof out over the front walk, tied to poles sunk into the front yard.

There were steps up to the concrete porch, and the monk, who looked as if he weighed scarcely more than the dog, gathered her in his arms and lifted her up. If this was an effort for him, he did not betray that. A small wind chime sounded as they entered into a small foyer. There was a shoe rack lined with black rubber sandals; the monk added his to the rack, and she wondered how anyone could find their own. She assumed she too was supposed to remove her running shoes, and she bent to fumble with the wet laces, which seemed to have fused into knots. Awkwardly, she slipped them off still tied. Her damp socks left small tracks on the polished wood floor.

Directly before them was a hallway that looked as if it led to the kitchen. To the right was a wooden staircase to the second story. On her left was the entrance to adjoining living and dining rooms with an open archway between them, forming one long room. At the far end was an altar with a golden statue of the Buddha. Facing the altar were several neat rows of maroon-colored cushions on the floor.

"Soon people come for evening meditation," the monk explained. He continued to urge the Labrador down the hallway. She had a hard time getting traction on the polished wood floor.

"What's her name?" Lorraine asked. It was the first thing she had asked him. Not: *where am I?* Not: *what am I going to do?* Not even: *what's your name?*

"Hakue," he told her.

"Does that mean something?"

His face lit up as he replied, "Pure Blessing." Then he and Hakue disappeared through another doorway.

Lorraine waited awkwardly in the hall. The house smelled of spice, perhaps from incense or from cooking, and of freesias, which were gathered in two tall vases on a small table in the hallway. From somewhere she could hear the persistent trickle of an indoor fountain and it reminded her bladder that she needed to pee. It was the first bodily sensation she could remember having in a while. She thought, *I could make my escape now*, but her limbs felt too heavy to walk out into the evening.

She allowed herself to wander into the meditation room; the windows must have faced east, because the light was dusky. She could make out a series of framed pictures on the walls, but not what they depicted.

She stepped more deeply into the room, toward the altar, where the Buddha sat on a low platform. Seated, the statue was taller than Lorraine. Scattered around its base was a thick layer of white rose petals; they had not begun to brown.

Francesca had been into Buddhism these last couple of years. Once or twice she'd cajoled Marielle into going with her to services at a small temple on the northeast side of L.A. She'd been glad for Francesca, because her friend's spiritual practice seemed to be helping her let go of her demons—including her tendency to become overly attached to entirely inappropriate partners—but the rituals and the rules of the place had not really spoken to Marielle.

Looking back on it, she must have disappointed Francesca; they had, in the course of their long association, often paralleled one another in their progress through life. They'd each moved to L.A. the same year. They'd weathered creative dry spells at roughly the same times. They'd both discovered their first gray hairs within days of each other, and had drunk champagne to celebrate. Marielle would often call her to say she was reading a certain author; Francesca would squeal and say, "I just bought that book!" Their couplings and breakups often seemed to follow similar cycles. Francesca's first solo exhibit happened within months of the release of Marielle's first novel, *Fear of Elevators*.

Her first novel. It would always be *her* first novel; no one could take that away. Even if they killed her.

With that thought, her knees begin to shake so hard she dropped to one of the cushions on the floor. She stared at the Buddha's impassive gold face. He had nothing to say to her. Still, what came tumbling from her mouth were syllables she didn't even realize she remembered. "*Om Mane Padme Hum.*" She kept repeating them, again and again, because it was the only thing that could stop her from bursting into tears.

"You are Buddhist?" The monk stood in the doorway to the meditation room, smiling expectantly.

Startled by having been observed, Lorraine abruptly clammed up. "No," she said a little too brusquely and did not explain further.

If he felt let down by her response, he didn't show it. "Forgive me for your waiting. I had to get Hakue her dinner. She is Buddhist dog; she likes ritual."

"How long have you had her?"

"She belonged to man who used to come to the center to meditate. He died of AIDS. He asked me to take her; she was already old. That was three years ago." He shifted gears. "May I give you some supper? Not fancy, just beans, rice, some salad from the garden."

"Nothing, thank you." She couldn't remember the last time she'd eaten. Her stomach felt twisted and raw.

"Perhaps some tea?" he ventured again.

She stood then. "I don't want to trouble you any further. I should just go."

"How will you go if your car doesn't?" The question was posed with the utmost innocence.

"I'll…I'll find someone with jumper cables." In Michigan, nearly everyone carried jumper cables in the trunk of their car, since winter cold could cause battery problems. This was not something you'd have in Southern California. This was something, like Triple A, that Lorraine should have, but *she* didn't.

"Wait till after the meditation. Koryo has jumper cables. He will help."

"I don't want to trouble you," she protested, but already her resolve was giving way. She no longer felt she could go back to the park and sit until she disappeared. Nor did she feel she could summon the will to ask a stranger to jump the car. There was really nothing else to do but wait for Koryo, whoever he might be.

The monk with frameless glasses peered at her. "Forgive me," he said, "I think maybe you are upset. I think maybe you have trouble in mind."

There was such kindness on his face that she nearly wept again. She was overcome with the irrational wish to sit him down and tell him the whole story—who she was, who she used to be, what had happened and what might happen to her. She wanted to tell him about the airport and the exploding cell phone and her funeral and Reza and the book and Garland and the black van. For a moment she even wondered whether Buddhist monks were bound by the same confidentiality constraints as Catholic priests who hear confession.

That was ridiculous because Buddhist monks, to her knowledge, didn't hear confession. And it was ridiculous because anyone who knew the truth about her could be at risk of serious harm. Or could prove a danger to her. About this, at least, Donald Watkins had been truthful.

"You are very kind," she told him then added, with as much lightness as she could muster, "I've just had a hard day."

Unless he was an idiot, he had to know that was the understatement of the year.

"Maybe I will have a little rice," she continued, less because she wanted it than to give him something other than her mental state to focus on.

"Maybe you feel better when you eat. Come."

Lorraine followed him down the hall to a cheerful kitchen. The walls were buttery yellow, the cabinets blond wood. Despite evidence that a meal had been recently prepared, the kitchen was immaculate. Hakue half lay on a flannel-covered dog mattress in one corner, hips trailing onto the wood floor, her great head resting between her paws.

She took advantage of a small restroom off the kitchen; it was as plain as it could possibly be, just a sink and a toilet in an area the size of a tiny closet. She tried to minimize the sound of the urine pouring out of her into the toilet bowl, suddenly conscious of being in a house of celibate men.

When she emerged the monk was pulling a small pale-green ceramic bowl from a cupboard; he filled it with a scoop of rice and a scoop of black beans. "Salad?" he offered again.

"Okay."

He indicated that she sit on a small wooden bench next to Hakue's bed. He brought over the green bowl, a white plate strewn with salad greens, and a pair of chopsticks. Then he poured a small mug of tea. He looked expectant, as if waiting for her to taste and comment.

She scooped a mixture of rice and beans into the chopsticks. She didn't think she'd be able to swallow or digest it, but once the spices of the beans reached her taste buds, she let out a small "Umm." All of a sudden she was ravenous and would have sworn no gourmet meal in a five-star restaurant had ever tasted this good.

The monk smiled, pleased. "I must finish the preparations for tonight," he excused himself. "I will be back to see if you need anything else."

The simple meal did seem to have a calming effect, or perhaps it was the lull of Hakue's soft snores. She had the urge to curl up on the dog mattress beside the Labrador and drift into blissful unconsciousness.

From the front of the house, though, she could hear the sounds of people entering, the tinkle of chimes as the door opened and closed. Soft greetings, "Namaste." She remembered Francesca started saying this whenever Marielle would see her, but she couldn't remember its exact meaning. Something more than merely hello.

Nearer, along the hallway, she heard a male voice sharp with reprimand. "Zenkei, is this another stray you've brought home? You will never advance as a monk until you learn to control your attachments."

A flash of maroon through the kitchen door. At first Lorraine thought it was her monk, but this man was taller and did not wear glasses. His face was long and thin, not round and pleasant like the other man. He didn't look especially pleased to find her in the kitchen. "Come, join the others," he said tersely, more an order than an invitation. It was the same voice she'd just overheard. Did that make her the stray that was retarding Zenkei's spiritual progress?

As usual, she bristled at being told what to do by a man, even if he was a monk. With defiance, she took a moment to lift her teacup and drain it. She set it down with a flourish before rising slowly, as if she'd been planning to get up all along, rather than doing as she'd been told. In this small act, she felt more like herself, but then she thought: *Who is that self?*

She trailed the stern monk out of the kitchen, back down the hall to the meditation room. She hadn't looked in a mirror to see what an afternoon in the rain had done to her, but if she appeared strange, none of the group assembled seemed to notice. About twenty-five people were seated on the cushions; another six were on folding chairs at the back of the room. As was the case when she'd gone to meditation with Francesca in L.A., the group here was eclectic; mostly but not exclusively white, a mix of young—perhaps as young as some of her students—middle-aged, and five or six who looked to be upward of seventy. A few glanced up as she entered, but most had their eyes closed, already beginning their practice.

She slid onto a cushion—near the door in case she decided to make a quick getaway. The candles had been lit and provided a warm glow in the near darkness. She was a little disappointed when the stern monk entered and took a seat on a larger cushion at the front of the room; it was he who would lead the meditation. "Her" monk, whom she now knew was called Zenkei, sidled up to her and offered a photocopied sheet containing the words to songs and chants that would be used throughout the evening. She cast a futile glance at her sodden watch and wondered how long the whole thing would last.

She hoped Dude was okay. Although Marielle was often out in the evenings when they'd lived in Los Angeles, since they'd been in Michigan her cat had grown accustomed to sitting beside her on the couch when she read at night. She tried to visualize the red bowl that held his crunchies—had it been full or empty when she'd left? Not that he couldn't have lived for a few days on his excess weight.

The stern monk began by leading the group in a song that most everyone seemed to know. The words—in English—were written on the page she held, but she didn't try to sing along. She just sat and let the sounds wash over her, as the rain had earlier.

The song was followed by a prayer. Then the stern monk began to speak about the nature of the mind and its illusions. "This floor beneath you"—he tapped it—"the cushion upon which you rest, these walls—all of it is only appearance to mind. Your attainments, your desires, your losses—these too are only creations of the mind. It is when we believe them real, when we grow attached to them, this is the cause of human suffering."

Although there was rigor to his belief, his cadence was monotone, and she began to grow drowsy. She couldn't hold onto the thread of his words, though they swirled around her. After a time he stopped speaking and began to provide instructions for the group to move into meditation. She'd never been good at meditating; keeping her mind quiet was impossible.

He reminded everyone to straighten their postures. She was starting to regret the decision to sit on the floor. Her shoulders had slumped forward; her lower back was aching. Still she struggled to right herself. "Relax your forehead," he said next. "I can always tell when the mind has started to take over, because the forehead tenses." This was harder than it sounded, as she attempted to melt the furrows downward.

"Begin to deepen your breath, and visualize that you are drawing in bright, white, cleansing light. Draw it deep into your body, let it circulate throughout your entire body." He demonstrated a prolonged inhalation.

"When you exhale, allow all darkness to leave your body—negative thoughts and emotions, hurtful experiences from the past, all anger and fear, any pain or fatigue you carry in your body. Visualize a stream of black smoke exiting through the nostrils, and then draw in more light. Fill up with light, release the darkness. And just continue in this way."

Despite her earlier obstinacy about participating, Lorraine allowed her breath to fall into the prescribed rhythm. *I'm doing this for Francesca*, she thought. It would make her so happy if she knew. Lorraine imagined her breath was bright light coming in, dark smoke going out. She imagined all the particles that made up that smoke—not only the recent losses, but the end of her relationship with Liana, as close to marriage as she'd ever come; being a finalist for but not winning the Pulitzer. She'd always believed she would win a Pulitzer. Not the Nobel, of course—her work wasn't weighty enough for that—but surely a Pulitzer.

She recalled the stern monk's earlier words about these illusions people become attached to—how much had she suffered because of a prize she didn't win? What would it have amounted to anyway—just another line in the obituary.

"If you find thoughts intruding," his voice cut in, "just watch them. Observe them without emotion and let them go." She appreciated this direction; it seemed a lot easier to watch her thoughts than to banish them entirely.

When at last he asked the group to come back to normal consciousness and open their eyes, she was sorry to leave the meditation. She felt emptier, and found herself wanting to hold onto that state.

The gathering closed with another song and this time she at least read the words that others were singing.

She felt awkward as the crowd broke up; many seemed to know one another. Both the stern monk and "her" monk were surrounded by devotees who had questions or who wanted to prolong their contact with these teachers. In a desultory way she observed people, wondering which one might be Koryo of the jumper cables.

A youngish woman, late twenties, she guessed, approached her. She had a mass of reddish dreadlocks surrounding a face dense with freckles. Her body, in T-shirt and jeans, was lean and pleasantly muscled, as if she came by it honestly, not from sculpting at the gym. "First time here?" she ventured. Lorraine noticed ropey arms laced with tattoos.

She nodded and hoped the young woman would leave it at that.

"This center opened about four years ago, and I've been coming since the beginning. I love it; I come Thursday and Sunday nights and, as much as I can, to the morning meditations during the week. I can't always make myself get up, though. I'm a musician."

Of course you are, Lorraine thought, then chastised herself. *She's just trying to be friendly*.

"I'm Tuna." The young woman extended a hand, its back also deeply freckled.

"Tuna? Is that what your mama named you?" Unbelievably, she heard a note of flirtation creep into her voice. *Stop it*, she told herself. *If you'd gotten pregnant young, you could* be *her mother*.

The woman blushed, always a charming quality in redheads. "Naw, she named me Darlene." Boldly she continued, "What did your mama call you?"

If you only knew. "Lorraine," she said, wondering if it sounded as false to Tuna's ears as it did to hers. There were women who did that, gave out phony names and phone numbers rather than simply say "No, thank you." She wouldn't want her to think she was doing that, and then she wondered why she cared what the young woman thought.

"Lorraine," she drawled, and it did sound better coming out of her mouth. "That's pretty. Listen, I brought my grandma tonight and I need to get her home. But if you're going to come here next week, maybe we can go out for tea or something afterward." It was a nice, simple approach, not sleazy or laden with ego. Also impossible.

There was a time in her life, not so long ago, when Marielle would have been flattered to receive the attentions of a woman her age, some confirmation that she was still desirable, despite being past her freshness date. Flattery was yet another thing Lorraine couldn't afford. "I'm just here for tonight," she said, without further explanation.

Tuna hesitated for just a moment. Perhaps she exhaled the darkness of feeling rejected. "Okay, that's cool," she said, "but in case you ever find yourself back here, let me give you my card."

The card, which was fluorescent green, read:

TUNA

SOUNDS

Her number was neatly printed beneath.

"Thank you, Tuna." She tucked it into a pocket, which was now only a bit damp.

"Namaste, Lorraine, nice to meet you."

She watched the woman's dreadlocks bob as she crossed the room to take the elbow of one of the senior women. Grandma was wearing a purple caftan and an amber *mala*, the string of prayer beads on which some meditators chanted continuous repetitions of their mantra. Francesca used to wear one made of moonstones. She'd tried to buy Marielle one made of lapis lazuli for her birthday last year but Marielle had discouraged it, saying she'd never wear it. *Why had I been such a bitch?*

As the room emptied, "her" monk came to find her. He brought her to the stern monk and reminded him, "This lady needs a jump for her car."

Great, she thought. *Of all people, this would have to be Koryo.*

The taller man looked so annoyed that she wondered for a moment if he really was a monk; weren't they supposed to be neutral and serene? Zenkei seemed undisturbed by his colleague's attitude; maybe he was used to it.

"Her car just on the next street."

With barely a glance at her, the stern monk said, "Come," in a tone that was plainly disgruntled. She had to run to the kitchen where she'd left her sodden purse, scurry to the foyer to retrieve her still-sodden shoes, and jam her feet into them just in time to keep up with his irritated stride as he exited the back door. In a small wooden garage, its door open, sat a battered

VW bug. The old kind, not the new. In the dark its color was indeterminate. He climbed behind the wheel and, before she could join him in the passenger seat, he barked, "I'll follow you."

So she walked back along the route traced earlier by her monk and his dog, and found the LeSabre still across from the park. Her shoes squished with every footfall. She fumbled to open the hood; she hated the car and hadn't taken the time to learn how it operated. Koryo seemed to sneer at her vehicle, then positioned his rear engine near the front end of her car. The interior of the car smelled of mildew. She sat in the driver's seat while the monk hooked the cables to the terminals and started his engine.

With a dismissive wave of his hand out the driver's side window, he indicated that she should turn the key in the ignition. The LeSabre groaned weakly; the lights on the dash lit briefly and then darkened again. She tried again. And again. Nothing.

"I'm sorry," she said. "It won't start."

The tall monk got out of the car and disconnected the cables. He appeared to be about to drive off, having discharged his responsibility, but Zenkei appeared then, walking toward them at the torpid pace that was all that Hakue, who was beside him, could manage. The dog seemed to like being out at night and waited on a patch of lawn while the bespectacled monk approached her.

"No good?" he asked her.

"It won't start."

He turned to confer with the monk behind the wheel of the VW. "We can loan the car. She bring back tomorrow, get a new battery."

Koryo rejected this idea out of hand.

"No Triple A," the sweet monk informed him. "It is night, no mechanics now."

Lorraine slumped deeper into her seat, trying not to overhear the exchange. She felt ashamed that this discord between them was because of her and irritated with herself for being in need.

Then the stern monk got out from behind the wheel and walked back toward the house without a word to her. Zenkei padded over, dangling the car key between his fingers.

"Check for gas," he advised. "Koryo never remembers to put gas in."

She gazed doubtfully at the VW.

"It's okay," the monk assured her. "Not go too fast, but gets you there."

Exiting the LeSabre, she promised, "I'll bring your car back first thing in the morning."

"I know." He grinned.

She handed him the key to the LeSabre. "For collateral." Then she settled into the worn leather seat of the VW. The door was lightweight, nothing like the LeSabre's. Glancing at the gear stick, she hoped she remembered how to drive a standard transmission; her dad had taught her decades ago.

"Thank you so much," she told Zenkei. "Thank you for helping me."

"You know how get to freeway?" It was as if he could read her mind. She hoped he couldn't.

"No," she admitted. "What's the best way?"

He fired off a few directions, punctuated with hand signals that she hoped she understood. He ended with, "Come back anytime, not just for car. Meditation very good for troubled heart." Under the streetlamp, Hakue seemed to smile in agreement.

She worried about driving away in front of him. What if the car stalled? What if she ground the transmission? But body memory took over, and after only a small battle with the gear stick, she was on her way.

Following the monk's instructions, it was only a few minutes until she reached the freeway entrance, not counting a quick stop for gas. She tried to pay attention to landmarks, so she could get back in the morning. By the road signs, it appeared she was on the outskirts of Ann Arbor, home of the University of Michigan. Like many a college town, Ann Arbor was a bastion of civilization, and she would have visited before this if she still had the heart for civilization.

It couldn't be that late, but traffic was relatively light on a Thursday night. The VW shook when she tried to go over sixty, but it didn't seem too long before she transitioned to the freeway that would lead her to the exit for Lorraine's townhouse. From there, the route was familiar. She was practically on autopilot as she made the series of turns that led her to the housing development.

It felt later as she turned in to the neighborhood. There were no other cars on the street and few lights in the windows. She felt self-conscious about the rattle of VW's engine disrupting the quiet air.

She started to turn onto her street, but then kept driving. She had an inexplicable instinct not to park the car in her driveway. Not even in her garage, where it wouldn't be seen by anyone driving by. She argued with that voice; it made no sense. Tired as she was, more tired than she could ever remember feeling, it was ridiculous to park blocks away. Yet her intuition—which used to serve her so well when she was writing—was insistent and she complied, parking a few blocks away. A bitter thread of complaint wound through her mind as she trudged in her still wet shoes to her front door.

Out of breath from nerves as much as exertion, she fumbled her key into the lock, and pushed her way in, slamming the door behind her and locking the deadbolt. Her time in the Zen Center and the meditation had almost made her forget the black van that chased her in the rain. She didn't believe they would give up so easily.

She entered the townhouse as if she'd never seen it before; it was cold and sterile as a hotel. No one lived here. Lorraine had made no effort to give it charm or any personal touches. Marielle's effects were still in boxes stored in the basement. The sofa still smelled new; the dining table had never been used for dining.

She noticed her coffee cup still in the kitchen sink. She would ignore that, but couldn't ignore Dude, standing at attention in front of his empty dish. He gave her a look that warned further measures would be taken if this problem were not attended to immediately.

As she began to be more aware of her body, she could feel every muscle aching. She bent to a low cabinet and opened a can of food, spooning it into his bowl. Dude made a sound of acknowledgment and began to devour the mound of odorous fish in bites that managed to be dainty even as they were ravenous.

She knew she should go to bed, but she could not climb the stairs, making it only as far as her sofa. Once her body sank into its cushions, she knew she wasn't getting up again.

She folded one of the throw pillows in half under her head and hoisted her throbbing feet onto the sofa. She didn't even bother to kick off her sodden shoes. She was already dozing when she felt Dude jump up and settle his body beside her hip, heard his purrs lengthen into soft snoring. That was the last thing she remembered.

The explosion seemed like a dream and yet it was so loud; its force threw her off the couch and onto the floor. She didn't know where Dude was. The stairs that stretched from the upstairs to the basement were already a column of flame; the heat of it seared her skin.

She had no time to think of anything; the living room was already filling with smoke. Lorraine crept along the carpet to the sliding glass door that led to the deck, to the backyard, and somehow managed to slide it open. The outside air fed the flames behind her.

She jumped from the deck onto the lawn that connected all the backyards of her street. The wet grass cushioned her fall. Somehow, she had her purse in her hands, though she couldn't remember picking it up. She should go back and get Dude. She should wake the neighbors on either side of her, make sure they got out. But dumb instinct made her run and she kept running even as she heard a second explosion behind her.

With an energy she could not fathom, she ran all the way to the monks' car. Once there, she found the keys still in her pocket and she got in. She sat there. She wanted to start it up and drive somewhere, drive all night, drive back to California, back to Marielle's life but it was all dead and she had nowhere to go.

Sirens now blared in the distance and came closer, multiple engines converging on what had been Lorraine's townhouse.

She thought of the boxes of Marielle's things, stored in the basement. She thought of her computer.

Her fingers turned the key in the ignition as if they had a mind of their own. She turned the car around and pulled out onto the main road through the complex. She yanked the collar of her coat up higher and slumped deep into the seat as she passed by the block where the house was in flames.

Risking a quick glance out of the corner of her eye, she noticed Donald Watkins on the street, shouting instructions to the firefighters. She could only hope he would not notice her in this unfamiliar car.

All that had happened on this day became a swirling ball in her nervous system; she couldn't think about the individual events, but the ball seemed to expand and threatened to swallow her. Instinct kicked in once more, and she shifted hastily into second and continued up the street, driving as fast as she could without calling attention to herself.

CHAPTER SEVEN

She had to move quickly, and she needed a good plan. She had to think of every detail and its possible ramifications, just as she did when writing a book. Harrison Unger in *The Disappearing Moon* forgot to dry the sink after he'd washed his hands; that's how the police knew he'd been in Marla Washington's apartment.

For the time being, the monks' VW was parked outside a body shop on Grand River Avenue. People sometimes left their cars there to be repaired if they couldn't drop them off during working hours; she'd heard her neighbors talk about it. People parked their cars on the lot and left their keys in a little deposit chute in the front door, so having a strange car parked here overnight wouldn't seem odd to anyone.

Despite an exhaustion that seemed rooted not in her body or mind but in her very essence, her nerves thrummed like an all-night diner after the bars emptied out: *we never close*. In her mind she replayed the events of the last six months, the last six weeks, yesterday and today. She needed to stop that wheel from whirling; she needed to slow down and make sense of it all, but instead her eyes could only seem to follow the churning craze of color.

She knew she had only a small window of time to disappear before Donald Watkins figured out how to find her. He might think she hadn't been home at the time of the fire because the LeSabre had not been in the garage. Would he think she had something to do with setting the fire? Or had *he* set the fire? To burn her out? To scare her? To make Lorraine disappear too?

She didn't know what to believe anymore. She could continue to believe that Donald's mission was exactly as he'd said: to protect her. Part of her wanted to believe that. But if he found her now, he'd want to put her in protective custody, and she'd spend the months until the trial in a locked room under guard. And after that—what? It was clear he couldn't keep her safe. Maybe no one could, but she didn't want to be a sitting duck.

And if, conversely, he wasn't really working to save her life? If he was instead part of some conspiracy she didn't understand? What exactly would her chances be against the law enforcement arm of the US government? Lousy, she figured, but no matter the odds, she had to play as if she had a chance to win.

As soon as the bank opened she would clean out her account. The Feds would know she'd done it, but she hoped that by the time they figured it out, it would be too late. She wouldn't be able to use Lorraine's credit cards, and she'd have to abandon her car. She couldn't even try to sell it, because the paperwork was somewhere in the blackened wreckage of her home. She should get a new battery and move the LeSabre, though. She didn't want it to be found so close to where she'd been.

From the size of the flames she'd seen last night, she couldn't imagine that anything in the townhouse had survived, but she had to make sure. She had to at least try to look for Dude. The Feds would have set up a crime scene, but she was betting they'd wait until morning to investigate. It was a risk she felt she had to take.

Even if she could have calmed her thoughts, spending the night in the front seat of an old VW was not conducive to rest.

She experimented with the breathing technique the crabby monk taught last evening—inhaling light, exhaling dark smoke. She found she could do it for a few minutes at a time and then her attention would be disrupted by another thought—*I have to call Garland! That gold scarf Francesca gave me for my forty-fifth birthday!* A constant litany of things to do and of things now irretrievably lost.

By habit, she kept angling her wrist at the streetlight to read the face of her watch; it faithfully reported the time as 3:24 every time she checked. Then she tried to close her eyes again and breathe. She thought about Reza. Then she remembered the manuscript of *Memory's Trail*, left unguarded in the back seat of the LeSabre. She shouldn't have left it; she should have stuck it in her purse. Then she reminded herself: *where's it going to go?* This was how time passed, how the darkness changed into not-yet-light.

When she imagined enough time had passed—the fire put out, the trucks cleared away, the looky-loos settled back in their houses and gone finally to bed, she drove back to the townhouse. She parked blocks away, so the noise of her engine didn't alert anyone to her arrival, and moved on foot through the neighbors' backyards, which in this complex were all connected by one wide swath of lawn.

She approached her house from the back. Even in the dim light, she could see that part of the roof was gone. Everything was quiet; there was no detectable movement inside. The thin band of police tape that cordoned off the property was laughable. Gathering her courage, she crept along the side of the house, its outer walls still hot from the fire. Peering around the front, she saw a blue sedan parked across the street; the two men dozing in the front seat must have been the agents assigned to keep an eye out for her or for anyone who might attempt to enter the property.

Both her house and the attached house next door had been devastated; she hoped the older couple who lived there had gotten out okay. The husband liked to tend a container garden out on his deck; since the weather had gotten warm she'd seen him outside every day. Lorraine believed his wife had some kind of medical condition, maybe cancer; she'd gone to the doctor a lot, but they'd never talked about why.

The lawn behind the house was littered with objects, barely distinguishable scraps of clothing, a pillow, shards of vase or plate, loose papers like an unseasonable snow. The sliding glass door facing the backyard was shattered and glass was strewn over the back patio. Something had blown up inside the house. *My God*, she wondered, *did someone firebomb my house?*

She'd be stupid to try to enter the devastated structure; there could still be hot spots from the fire that might flare. The floor might collapse, trapping her. Whatever scraps of Lorraine's or Marielle's life that were still able to be retrieved were on the lawn in a rubble it would take daylight to sort through. She didn't have the luxury of daylight.

Still, she stepped carefully around the pile, willing her night vision to grow stronger, trying to identify something of value. The cover of *The Flat Earth* by Marielle Wing taunted her; the insides had been torn away. She recognized a soup pan from her cookware set purchased at Walmart when she first arrived, a part of a mug the mother of one of her students had given her—Teacher of the Year. It was amazing how little any of this meant to her.

She didn't find her computer. Either it had blown up, or whoever set the bomb had taken it before the explosion, or Donald Watkins had confiscated it before he left last night. A week ago she'd burned a backup disk and put it in her safety deposit box. What prescience had driven her to do that? She would retrieve that when she closed her account.

She could see an edge of pale yellow beginning to appear on the horizon and the sky was becoming a distinct gray. The birds were beginning their wake-up song. Time for her to go. Still she had to try one more thing. Dropping to her knees on the lawn, she softly called, "Dude! Dude! Kittykitty." She waited a few seconds, then tried again. She didn't dare call any louder. After the third attempt she heard a small answering cry. It seemed to be coming from under the house of the neighbors on the other side of the lawn.

As she walked toward the sound, she continued calling softly, "Dude, Dude. It's me. Come out, please."

The sky was getting more and more light. If she hadn't already awakened them, her neighbors would be getting up at any minute. It was Friday morning. People would be going to work. She knelt again beside her neighbor's house and visualized her cat appearing, his enormous orange fluffy body emerging from his hiding place.

Then he did. He was sooty and trembling all over as she scooped him into her arms and held him close to her heart. "Oh, my big boy," she crooned. "My main man. How did you survive?" she asked him, but he wasn't telling. She remembered the adage about cats having nine lives, and wondered if Dude would have one less now, if he'd come back somehow to be with her.

She checked him quickly; no bleeding that she could see, no broken bones.

"It's going to get a little worse before it gets better," she warned him. "Please cooperate." It was time to go. And if it had been difficult to walk six blocks unnoticed in predawn light, it was all that much harder carrying a nineteen-pound cat as the sun was coming up. Luckily, he was frightened enough to be docile; he clung to her shoulder with his front paws. Usually he was only this passive at the vet's.

She walked as fast as she could back to the monks' car, which in the morning light she could see had once been a midnight blue, and loaded her cat into the passenger seat. Dude hated being in a car. He hated the noise; he hated the movement, and usually nothing she could do would calm his loud complaints. She took off her raincoat and wrapped him inside it; he was traumatized, and she hoped being contained would be comforting. She'd need to get food for him, and water. And something—she wondered what—for shock.

It was crazy to have dragged him to Michigan in the first place; how could she now subject him to a life in which she didn't even know where she'd be sleeping tonight? Cats needed routine, stability. But there must be a reason he'd survived, she argued with herself. And he'd come out of hiding at the sound of her voice.

She started up the VW and drove away. It was both a worry and a relief that Dude didn't start to howl. She was guessing the time was about six thirty. She needed to find a place to wait until nine. She wondered if she were on the news; she wouldn't put it past Donald to be broadcasting her face on the early morning shows to try to locate her. On the other hand, he might have thought it too risky; did Lorraine Kaminsky really look all that different from Marielle Wing? Even if the people who knew her didn't figure it out, the people who wanted to kill her might. And if those people had tried to kill her, would Donald want to make it known that she was alive and lost to him? Or, what if Donald was one of those people who wanted her dead?

Unable to find a reasonable solution to this most unreasonable situation, she decided to proceed for the next few hours as if she were invisible. Lorraine was the kind of woman who could be invisible. She would drive to Meijer's and buy crunchies for Dude, a jug of water, perhaps a few basic toiletries for herself. Maybe a change of clothes. There would be surveillance cameras, no doubt, but, smart as he was, it would take Donald Watkins a while to imagine she would go grocery shopping less than a mile from her bombed-out home. By the time he did think of this, she would have left the immediate area.

Then she would take herself out to breakfast, someplace mundane and anonymous, Denny's perhaps, and wait for the bank to open.

* * *

She picked at the greasy eggs on her plate, sipped the bitter coffee the waitress automatically topped off each time she passed. The restaurant was slowly starting to fill with people on their way to work. The busier, the better, Lorraine thought. Her new watch, a utilitarian Timex from Meijer's Thrifty Acres read 7:54. Could she stretch her stay another hour?

The firebombing hadn't made it into the morning edition of the newspaper and there was no television in the restaurant, so she couldn't tell how her disappearance was being reported, if at all. Would Donald find a way to hush it up?

Her training as a novelist had prepared her, she realized, for inventing scenarios and imagining what people were thinking. That should help her in this situation. She needed to stay a step ahead of everyone. On the back of a napkin, she began to make notes.

If the people in the black van were part of the terrorists' network, why hadn't they killed her in the parking lot of Farmer John's? Or kidnapped her? If they were from the Feds, why were they trying to terrorize her?

If the terrorists had firebombed her house, what were they after? If they knew her car from following it yesterday afternoon, why had they bombed the house without her in it? But why would the Feds have firebombed her house? Why would they want to get rid of their own witness? But they, too, would have known her car wasn't in the garage. What was the point?

And who was trying to posthumously publish a book by Marielle Wing that she didn't write? She was furious with herself for leaving that manuscript in her back seat. Furious too with having run down her battery by leaving the headlights on. She hadn't been thinking, and while this might be understandable given the circumstances, unconsciousness was a luxury she couldn't afford.

There's a shadow world beneath the world in which most people conduct their daily lives, she reflected. The novelist may imagine this but never expects to live it. Having imagined it does not make it any easier to live it.

"Do you want anything else?" The waitress, whose hair had withstood a few too many bleachings, stood poised to plop Lorraine's check onto the table. She was counting on her saying no. She wanted to turn over the table, have a chance at another tip.

"Actually, do you have any fresh fruit?"

The waitress' response was automatic. "Grapefruit, banana, fruit cocktail," she intoned, masking her frustration with an attitude of boredom.

"Grapefruit, please."

She disappeared, returning a minute later with a bowl in which rested a dry half of a white grapefruit, which looked like it might have been cut a few days ago. She plopped it down beside the plate with the half-eaten scrambled eggs, then spilled more coffee into Lorraine's cup. No matter. It had bought her more time in the booth, which felt secure and unassailable.

She couldn't quite imagine the minds of the terrorists, how they thought. Marielle had always had a facility for putting herself into the skin of her characters; her reviewers often noted that. Now she kept thinking about the two men she'd seen in the airport, the two who'd allegedly planted the bomb, how they looked like boys she might have seen at the mall or in her classroom. But much more motivated, evidently. The boys in Lorraine's classroom had seemed motivated only by hormones, or peer pressure. Occasionally, but rarely, by their parents, when they'd threaten things like, "If you don't raise your grades, I'm going to take away your car."

"Go to Magda," the one bomber had instructed the other. Or that's what she'd imagined she'd heard, in that split second after the blast and before the screaming began. Could Magda have been a girlfriend, a Helen of Troy who'd inspired these young men to war? Could she have been a passenger in the black van? Or the driver, determined to keep this witness from sending her boyfriend to the electric chair? But the bombing had been in New York. What would Magda be doing in the suburbs of Detroit?

Or perhaps it was a mistake to link events. Maybe Marielle's death, Reza's disappearance, and the black van had no connection to one another. Could the van have belonged to the parent of some student she'd flunked? Life, as Marielle had often reminded the aspiring writers who sent her their work to read, is not like fiction. Life can be just a series of random and meaningless events.

She sighed into her bitter coffee. Donald Watkins, on the other hand, was easier to figure out. Not the government bureaucracy behind him; its motives were never what they seemed. But Donald had always appeared to be a by-the-book guy. He believed in his job, was committed to putting away bad guys and saving the lives of witnesses, no matter how unwilling. He would of course be worried about the loss of a star witness in the case, but if she understood him at all, she believed he would also be worried about her as an individual, worried that she'd been hurt or killed. This was going to rankle him as an unforgivable lapse in professionalism, but it would also make him afraid for her.

Reviewers had commented frequently that Marielle did a remarkable job of depicting male characters in her fiction. What she knew was that Donald Watkins was both concerned that he screwed up and that he'd let her down. She believed he would do everything in his power to find her and return her to what he imagined was protective custody. He would stake his entire reputation on it.

Or at least he would if he was legit. On the one hand she had an implacable sense of his character—upstanding, fighting for what he believed was right. At the same time it was increasingly implausible to her that a small band of disgruntled guys from New Jersey could reach so deep and so wide as to affect the events that had taken place. It was like a bad novel; the plot and the characters didn't match up.

What she also knew was that Donald had no idea what she was thinking. Skilled as he might be in reading the criminal mind, Donald Watkins did not understand women. Most men didn't. He might imagine her captured, tortured, dead; he might imagine her as a threat that had to be eliminated; but he couldn't imagine her free to eat a crappy breakfast at Denny's at eight-thirty in the morning. He couldn't imagine her with her cat banging around in an ancient VW belonging to a couple of monks. He couldn't conceive of her deciding she'd do better on her own than with the forces of the US government behind her.

Still, she felt a little sorry for him—and wasn't this always women's undoing with men? It made her want to send him a postcard, or leave him a phone message letting him know she was okay. He'd know within a couple of hours—she hoped it would be that long—that she'd cleaned out her bank account. He'd watch the videotape of the transaction and confirm that yes, that's her. He'd know then that she was alive, but still he would scour the footage for some sign of another presence, someone who was forcing her to do this. He'd round up everyone else who appeared on the surveillance tapes and ask them what they'd seen, had they noticed her, was she with anyone, what kind of car did she get into or out of?

Good for her to remember that he'd look for that. She had to keep the monks' car out of the picture. Maybe she'd leave the car in the lot here, and walk to the bank. It was just about ten blocks. Of course, she was a more vulnerable target on the street. But then she reminded herself: *for the next few hours, I'm invisible.*

She signaled the waitress for her check.

* * *

The teller initially made no argument when Lorraine asked to close her account, but when he saw the amount, he informed her it would take three days to get the full amount in cash; the bank didn't keep that kind of money—$300,000—in its vault.

"How much may I withdraw?" She struggled to keep panic out of her voice.

"I think we can give you $50,000 today," the teller replied, "and the remainder next week, Tuesday or Wednesday. But I'll need to get the manager's authorization for a withdrawal of that amount." Her heart dipped but she knew that some cash would be better than no cash. She'd have to stop using Lorraine's credit cards immediately, so she had to keep her cool.

"And," the teller continued, "we have to notify the Feds of any transaction over $10,000."

"Notify them?" Was Donald going to show up here before she ever walked out of the bank?

"There's just a form to fill out," he explained. She nodded her agreement, trying not to convey the urgency she felt about how long this was taking.

"Buying property?" the manager asked in a gruff, avuncular voice. He was a tall man but bent; he looked as if working at the bank had squashed him, diminished his stature.

"I'm moving," she replied.

"It's a lot of cash to carry." He enjoyed giving her fatherly advice. "We could just transfer it to one of our branches after you get settled."

"I'm leaving the country," she said brightly, as much for Donald Watkins as for the bank manager. This would be a good idea; Canada wasn't far away, but although Lorraine Kaminsky had a birth certificate and Social Security card, she did not have a passport. Could she somehow cross the border without a passport?

"No place like the good old USA." He dared her to contradict him. She just smiled. "Hundred dollar bills?" he asked, resigned that a share of the bank's money was about to walk out the door.

After he'd watched the teller count and recount the pile of bills, the manager said, "Anything else we can do for you today?"

"Yes." She surprised him. "I have a safe deposit box. I'll need the contents."

She thanked the teller and folded the bills into a large compartment of her oversize purse. Its lining had almost dried out from yesterday's soaking. Then she followed the tall gray-haired bank manager through a door leading off the main lobby of the bank. She imagined his interview with Donald Watkins. "It's not usual to have someone just walk in and withdraw that amount of money, but she had her ID and there was nothing I could do to stop her. I was kinda worried about her but she was cool as a cucumber." And Donald would wonder if he'd had her wrong from the beginning.

The bank manager was required to leave her alone in a small room as she gathered the contents of her safe deposit box. As she turned the key in the lock, she congratulated Lorraine on her prescience—Marielle would never have such a thing as a safe deposit box. Marielle had believed her world would go on forever as it always had; her books would always remain in print; her reputation would continue to grow. Marielle's biggest problem in life was not receiving an award she'd thought she deserved, or not making her goal of producing a certain number of pages in a given day.

Lorraine was practical. Watchful. Self-preservative. She knew that dangers lurked. For all Marielle's sophistication, Lorraine was the more worldly.

There was the thumb drive with the contents of her laptop as of last week; this included all of Marielle's books, as well as the first seven chapters of *Weeping Minerva*. She hoped that her laptop had burned in the fire, but she couldn't count on that. If the terrorists had it, they would know for sure that Lorraine was Marielle.

Lorraine had stored other items in the box—a sheaf of photographs from her former life. There she was with Francesca at the opening of her first one-woman show at a now-defunct gallery on La Cienega. They both looked painfully, tenderly young, they who'd thought themselves so knowing and urbane. There were her parents in the stateroom of the cruise ship that would carry them to Greece. And one of Liana and her at their commitment ceremony, barefoot and wearing loose white linen shirts and pants above the ocean at Big Sur.

She couldn't bear to look at the rest. She scooped them up and placed them in the manila envelope the bank manager had graciously provided.

There weren't many official documents. The marshals had confiscated all of Marielle's IDs: her birth certificate, driver's license, credit cards, passport. They'd told her at the time they didn't want her to have anything in her possession that would betray her real identity.

Here was Lorraine's fake birth certificate and fake Social Security card. Here was the deed to her bombed-out townhouse; she wondered what Donald would do about the insurance claim. Unfortunately, she'd neglected to include the pink slip from the LeSabre.

Her new Timex read 9:18. The longer she remained, the more likely she was to be found out. She swept clean the metal box, cramming everything in the envelope, and exited the small room. As she opened the door to the main lobby, she spotted the bank manager talking with two policemen. Guns hung from their belts. They appeared to be looking in her direction. The hair on the back of her neck bristled. She poked her head back in and looked around for another exit. There was a door that said, "Bank Employees Only," and she ducked into a break room with a table, a microwave, and a small refrigerator. At 9:24, no employees were on their break, although a smattering of half-filled coffee cups had been left in the sink. At the other end of the room was a door and she opened it, grateful to find herself in a parking lot outside.

She expected an alarm to go off as she exited the door, but if it had, she couldn't hear it. She quickly scanned the surroundings and, clutching her bag against her ribcage, veered down a side street. She followed a circuitous path back to the VW, walking briskly down one block, then cutting over to the next street for another block, stealing glances over her shoulder, all the while reminding herself that she was invisible. It didn't appear as if anyone was in pursuit, but she'd learned to distrust appearances.

Back at the monks' car, the orange cat was asleep in the back seat. He'd used the litter box she'd set up for him, leaving the car redolent with cat feces. She thought of the Koryo's stern face when he next drove the car and despite or perhaps because of her fear, she couldn't help but chuckle.

That was her first order of business—to return the monks' car to them and make a plan to deal with the LeSabre. But what was she going to do with Dude?

Okay, first she'd find a motel and check in. Someplace under the radar. Not part of a chain. Someplace without security. The kind of place that wouldn't care that check-in time wasn't until afternoon. She'd get a room and set Dude up there before she returned the car.

She'd find a motel, gas up the car, then locate a place to buy a battery for the LeSabre. Then she'd drive it someplace and abandon it. She wondered where. She'd have to figure out how to get back to the motel from there; you couldn't call a rideshare without a cell phone and a credit card. She'd have to buy a used car, not at a dealership, but from an individual. She'd answer an ad in the paper. How long would all this take? Marielle had been good at figuring out things in her head, when it concerned a character in her books, but these kinds of real-world tasks could send her to bed with a tumbler of rum. Lorraine needed to be good at navigating the real world.

Before starting the VW she had a moment of being overwhelmed; her shoulders sagged over the steering wheel. Who did she think she was that she could pull this off?

She had no idea who she was anymore. But alive, at least, she could figure that out.

The sooner she left the area, the better. She'd have to think about where to go. But first, she needed to deal with what was directly in front of her.

She squared her shoulders, turned the key in the ignition. "*Vamanos*, Dude." It was something Liana used to say.

* * *

It was a good plan. It should have worked. It almost had. Almost.

Although it had taken a little driving around, Lorraine had found the perfect motel, a rundown beige courtyard circa 1950s, what Francesca would have called a "Mr. and Mrs. John Smith" motel, meaning the kind of place you went to have an affair with someone who's not your spouse, the kind of place where you registered under a phony name and no one asked for ID.

Dude did wake up about five minutes into the drive, and spent the rest of the time serenading her with howls that no amount of coaxing would allay. She was thankful he'd stayed in the back seat and hadn't started prowling around the car. She'd need to get him a carrier. She drove back roads instead of freeway, and that's how she'd found the Twin Pines Motor Inn, just a little east of Ann Arbor. She'd waited a while at the "front desk"—the foyer of a living room cluttered with a good ten years of newspapers and a collection of dolls with vaguely threatening ceramic faces. From an unseen room, she could hear the sound of radio preaching, the volume loud. She'd called, "Hello, hello," at intervals for some minutes, until a defeated looking woman in her seventies slowly limped into the room. Her housedress was of some shiny, impossibly bright flowered synthetic that belied everything else about the environs.

"Thirty-nine a night," she said, not looking at Lorraine, "even if you don't stay the night. Two-ten a week."

Lorraine pulled two twenties from her wallet. "I think I'll just be here the one night." She sounded a little apologetic. Lorraine had already acquired that Midwestern kind of politeness that assumed she was to blame for everything.

The old woman could have cared less. There'd been no paperwork to sign. The minutes Lorraine had spent trying to decide what name to use were wasted here. The old woman stuck the twenties into the pocket of her housedress and handed Lorraine a key. Room six.

She had a momentary impulse to confess she had a cat with her, but it appeared this innkeeper made it a habit to know as little as possible about what went on in her establishment. Lorraine wondered what this boded for the condition of the room, but reasoned it was bound to be better than the front seat of the VW.

She drove around to the back, glad that the room did not face the main road, and grabbed Dude, wrapped in her raincoat, and hustled him in. After the commotion of the ride, he was once more pliant. Room six was painted Pepto Bismol pink, but a long time ago. There was a dirty red carpet, a double bed with a paler pink coverlet that clashed with the other hues, and flowered drapes that reminded Lorraine of the innkeeper's housedress.

There was a nightstand beside the bed, no telephone. There was a low dresser with a mirror propped on top, an old television set in the corner. She expected to see old shows, like *Lucy* or *Petticoat Junction*. But there was nothing except talk shows at that hour of the morning. Impatient, she turned it off and completed her exploration. The bathroom had salmon-colored tile and was surprisingly clean. This, at least, was a relief.

Much to his displeasure, she closed Dude in the bathroom while she unloaded the other things from the monks' car. The cat box, the bags of cat food and cat litter she'd bought, the plastic bowls and the jug of bottled water. On her next trip, she brought in her shopping bag, which had toothpaste and brush and floss, a washcloth and soap, deodorant, some cheap moisturizer, shampoo, and a hair dye kit that promised to turn her color to "Autumn Flame." She'd also bought a T-shirt, a sweatshirt, underwear, and socks. People in the Western world believed they needed so many things. When Marielle had traveled in Malawi some years ago researching a book she never did write, she'd met people who felt lucky if they owned a bowl.

Lorraine's sojourn in room six evoked a combination of feelings, including disgust, relief, utter exhaustion, and pride in having found such a good hideout. She gave herself the opportunity to stand under the thin stream of rust-colored water that came from the shower, washed her hair (she couldn't color it until after she'd returned the VW to the Zen Center) and dried off on one of the scratchy towels. She washed her face with the tiny motel soap, brushed and flossed her teeth, and dressed in her new clothes. She had to put back on her bra from the day before, and then new jeans and sneakers. She wanted to take her old clothes and burn them, but perhaps she'd feel differently after a trip to the laundromat. She hadn't been in a laundromat since she was twenty.

She checked herself in the mirror and found no trace of Marielle, but she looked very much like Lorraine: practical, no-nonsense, someone without high expectations of life.

She had to fight the urge to lie down beside Dude, who'd jumped onto the middle of the pink-covered bed and curled his large frame into a half circle. Her head was spinning with a million things she needed to do, but she was so tired she began to feel she was hallucinating, as if she were watching her body and its actions from a great distance. But she'd promised the monks she'd have their car back in the morning, and her new Timex said 10:50.

She whispered a promise that she'd be back into Dude's ear and slipped out the door. The day was beautiful, hot without being punishing, summer in Michigan at its most beguiling. The trees along the road to Ann Arbor were deep green, and flowers seemed to peek out from every bit of unpaved ground. As she neared the city, she stopped and filled the old car up with gas and put in a quart of oil. She bought pine-scented deodorizer and washed the windshield and did what she could to leave the VW better than she'd found it. She asked the station attendant for directions to the freeway, hoping she could figure out her way back to the Zen Center from there.

Luck was with her and with only a few wrong turns, she navigated through the curving streets of the college town. She was excited to recognize the little park where she'd sat yesterday in the rain, where Zenkei and his aged yellow dog had found her. She once more regarded the bench where she'd sat, the slides and merry-go-round, the maple trees. The plan had been working beautifully up to this point.

But the LeSabre was gone.

At first she thought she must have forgotten where she'd parked it, but that was ridiculous. She remembered exactly on what bench she'd been sitting, could picture clearly that it faced the street where the car was. She parked the VW, walked to the bench, and sat again, in case she'd somehow missed seeing her car.

She'd been feeling oddly buoyant for the last hour or so, confident that she'd get away with this, congratulating herself on her strategic thinking. All that drained from her, fear flooding her nervous system. As she inched her way back to the monks' car, she tried to appear casual as she scanned the surroundings. Were there cars parked with passengers in them? Was someone watching from a window in one of the brick houses? She couldn't see anyone, yet she sensed a presence like cold fingers inching up her spine. She had just enough time to lean over the curb before she abruptly retched and emptied the contents of her stomach into the street.

She was shivering all over on this eighty-degree day. Still, she wiped her mouth, started up the VW, and drove the short block to the Zen Center. She realized she might be putting into danger these monks who had tried to help her, yet she couldn't not return their car. She had to hope their Buddha would protect them.

She drove up in front of the Zen Center just as Zenkei was letting himself and Hakue out of the front gate. His face stretched into a wide grin at seeing her.

"I tell Koryo you be back!"

She tried to stretch her mouth in an approximate response, but she could feel the tightness in her cheeks, the grim set of her lips.

Then the monk said, "So sorry about your car."

"What do you mean?" she snapped.

"Police come early this morning. Hakue needed to go out very early, before sunrise. I see them tow your car."

"The police towed it?"

"I'm sorry." He bowed a little. "I want to tell them it broken, that you'd be back, but Hakue was having trouble walking and I couldn't leave her." As if on cue, the Lab's back legs gave way, and she sank to the sidewalk. The monk gently boosted her back to standing then leaned his own legs against her for support.

The police towed the LeSabre. She turned this information over in her mind, trying to make sense of it. She didn't know whether to be relieved or more afraid. The police had saved her the trouble of dumping the car. That was the good news. But on the other hand, why would the cops tow *her* car at five o'clock in the morning just after her house had been firebombed?

"Was I parked in an illegal spot?" she asked the monk.

"No, no," he assured her. "Okay to park there. I would have told you."

It was too weird to be a coincidence. If they'd towed other cars, surely Zenkei would have noticed that. Why would they tow a legally parked car with no outstanding warrants on it before sunrise? There could only be one explanation.

The monk's eyes studied her from behind his glasses. "You are worried. Don't worry. We drive and get your car. No problem."

She shook her head. How could she ever begin to explain what she was and was not worried about?

"It okay," he persisted. "Couple hundred dollars. If you don't have, we can loan it to you." He smiled slyly. "Just don't tell Koryo."

Of course, she had no intention of presenting herself at the impound yard to retrieve the LeSabre. She tried to think whether she'd left anything inside it that she would want or that she'd rather the police not have but her mind was blank.

Then she remembered: in the back seat of her car was the manuscript of *Memory's Trail.* The manuscript she'd waited weeks for, that she might have endangered Reza to get her hands on. The manuscript that might have explained what the terrorists had in mind for her. It was gone.

She took the key out of the VW and rolled up the window. She stepped from behind the wheel and handed the key to Zenkei. "Thank you very much," she told him. "You've already been so helpful. I don't want to impose on you any further. I'm fine." She made a better effort at smiling this time.

Her nerves were hair-trigger. She kept expecting something terrible to happen—gunfire or an explosion. She wanted to get away from this gentle man, his ailing dog; she didn't want her karma, whatever that might be, to infect them. And she needed to get off this street in a hurry.

Because she knew that if the police had towed her car, it was because they were asked to find it. And now that they had found it, Donald Watkins for sure knew that she had been, or still was, in Ann Arbor.

CHAPTER EIGHT

It was only after she'd said goodbye to Zenkei and was walking up an unfamiliar street that the numbness dissolved and Lorraine started to feel the enormity and impossibility of what was before her. However well she might understand Donald Watkins as a man, she did not have a good grasp of the resources at his disposal, which now seemed limitless. She had to wonder if there was a tracking device installed in the LeSabre—so much less labor intensive than actually having to have her followed.

How could she make a plan if she didn't know what he knew? He could be watching her at that very moment. From anywhere. She couldn't help but stop for a moment to scan the street again, pivoting 360 degrees on the sidewalk. It was a quiet street; most of its residents must have been at school or work at this time on a Friday morning. A white cat walked along a low wall. A dog barked in a backyard. A mail carrier lugged his bag from house to house. A few cars passed, but no one stopped. The quiet felt unimaginably dangerous.

What if he'd implanted something in her brain and could read all her thoughts? She prayed this was just a paranoid fantasy, the cheap stuff of summer blockbusters. Two of Marielle's books had been made into movies—one they ruined, but the second one was more faithful—though neither of them had become summer blockbusters.

She tried to think but her mind was too agitated. Once more she tried the breathing technique taught by the crabby monk, but she could only seem to inhale and exhale in ragged gasps. Breathe in light. *How am I going to get away from Donald without a car?* Breathe out darkness. *How am I going to get back to Dude without a car?* Breathe in—*how can I possibly get a car without Donald finding out? And then what am I going to do?*

She wasn't sure if she was walking toward town or away from it, or which strategy would be best. Lorraine might be practical, but she wasn't brave; she needed Marielle to make an appearance, fearless and attitudinal, and get them out of this.

All of a sudden, she saw a fuchsia-painted van driving up the street. It slowed as it came closer and seemed to be headed right for her. A wash of dread filled her mouth with saliva. In a split second she imagined men leaping from the back to grab her and drag her in, the van speeding away with only the anonymous white cat as witness. She imagined men with face masks and sub-automatic weapons jumping out, spraying her with bullets, shouting, "This is for Magda," as she lay in a bleeding heap while they speed away.

She considered running, trying to make a break for it, maybe slipping into someone's backyard, but as the van rolled up beside her, another part of her brain thought, *Would either the Feds or a group of terrorists really use a purple van with a big fish painted on the side to do their covert work?* Then she heard, "Hey, Lorraine!" and she saw Tuna's face grinning through the open window.

Her white teeth flashed behind a broad smile. Her dreadlocks swayed slightly around her face. "It's me, Tuna. Remember?"

She managed a weak, "Hey," trying to arrange her face into an expression that might approximate normalcy.

"I was just thinking about meetin' you last night," she continued undeterred. "Hopin' I might run into you again."

"I'm just on my way out of town," Lorraine answered, hoping Tuna would drive away.

"Can I give you a ride to your car?" Her persistence was both charming and maddening, but she didn't have time for either.

"No, thanks..." she began, but the younger woman interrupted.

"Ahh, come on. You look a little lost. Climb in."

Then she saw a black van turning the corner. She couldn't tell if it was the one that followed her yesterday, but she had no time to assess the situation. She raced to the passenger door of the purple van and yanked it open.

But Tuna had to clear an empty yogurt carton, wrappers from a couple of Power Bars, and a drained bottle of green tea before she could settle onto the sheepskin-overed passenger seat. As she hung awkwardly half in, half out the door, the items joined a half-foot-deep pile of trash on the floor. When the van passed them, Lorraine saw that its driver was a woman with a bowl haircut not unlike her own; she had a boisterous Irish setter in the passenger seat. Part of her wanted to change her mind about getting into the van, but her heart was racing so fast she didn't want to be alone on the street.

"Sorry." Tuna smiled with embarrassment, but Lorraine could tell this was how the van always looked. She imagined Tuna had dated women who'd given her a hard time about it. She wondered what her grandmother said, or if they took *her* car when Tuna drove her places.

She thought of Liana, who could spend hours polishing her vintage Comet to a cool sheen, who'd have a meltdown if Marielle so much as left a used tissue in the front seat. Her pulse slowly returned to normal.

The inside of the van smelled like patchouli oil, like a flashback to her teen years. It made her want to roll her eyes, but it was also deeply comforting. There was music coming from the CD player—a kind of jazz and tribal fusion that sounded as if it were being channeled from another planet.

"Like it?" Tuna nodded toward the dashboard. "That's my band."

"Hmm." She nodded back, but she was distracted. She kept looking out the passenger window, trying to see who might be seeing them.

"Are you okay?" Tuna asked. "Were you waiting for somebody?"

"No, sorry, I'm fine." Her tone, more Marielle than Lorraine, said, *drop it.*

"Where do you want to go?" Tuna squared her shoulders and gripped the steering wheel, resigned to her companion's rude behavior.

Where indeed? What was she thinking, getting in this van? Her lack of sleep was starting to take its toll; she wasn't reasoning clearly. She needed to get out of the area and find a place to regroup.

Just then she heard a helicopter overhead—a common sound in Los Angeles, but not one she was accustomed to hearing in Michigan. Involuntarily, she ducked, so as not to be visible to whoever was up there.

"Lorraine, what's going on?"

Tuna reached to touch her arm. Her hand was large and warm. Lorraine was surprised to find that she wanted to sink into it.

"Let me help you." The younger woman's brown eyes were so bright and innocent, so eager.

This time she didn't play it off like everything was fine. "You can't help me," she told her, with genuine regret. She gently removed her forearm from underneath Tuna's hand. The helicopter had moved on.

"Why not?" This amused her; she liked the challenge of being told she can't.

"It's dangerous."

Tuna was still smiling. She was looking at Lorraine, this nice little suburban lady with an inexplicable edge, who seemed a little unhinged, and she was thinking, *what could be so dangerous?* She wanted to be the big strong protector; her youth made her want it even more. With the insight into human nature that was Marielle's gift, Lorraine understood these things about her driver.

How could she explain? She was battling within herself because more than anything in the world right now she wanted help. She was tired and scared and she didn't have a clue what she was going to do. She wasn't even sure who she was anymore, and Tuna's attention was helping her forget that.

"It's my ex-husband," she told her, without meaning to. As she heard these words, she wanted to take them back, but now that she'd begun, she couldn't seem to stop. The lie spilled forward, sounding more convincing with each syllable. "Ever since we broke up, he's been stalking me, threatening me. He's following me. He says he'll kill me. He just had my car towed away."

She was ashamed of herself. Marielle would never have portrayed herself in this kind of victim role. It was one of the things reviewers always said about her female characters, how she never drew them as victims.

There was a look in Tuna's eyes that shifted, just slightly, probably nothing she was even aware of. The tough, elusive woman she thought she'd met, whom she wanted to help because she didn't need it, had devolved into another needy female. A needy, heterosexual female at that. She remembered that same look in Liana's eyes, the only time Marielle had let her guard down.

But Tuna had been better brought up than Liana, because rather than finding an excuse to slip away, she said, "Let's get you someplace safe." She began to drive with purpose.

"Have you gone to the police?" the younger woman asked as she turned at the corner, carrying her away from the park and the Zen Center.

"He's an ex-cop," she blurted. "They won't do anything to help me."

The van took a left. Tuna was looking in her mirrors. Did she think someone was following?

"I need to get a car," she told Tuna. "I need to get a car that I don't have to register, because I don't want him to be able to trace it." Then she told her about Dude and the motel, but she didn't tell her which one. "I should leave the area. I should leave the country. But he took my passport."

"You can go to Canada without a passport," Tuna said. She took another right. "But only if you drive over the border. Do you have other ID? A birth certificate?"

Lorraine wanted to throw her arms around the lanky woman, so relieved was she to get this information. But then the van turned left again, and the thought crossed her mind, *What if she's not trying to elude someone else, but trying to make sure I can't trace the route we're taking?*

Even though she'd told Tuna a lie, she knew she'd told her too much. She knew Lorraine was thinking about Canada. If she helped her get a car she'd know what car she was in.

Tuna was unaware of the storm bursting in her head. "We could steal a car," she offered.

Lorraine said, a little aghast, "Whatever happened to Right Action?" recalling one of the Buddhist principles the monk had talked about last night.

"I'm totally kidding," Tuna assured her. "I've got a buddy, Hatch," she said, as she steered onto a busy thoroughfare, "who's a drummer. He used to be in my band, but then he got this gig touring with Daisy Heart in Europe for, like, a year. He left me the keys to his Ford Focus and asked me to drive it once in a while. You could take that."

This youthful logic astonished Lorraine. "Given that my ex-husband wants to kill me, and I'm trying to leave the country for good, do you really think it's a good idea for me to borrow your friend's car?"

"You'll come back," she said breezily. "Your ex'll hook up with someone else and get over it. And if it turns out to be a while, maybe you could send Hatch some money or something. It's not a big deal, I swear."

She recalled herself before age thirty, when the stakes were low and everything still seemed possible. Francesca had been the same way. Nothing was a big deal; every problem could be solved by not taking it too seriously.

"So do you want to get your cat before we get the car?"

She was thinking *I should get the car, lose Tuna, pick up Dude, and head across the border*, but she couldn't exactly say that. "If I get the car first, then you can just go on to whatever you were on your way to do. I don't want to put you out any more than I have already."

"It's no trouble." She turned up the volume on the CD player, grooving on her own riffs. Then she looked in the rearview again. "What kinda car does your ex drive?"

"Is someone following us?" She prepared to duck down onto the floor again.

"Lorraine, I'm not gonna let anyone hurt you, I promise." She made an abrupt turn down a side street. In the passenger side mirror, Lorraine saw no one behind them.

She was furious with herself for lying to this woman. Now Tuna thought this was some kind of man-woman thing, something to be resolved with fists, where youth and being a lesbian would be in her favor. She had no idea the seriousness of the situation, that she could be killed, or implicated in something even Lorraine didn't fully understand.

In another few minutes they pulled into the driveway of a wood frame house, two stories painted a pale blue that had weathered to almost gray. There was a neat front lawn, but nothing as manicured as the gardens in the neighborhood of the Zen Center. There was a porch with a couple of straight-backed chairs, and lace curtains in the front window, from behind which a tortoiseshell cat peered.

"This is my grandma's house." Lorraine looked at her quizzically. She blushed, then explained, "I'm kinda between places right now, so I'm staying here. She's got the room, and since I'm around I can do things for her."

Tuna jumped out and came around to open her door; she was unused to such courtliness in men or women. But Lorraine couldn't move. She didn't want to walk into this grandmother's house. All she could think of was that she didn't want to endanger the life of an old woman who wore caftans and meditated.

She tried to think back to the chain of decisions that had led her here; it seemed like she hadn't been thinking clearly since she'd found out about the novel, the one someone wanted to publish in Marielle's name. Seven weeks ago.

"It's okay," Tuna said, sensing her hesitation. "I think she's at her book group this morning." As if that were Lorraine's concern, as if she were a schoolgirl worried about the approval of someone's family. "Not that she'd care. My grandma would like you just fine. She can talk to anyone!"

She had no way to explain her reluctance. All she could do was get the keys to Hatch's car and get the hell out of here.

As they entered, the cat came to the door to greet Tuna, but turned and ran when she saw Lorraine. The house had a layout similar to that of the Zen Center; the front door opened into a long hallway, at the end of which was the kitchen. A staircase framed the right side of the hall, and a living room opened to the left. The walls were painted in bright colors that suggested grandma may have once been a hippie. Like grandma, like granddaughter. The furniture was cheerfully mismatched. She wondered if Tuna's parents lived some buttoned-down life in the suburbs.

Tuna led her along the hall, through the kitchen, and down the stairs to a finished basement. Here the décor resembled the van, clutter being the main theme. Lorraine counted four guitars on stands planted like sculpture throughout the space, an electronic keyboard, a scattering of African drums.

The young woman offered her some tea, but she declined. She wanted to get out of there, go pick up her cat. She conjured the image of Dude stretched out on the horrible pink coverlet, and hoped he was resting as she'd left him.

Tuna confided that she wanted to get a dog, but because she was gone so much playing music, thought it might be too much for her grandma. She attempted to excavate the cushions of a battered brown leather sofa from the piles of mail and other paperwork that buried them. "Have a seat."

Shut up, give me the keys, was all Lorraine could think. Then she felt ashamed. This young woman was nice, was trying to help her, she reminded herself. The least she could do was give her the time of day. So she perched on the edge of the seat, a bird ready to fly in the next instant.

Tuna was puttering around, looking through a pile of mail in a leisurely fashion, checking her cell phone for messages. Lorraine attempted deep breathing again, to keep her impatience from exploding.

Tuna filled a teakettle with water from the faucet of the laundry sink and set it on a hotplate atop a long wooden folding table. She pulled down a couple of dubious mugs from the shelf above the washer and dryer and ran them under the tap as well.

"I don't mean to be antisocial"—Lorraine struggled to keep a measured tone—"but I've got to get out of town fast. If my ex were to find me here with you, it would be really bad for both of us."

For just a moment, disappointment threatened to undermine the young woman's natural optimism, but only for a moment. "No one's gonna find you here." Lorraine thought she ought to find these words ominous, but before she could register them, Tuna came up behind the back of the couch, and took her shoulders in her big, warm hands. Surprisingly strong fingers began to knead the knots and lumps in her muscles. It felt better than Lorraine could let herself admit.

"You're all tense," Tuna admonished, then, lest Lorraine think her critical, added, "'Course, anybody would be with some crazy guy givin' them a hard time. If you can just relax a little, you'll be able to figure out better what to do." Her thumbs were more persuasive than her words; they seemed able to find and read each pocket of stress that had accumulated in the tissue over the last days or months. The pressure of those hands threatened to unwind the whole careful construction of Lorraine Kaminsky, but she couldn't afford that.

"Please, you're very kind—" she tried to protest, but couldn't seem to summon any words to stop those hands, nor any will to propel herself off the sofa. The fingers were warm across her neck. Her skin seemed to rise of its own volition to meet their touch.

She thought back to when she'd last been touched by anyone. It was when she had still been Marielle, at that PEN conference in February, too much rum, that journalist. It was the day before the bombing at JFK, before her life changed. Ended.

Lorraine, in her short life, had never known this kind of intimacy; under this woman's freckled hands, she found herself as shy and desperate as any fifty-something virgin. She could hardly believe she was in the midst of this flirtation while there were people trying to kill her, but she supposed it made a kind of sense. *Eros and Thanatos.*

When Tuna's hands slipped down, almost as if by accident, to cup her breast, Lorraine felt warm all over and her limbs became liquid, like when she and Francesca used to drink Ouzo in that Greek bar in San Pedro. She knew she was not in her right mind, was not capable of making good decisions, but she decided right then and there that if she were going to die in the next few hours or the next few days, she wanted to have this experience before she passed from this world.

The shift in her breathing must have signaled to Tuna that she was with her because the grip grew less tentative, more insistent. Her nipples hardened beneath those strong fingertips. She could feel wetness spreading between her legs, and she turned her body to kneel on the couch cushions, so she could pull Tuna's body toward her. As their mouths met—the young woman tasted of licorice—Lorraine pulled harder until Tuna's body tumbled nimbly over the sofa back and on top of her.

She could tell that Tuna would be a gentle lover but Lorraine did not feel gentle, not now. Some force had been unleashed and it had its own momentum. She tore at the young woman's shirt because she needed to feel her skin; she bit the muscled chest, the small, perfect nipples. She pulled her dreads. She could feel Tuna's wetness through her jeans, and she thrust her hips toward her. She wanted the young woman to grind against her until both Lorraine and Marielle were annihilated, and only some raw essence remained.

She didn't have time to care that she was wearing a shapeless bra and unflattering panties from Meijer's Thrifty Acres. Or that her thighs were not those of a thirty-year-old. She was shedding her clothes as fast as she could without losing contact with Tuna, tugging frantically at the young woman's zipper at the same time.

"Easy," Tuna cautioned with an embarrassed grin. "I'm not wearing any drawers."

Lorraine didn't care if she hurt her. Her need was bigger than caring. Or she needed to hurt someone. But she let Tuna take over the job of peeling off her jeans.

"Would you rather be on the bed?" It was touching to her that this young woman was courtly, while she, the older woman, was carnal, an animal.

"No," she managed to gasp, but Tuna ignored this. She scooped Lorraine up in her muscled arms and carried her over to a corner of the basement, where she plopped her onto a waterbed, which swayed with the impact of their bodies. This brief delay only served to intensify her desire, and with no further preliminaries she flipped herself on top, guided herself onto Tuna's long fingers, and rode them in a frenzy.

In a matter of moments, she was coming, emitting sounds she hadn't known she contained; it seemed to go on and on, and when the weeping erupted, she couldn't pinpoint the moment of segue. She sobbed the way a newborn cries, wailing without inhibition, releasing some kind of primal distress while Tuna discreetly slipped her fingers out of her and wrapped her arms around Lorraine's shoulders.

The weeping went on for a long time or seemed to. Snot and tears poured down her face, over Tuna's shoulder, onto the pillowcase. Tuna rubbed one hand on her middle back and cradled her head with the other.

When at last Lorraine grew calm, she said, "I'm sorry." Her whole face felt swollen with crying.

"Shh, Lorraine," Tuna whispered as if to an infant. Tuna handed her a T-shirt from the floor to use as a handkerchief. "You don't have to be sorry about anything."

She must have dozed a few moments, because she woke with a start, not sure where she was. Tuna was propped on one elbow, staring at her intently.

"You look like somebody, but I can't figure out who," she said. "Somebody famous."

A stab of terror split her chest. "No," Lorraine told her, "I just have one of those kinds of faces. People always think I look like someone—some actress, or their cousin, or their third-grade teacher—never the same person." She wished she didn't like Tuna so much; it would make it easier to lie to her.

"No, it's somebody. Damn, it'll come to me later." Then she asked, "What's his name?"

"Whose name?" She didn't follow the change of subject.

"Your ex. The one who made you cry like that."

She hesitated. Her fictional capacities seemed to desert her; she couldn't imagine this invention she'd created, herself as a heterosexual housewife, this abusive former spouse. Yet the pause was too awkward after their intimacy, so she said the next thing that occurred to her, "Donald. His name is Donald."

Then wished she could take back the answer.

"Donald is a damn fool," Tuna pronounced, and began kissing the back of her neck.

But that impulse had been sated; if Tuna was expecting reciprocity, she was going to be disappointed. When they'd first gotten together, Liana had accused her of being a "pillow queen," more interested in receiving sexual attention than giving it.

Lorraine couldn't care about that right now. Her nerves were beginning once more to crackle with anxiety; it was as if a switch had been flipped and there was no trace of the passionate woman of a few moments earlier. "I'm sorry," she told Tuna. "I shouldn't have started this at all. I really have to go. I mean now."

With these words she was up, recovering her clothing from where it was strewn beside the couch. Her cunt was aching, bruised from the force of their lovemaking, and her head was spinning from sleeplessness and fear. She had to think carefully about what she'd brought with her here—her purse with its considerable wad of cash and the manila envelope with her papers and computer backup. She longed for coffee, and realized she needed some food as well, but for now she had to concentrate completely on getting on the road.

Her mind was already planning—*Take Tuna's friend's car, go back to get Dude, and get across the border. Will they let me take Dude across the border? I'll hide him in the trunk and hope they just wave me through.* She wouldn't go through Detroit to Windsor;

she figured that was likely to be more patrolled, but there was another point of entry further north through Port Huron to Sarnia. One of the other teachers had talked about using this route for a camping trip to Ontario with the school's soccer team.

"I don't want you to go by yourself." Tuna's voice interrupted her thoughts. She'd almost forgotten about her. The young woman was zipping up her jeans and Lorraine saw she'd left a bite mark on her left shoulder. "I want to make sure you're safe."

"I'll be fine," she protested.

"I don't want to take that chance." Tuna was pulling on a clean shirt; Lorraine had popped the buttons off the old one. This one was lime green and looked good with Tuna's hair and skin tone. "You'll be less conspicuous traveling with someone. He'll be expecting you to be alone."

She had a point, but it was hard to imagine Tuna being inconspicuous. Besides, it was unthinkable. "Really," she said, "I need to do this by myself."

The young woman misunderstood. "Look, I'm not trying to tie you down to anything. In your situation that's the last thing you want; I get that. We'll just take the Hatchmobile and get you across the border; then I'll take the bus home. No obligations, no attachments."

Of course, she was trying to be nice, but to Lorraine it sounded like Tuna was saying that she came with the car, a package deal, take it or leave it. Maybe Lorraine should just walk away and find some other mode of transportation. Or maybe it would be good to have another head to strategize this, given her own lapses in the past few days. Including this one.

"Okay, but we have to go right now," she insisted.

Tuna slipped, sockless, into a pair of worn black cowboy boots, grabbed a jacket and her wallet, then fished out a ring of keys from the drawer of an end table. "Let's go." Tuna flashed her a warm smile, as if she was looking forward to an adventure.

Lorraine couldn't remember the etiquette of how one related to the complete stranger who'd just fucked you senseless. It was a circumstance at which Marielle was rather gifted, but

Lorraine had no clue. Tuna gestured to her to go first up the stairs, and then followed her.

In the kitchen, the younger woman paused and asked if she wanted something to eat.

"Only if it's something we can eat in the car." This came out sharply, although she was salivating.

Tuna grinned, as if she was used to dealing with moody and demanding women, and rummaged for a couple of apples, a bunch of bananas, and a box of granola, which she jammed into a backpack. She surveyed the kitchen to see if there was anything else that met the criterion. She added a bag of potato chips to the cache.

Lorraine didn't want to take the time, but she needed to pee, especially after sex. Tuna guided her to the first floor bathroom. Afterward, she took a moment to try to repair her face; her lipstick was smeared across her cheek and her hair was disheveled in a telltale fashion. The more she tried to hurry, the more her actions seem to be occurring in slow motion.

Then she heard a phone ring in the next room, two rings, then a click. She stepped out of the bathroom just in time to hear the answering machine pick up. "Hello," the recorded voice of an older woman announced. "You've reached the home of Magda..."

CHAPTER NINE

After the beep, there was only a click. The call was a hang-up. Lorraine locked herself inside the bathroom and ran water in the sink to buy time. Could it be anything more than coincidence that Tuna's grandmother was named Magda? But how could anyone believe such a coincidence?

She tried to think back over the chain of seemingly unrelated events of this morning. She'd assumed it had to be the Feds who'd gotten her car towed, but what if that was wrong? Could it be the terrorists? But how would they have access to police uniforms, tow trucks? Maybe it was a bigger organization than had been suggested in the press. Maybe they wanted to make it sound small and marginal to keep people from freaking out.

But how could Tuna's grandmother be the head of a large terrorist organization? And had she just fucked someone who was out to kill her? If Tuna was supposed to kill her, why have sex with her first? Maybe she figured that would relax Lorraine's vigilance, get her in the car on the way to Canada?

But why go to all the trouble? Tuna could have popped her while they were in the van and dumped her body in a field.

Lorraine didn't exist, so what was the problem? Was it possible she'd misunderstood the name Magda in the first place? In the noise and confusion that followed the bombing at JFK, that young man could have just as easily been yelling, "Go to Moscow" or "Go to Baghdad."

She stared at her face in the mirror, the skin reddened with what Liana used to call "sexual flush." She didn't want to be reminded of what she'd just been doing, so instead she rummaged in grandma's bathroom cabinet, in search of something—what? Cyanide pills? Capsules to make her invisible? A straightedge razor? She found only a jumble of lotions with organic ingredients and supplements from the health food store. Not what you'd expect to find in a terrorist's cupboard.

Then she thought, *Maybe Tuna works for Donald*; maybe the phone message was just a ruse to scare her into going back into protective custody. Maybe the sex was just to give Donald enough time to get here to apprehend her. "Stall her," she could imagine him instructing the younger woman, "we're on our way."

"Lorraine, are you okay?" Tuna knocked on the door. She sounded more concerned than impatient.

"Just a minute," she answered. She was trying to calculate the odds of going out the small bathroom window; could she disappear down the street before Tuna figured it out? Doubtful; if she was right outside the door, she was bound to hear her do it. Then Lorraine's hand would be tipped, and Tuna would know she was trying to get away. Whereas if she just played along, went with her as far as the Twin Pines Motel, perhaps then she could find another moment for escape. Assuming Tuna didn't kill her first. Assuming Donald was not outside the door with a big butterfly net.

On impulse, she borrowed a touch of grandma's lipstick—a burnt orange that was a little wild for Lorraine but not out of harmony with her ash-brown hair. Blond Marielle could have never pulled it off. She felt powerful, wearing the lipstick of the woman who might be trying to kill her, like warriors who smeared their torsos with the blood of their slain enemies. She took a deep breath and opened the bathroom door.

Tuna leaned against the wall outside the bathroom, waiting for her.

"Sorry." She flashed a grin. "I had to clean myself up a little." She called on Marielle's flirtation skills and grabbed the younger woman's belt buckle, making her voice a little breathless. "I must say I'm sorry to have to rush off like this."

Tuna blushed.

"Are you sure we have to go right now?" she asked.

Lorraine had hooked her. In fact, now she wanted to stall, to buy some time to peruse her bookshelves, examine other parts of the house, try to figure out whether this was all a strange but random concurrence or whether she'd fallen into a trap. But her best bet was still to get going. The farther she traveled from here, the more likely she was to be safe, at least for a while.

"Maybe once we get to Sarnia, we can get a room. Maybe you won't have to rush right back." She ran her hand down the front of her shirt.

"Maybe I should bring a toothbrush," Tuna flirted back. She appeared delighted by the turn events had taken, after Lorraine's initial resistance.

"And another shirt," she suggested. Tuna hurried back down the basement steps, and she took the opportunity to rummage through the backpack.

The food for the road was stashed in the largest section; a few guitar picks littered the bottom of the bag. In a front pocket, Tuna's wallet; only $34 in cash. If this were planned, you'd think she'd be better financed. Her driver's license said, "Darla Tone." Her birth date was April 23, 1989. Lorraine wasn't quite twice her age, but damn close.

She kept searching. In an inside pocket of the backpack, she felt something heavy and square. She unzipped the compartment and grabbed it.

Marielle's face stared up at her from the back jacket of *Hard-Hearted Monday*, her second book. In hardcover. Although the photo was black and white, the blaze of the blond hair was unmistakable. The face was younger, eyes still brittle with ambition. Life had not yet cracked her open when this picture had been taken. *You look like someone*, Tuna had said to her earlier, *somebody famous*. Had she just been playing with her?

Tuna came bounding up the stairs two at a time; she reached the kitchen before Lorraine could put everything back. Would she be mad at her for going through her stuff? She'd kill Tuna if she took one step toward her purse.

"Sorry," she said quickly. "I needed some of those potato chips; I couldn't wait till we got on the road. Say, is this any good?" She hastily turned over the book and showed her the front cover with an illustration of a buxom brunette consulting a well-thumbed date book. She'd always hated the cover; after that book sold well Marielle had started to demand approval of book design in her contracts.

"I've read everything she's written," Tuna said, giving it just a casual glance. "My grandma got me started on her."

This surprised her. She'd never imagined someone like Tuna being part of her fan base. For a moment she felt good; her work had crossed over more than she'd known.

Then she remembered her ego had no place in this interaction. She shoved the book back into its pocket and ripped open the potato chips, conspicuously ingesting a handful. "I've never read her." Her voice was indifferent. "I don't read a lot of fiction."

"Did you know she died this year?"

Her heart began to rattle in the cage of her chest, like a prisoner trying to break out. Was she testing her? "Who?" She tried to sound nonchalant.

"That writer. Marielle Wing. But I read she's got one more book coming out." Tuna reached into the potato chip bag for her own handful.

"How can she have a book out if she's dead?" Lorraine asked. She wondered if Tuna knew something about that new book.

"I don't know. I guess she was almost done before she died."

She found herself wanting to argue the point, defend Marielle's reputation against this imposter book. She wanted to tell her that *Weeping Minerva*, less than half finished, was taking Marielle in a whole other direction as a writer. Of course she couldn't say any of this. It seemed increasingly likely that the book was a ruse to get her to reveal herself. But to what end?

It was for *Hard-Hearted Monday* that Marielle had done research about how you could tell if someone was lying. There were telltale clues like avoiding eye contact, or fidgeting with the hair or earlobes, or talking too much. If someone had been trained to lie, they would studiously avoid all those clues; they'd look directly at you and never blink, and this was also an indication they weren't telling the truth.

Tuna seemed neither excessively nervous nor preternaturally calm. If she wasn't sincere, she was a terrifyingly good actor. Lorraine, on the other hand, who had been lying through her teeth since the moment they'd met—what signals was she sending out?

"We should go," she urged.

Tuna casually closed the backpack without looking to see if anything was missing. She checked all the burners on the stove to make sure they were off, then turned out the kitchen light. She opened the back door and gestured her to go ahead.

Her extremities grew cold. If Donald was waiting outside, should she try to make a run for it or just go along quietly? Would Donald shoot her if she fled?

Why would he? She hadn't done anything wrong. That was getting harder to remember. She was a witness; she had value to him, at least until the trial. Unless the whole thing was a sham. She knew one thing—Donald Watkins was too smart to let her slip away again.

They stepped off the porch and outside into the yard. She scanned the street.

"You okay?" Tuna was walking over to the "Hatchmobile," a once-white Ford Focus that looked like it hadn't been washed all summer.

"I'm just afraid he's going to find me." For all she knew, he already had.

"He wouldn't in a million years know you're here."

"Unless he's watching me."

"You poor thing. He's really got you spooked." Tuna opened the passenger door for her, and she climbed in.

No one in her life had ever called Marielle "you poor thing." She would have stabbed them with her fountain pen. The role of helpless female made her seethe, but she had to play the hand she'd dealt herself.

"Oops, I've gotta move the van," Tuna said. "Can you take over, so I can pull out and pull back in?" She handed her the keys and climbed out.

Taking Tuna's place in the driver's seat, she couldn't believe her moment had come so soon. And so easily. Once the VW backed out of the drive, she could gun the Focus and take off.

She heard the van sputter to a start, watched Tuna effortlessly steer in reverse toward the street. The driveway was clear. She started the Focus, stepped on the gas. But it didn't have much pick-up. By the time she cleared the driveway, Tuna had hopped out of the van and stood directly in her path with her thumb extended like a hitchhiker and a goofy grin on her face. There was no room to steer around her. Even Marielle wouldn't have run down a woman who'd just fucked her till she wept. She had no choice but to slam on the brakes.

The Focus stopped a few feet from her. "Easy there, girl," Tuna said as she opened the door. "You're still shook up. I better drive."

She considered insisting on remaining in the driver's seat, then changed her mind. If shooting started and she needed to duck, she'd rather not be driving.

"So the first stop is to pick up your cat?" Tuna asked, once they were on the road. She nodded. It was crazy to think she could keep Dude with her, but he was all she had left of Marielle's charmed life, and she didn't want to give him up.

"Where is that motel?"

Lorraine didn't want to tell but didn't know the area well enough to mislead her without getting hopelessly lost. So, she described as best she could the route she'd followed into town this morning, and Tuna seemed to understand.

"Can I eat one of these apples?" She was hungry, and the potato chips were greasy and now lay heavy on her tongue and in her belly. The sensation reminded her of the nausea she'd felt earlier that morning when she'd seen the LeSabre was gone. Tuna passed the backpack toward her; she reached in and grabbed a Red Delicious. It was too early for apple season—who knew where this one had been grown?—and its texture was not all it might be.

"Give me a bite." Tuna steered the Focus onto an eastbound freeway. She held the apple to the young woman's mouth, and she bit down happily. *This is what people do when they're intimate; they share their food.* This realization was so startling she wanted to vomit or scream.

Perhaps it was the collision of terror and tenderness, the longing to surrender and the complete inability to trust that began to short-circuit her system. The intensity of her reaction seemed to startle her awake, although she hadn't known she'd been on autopilot. *How long have I been walking around in a state of shock? Since last night? Since yesterday afternoon? Since I died?* The blessing of shock was that it masked unbearable pain. Now that the shock was lifting, she longed for its balm again.

She regarded the young woman beside her, young enough to be her daughter, this stranger with whom she'd exchanged bodily fluids. She looked at the gray concrete freeways walls looming on either side of her, the gray stretch of pavement before her. The car behind them might contain a federal agent or a terrorist. The young woman beside her might be a terrorist or a federal agent. She couldn't say who had the greater power to destroy her—terrorists or federal agents or her own unhinged mind.

She'd never had a panic attack, but Marielle had researched them because Antoine Battavia, the antagonist in *Hard-Hearted Monday*, was stricken with them every time he broke the law. She knew enough to diagnose what was happening to her. Even though she could scarcely draw breath, she felt like she was going to start screaming and never stop.

"Stop the car!" she gasped.

"What's wrong?"

"Pull over, pull over right now."

This wasn't easily accomplished on a southeastern Michigan freeway on a Friday afternoon, but Tuna pulled to the right, managing not to be hit and not to crash into the concrete wall. Lorraine burst out of the car onto the narrow shoulder.

"Lorraine, you could get hit!" Tuna yelled and followed her out of the car.

The trucks speeding by created their own wind on the side of the freeway. She wished she had the guts to dash out into the oncoming traffic; she could be dead before the driver would know what he'd struck. But her will to survive was too strong, or her courage to die was too weak. All she could do was to stand on the shoulder with the other refuse and scream at the top of her lungs, arms flailing at Tuna's attempts to bundle her back into the car. Whatever words she was saying were lost in the roar of the freeway and the siren wail emanating from her throat.

There was never a cop when you wanted one, but always one when you didn't. A white patrol car, red and blue lights flashing, pulled sharply in front of the Focus. COUNTY SHERIFF was spelled out on the door. Two white men with short-cropped hair and wearing blue uniforms got out of the car, their batons drawn.

"Let her go," one said to Tuna. "Ma'am, are you all right?" The other officer grabbed Tuna and shoved her up against the freeway wall. "Did this woman carjack you?"

This sobered Lorraine up quick.

"Officers, I'm sorry. This is a misunderstanding." Her head was spinning. She didn't want them to run her ID. She didn't want them to search her purse. "My friend was giving me a ride and, I don't know how to explain it—I just got claustrophobic in the car." Trixie Grenoble was a claustrophobe; she'd made a scene in an elevator in *The Disappearing Moon*. She was only a minor character. "She was trying to help me."

"Does your friend have a name?"

"Yes, it's Darla Tone. Her birthday is April 23, 1989. Her ID is in her wallet in the backpack in the front seat of the car."

If Tuna was surprised that she had this information, Lorraine couldn't tell, because the young woman's face was still pressed against the freeway wall by the other officer's meaty arm.

Sheriff Number One went to check it out. She prayed there was no pot in the car; it wouldn't be out of the realm of possibility. She hoped Tuna wouldn't be stupid enough to try to cross the border with it. "Where's the registration?" the cop wanted to know.

Tuna admitted, "I don't have it. This car belongs to a friend. I'm keeping it for him while he's in Europe. He asked me to drive it once in a while."

"Okay," Number One decided, "let's sort this out at the station." He turned to Lorraine. "That'll give you the chance to figure out if you want to press charges."

"I *don't* want to press charges. I *told* you, she was helping me. Can't you just let us go, or give us a ticket or something?"

Number One looked at her with feigned amusement. "We've got suspected domestic abuse. We've got a suspected DUI. We've got disorderly conduct. We've got a suspected stolen vehicle." He ticked off each potential crime on his fingers. "Who knows what else we're going to find when we search the car? Whaddaya think, Hank?" he said to his partner. "What kind of ticket should I write them?"

Lorraine could not let this happen. She could not let herself get put into the system. How could she have been so stupid? *Stay below the radar*, that's what Donald had told her from the beginning.

"Officer, there's no domestic abuse. There's no DUI. I'll take a breath test, I'll walk a line." She couldn't help Tuna with the stolen car problem; how had she thought they were going to get to Canada with no registration? It was crappy to think of talking her way out of this and leaving Tuna in the lurch, but if she didn't have drugs on her, she'd be out in a few hours, and Lorraine could send her some money to get the car out of impoundment.

The patrolman looked at her for a long moment, sizing her up. Then he said, "Sorry, ma'am. I got a feeling that there's more here than meets the eye. I gotta bet my hunch. You're both coming with us."

They hadn't asked for her ID yet, but it was only a matter of time. Would it take five minutes or an hour or a day to find out she was in witness protection? Would Donald be waiting for her at the station, or would he come later?

The patrolmen put both of them in the back seat of their patrol car. No door handles on the inside. "I'm sorry," she said to Tuna.

"I never should have stopped the car on the freeway," she murmured, "I should have waited for an exit." She looked dejected, like this wasn't the first thing she'd fucked up in her life. Lorraine wanted to console the young woman; she couldn't bear her feeling responsible for her stupidity. Unless this was all part of an elaborate plan. Was it just because they'd had sex that she wanted to trust her?

She watched "Hank" put a tag on the antenna of the Focus to signal the tow truck, while his partner called the station.

"Do these guys know your ex?" Tuna whispered.

"I don't know what they know. But if I don't get out of this, would you go find my cat and take care of him? Twin Pines Motel." Now that she thought about it, Dude would get along well with this young woman.

Then the two patrolmen climbed in the front seat and Lorraine and Tuna stopped talking.

* * *

Once the sheriffs delivered them to the station, she did a quick scan for Donald. She didn't see him. The minute she was released from the back seat of the vehicle, she became argumentative. Reza always seemed to lead with belligerence, and it often worked. Just thinking about Reza threatened to revive the panic attack, but she had to remain clear-headed.

"Are you charging us with something?" she demanded to know. "Because if not, you can't force us to stay here." She didn't know whether that was true or not, but she'd heard it on TV shows and it always seemed to make cops nervous.

"You only gotta stay here till we get to the bottom of this," said Number One wearily. He herded them into the lobby.

"I keep telling you, there's no bottom to get to!" If she was a big enough pain in the ass, maybe they'd just be happy to be rid of her.

Her approach made Tuna nervous. She kept shooting Lorraine these looks that said, *Just calm down. Don't make more trouble.*

No doubt that would have been Lorraine's approach, too, but that was before she'd been chased by a black van, before her house had been firebombed, before her car was towed under mysterious circumstances. She just needed to get out of there before the cops figured out who she was. Of course, how she was going to transport herself was once again a problem.

As if Officer Number One had decided the best strategy was to divide and conquer, he grunted to Hank, "You get *her* story," then told Tuna to follow him. As Tuna gazed balefully at her, she realized that—if she was indeed just a nice millennial hippie dyke Buddhist musician with a thing for older women—she was going to tell them everything, including her story about being stalked by her abusive ex. *Donald.* The ex-cop.

But on the positive side, she didn't think Sheriff Hank had formed any particular impression of her yet. It seemed they'd assigned her to the muscle of the duo; Hank looked like the kind of guy who didn't trouble himself with too much thinking. She'd need to keep it simple with Hank.

He didn't escort her into a separate room but sat down beside her on a plastic chair that didn't offer much hospitality to his square-built frame. He grasped his pen earnestly; he had not been a good student in school and writing had always been a difficulty to him. She could see the young boy of him, hunched over his desk.

"May I see your ID, ma'am?" he asked politely. Despite the circumstances in which he'd found her, she still appeared—more or less—like a nice middle-class lady and he'd decided to treat her as such until he had a reason not to.

She fished her driver's license out of her purse. He dutifully copied the information onto a yellow pad in blockish letters.

"Is this your current address?" he asked.

"Yes." What would he think when he ran the address and found out the townhouse was firebombed last night?

She was blessed that he appeared to be utterly lacking in curiosity. If she just played it cool, she might be walking out of here in no time.

"Wanta tell me what happened back there on the freeway?"

"I met Tuna yesterday." Car trouble would ordinarily be a good angle but she didn't want the sheriff's to connect her in any way to the car they towed this morning. "I spent the night in town and ran into her on the street today. She offered to drive me home."

She stopped, waiting for Hank to catch up.

"And?"

"I just...well, I started my period, and that always makes me a little crazy." Men never liked to hear a woman talk about their period and she figured Hank was no different. "I began to feel claustrophobic in the car and begged her to pull over. I just needed air, but she wanted me to get back in the car because she thought I wasn't safe. I'm afraid I wasn't cooperating." She grinned ruefully, appealing to his stereotype of every woman who'd ever gotten herself in trouble and made his life miserable by refusing to cooperate.

She let that sink in, then added, "That's when you pulled up."

She could tell it made sense to him: *Women can just go crazy on you all of a sudden; it's the hormones or some damn thing. They won't cooperate and that's why men need to run everything.* He wrote it down, then told her, "Okay, I'll be back in a minute. This shouldn't take too long."

He got up, then turned back a moment. "What about the car?"

"I don't know," she told him. "It was parked in her driveway. She told me it belonged to a friend who's on tour."

This seemed to satisfy him. He walked down a hallway and disappeared.

She was counting on Hank to not be an over achiever, so she began strategizing her next moves: She needed to get a car. How could she buy a car without leaving a paper trail? She wasn't going to hotwire one. She wasn't going to carjack somebody. Maybe she could just buy one to get her over the border, and then abandon it. No car dealer would file the paperwork in the next few hours.

It was just possible she could pull it off. The system was porous and lazy, and she supposed that was bad for keeping citizens safe against terrorism but for now it was going to work in her favor.

Sure enough, Hank came back down the hallway. He handed back her driver's license and said, "Sorry for the inconvenience." He'd probably only checked to see there were no outstanding warrants, and there weren't. "You're free to go."

She didn't ask about Tuna. She didn't ask any questions at all. She thanked him quickly, gathered her purse, and left the station on foot. A light rain had begun, and she wasn't at all sure where she was. She crossed the street and had stepped into the doorway of a Starbucks to get her bearings, maybe ask directions, when she saw three black sedans tear into the parking lot of the sheriff's station. Seven men in suits burst out of the doors and one of them was Donald Watkins.

CHAPTER TEN

Lorraine stepped up to the counter, grateful there was no line. Grateful too there were no sheriffs here at this hour of the day. A young man with a stud in his tongue and a ring through his eyebrow was behind the register. She ordered a latte and paid for it, then asked, "May I have your restroom key?"

She knew this was a temporary solution. She knew that once Donald found out she'd been released, he'd waste no time in canvassing the area. He'd go to the counter and show the pierced young man her picture, and the young man would say, "She asked for the restroom key. This is her latte."

She prayed to be spared the humiliation of being hauled out of a public toilet at Starbucks by federal marshals. Maybe she should just go back across the street and surrender to Donald Watkins. She didn't know for sure what would happen to her—could it be any worse than what had already occurred?

But she thought about seeing him backlit by the smoldering ruins of her townhouse. She opened the door to the women's restroom, left the key inside, locked the door and closed it again.

She hoped that would be a small deterrent, give her a few more minutes before they knew she was really gone.

This Starbucks had a back door, and she opened it cautiously onto an alley and slipped outside, searching for possible avenues of escape. Despite the rain the air was hot, compared to the air-conditioning inside Starbucks. She snuck around into a space between buildings to observe what was going on across the street. She saw two of the suited men leading Tuna out of the sheriff's station, putting her in the back of the car. Did that mean she'd been working for them all along? Or that she'd just ratted her out? Or that she was a terrorist? Or maybe they thought Lorraine would come back for her?

She saw other marshals fanning out in each direction from the station. She saw Donald crossing the street. She ducked back into the alley.

A few doors down, a delivery truck was parked. She recalled noticing the driver taking a break at one of the tables, eating a muffin. She sidled around the panel truck. If she could get inside, maybe she could stow away in the back.

But this must be an unscheduled break, because the door was open and the keys were in the ignition. She didn't have time to think about it. She jumped behind the wheel and started the truck. She prayed the piped-in jazz-lite in the coffee shop would be loud enough to cover the sound of the engine starting. She resisted the urge to gun it and proceeded instead at an orderly pace. It would take her a bit to become adept at steering this large a vehicle; fortunately the LeSabre had been good practice. She found the windshield wipers just before she took a left at the end of the alley, driving away from the sheriff's station and the men who were looking for her.

Now you have completely lost it, she told herself. *Now you've actually committed a crime.* Would they put out an APB? Would they shoot to kill? *Don't be dramatic. They still want you alive to testify*. Or did they?

From the looks of the beat-up panel truck, she figured it was not equipped with a Lo-Jack or other tracking system. But, although no one was pursuing her now, it wouldn't take long for them to realize she'd left the building and that the truck was gone. It certainly wouldn't be hard to spot her in it. Perhaps the marshals already knew about the Twin Pines Motel; how would she ever get to Dude before they did? Tuna would certainly tell them about her plan to go to Canada. Even if the young woman was innocently caught up in this, why should she be loyal? After all, Lorraine had ditched her without a second thought, thrown her to the Feds without so much as a heads-up.

There was a chance she might get to the motel first. Maybe Tuna hadn't said so much at the police station. Maybe she'd forget about the cat until the Feds interrogated her. Maybe Lorraine could go get Dude and be on her way.

It was crazy to keep this vehicle. The longer she had it, the more likely she was to get caught. But the time it would take to rent or buy a car could use up any small window she might have to get to Dude. She knew it was even crazier to risk her life for a cat, but she couldn't imagine dumping Dude at the Twin Pines where it might take the proprietor weeks to find his lifeless body. He'd been a good companion to her in exile, and she owed him something. *Like those people in New Orleans who stayed on their roofs for a week rather than evacuate without their dog.*

Then she had another idea. This might be the most deranged of all, but the minute she thought of it, it felt right. She pulled into the parking lot of a grocery store. It was a big shopping day and the lot was full of cars and vans, even a few trucks like the one she eased into a space. She parked and left the truck in the middle of an aisle in the middle of the lot—it wouldn't be easy to spot from the street. She took the keys with her in case she needed to change her mind. She didn't bother to wipe off her fingerprints or anything—they'd know who'd taken the truck.

The rain was little more than a mist, enough to fog Lorraine's ersatz glasses but not enough to soak her. Not like yesterday. She hightailed it up the street, walking a few blocks before she found a gas station with a payphone. It smelled like piss and vomit inside the glass booth, but the phone seemed to be in working order. Luckily she had change from her latte. Of course there was no phone book, so she called information and found the number for the Zen Center.

She prayed she wouldn't get an answering machine. After four rings, a voice said, "Ann Arbor Zen Center" and she recognized the voice of Koryo.

"Is Zenkei there?" She resorted to deep breathing again to force her voice to stay calm.

She heard the receiver crash down and for an instant she thought he'd hung up on her, but the line stayed open and she heard the clatter of footsteps. The stern monk seemed to be delivering a lecture about personal phone calls, but she couldn't hear the words, only the tone.

After what seems like minutes, she heard "Hello?" It was Zenkei.

"It's Lorraine, but don't tell anyone you're talking to me. Don't tell Koryo."

"He already know. He tell me you call."

That could be a problem. A really big problem. Nevertheless, she forged ahead.

"I'm sorry to bother you, but I need your help again. I don't really have anyone else I can ask." She told him about her cat, how he needed a place to stay, how she couldn't go to get him herself right now. "If you could just go get him and keep him for a day or two, then I'll come get him, and make a generous donation to the Center."

"A favor is not done for money," he replied. She could see he was trying to puzzle out her strange and strangely urgent request.

She gave him a few terse directions to the Twin Pines. "But here's the thing. I need you to go right away. The longer you wait, the more dangerous it might be."

"How so?" She could tell he was being discreet; he didn't repeat the word "dangerous."

"I can't explain now, but I promise I will. Nobody is going to hurt you." She could only hope this was true. "But there are some people who are after me, and they might know where my cat is and be waiting for me. But you don't know where I am, so you can't help them."

She realized that if they did apprehend Zenkei, the Feds would just wait for her to contact him. "I'll call again later tonight. If you have the cat and everything's fine, you can tell me that. But if there's a problem, just tell me 'You need to correct your delusions.'"

"You need to correct your delusions," he repeated. "Are you all right?"

"I don't know," she answered truthfully. "But if you manage to pull this off, I will be a lot better."

"How do I get in?" Again, his discretion. He made no mention of the cat or the motel.

Shit. She had the key. She remembered the rattletrap structure; it wouldn't be hard to break in. But she couldn't suggest that to a monk. "There's an old lady who runs the place. She must have an extra. I don't think she'll give you a hard time. She, uh, doesn't know I brought a cat with me."

"Okay, okay," he said. She could scarcely believe he was agreeing to such a scheme, which must seem very bizarre to anyone outside it. Still he said, "I'll go now. You call later."

She hung up and felt a little giddy. Her Timex told her it was 4:12 p.m. and she had not been killed by terrorists today, nor was she in federal custody. Although she could imagine twenty things that might go wrong, she knew at least that Dude would be safe. *If* Donald hadn't already gotten to him.

Still, she worried. Was she putting Zenkei at risk? And could Koryo be trusted? There were brief moments when she felt ingenious, an intrepid solver of problems, but just as quickly those moments would collapse and she knew she was a fool with no clue about what would result from her actions. Indeed, she needed to correct her delusions.

Humility, Francesca would say. Since she'd started meditating, that was a concept she'd talked about a lot. *There's relief*, she'd told Marielle, *in accepting that we don't have all the answers*. Marielle never bought it, but Lorraine might have no choice but to embrace this virtue.

Francesca. Her longing for her best friend welled in her as she huddled inside the fetid booth, keeping her back to the street to thwart being identified by a passing unmarked car.

With the rain picking up outside, she had no idea where to go next, how to pass the hours until she could find out if her orange tomcat was safe.

Francesca. Lorraine could hear her laughter, a deep guffaw that sounded booze-soaked, but wasn't. She could see the way her friend would toss her red hair before she was about to say something serious. Lorraine needed her to tell her something now.

She still had coins in her pocket and more in her wallet. Without allowing herself to think about the consequences, she was loading quarters into the phone, punching in Francesca's number from memory, a number Marielle used to call nearly every day.

It would be early afternoon in Los Angeles. She could be anywhere—in her studio, at her gallery, having lunch, playing hooky to take a hike in Griffith Park. She could be meditating. With each ring, Lorraine prepared herself to hang up when the message machine kicked on.

Instead she heard a breathy, "*Digame*" the greeting an affectation Francesca had picked up after a summer residency in Barcelona a few years ago. The sound of her voice sent a warm current up Lorraine's spine.

Lorraine hesitated a moment, and concern crept into Francesca's voice as she said, "Hello?"

"Fresh…" Lorraine began. She was afraid to say much more.

"Oh my God, it's true." Francesca, who could never disguise her emotions, began weeping.

"Be careful," Lorraine cautioned. "We can't know who might be listening."

"Where are you?" her friend demanded.

"I can't tell you, for that same reason. Someone could be monitoring the call." For that matter, she thought, they could be tracing the call. She wondered how long that took. And was it harder or easier with a pay phone? "It's safer for you not to know."

"I never believed you were dead," Francesca sobbed. "You wouldn't just leave me like that. And to never be able to see the body…I told Reza…"

"Is Reza okay?" Lorraine asked sharply. "Have you seen her lately?"

"Not for a few weeks, I guess." She was not concerned about Reza. "And then I got that card..."

"You got it? It wasn't opened or anything?"

"Not that I could tell. I was so relieved, but..."

"Fresh, we shouldn't talk any more now. I don't know if your phone is safe."

"What's going on?"

"I wish I could tell you..."

"Let me help you."

"You can't. I'm sorry. I shouldn't have called. If something happens to you, I'll never forgive myself."

"Nothing's going to happen to me," Francesca said, with all the certainty of ignorance, as if her insistence alone could make it true. "Call me back at the dirty place. One hour," she commanded, then hung up.

The dirty place—their nickname for a café where they'd sometimes meet for breakfast. One cup of coffee was all it took to understand the appellation, but no one listening in would know where she meant. *My brilliant Fresh.* Lorraine sagged with relief against the window of the booth, grateful to have spoken to her, not quite believing that she'd have the chance to speak with her again.

Unless they'd been listening to the call. Unless they followed her.

She had to leave this phone booth right away. In case they'd been listening. In case they'd traced the call.

She stepped out into the rain, now falling hard enough to obscure her vision. She thought about going back to the grocery store, pushing a cart up the aisles for an hour, but decided it would be better to put some distance between herself and the stolen truck. This stretch she was on was an industrial strip—she couldn't think of any reason to step into an auto body shop or an upholsterers. But she had to get off the street; if they found the truck, they'd search for her in the area. She kept walking away from the grocery. The rain and Friday afternoon rush hour had congested the traffic on the street. It was bumper to bumper.

She considered sticking out her thumb to hitch a ride. How would she appear to the people in their cars—a soccer mom turned homeless? And if someone did stop, where would she say she was going? Then across the street she spotted a truck stop diner and, right next door, a cheap two-story motel.

She took her life in her hands to cross the eight-lane highway, but thanks to rush hour traffic she managed to do so, and slogged her way to the motel office. She stood for a moment just inside the door, shaking the rain from her hair and rubbing her glasses on her soggy T-shirt.

This was the other end of the sleaze spectrum from the Twin Pines. The office was white-tiled and lit by relentless fluorescent light. It smelled of gasoline. She looked up to see a tiny Asian woman slumped behind the counter.

"Can I get a room?" Lorraine asked her. The clerk didn't bother to look at Lorraine. A more observant person might notice that she was anomalous here, neither trucker nor hooker, but the woman at the counter had trained herself not to observe who came and went. She might not even recognize Lorraine if Donald showed her picture.

"How long?" she wanted to know.

"One night, maybe two."

"All night?" she asked without amusement.

Lorraine shrugged. "Is there a phone?"

The clerk nodded. "Forty-five dollars." She didn't ask for ID. There was no paperwork at all.

Lorraine handed her a fifty dollar bill. She returned five singles and a key. "Two-seventeen," she mumbled and then blanked Lorraine out of her mind.

The elevator doors opened. A burly man in a black T-shirt stepped out, followed by a too-skinny woman in a too-short skirt and a halter top. They were not spending the night. Lorraine entered the elevator, which smelled of beer and sex in the couple's wake, and suppressed a shudder as the doors closed and the car began to move up.

Room 217 was plain and tidy, but on close inspection she couldn't escape the feeling that nothing was truly clean. The sheets were laundered, but the polyester bedspread felt sticky. The uncarpeted linoleum appeared caked with debris. There were stains on the ceiling she didn't want to know about. The bathroom was over-lit, with one of those little paper seals across the toilet bowl. There was a shower stall, but no tub.

Still, she eagerly stripped the wet clothes from her body and stood under the stream of hot water. She used the paper-wrapped chip of hotel soap to scrub between her legs. She could scarcely fathom that a few hours earlier she'd been fucking a woman almost thirty years her junior, but she wanted no trace of that experience on her. She wondered: *Was Tuna truly just an innocent guitar player who'd gotten caught up in her situation?*

If Francesca were here, she might laugh, as she always had, at Marielle's choice in partners. "You know how to pick 'em, girlfriend," her friend would tease. Lorraine dried herself with a rough towel, wishing she had the moisturizer she'd bought this morning. Had it been just this morning? She could barely take in all that had transpired this day, and experienced a flicker of nostalgia for the boredom she'd felt when she first got to Michigan.

She had no dry clothes to change into, so instead she ran across the tacky floor and jumped her naked body in between the sheets. She consulted her Timex on the nightstand. 4:50. About twenty-five minutes before she was supposed to call Francesca at the dirty place.

Then she realized there was no phone in the room. The nightstand had a lamp, but no clock and no phone. Hadn't the woman downstairs said there was? She recalled having passed a pay phone in the hallway; was that what she'd meant?

Now she would have to crawl back into her wet clothes and stand in the hallway as the hookers and their tricks passed by. Anything she said to Francesca might be overheard by anyone.

Unless she didn't call her back.

Unless she let the next twenty-five minutes pass into the next twenty-five and then the next, and sooner or later Francesca would leave the dirty place and go home. Or go somewhere, off into her life. She couldn't believe she'd dragged her friend into this. Liana used to tell Marielle she was selfish, and Marielle had always considered it a virtue. But this was perhaps the most selfish thing she'd ever done.

Maybe it wasn't too late to undo what she'd set in motion. Even if Francesca's phone was tapped and they followed her to the café, if nothing happened there, if no call came for her, they'd leave her alone, wouldn't they? Okay, maybe they'd keep tapping her phone; maybe they might follow her around for a while, but if Lorraine didn't bother her again, that would stop eventually, wouldn't it?

Am I so lonely and desperate that I would inflict my own miserable circumstances onto her? And Lorraine found that the honest answer to that question was: maybe.

But maybe everything was fine. Maybe the Feds hadn't found the truck yet. Maybe there was an APB on it and they were searching all the highways. Maybe they wouldn't guess that she'd drive it a few miles and abandon it, let alone that she'd use precious getaway time to attend to her cat and reach out to her best friend.

She couldn't know what they knew and therefore she didn't know how best to keep safe those she cared about. Let alone herself. She wasn't even sure if she was running from Donald Watkins or the terrorists or both. Or if there was any difference between the two.

If she didn't call Francesca back her friend would be frantic. She wouldn't just sit there for an hour and then shrug and go off to Pilates. She'd make trouble; she'd try to call Reza; she'd go to the police; she might even go to the media. She'd put herself in danger to try to find Marielle. *I've put her in danger by letting her know I'm alive.*

So she had to follow through. She reluctantly pulled on her underpants, her sodden jeans, her wet bra and T-shirt. Her soaked shoes. She didn't bother to look in the mirror or assess her appearance. She counted out a pocketful of coins and hoped it would be enough. She took the room key and her purse, just in case. In case of what, she didn't bother to speculate.

She walked down the hallway, brightly lit as was every part of that establishment. At the moment, no one was in the corridor and no one was on the pay phone. She plunked in quarters and called Directory Assistance for Los Angeles. "I'd like the number of Café Granada on Sunset Boulevard."

She punched in the number with trembling fingers, more worried for Francesca than for herself.

"Café." Lorraine recognized the slightly accented voice of the owner. As always, he sounded hurried and resentful of the intrusion. He used this same tone for customers. For some reason, his crankiness had always endeared him to Francesca, who called him The Grouch.

"Yes, is there a woman there with red hair? She comes there frequently. I was supposed to meet her and I need to speak with her."

"What am I, a secretary?" She thought he was going to hang up on her, but he just slammed the phone down and after a minute or so, Francesca was on the line.

"What in hell is going on?" she asked immediately.

"Francesca, you need to be very careful. Is there anyone listening to your conversation? Is there any possibility you were followed?" Lorraine was clutching the receiver so tightly her knuckles were white.

"Marielle, you're scaring me! The place is completely empty except for The Grouch."

Her grip relaxed just a bit. She drew a breath. As briefly as she could, she told her friend about the events since last February—the bombing, the Witness Security Program, being dead, the imposter book, Reza—and then the events of the last two days. Periodically, the automated voice of the operator interrupted, demanding she insert more coins. "I don't know any more, Fresh, what to believe."

"Where are you now?"

"I'm in a hooker motel on the outskirts, I think, of Ann Arbor."

"Colorful. So you're gonna see if the monk was able to get Dude and then what?"

"I don't know. I thought Canada was a great idea, but now I'm sure they'll be watching for me."

Just then the elevator ascended to the second floor. The door crept open and the same too-skinny woman stepped out, followed this time by a sheriff. Every muscle in Lorraine's body tensed; she would have hung up the receiver if only her limbs weren't paralyzed. Only her mind sprung into action. *Did they find the truck, then somehow track me here, put pressure on the hooker to say she's seen me?* She couldn't draw a breath.

She tried to observe him without letting him know she was looking at him. From his build he looked like an ex-high school football player. She was relieved to see his expression was not one of alertness, but of boredom. Did he do this every Friday afternoon? Neither he nor his date paid any attention to Lorraine; still she remained frozen until they'd opened a door at the other end of the hall and closed it again. Only then could she inhale.

"Are you still there?"

"Yes," she said quietly.

"You need help," Francesca decided. "You can't do this by yourself. Let me snoop around a little bit and try to find Reza."

"She's either been threatened by somebody and is hiding out, or she's in on it."

"But it would be good to know which. Then I'm going to get on a plane and come to Michigan and figure out how to get you out of there."

"Fresh, you can't. This is serious. You could get arrested. You could die."

"We all could die at any moment." This was her Buddhist philosophy.

"You say that because you don't know what it's like to be dead." Lorraine pouted.

"You don't either. If you were dead, you wouldn't care anymore about your career."

The automated operator broke in again.

"I'm down to my last couple of quarters," she told Francesca. "I have to go."

"Call me tomorrow. Call me here again at eight a.m. L.A. time."

"I have no idea where I'll be at eight a.m. L.A. time tomorrow," Lorraine whined, "but I'll try."

"Honey, listen to you! You need to get back your fighting spirit."

"Oh, Fresh," she sighed, "being dead takes it right out of you." The phone went silent then, and she had no more coins to feed it.

But something had shifted, she could feel it, because she hung up hungry, and instead of going back to the dreary little room, she decided to go down to the diner. She took the stairs instead of the elevator and made a mad dash through the rain across the parking lot.

CHAPTER ELEVEN

There was a little counter in the front of the diner that sold gum and mints and candy and a random collection of souvenir T-shirts. One was from Las Vegas, with the words "Hot Hot Hot" over three windows in which appeared red chili peppers, as if they'd just come up jackpot. Another was from the Alamo, with a graphic reproduction of the site. Still another read, "Support Our Troops," and a fourth with the message: "How to impress a man: show up naked, bring beer." She should have been glad to see them. She needed to buy a T-shirt; the one she had on was soaked through, but she was confounded by the options.

A tired-looking hostess sat her in a booth by a window that faced the gas pumps rather than the street. Without asking, she brought coffee, and Lorraine drank it down in one gulp. It wasn't the latte she'd abandoned at Starbucks, but it was nice and strong. An older waitress in an ash-blond wig piqued her curiosity—was it vanity or chemotherapy that necessitated the hairpiece? Or maybe she too was in hiding. Her nametag read "Dinah," and she looked like she'd seen it all. She refilled Lorraine's cup and took her order: a club sandwich, french fries, and a salad with blue cheese dressing—Lorraine was ravenous.

"Is there a little drugstore or something anywhere nearby?" she asked Dinah.

Dinah's already weathered face creased as she thought about it. "There's a 7-Eleven about three blocks that way"—she pointed—"and there's a Kroger's about six blocks the other way."

"Thanks." She calculated that the Kroger's might have hair dye, but it must be the same store where she'd parked the stolen panel truck. Part of her wished she still had that truck. The 7-Eleven might have shampoo, a few basic toiletries. She should have told Zenkei to get everything from the Twin Pines. She wondered if he'd managed to pick up Dude without being apprehended.

These thoughts receded as her food appeared and she began to eat as though she'd never in her life had a concern for her weight. She ingested every morsel of iceberg lettuce, every glistening french fry studded with salt. She polished off the triple-decker club, drank cup after cup of the truck stop's strong, black coffee—she'd never sleep tonight. Despite the caffeine rush, she could feel her nerves calming down, her thoughts clearing; it was amazing how the body responded to fuel.

When the waitress asked if she wanted dessert, Lorraine inquired, "What's good?"

Dinah said, "The peach pie. Audrey makes it right here in the kitchen." Lorraine ordered it a la mode. It occurred to her—*I'm eating like Lorraine, not like Marielle.* She hoped she wouldn't have to run anywhere for a while, because she wasn't sure she could move.

The pie was every bit as good as Dinah had promised. It tasted like it had been made from peaches grown down the road. Lorraine was just about to put the last forkful in her mouth when a couple of state patrolmen sauntered into the diner and were seated a few booths away. A bolt of anxiety threatened to send the contents of her dinner back up her esophagus, but she used Koryo's deep breathing technique. Thankfully, they were not the two in whose car she'd ridden earlier that afternoon, and they seemed to have no more on their minds than dinner.

The younger of the two flirted good-naturedly with Dinah, and she swatted at him with her pad of checks. The other, his back to Lorraine, was engaged in a running monologue with his partner.

Lorraine signaled to Dinah for the check. As she laid it face down on the table she said, "Pay up front," and gestured to the counter near the door. Lorraine left her a ten-dollar tip and practiced being invisible as she made her way toward the entrance. There she paid her check, bought the Las Vegas T-shirt, a talisman of hope that her luck would hold out. The only size they had was men's extra large, but after that meal, she was certain it would fit. She also bought a roll of quarters; she'd be spending some time at the pay phone.

She stole a glance back at the two patrolmen; they appeared not to have noticed her at all. She folded the new T-shirt into her purse and dashed back through the rain to the motel. Instead of the woman who'd been at the front desk earlier, there was now an extremely slender man, rocking his body to something playing through the headphones in his ears. He didn't look at her, which seemed both relieving and worrying from a security perspective. Instead of the elevator, she took the stairs, hoping the exercise might dissolve the overly stuffed sensation in her gut.

When she reached the top of the stairs she saw someone standing outside the door to her room. He was a small, compact man whose tawny complexion might be Central American; he was trying to enter room 217 with a key card. Lorraine stayed in the shadow of the stairwell as she watched him stick the card in the slot in the door, again and again. Each time his offering was rejected he stood back and regarded it with perplexity, swaying a little on his feet. It occurred to her there might be a simple, rather than sinister, explanation. As she approached, she could smell the beer on him.

"What room do you want?" she asked him.

He flinched a little, as if he expected to be hit. His eyes narrowed with suspicion, incomprehension.

"*¿Que número?*" She hoped that was the right way to ask it. Marielle had the lazy Spanish of many Anglo Los Angelenos, who heard it spoken all the time but never bothered to learn it.

"*Doscientos dieciséis,*" he responded.

"*Diecisiete.*" She pointed to her own door. "*Dieciséis.*" She pointed across the hall.

"*Perdoneme,*" he muttered, and staggered a little toward his room. She was as relieved as he was when his card worked in that door and it closed behind him.

Sequestered once more in room 217, Lorraine stripped off her wet T-shirt and slid into the Vegas shirt she'd just purchased. She took off her wet jeans and hung them over the towel railing in the bathroom. A nicer motel might have a hair dryer and she could have tried drying the clothes by hand, but this place offered no such amenities.

Her Timex revealed it was 6:45. In a little while she could try calling Zenkei to see whether he'd gotten Dude or not. She wasn't sure what she'd do if he hadn't. A thousand things might have gone wrong: the old lady at the Twin Pines might have refused to let him in the room; the traumatized cat could have run out through the open door; Donald Watkins might have gotten there before Zenkei; Donald Watkins might have busted the pleasant monk.

To distract herself she turned on the battered TV that sat across from the bed. All three networks were running national news; Fox was running *Access Hollywood*. She had scant attention for stories about the economy, the ongoing wars, or the latest scandals. She burrowed back under the scratchy sheet, and channel surfed haphazardly. When the seven o'clock hour came, she saw her choices included *Bernie Mac*, *Wheel of Fortune*, and *Dr. Phil*. She was about to turn it off when she clicked to channel seven and saw they were rerunning their local news.

She leaned a little closer to the TV as she heard the reporter say, "In a late-breaking story, a crucial witness in the government's case against the JFK airport bombers is missing after her house was firebombed last night." There was footage of the charred wreckage of the townhouse, and then of her image on a blurry surveillance tape at the bank that morning. She heard her name—Lorraine's name, that is—and then, "If you've seen this woman, please call..." as a number flashed on the screen.

Had Tuna seen this, or had she known it all along? If Zenkei saw it, would it make him less willing to help her? If Koryo saw the news, she was sure he'd turn her in right away. But could anyone really identify her from this snowy videotape?

Donald was taking a risk to broadcast it. What did it do to the government's case against the suspects? If he were really worried about the terrorists finding her, he wouldn't do that, would he? "Missing" was such an ambiguous phrase. It didn't tell her their theory of Lorraine's whereabouts—abducted, in hiding, disappeared.

But Donald knew she'd been at the state trooper station that afternoon. It was almost certain he now knew she'd stolen the truck. And with her name in public circulation, using her ID was not an option. She couldn't fly, rent a car, or even risk buying a car unless it was under the table. Francesca was right—how could she possibly do this by herself? But how could she justify involving anyone else?

The news moved on to other segments: a carjacking, an apartment fire, another loss by the Tigers. Lorraine continued to fret in a nervous, unfocused way. At 7:30 she put on her wet jeans, and went back out to the hall phone. She dialed the number of the Zen Center; the phone rang with no answer. Anxiety spiked; had Zenkei been apprehended? Had Koryo gone to bail him out? What would happen to Dude and to Hakue?

She went back to the room and paced for ten minutes before trying again. This time, the pay phone was in use. A diminutive Black woman in tight jeans and a tube top was clutching the receiver with one hand, smoking a Virginia Slims menthol cigarette with the other. Her small size didn't prepare one for her truculence. "I ain't drivin' all that way," she protested into the receiver, "unless that sucka's gonna give up some gas money."

Then she saw Lorraine eying her and snapped, "I'll be off when I'm good and ready."

Lorraine retreated to 217. She could pace the length of the room in six strides. She walked back and forth, making herself count to three hundred before she cracked the door a bit to see if the phone was still occupied. It was. Three hundred more. She tried to focus on the movement, on the counting, to drive the other thoughts from her head. It occurred to her that everyone would have been better off if she had been blown up with her cell phone on the front steps of her Hollywood home.

Thinking back to that morning, she realized she'd never questioned how Donald Watkins just happened to show up at the precise moment she'd picked up the cell phone. If someone else had left it at her door, how would Donald have missed him? How could he have arrived right in the nick of time?

She stopped in the middle of step 246. It had to have been Donald who put that phone on her welcome mat, primed to explode. To scare her? To kill her? Then why save her? If she were outside of this web, she might be able to follow the strands, tease them apart and see how it was woven, but from inside it, she just kept getting more tangled.

The next time she looked into the hallway, the coast was clear. Once more she dialed the Zen Center; this time Zenkei answered. "Thank goodness you're there," she burbled. "Are you all right? Did you find Dude?"

"Everything all right," he said, but she sensed an odd tone to his voice, as if there was someone listening and he didn't want that person to know what he was talking about. Was it Koryo or someone else? He didn't use the code, though, but she wondered if he remembered it.

"Do I need to correct my delusions?" she asked.

"No more so than rest of us," he answered, and she was relieved to hear he still had his sense of humor. Things couldn't be that bad.

"I come meet you," he offered.

This option worried her, but how else did she expect to get her cat? It wasn't like she could walk back to downtown Ann

Arbor. Still, she'd driven that beat-up VW to her house last night, sped away from the fire in it, and driven it back to the street from which the LeSabre was towed. How could it not be on Donald Watkins's radar, especially after Tuna must have told them where they'd first met? On the other hand, if Zenkei had gotten to Dude first, maybe Tuna hadn't spilled the beans.

Then it occurred to her: what was she going to do with her cat in this motel, with no vehicle?

"Is Dude somewhere he can stay for a little while?"

"Yes." Still, that caution.

"Meet me, but don't bring him. I can't keep him yet."

"Okay. No problem. Where should I come?"

She was afraid to tell him. Either someone was in the room listening to his conversation or his phone was tapped. Perhaps Donald Watkins had merely watched from a distance as Zenkei retrieved Dude, then followed him, believing that eventually he'd be led to her.

But she heard Francesca's insistent voice, "You can't do this all by yourself," and Lorraine knew she was right. So she told him the name of the motel. She knew the street it was on, but not the exact location, and she apologized for this.

"No problem," he said. "I look it up."

"It's..." She hesitated. "It's kind of a rough place."

"I was born in Vietnam," he told her. "Rough place...I'm used to."

CHAPTER TWELVE

She knew she needed to stay sharp, at least as sharp as someone on her thirty-seventh hour without sleep could be, but God, she needed a drink. She wondered if there was a liquor store in the area that delivered. She could imagine the glass in her hand, frosty with ice, fragrant with white rum. The bite of the alcohol on her tongue and the warmth spreading down the throat and throughout the network of veins. How her nerves would unclench. How she could slide into a dreamless sleep.

She must have dozed just thinking about it, because the knock startled her. For a moment she couldn't remember where she was; then, she couldn't believe she'd nodded off. A string of drool had slid from the corner of her mouth onto the hard, flat pillow against which her cheek was pressed.

She scrambled up, wiping her cheek on her hand, her hand on her damp jeans, checking to make sure she was fully dressed, and hurried toward the door. "What?" she called, in a voice as gender-neutral as she could manufacture.

"Zenkei," she heard from the other side of the door, and she unbolted it. Trying to keep herself hidden behind the door, she reached one arm out to gesture to him to come in.

"Did anyone follow you?" This, before making any kind of greeting or offering an expression of appreciation.

The monk blinked from behind rain-spotted spectacles. Who knew what he was thinking about any of this? "Who you running from?" he asked. "With your yellow cat?" He seemed amused, as if he was convinced she'd invented all this drama.

Instead of lying to him, she asked, "Did you see the news tonight?"

He shook his head. "I don't watch news." He paused to clean his lenses on a clean handkerchief, then returned them to his face before adding, "Koryo watch news."

Her face asked the question.

The monk nodded. "He come tell me about it. It hard to understand. You in trouble with the government?"

"Is he going to turn me in?"

"Koryo? Why he do that?" The question seemed to bemuse him.

"He clearly doesn't like me. And he seems to do everything by the rules." She stopped herself from adding, *And he's so mean.*

Zenkei looked at her deeply, as if he wanted his words to penetrate. "Emotion make commotion inside the mind. Who like, who not like. Buddhism not about that.

"Like me, Koryo was born in Vietnam. When he was a child, he saw the war. So much suffering. So many died. Koryo would not help government."

She felt a little chastised. Of course she hadn't given any thought to the events that might have shaped the nature of the stern monk. Still, she was relieved to hear he wasn't likely to betray her. But another worry nagged.

"By helping me, you could be in danger."

Zenkei dismissed this with a wave of his hand. "I leave Vietnam on a fishing boat, very unsafe. Pirates try to rob us, but we have nothing. Not even food or water. Three years in a refugee camp before I come here. If 'danger' mean we might die, we are always in danger."

Lorraine felt like a very stupid American, her worldview confined, limited by privilege. With all her skills at fiction, she couldn't imagine the lives these monks had lived.

As if reading her mind, Zenkei said, "Now you know our stories. What about you?"

She wished he'd brought the yellow dog with him, though of course no dog would want to be out in this downpour. Still, she missed Hakue's placid energy; she wanted to curl against the Lab's ample body and whisper her story into one silky ear.

She offered Zenkei a seat on the bed and hoped it wasn't an inappropriate gesture toward a monk. He declined and sat instead on the grungy linoleum, arranging his robes over his crossed legs.

She'd planned to say only a few things, but once she began to speak the entire story came pouring out, unstoppable as the rain still falling outside. She told him about the secret phone calls to Reza, about the card to Francesca, about leaving Tuna at the sheriff station, about stealing the truck. He nodded, taking it all in, but asked no questions, which made Lorraine wonder how much he actually understood.

Then he closed his eyes and she feared she'd put him to sleep. Her stomach sank as she realized how much hope she'd invested in this monk, as if he had magical powers to help in her situation for which there was no help.

They sat in silence. She could hear the rain outside the building and traffic on the road and the elevator chugging its way upward. In the quiet, she could hear the couple in the next room engaged in joyless, acrobatic sex, and worried the sounds might embarrass Zenkei. Though what he might have overheard in a refugee camp had probably eliminated his capacity for shock. The monk was so still, he made her want to start pacing again.

A few minutes later he opened his eyes and smiled; he looked refreshed, as if breaking the surface of the water and returning to light. "I know where you can stay," he announced. "Zen

Center has a retreat house in Brightmoor. Someone donate it. Nobody look for you there."

Lorraine had no idea where Brightmoor was, but the words "retreat house" summoned an image of a wooden cottage on the tree-lined shore of a placid lake.

"I can't just hide out in the woods for the rest of my life!" It was only after the words were out of her mouth that she heard how ungrateful she sounded.

"Rest of life?" He lifted his eyebrows in mock surprise and grinned. "Rest of life could be long, could be short. We don't know." He shrugged. "You have many problems right now. Too many to solve at once. Zenkei just trying to solve one problem, short-term. If you like better, you stay here." He gestured toward the wall behind which the guttural moans had gotten louder.

"I'm sorry," she backtracked. "I am really grateful for your help. You're right; I don't have a lot of options. I just—" Unexpectedly, her eyes flooded. "I just don't know what I'm going to do."

Just a week earlier she'd thought her biggest problem was being stuck in a loser lifestyle for an undetermined period of time. Now if only she could have returned to the security of the townhouse, the quiet evenings spent with Dude, and the pleasant afternoon routine of reading to Garland.

"Only need to live one moment at a time. This moment. This moment. See, in this moment you're okay. Nothing to worry."

She could have argued that point, but Zenkei did have a calming effect on her.

"Okay, how will I get there?"

"I take you."

"Do you think anyone is on to you? Do you think someone saw you at the Twin Pines? Do you think they've tapped your phone? Did anybody follow you here?'

He placed his hands to either side of his head, in an affectation of Munch's *The Scream*. "Your mind is so busy. So much worry." He grinned. "Saw nobody at Twin Pines." Delighted with himself, he admitted, "I broke in. Easy—lock very old. Not good for security."

"But I wonder if Tuna told them where she met me."

"Tuna's okay. She's not going to do anything to hurt you. I know her and her grandma a long time."

Her grandma. Her grandma, Magda. Was it possible that everyone was connected to this conspiracy—even her lock-picking monk? But Lorraine's mind was too exhausted to embrace this idea. She needed to believe in someone. Even if his judgments about others—first Koryo and now Tuna—turned out to be overly optimistic, she couldn't see Zenkei as capable of harming anyone.

"I think you should sleep now. I come back tomorrow. Figure out plan then."

He was right. Lorraine had nothing left in her—not for cunning or strategy, not even for paranoia. She couldn't even hold onto her anxieties. The mere act of sitting up suddenly seemed more than her body was capable of.

"Thank you," she said woozily. How could any words compensate for the effort he'd made, the efforts he intended to make?

She followed him to the door and bolted it behind him. Then she stumbled to the bed and, despite her caffeine intake, was asleep before her body hit the sheets.

* * *

The rain had stopped by the time she woke, although the sky was still overcast. Her clothes, in which she'd slept, were sour. With her face on TV, she didn't dare risk going back to the diner, not after seeing the troopers there the night before. Her invisibility powers were lost. Every cell in her body longed for caffeine, but she felt the more urgent need to lay low. Luckily, the denizens of this motel seemed unlikely to be people who followed the news, so she believed it was safe to remain here at least another day.

She checked her Timex; it was close to nine a.m., two hours before she could call Francesca. She stared at the dingy room with nothing to read, nothing to eat, no coffee. Saturday morning television had nothing in the way of information, and she didn't have the patience to be lulled by the stupid or the brutal, so she clicked it off.

She missed Dude. She hoped he was getting along okay at the Zen Center, that he'd managed to do something to annoy Koryo. If her cat were here he would curl his body against her hip and lull her to sleep. She tried to will herself back to unconsciousness, but her nerves were thrumming. The questions began to tumble in her head again, but she had no more answers than she'd had last night. *Why am I in danger? What did I do? How will I ever get back to my life?*

Her heart began to race and she couldn't seem to draw a full breath; she wondered if she was having another panic attack—she, who had always been the calmest person in the room. She folded her legs under her on the mattress and tried to concentrate on her breath, drawing in the light, exhaling out the dark. She tried to focus on the sound of the air moving in and out of her nostrils, to allow the sound to wash away the clamor of thoughts that hammered inside her skull.

This moment, she reminded herself of Zenkei's words last night. *In this moment I am fine.*

Her mind yammered on relentlessly and she was convinced the meditation wasn't working but she kept going anyway; there was nothing else to do. Time passed and she didn't even notice the moment her breath descended deeper into her pelvis and her heartbeat slowed. It was only after her legs went to sleep that she unfolded herself and looked at her watch. She was amazed to see an hour had passed and even more surprised that she felt more stable.

She was about to risk the shower when she heard a knock on her door. "What," she barked.

"It's Zenkei."

Lorraine opened the door. He was carrying a satchel and grinning ear to ear. "I have idea."

She pulled him into the room, cautioning him not to talk in the hallway.

He plunged his hands into the satchel and pulled out a maroon-colored robe not unlike his own. "You wear this," he offered.

She was taken aback. She knew that monks had to undergo some kind of lengthy initiation before they were allowed to don their robes; surely one couldn't just put one on like a Halloween costume. Besides, who was going to buy her as a Buddhist nun?

As if he knew her thoughts, Zenkei produced an electric razor. "We shave your head."

"Oh, no," she gasped before she'd even formulated an argument. *Not bald*, she thought, *anything but bald.*

"I'll be too visible," she protested. "No offense, but you don't exactly blend in."

"But no one will know it's you." He'd clearly anticipated her objection. "People notice the robe, yes, but they don't see the person inside it."

He'd also brought with him the bag of items she'd purchased at Thrifty Acres the morning after her townhouse was firebombed. Yesterday morning, she remembered with a start. Clean underwear. Deodorant. Lotion. A comb. And the box of hair dye.

But Zenkei was right; changing the color of her hair alone wouldn't make enough of a difference if law enforcement was looking for her. The robe would hide the shape of her body and the baldness would remove any remaining vestige of Marielle. *But, bald?*

"It grows back," he assured her. He'd also brought a pair of round, rimless glasses not unlike his own. He laid out these items on the unmade bed like a chambermaid, delighted with his cleverness. Even though Lorraine resisted this plan in every cell of her body, she had to admit that it was just crackpot enough to work. It wasn't as if she had a better idea.

The last item he pulled from the satchel was a shopping bag containing a thermos of hot tea, a plastic baggie full of granola and a carton of soymilk. He'd even thought to bring a banana, a bowl, a knife, and a spoon, and he arranged it all on the small night table beside the bed. She couldn't remember when she'd felt so well taken care of.

"When will you call your friend?" he wanted to know.

"In about forty minutes," she mumbled through a mouthful of cereal.

"We should change your appearance after the call," he decided.

Great, no rush, really. She felt her head clearing, her energy getting stronger as she ate. She washed her breakfast down with green tea that had roasted grains of rice in it; she'd had it before in Japanese restaurants. She was grateful it was caffeinated.

Zenkei asked if she could afford to spend another night here. She assured him she could. She wondered if he was helping her because he thought she was poor, if he'd be turned off to learn of the wad of cash in her purse. She hadn't even dealt with how crazy it was to be carrying that money around, but where would she stash it, especially now? Perhaps she could find a way to give some to the Zen Center without revealing the total amount.

Her mind spun from one preoccupation to the next until the monk brought her back to his original question. "Are you okay to stay here until your friend arrives?"

When he said these words, it penetrated that Francesca really might be coming. Oh, how she'd laugh to see Marielle gotten up as a Buddhist nun.

All of a sudden she wanted nothing more than to see Francesca. Tears spilled as she realized part of her had believed she'd never see her again.

At precisely eleven o'clock, they made their way to the pay phone in the hall. Lorraine asked Zenkei to join her since he would have a role in their travel plans. A squat housekeeper was laconically pushing a cart at the other end of the hall but otherwise the floor was deserted. Lorraine loaded up the phone with change, then dialed the number of the dirty place. Again the grumpy response, and she heard the proprietor admonish Francesca, "I'm not your receptionist!"

"Hey." Francesca's greeting held none of her usual enthusiasm. It was the tone Marielle remembered from when her friend had called to tell her she and Benny were getting divorced. Lorraine was instantly afraid.

"Fresh, are you safe? Is someone watching you there?" She was calculating how much time it might take for someone to trace this call if they happened to be tapping the phone in the café.

"No, it's okay. I *think* it's okay. Mar, I had a visit this morning from Donald Watkins."

"You're fucking kidding me!" She looked over to the monk to see if she'd offended him, but he only looked concerned at her anxiety.

"Fresh, if he knows we're in contact, he for sure is having you followed and he's probably tracing this call right now…"

"I don't think so. My home phone maybe. But they wouldn't expect me to get a call here."

"Did anybody come in after you?" If she were being tailed, they'd see her on the phone.

"There's nobody else here except The Screenwriter." The Screenwriter was a fixture at the dirty place; he drank coffee all day long, tapping away on his laptop. If you sat next to his table, he'd move, sure you were trying to steal the concept for his latest blockbuster. She had a momentary wave of missing him and the other characters who'd populated her former life.

"Did Donald happen to tell you I wasn't dead?" *Why would he do that?*

"No. He didn't say this had anything to do with terrorism or with you being a witness—nothing. He said he was from the government and that there were some questions about your estate, with this new book surfacing. He asked if I knew Reza and if she'd been in touch with me."

"He's fishing. He's trying to see if I've been in touch with anyone."

"I didn't tell him anything. I just kept saying how I couldn't get over you being gone."

"And what about Reza? Did you find out anything about her?"

"Not yet. I was going to go by her house later today—I remember we went there to that fundraiser for the women's shelter last year—but now I think that's a dumb idea. It's likely they've got her under surveillance."

"I'm so sorry I dragged you into this."

"Are you kidding? I'm so sorry *you* got dragged into this. And I wish I were smarter and had a better idea of how to help you."

Lorraine hesitated. "There is a way, but it's crazy."

"I specialize in crazy," her friend responded.

In Marielle's novel *The Time Before the Last Time* Coraline Avery needed fake ID to get away from the man who was stalking her. Marielle had researched the vast market in counterfeit papers that was transacted in L.A.'s MacArthur Park. Run by the Mara Salvatrucha, a criminal gang from El Salvador, you could get pretty much any documentation you needed in a couple of hours.

"I need a passport and a driver's license." She explained where to go and what to do.

"Do you think they'll talk to a white woman? Oh, I know; I'll take Ernesto." Ernesto was the young assistant in her art studio.

"You can't tell anyone about this!" Lorraine insisted.

"I won't. I'll just ask him to help me flag down one of the dealers, and then get lost."

It was sounding crazier and crazier. "Are you sure, Fresh?"

"Yes," was all her friend said, but this one word was filled with so much feeling.

"I think it will cost about three hundred dollars; they'll charge you the gringo price. And you'll need some photos of me; not the same one for both."

"Can I use the pictures we took on our hike last New Year's Day?"

Lorraine thought back to that day as though it had happened in another world, decades instead of months ago. "I don't look anything like those pictures anymore."

"That's okay. Women change their looks all the time. The basic shape of your features is the same, isn't it?"

"God, what if they're using face scanning technology? The Feds must have put me in the database."

"We have to hope that budget cuts have prevented them from installing the latest technology. What name do you want me to use?"

Lorraine remembered how at first she'd wanted a name borrowed from one of her characters, a clue for someone to catch a long time in the future. How silly that all seemed now. Still she answered, "Minerva Turnbull." That was the name of her protagonist from *Weeping Minerva*, a book she now knew would never be read by anyone.

The automated operator demanded more coins and Lorraine fed them into the phone. She looked to Zenkei for signs of impatience but his face was calm and attentive.

"Fresh, I'm sure they're going to be watching you. If you book a flight to Michigan, they're gonna know what's up."

"Well, what if I fly to New York or Chicago? And get a car and drive there. I could be going to New York *or* Chicago on my own business."

"But there'll be a record of the car rental."

"Okay, okay." She could hear her friend trying to think her way through the problem. "I have an old boyfriend in Chicago—Armando..."

"Why have I never heard about Armando?" Lorraine interrupted. It wasn't the moment for girl talk, but she felt starved for this kind of normalcy, dishing with a friend.

"Ancient history. Before I knew you. But we're still in touch. Go figure. What if I fly to Chicago, borrow his car, and drive to where you are?"

Lorraine didn't ask why an old boyfriend would loan her his car. Francesca had always had a knack for getting men to do what she wanted. Since they'd broken up, Francesca had exclusively dated men, even marrying for a few years. For some reason, this had stung Marielle, and she'd once asked Fresh if she'd stopped being attracted to women.

They were taking a hike in Griffith Park on a late December day. It had rained recently, and the air was clear and cold, the chaparral beginning to green.

Francesca had stopped walking and turned to face Marielle. "It was never about 'women,'" she'd said. Her tone was level, but her eyes were fierce. "It was only ever about you."

Lorraine forced herself to bring her awareness back to the present. This plan seemed so risky; and involving another person, however peripherally, just made it worse. But, she reminded herself, even standing here at the pay phone in this truck stop motel was a risk, not just to herself but to her patient monk. And without ID she wouldn't be able to get out of the country. "Okay," she agreed.

"Where are you?"

She remembered the moment, a few weeks ago, when Reza had asked this same question. Lorraine had been reckless to answer then; was she just as foolhardy to give away her whereabouts again?

"I'm not going to stay here much longer. But the monk I told you about has someplace he's going to take me."

She put Zenkei on the phone then, and he gave her directions to the Brightmoor retreat. She tried to listen so she too would know where she'd be going, but his voice was soft and she couldn't really follow the instructions. She thought how Fresh had never been good with directions and wondered how in the world they'd be able to pull this off.

The monk signaled that he was done. She reached once more for the receiver.

"I'll do some calling around about Reza," Francesca told her. "I'll get a passport and driver's license for *Minerva*. And I'll get a flight out tomorrow morning. I think taking the red eye tonight might seem too conspicuous. I should get to you sometime late tomorrow."

"If something goes wrong…"

"Nothing will go wrong," she assured her, but Lorraine was unconvinced.

"How will I know?"

Her friend sighed. "I'll buy a cell phone. One of those disposable ones. I'll call your monk when I get to Chicago. He gave me his phone number, okay?"

They could still nip this plan in the bud. There were so many things that could go wrong. She would never forgive herself if Francesca were hurt. But if not this plan, what would she do? Go to the woods and become a hermit?

"Fresh? I haven't asked anything about you, about how you're doing."

"A lot better now that I know I'm going to see you tomorrow."

Once she'd hung up, she thought of a thousand questions she'd wanted to ask, but she couldn't risk calling the dirty place again. She tried to imagine what her friend would do next: whether she'd stay for breakfast or hurry out of there. She wondered if Fresh felt as brave as she sounded or if she was putting on a face. She remembered that Reza had always sounded brave too. She wondered if Donald had realized that something had gone wrong with Reza.

What she'd once considered problems seemed laughable to her now. Getting a bad haircut. Being unsatisfied with the prose she'd produced that day. Having too many requests for her time.

How she wished someone would request her time. She thought about the long day ahead of her, stuck in the dreary motel room, alone because Zenkei couldn't be too long away from Hakue who couldn't go out by herself.

They agreed that she shouldn't transform herself into a nun until she was ready to leave the motel, sometime tomorrow morning. One more day of having hair. She eyed the box of dye she'd purchased yesterday; she might as well make use of it. When housekeeping knocked at the door, she sent them away, but not before she asked for a couple of extra towels.

She opened the package. She'd been dyeing her hair brown for six months now; she'd gotten to be a pro at home dye jobs. In about fifteen minutes, her head was slathered with color; the applicator was empty. The slight stinging of her scalp signaled it was working.

She stared at her face, greenish in the hideous fluorescence of the bathroom, her features surrounded by a hood of deepening burgundy. She looked for signs of who she'd once been, but nothing seemed familiar. Exhaustion made her look older, or perhaps made her look her age. Marielle had never wanted to look her age. The mouth, once proud, was pinched and downcast; new lines had sprouted on the forehead. She wondered if Francesca would be able to find her in this face, or if Marielle Wing had truly died.

Zenkei had been kind to leave her a book, but it was a book of Buddhist teachings. Its passages seemed both too obvious and too profound. Unlike a good novel, she couldn't lose herself in it; her mind wandered quickly. The monk had promised to return with dinner and said he'd bring a newspaper and a writing pad at that time. Although what he imagined she'd be writing, who knew? It occurred to her that she should buy a laptop to take to the woods; could she risk going shopping dressed as a Buddhist nun? And she'd definitely want to get some white rum, maybe a case of it.

A quick peek out the window showed not even a hint of sun breaking through the clouds that were suffocating the sky. She checked her Timex; there was still about fifteen minutes before she could wash the dye off her hair. She flipped through the phone book in the drawer of the nightstand and found an Apple Store in a mall in Ann Arbor. Briarwood Mall—another tree name.

She had the irrational wish that Tuna would appear at the door to visit her; this room would hardly be a comedown from the rancid basement where they'd fucked yesterday. It was preposterous to find herself feeling horny as a teenager, but she'd never been good at handling boredom. While it was probably true that her passion the day before was fueled by fear and nervous exhaustion, it was also true that these states persisted.

In her fantasy, Tuna showed up *after* she'd washed the color out of her hair, which had miraculously grown long again and possessed the body and coppery shine of a model's tresses in a TV commercial. She was no longer dressed in stinky clothes or in the Buddhist robes, but in a satin negligee that had fortuitously appeared out of nowhere. It was a lime green that complimented her newly auburn locks. She was listening to jazz on a radio that had likewise materialized just for this moment. When she heard the knock on the door, she already knew who it was, and she was ready for her.

This wasn't helping anything. She shook her head to clear it, careful not to send splatters of dye onto the bed or walls. The fantasy subsided.

The motel didn't offer cable TV and the local stations had only sports, painfully dull ones to watch: baseball and golf and car races. Too early for football; too late for hockey. Not that she was a fan of any of these; she was just craving mental stimulation. Still, she left a baseball game on turned low, just to have sound in the room besides her own thoughts. Marielle had always felt contempt for people who used the television for company, but Lorraine understood them now.

She returned to paging through the Yellow Pages. She looked up Escort Services; there were several listed, one specifying "female and male escorts." Then she browsed Restaurants, imagined ordering take-out food. She flirted with the idea of calling a crisis hotline and chatting them up a bit.

Then she thought about calling Donald Watkins; would she be able to get any information out of him before he traced the call? Now she'd really lost her mind. *This is how people get caught*, she reminded herself. Like Winston Klein in *Hard-Hearted Monday*, who, in a fit of wounded pride, left a note after killing Lakshmi Davenport. The note said, "She broke her promise." It was all the police had needed to link him to the crime.

Still, the more perverse she understood it to be, the more the idea compelled her. Donald knew who she was, or at least who she had been. Donald might know other things that could help her, if she could get the information out of him.

Thank God it was time to wash her hair. She turned the shower up as hot as it would go and hoped her self-destructive notions would swirl down the drain along with the last remnants of burgundy suds. When she'd scrubbed her scalp raw she used a generous helping of the cheap conditioner, which smelled of chemicals and hand lotion. She lathered her body with the hotel soap; she used the razor that Zenkei brought from the Twin

Pines and shaved her legs. When she stepped out of the shower, she wrapped her hair in one towel, and dried her body with the other. The moisturizer felt soothing to her parched skin. And deodorant—what an invention!

But there was no getting around the fact she had to climb back into her putrid clothes. She should have asked Francesca to bring her some things to wear. Then she remembered that tomorrow she'd be donning the nun's robe.

She took a brush to her hair. She did this without looking into the mirror; she wanted to style it before she discovered what she looked like as a redhead. Although she'd grown used to its shorter length after a lifetime of letting it curl halfway down her back, in her mind she believed she'd end up with *long* red hair. Still, by tomorrow at this time even this would seem like an extravagance of tresses, once she'd let her head be shaved.

She took a breath and turned toward the mirror. It wasn't, of course, the fabulous red of Francesca's hair, although perhaps even hers would dull under the abysmal light of the bathroom. Still, it was much more lively than the light ash brown that Deputy Orellano had assigned to Lorraine. It brought a warmth to her skin tone she'd been missing. It was crazy how a cosmetic change could shift the way she felt about herself but as she stared at her face, she felt a little crackle of energy. Now she wished Tuna would show up here for real. Not that the young woman would ever want to speak to her again.

Just then her eyes happened to glance at the TV. A banner read: Breaking News—Suspects in JFK Bombing Dead. Her hands shook as she reached to turn up the volume. The announcer looked gravely at the camera and said, "In breaking news, the two men accused in the February bombing of the American Airlines terminal at JFK were found dead this morning in their maximum-security cells. Prison officials are initially calling each a suicide, pending an investigation."

She thought of the young men she'd seen running at the airport. She never did know for certain if those men were the suspects but Deputy Orellano had confided, "Your testimony was very helpful." And what of the man in the uniform, the one who'd said, "We'll find you"? Had Homeland Security ever located him?

As she sank onto the mattress, her body was trembling. She recalled Donald's warning from months ago: "We can't guarantee your safety in prison." Donald. She had to talk to Donald.

She wouldn't call him from here. She'd walk until she found a pay phone. She put on the rimless glasses Zenkei had brought her. There was nothing to be done about the clothing, but no item was remarkable, unless the stench of being unwashed could be considered memorable.

Although she'd slept in the Vegas T-shirt, she put that on again; no one but Zenkei had seen her in it. She did a quick check of her purse to make sure the cash was still there, along with all the other relevant material gleaned from her safe deposit box. Everything that mattered—except for Francesca and Dude—was in this leather bag.

She again took the stairs. Yet another new person was sitting at the front desk. She paid Lorraine no more mind than had any of her predecessors. The young woman was watching a movie on her iPad. Even when Lorraine handed her some money and told her she'd be staying another night, the clerk barely paused to note this in the registration book. So much the better.

Then she was out on the street. The humidity was oppressive; three days of rain hadn't broken the back of the heat wave. She walked in the opposite direction from where she'd come yesterday.

Despite her copper hair, which would be gleaming, she was sure, if the sun were out, she felt relatively invisible, even when a couple of truckers honked at her to see if she wanted a ride. The road seemed not much used by pedestrians. There were auto parts places and industrial parks, about which nothing was park-like.

She saw the 7-Eleven but it had no pay phone.

In a few more blocks she spotted a gas station that did have a phone booth tucked in the far corner of the drive. She asked the cashier for change and he gave it to her. All the arguments against making this call were drowned out by the terrible need to find out what was going on.

It was only a little disconcerting to find a pair of women's panties—black cotton with printed pink hearts—stuffed into one corner of the glass booth. The phone was in working order. She plunked in coins and dialed Donald Watkins's number, which she recalled as if it were tattooed on her memory.

She heard his voice in the receiver. "Hello? Hello?" He sounded annoyed. He sounded like he hadn't been getting enough sleep. She knew how he felt. "Is someone there?"

"I'm not sure," she told him.

"*Lorraine?*"

"Lorraine's dead." She didn't have time to play games with him. Every second she spent on this call brought him closer to tracing it.

"Marielle?"

"Marielle's dead too. I know you're tracing this call," she told him.

"Where are you?"

She just snorted. "Where are *you*, Donald?"

"I'm in Michigan, looking for you. It's critical I find you, Lorraine. You're in more danger than you realize."

"You think I don't realize? It wasn't *your* house that was firebombed."

"We found the manuscript in your car. You got it from Reza. You were in touch with her. Even though I told you not to be."

"This wouldn't be a good time to lecture me on obedience."

"You think the rules don't apply to you, Lorraine? Reza is dead."

"Yeah, there's a lot of that going around. Where did you send her—South Dakota?"

"Listen to me. Reza Caldicott was found two nights ago on the bank of the L.A. River near Elysian Park with a bullet between her eyes."

The statement tore through her body as if she were the one who'd been shot. She felt bile rise in her throat. "I'm hanging up now."

"Lorraine, please. It's not too late for me to help you."

"It *is* too late. I saw on the news the suspects are dead." Then she gasped. "Or is that just another sleight of hand trick?"

"No. No trick. They were executed in prison."

She slid open the glass door, taking in deep breaths to try to keep from vomiting right there in the booth. She scanned the road before her, half expecting a battalion to pull up any minute to apprehend her.

"Well, I guess I gave up everything for nothing then. You don't even need me anymore now."

"Let me come get you, Lorraine. Let me help you." His usual cool detachment was gone; he sounded—what? Desperate? Defeated?

The part of her mind that was scared, that was exhausted, that was confounded about what to do, was almost persuaded. Lorraine wanted to rely on Donald. But Marielle was still inside her and was the stronger. If Donald was desperate, he'd be of no use to her. She had a lifetime of relying on herself.

"If you wanted to help me, why did you put my face on TV?"

She slammed down the receiver and exited the phone booth like it was on fire and crossed the road against the light. She needed to get as far away as possible. She wanted to break into a run, but that was too conspicuous; no one would mistake her for a jogger on this strip of road. So she walked as fast as she could, trying to outrace her mind.

What had she learned, risking so much to place that call? It was Donald who'd had the LeSabre towed. The morning after her townhouse was firebombed. If he'd only waited, she would have come back for it, and he would have found her. Was he impatient, like her? Or had he been trying to keep someone else from finding the car, and therefore her, first?

The young men from the airport were dead. *If* Donald was telling the truth; it had sounded like he was. But who wanted them dead? The terrorist group, afraid they'd reveal secrets?

She tried to stand back from the information, to think about it as a story, the way a novelist would. The same people who had written the fake book, the people who wanted to kill her, were the people who'd killed those young men. Who were they and what did they want?

Her mind was going to elaborate lengths not to accept the other information Donald had given her. Reza was dead? She wanted to be cynical. It would be easier to doubt. But somehow her intuition would not let her retreat into denial.

If Reza is dead, then I got her killed. This recognition brought the contents of her stomach heaving up; she dropped to her knees in the weeds beside the road and spewed a sour stream of vomit onto a patch of dandelions. She'd been told again and again not to contact anyone from her former life; she'd not only flouted that in the beginning but had continued to do so.

And now she'd done the same thing with Francesca.

Then she remembered something else. Donald had said he was in Michigan looking for her. She'd seen him yesterday across the street from the Starbucks. How then could he have been in Los Angeles just this morning visiting Francesca?

CHAPTER THIRTEEN

At first she couldn't remember where she was. Or why the pain in her head was so severe that she was compelled to close her eyes the minute light struck them. Her limbs were heavy and beyond her control. Her throat felt as if it had been packed with cotton.

It seemed safest to surrender, slide back into unconsciousness, but her bladder sent an overwhelming signal—it must have been this that had awakened her in the first place—so she began the delicate and tortuous maneuver of bringing her body into an upright position. The move from horizontal to vertical caused everything to spin until she had no choice but to lower herself back onto the bedspread. Then she remembered: The truck stop motel. Her call to Donald. Reza. The bottle of white rum.

It made all the sense in the world to drop down instead of stand up, to lower herself to her hands and knees and make her slow way across the sticky linoleum to the bathroom. Once her knees felt the cold of the tile, she painstakingly hoisted her body onto the toilet; once more her head spun and she had to carefully hold herself motionless, lest she fall from her precarious perch. Still, her bladder was insistent, and began to let loose a stream that seemed to go on for several minutes.

She was still peeing when she heard the knock on the door. She had no idea what time it was—all the shades were drawn in her room. Could it already be time for Zenkei to pick her up? What a disaster! She needed a shower; she needed some coffee; she needed to sleep for another few days.

"Just a minute," she called, forgetting she was trying to disguise her voice. Her voice echoing off the tile sounded way too loud. Wasn't she supposed to be quiet? She couldn't remember why.

Once you've started to pee there's no way to make yourself stop and no way to speed the process, so she remained on her seat. How much could she possibly have drunk?

In anticipation of company, she tried to survey her current state. She seemed to be wearing a T-shirt, but nothing below the waist. She'd have to fix that before opening the door but she wasn't sure how. She could mentally form the image of pants and even imagine they were somewhere in the disheveled room, but she couldn't quite think of how to locate them. She pressed her aching head against the bathroom wall and hoped nothing further would be asked of her.

The knock came again. Had it been just a second or several minutes since the first time? She summoned what used to be her willpower and stood, placing her hands against the basin and then the wall to help her counter the force of gravity. Every nerve in her body throbbed in protest of her movements. She'd almost gained the door when she remembered she was naked from the waist down.

When she looked down, her pants were on the floor. She felt lucky to spot them, but not lucky in her descent to retrieve them. She lost her tenuous balance and crashed down. She was tempted to remain sprawled on the carpet, but the knock came again. Slowly her legs recalled, seemingly independent of her brain, how to push themselves into each leg-hole. Buttoning them was more difficult after her nighttime snack of Cheetos and Kit Kat bars; she had to lie down to make the fabric close around her belly and feared she'd never get up. Rolling onto her side, she managed to press herself to standing, then lurched for the door and pulled it open.

She expected to see the welcoming face of Zenkei, who might be dismayed at her condition but who would not judge her. But in his place stood Koryo. The very erectness of his posture seemed a rebuke to her and his customary scowl grew even sterner as he took in her appearance. It was as if he could read all of her recent history just by looking into her face.

Reluctantly, she motioned him into the room and just as reluctantly he entered. The room smelled like alcohol and anxiety and dirty clothes.

"Is Zenkei all right?" she asked.

"His dog"—his tone conveyed a weary disapproval—"has an infection. He had to take her to the emergency animal hospital in the middle of the night."

"Is she going to be okay?"

"Someday she will die, as will we all. But not, apparently, today. She's back at the Center, resting, but Zenkei does not want to leave her. Therefore, I am here to do his errand." He couldn't have sounded less thrilled about it.

Lorraine wondered how much he knew about what Zenkei had planned. Maybe she should just call off the whole thing.

Then he added, "Your friend called just before I left the Center. She arrived in Chicago and is on her way to meet you."

Francesca! Lorraine couldn't call it off; she had to be there when Francesca got to the retreat center.

"Okay." Her body sank onto the unmade bed. She was too hungover to finesse this conversation. "I know you don't like me and before the day is over you may not like me even more."

He made no effort to dispute this, just waited for her to continue.

"Before we go to Brightmoor I need to buy a computer. I can't just park myself up in the woods with nothing to do."

"The woods?" The monk sounded surprised.

"Isn't this retreat center out in the woods someplace?"

The monk shook his head. "Retreat center is not in woods. Is in Detroit."

"Detroit? I thought Zenkei said Brightmoor."

"Yes," the monk affirmed. "Detroit."

It was like some Zen riddle, and she didn't have the patience or clarity to solve it right then. So she kept on. "And I need to buy a car. Well, what I mean is I need you to buy me a car. I have the money to pay for it; I just can't transact any business in my name. In either of my names."

The monk looked at her. "A monk is not allowed to own anything."

"What about the VW?"

"A supporter gave that to the Center. It's still registered in his name."

She pressed her face into her hands. Her head was pounding so badly; how was she supposed to figure any of this out? If only she had some coffee. Unlike Zenkei, this crabby monk had brought no breakfast, no mug of green tea.

Koryo offered no solution. "Are you ready to go?" His glance around the room indicated he doubted it.

"Aren't you going to shave my head?"

"Excuse me?"

"Because my face was on TV. It may not be safe for me to be seen in public. Zenkei brought me a robe—" She stopped, suddenly worried that she would be getting the kind monk in terrible trouble.

"He was going to dress you as a Buddhist nun?"

She nodded.

Koryo shook his head. "He is too much in the intrigues of the world." He was silent for a moment, perhaps contemplating the fate of his comrade. "But it *is* a practical idea."

She was surprised that he'd gone for it and more surprised when suddenly he was all in motion. He would go out and find a place to purchase scissors and a razor. Lorraine was to pack up everything she was taking with her and get herself cleaned up. "Save that bag." He indicated the paper sack that had held her rum, Cheetos, and candy bars. "We'll put your hair in it, so nobody finds it and figures out your disguise."

Marielle might have bridled at such directives, but Lorraine was grateful that Koryo was organizing her. She was not equipped to be in charge today.

"I hate to bother you," she said, "but is there any chance you could bring me a cup of coffee when you come back?"

He neither agreed nor disagreed, but as he pushed out the door on his mission, he said, not unkindly, "You should drink some water. Dehydration makes your symptoms worse." She wondered if he was speaking from experience.

* * *

She was surprised that Koryo did bring coffee when he came back. A tepid, tasteless coffee—the kind a non-coffee drinker would think was just fine. She didn't care; she gulped it gratefully to help dull the pounding in her skull.

It was no easy task to sit and listen to the clipper buzz against her cranium, to see the locks of coppery hair drifting to the tile. The drone of the clipper bore like a dentist drill into her brain. She'd anticipated that Koryo would be rough with her, but his hands were gentle, if not tender, as he held her head steady and stripped it bare.

An hour later she was gazing into the mirror, wondering who was looking back at her. Without her hair, *any* hair, the shape of her face was starker, cheekbones sharper, eyes hollowed out. The mouth lacked softness; it lacked kindness. It was as if a mask had been lifted and exposed her ambition and drive, leaving her no place to hide. The round rimless glasses only partially mitigated this.

If someone were casting this for a film, they would never buy her as a Buddhist nun. Her movements were not fluid or graceful; she kept kicking the robe out of her way when she took a step. She had the sudden implausible thought: *What if Tuna could see me now?*

"You need a name," Koryo suggested.

"Great," she snapped. "I'm about ready for a new one."

She had never seen the man smile, but she detected an unmistakable grin as he said, "Let's call you Chiko."

"Does it mean something?" She expected the worst.

"It means 'small tiger.'" He actually chuckled, pleased with himself.

She didn't know whether to feel flattered or insulted, but she didn't have the energy to figure it out. It was the monk's concentration that helped her to collect her small pile of belongings—her purse, her toothbrush, the ragtag bundle of dirty clothes. The trash—the Bacardi bottle, the half-empty bag of Cheetos, the plastic cups she'd used to drink from, the shards of hair—they would dispose of elsewhere. At his suggestion she checked the room a second time to make sure she was leaving behind nothing that could indicate she'd ever been there. Indeed, she'd almost left behind her Timex, to which she had developed a certain attachment.

They descended in the elevator and floated past the front desk as if they were ghosts; the young woman sitting behind it never looked up from texting on her phone.

Once at the car, she spotted Dude in a carrier in the back seat. "Dudeman!" she exclaimed in a manner that was decidedly not nunlike. Apparently unfazed by the change in her appearance, the cat yowled at the sound of her voice. "Thank you for bringing him!" she said to Koryo. She wasn't sure it was a good idea; she had no idea how this sojourn was going to go or how long it would last, but she'd missed her orange tom.

He seemed none the worse for wear, given what he'd been through. She reached into the carrier and pulled him out. Although he wasn't fond of being held and less fond of being in a moving car, the cat purred as she held him close to her heart, and suffered her kisses on his ears.

"So you want what again?" Koryo asked. His tone displayed the slightest disdain for the need to acquire.

"A laptop." She was glad he'd reminded her. "I think there's an Apple store in the mall."

If the prospect of the Briarwood Mall on a Sunday was slightly less appealing than a root canal, the monk didn't let on. He dutifully drove her to the mall, asked if she needed him to accompany her and, when she said "No," parked and told her where in the mall to find the store. She wondered how he knew.

Dude was reluctant to go back into the carrier, but she understood without asking that the monk was not a cat person, perhaps not an animal person at all. He seemed to have decided that she was one of his spiritual trials and he'd win karma points by putting up with her without complaint. Or so she imagined.

As she stepped out of the car, she felt the sun on her bald head. Through the haze of her hangover, she'd managed to avoid until now the recognition that she was out in public dressed as a Buddhist nun. She was not doing this in Los Angeles, where presumably people were accustomed to all manner of diversity, but in Michigan, where most people worked hard to fit in. As she entered the mall, she felt the stares of dozens of people. It wasn't any better knowing that her presentation was utterly fraudulent.

She quickly realized, though, that Zenkei had been right. They were not looking at *her*, only snickering or pointing at her outfit. A bald woman. Someone dressed in a floor-length robe instead of ill-fitting khakis and a polo shirt. It was in this way a perfect disguise. Her only concern was with the possibility that Donald had traced the call, or at least enough to know she was still in Ann Arbor. Would he look for her at the Briarwood Mall? He certainly wouldn't look for her in a nun's robe, or so she hoped.

Still, she tried to remain as vigilant as she could, given how lousy she felt. Her business at the Apple Store was transacted quickly. If any staff was aware of the fact that monks and nuns were not supposed to own anything, they didn't bring it up. She purchased the newest version of the same model as her old laptop; she bought and had the staff install MS Office; she added a backup drive and a modest printer. *What are you doing? What do you need all this for? How are you going to cart around all this crap?* Her brain screamed at her, but she impassively handed over the cash. If she was going on retreat, she needed a computer. She couldn't have said exactly why in this moment, but she was absolutely convinced it was true.

Many items in the mall suggested themselves to her: she was going to need some clothes and shoes and a hat until her hair grew out. She'd need toiletries and reading material. She would need a ream of paper. But her sodden brain could not organize this activity right now, even if she hadn't had a reluctant monk waiting for her in the parking lot. Besides—how does a nun shop for underwear? She wondered what consumer options might be available to her in Brightmoor; she was afraid to find out.

She considered whether she ought to eat, but the smells arising from Chipotle made her stomach flip over and she hurried past. On her way back to the car, she passed a kiosk selling cell phones. She stopped to inquire about a prepaid phone and whether she could just pay cash for it. She could and within minutes after filling out some paperwork with phony information she pocketed a cell phone with 90-day access and 1000 minutes. Lorraine had been fearful to have another cell phone but Chiko—a small but mighty tiger—had no such apprehension.

Her last stop at the mall was at the Starbuck's kiosk where she purchased a venti black coffee and two bottles of water. *Should I have brought something back for Koryo?* she wondered, but she couldn't think what he might want.

She was weighed down by her purse and her packages as she slogged back to the car. She had a momentary concern that the monk had grown impatient and driven away, but the VW was parked just where she'd left it. As she approached the car, she saw Koryo sitting in the front seat, his eyes closed; he was meditating. She hated to disturb him, so she quietly opened the passenger door.

Dude yowled at her immediately, as if to say, "What took you so long?"

Koryo said nothing, merely started the engine as she loaded her packages into the back seat and brought Dude and his carrier up front to sit on her lap. She was grateful for the monk's silence. Having accomplished her immediate tasks, she was ready to lapse back into her hangover and leave Ann Arbor behind. She nursed the strong coffee as Koryo began to drive.

I should be paying attention, she told herself, and forced her eyes open to note that they were on M-14. But her lids would not stay up. The caffeine eased her headache enough that she could relax and, still clutching the to-go cup, she drifted into sleep.

She didn't know how long she'd been dozing when she woke, stiff from the bumpy ride in the old Bug. Her thighs had gone to sleep under the weight of her slumbering cat. He must be traumatized; she'd never known him to be this calm in a car.

"I'm sorry," she said to Koryo. "The passenger is supposed to entertain the driver."

"The scenery is very absorbing." He nodded toward the view beyond the windshield.

It was true. At the side of the road there were green woods with the afternoon light speckling the leaves. Her view of Michigan had been limited to the suburbs, clotted with housing developments and chain stores. Now, if she looked out the passenger window, she could almost imagine this land as it had been when Indians roamed it.

They were supposed to be heading toward the city; she'd expected more density, not less. But she had no real idea where she was and Koryo didn't seem inclined to play tour guide.

"Have you ever stayed here?" she asked Koryo.

"We come once or twice a year for retreat," he answered.

"Do you like it?"

He was quiet for a moment. "Buddhists don't cultivate preferences the way you do in the West. We practice to find contentment with everything and attachment to nothing."

"I don't know how you do that."

"In the West, you are trained just the opposite. Very hard for Westerners to become neutral."

She couldn't help but feel a little rebuked—she supposed that must be attachment to something—but she couldn't really argue with his statement. It made her feel grumpy and she abandoned her efforts at conversation.

Of course she'd heard about Detroit: The once glorious metropolis, birthplace of the auto industry, famed for its Art

Deco architecture and the Motown sound. Now much of it lay in ruins, houses abandoned or burned down. Several years ago she'd seen a photo essay in a magazine, created, she thought she recalled, by two Frenchmen documenting the decay with an aesthetic eye; some commentators had objected, dubbing it "Ruin Porn."

When she'd first started teaching at Novi High she'd asked another teacher about going into the city. The blond biology teacher had looked concerned and admonished her, in her flat Midwestern tones, "You don't want to do that." Her tone held a great deal of significance, although she didn't explain further.

Once in a while Lorraine's students would mention Detroit, always in a disparaging way, which she'd determined had to do with race or class or both. She imagined they learned it from their parents rather than direct experience.

Lorraine hadn't cared much for the local Novi paper, but still she'd caught glimpses of the news of Detroit—a corruption scandal with the city government, allegations of racial discrimination by several businesses, the pathetic showing of all the city's sports teams. It seemed no accident that she'd landed here beside this sad place of drastically reduced circumstances.

Still, she hadn't once ventured into Detroit in the months she'd been here and she had to admit it was because of fear. Marielle would have gone right away, as much to assert her fearlessness as out of a deep curiosity about the place. Lorraine was more cautious; there was no need to go looking for trouble. But trouble had found her anyway, and now she and Koryo were headed for Detroit.

As they entered the city, she saw that buildings were older, more dilapidated, and sparser than in the suburbs.

Koryo made a turn and then another. A ragged sign proclaimed, "Welcome to Brightmoor," which she now guessed was the name of the neighborhood. Beneath the letters, a tagger had scrawled "Blightmore."

At first, Lorraine couldn't help but be struck by how green it was, the tall old trees and wide swaths of grass, like a park. Then she understood that this had once been a residential neighborhood, where neat brick houses must have stood on every lot. Now only a few houses occupied a block, and if she looked more closely, many of these were boarded up. The sidewalks were cracked or had been swallowed up all together by field, and the pavement was potholed.

A commercial strip showed more obvious signs of decay—buildings boarded up, many missing altogether, the vacant lots like missing teeth. The occasional business still in operation might be a liquor store or an auto parts place, maybe a gas station or a fast-food joint, all heavily fortified against intruders. Every few blocks there was a church, but even some of these appeared burned out or abandoned.

Where did residents go to get their groceries? Where did they go to the bank? Where would she go, once Koryo left her here without a car?

The weariness of this city, all it had suffered and lost, entered her bones, weighted her down.

"This is where you go for retreat?" she asked the monk, whose face was impassive as he drove the wide streets.

In a calm voice he said, "As monks, we are committed to relieving suffering. It makes sense to go where suffering is."

He made a right-hand turn onto a street that seemed to no longer have a street sign and added, "I appreciate the city of Detroit. Everything is as it appears to be. It's harder to practice in Ann Arbor, where people are filled with more delusion."

They drove more blocks. Only a few houses remained standing. Between them were vacant lots overgrown with weeds; some of these were being used as dumps for garbage, old tires, construction materials that could not be reused. She stared out at a streetlamp, trying to figure out why it looked wrong; then she realized that its base, which contained all the electrical workings, had been gutted. When night fell, it would cast no light. Nearly all the streetlamps they drove past appeared in the same condition, stripped for wiring.

Some of the driveways had cars parked in them, but although the late Sunday afternoon was warm, she saw no other people on the street. Fear rippled between her shoulder blades.

"What would you do," she asked the monk, "if something bad happened? Would you call the police? Are there even police?"

"We don't think that way," he told her. "Not good things and bad things. Every moment there is breath, and we meet each moment with the inhale and exhale."

Then Koryo turned in to a driveway beside a two-story red brick house. While some of the houses they'd passed looked as if they'd been built in the 1920s, this style seemed more in keeping with houses built in the fifties. Koryo parked the car in front a wood-frame garage painted red with gray trim. The modest backyard showed signs of care; the grass was trimmed and bordered by a bed of petunias.

Stepping out of the car, she could feel humid air pressing all around her, even more cloying with the heavy robes that draped her. Shifting Dude's carrier onto the passenger seat, she walked down the driveway to gaze into the street. There were only two other structures on this block, one on the same side of the street a few lots down, and one across the street at the other end of the block. Next door to that house were the collapsed ruins of another structure that had been burned. She was glad Fresh hadn't arrived ahead of them. She didn't want her friend to have to deal with the area on her own.

Koryo had gone on ahead and climbed a few concrete steps leading to a back door. He rooted under a flowerpot and retrieved a key to let himself in. She wasn't sure if this practice made her feel safe because the monks weren't worried about break-ins or fearful that the place had no security.

The monk did not take any trouble to carry her things into the house, so she began by hauling her purse and Dude's cat carrier up the back steps. The cat's meditative calm shattered, Dude was announcing himself to the neighborhood at full volume. As soon as she got him into the wood paneled kitchen and opened his carrier, he wanted to make a beeline for the outdoors, which she thought inadvisable. She managed to slam the door just before he got to it, whereupon he squatted and peed a voluminous river on the linoleum floor, looking up at her with a deliberate gleam in his eye.

"Okay, you made your point," she conceded, searching for a sponge beneath the old-fashioned country sink. Had Koryo thought to bring the litter box from the Zen Center? Still awkward in the robe, she bent to wipe up the cat pee and found some Pine Sol to cover the odor. Dude was twitching his tail in an ominous way that signaled he was getting ready to embark on a Search and Destroy mission. Discovering a half bath off the kitchen, she scooped up the indignant feline and locked him in the small room until she could unload the rest of her things from the car. As much as she felt as if she no longer had any worldly possessions, it still took a couple of trips.

Placing everything except the litter box on the table of the breakfast nook, she went in search of Koryo. She wandered through what must have been a large dining room that was notable for the absence of a table. This space opened to a larger living room that seemed to stretch the width of the house. The living room contained a modern brick fireplace; a stone statue of the Buddha had been placed before the hearth. Through a foyer, the front door hung open and she saw Koryo in the front yard wrestling with a hose. She wanted to laugh at the sight of the monk attempting yard work.

She checked her Timex; it was almost four o'clock. Francesca would have left Chicago about noon. Wait, there was a time difference. It was only three o'clock in Chicago. She didn't know how long the trip would take, though she was sure Francesca wouldn't drive as slowly as Koryo had. She wished she'd gone shopping for food; she'd love to surprise her friend with a sumptuous meal.

It's not vacation, she reminded herself sharply. All the waiting around and the hangover and the long drive couldn't lull her into forgetting why she was here: because people she didn't even know were trying to kill her. She was bald and on the run; she was Chiko, a small but ferocious tiger.

This realization seemed to awaken the sensation of hunger in her. Returning to the kitchen, she searched the cabinets, but the pickings were slim. There was a canister of rice, another of lentils, a few canned soups, a bottle of cooking oil. The refrigerator had been unplugged, its door left ajar, only a box of baking soda on one shelf. She plugged in the appliance and was gratified to hear it rumble to life, to see the interior bulb light up. She tested out the faucet in the sink. Its initial outpour was reddish, but after a moment it ran clear. The pilot light was out on the gas stove and she had to rummage in several drawers before she found a book of matches. She was slightly concerned about blowing the place to kingdom come, but luckily the pilot lit easily.

A loud protest from the bathroom reminded her that Dude hadn't eaten in a while either. Rummaging in her bags, she located the cat food. She took two bowls from the mismatched collection of dishware in the cupboard, spooned cat food into one and filled the other with water and carried them into the bathroom. The room was too small to contain Dude for long, but she had to check out the rest of the house for possible escape routes.

The cat eagerly attacked his bowl of food, so she left him with it and began searching the house. She went back to the living room and saw through the window that Koryo was now wielding a rake. If it had been Zenkei she would have gone out to keep him company, but there was a quality to Koryo that did not invite camaraderie. She continued on into a small study that was lined with books; she would explore them later. So far, she'd spotted no television or radio.

Heading upstairs, she found four bedrooms, each appointed with modest cots, sometimes as many as six to a room in the larger spaces. These austere appointments reminded her that the house was now used as a retreat center for the monks and that she could kiss goodbye her fantasy of a thick mattress and luxurious sheets. Nothing hung in the tiny closets but a few bare hangers. The air upstairs was stuffy and smelled of mildew. In each room she entered, she wrestled open a cantankerous window, grateful to note the presence of screens. There were two serviceable bathrooms on this level and the plumbing worked.

At the end of the hallway she found an additional door. It stuck and she had to yank on it before it yielded to a flight of stairs that led to an attic space, even stuffier than the second-floor rooms, but also arrayed with facing rows of neat cots. She felt a pang of sympathy for the monks who would draw this attic dormitory for their rooming assignment.

She wandered back to the first floor and out into the front yard. It would be light for several hours but she saw no neighbors in their yards or out on the street. An occasional car passed; every person in those cars was African American. She wondered what they made of the monk—two monks, she reminded herself—set down amidst the rubble.

"Are you getting hungry?" she asked Koryo, who was pulling weeds from a flowerbed.

"Do you mean to say that you are getting hungry?" he replied.

She felt a flush of shame for her bodily needs, her human cravings. Then she was mad about being shamed. "Am I the only one here in a body?" she asked.

"Buddhists train the body, train the mind, so we are not subject to our impulses."

"We mere mortals need to eat once in a while. Is there a store anywhere nearby? I could take the car and fill it with gas while I'm at it."

"Are you already bored as well?"

Every word out of his mouth seemed to chastise her. She was about to ask him whatever had happened to compassion when a red car pulled into the driveway, a Cadillac CTS. A cascade of red curls appeared in the open door. Fresh!

She forgot she was trying to remain inconspicuous as she rushed to enfold her friend in a deep embrace. Fresh stared at her as if she'd gone crazy. It took a second to remember she was bald and in a nun's habit.

A slow, teasing smile spread across her friend's face. "If only Liana could see you now."

"I know." Chiko grinned back. "Do you have stuff to bring in?"

Of course she had stuff. Francesca went everywhere with multiple suitcases, at least one crammed with art supplies. But she paused from unloading the Cadillac's big trunk to look again at Chiko. Tears welled in her eyes. "Oh, Mar, I can't believe it. I thought I would never see you again."

Chiko's eyes filled too. Francesca had really come! Even after a day's travel, she looked elegant in black silk pants and a long shirt with an ivory scarf and oversized silver jewelry. She looked like a woman who should be getting out of a Cadillac. Although Chiko felt like weeping, this was no time to indulge it.

"Please don't call me Mar," she said in a quiet voice.

"Right! It's Minerva now." Fresh rummaged in her leather purse and handed over an envelope. Inside was a passport and Indiana driver's license for Minerva Turnbull, each sporting a photo of Marielle. The woman pictured looked stiff and artificial, somehow, not as beautiful as she'd once believed herself to be.

"Did you have any trouble?"

"It was easier than going to the DMV," Francesca assured her. "Although the guy told Ernesto—in Spanish—I was too old to have his babies and he should get a younger girlfriend."

Chiko brought Francesca over to meet Koryo, who was watering the front garden bed. She pressed both palms together at her heart and bowed before the monk. He bowed in return. Here Chiko was dressed in this outfit and she didn't even know the secret handshake!

Koryo turned off the hose and picked up the largest of Francesca's bags and carried it into the house. Even this monk was not immune to her friend's charms! The two women followed with the remaining bags.

He offered to make some tea and disappeared into the kitchen. She invited Fresh into the living room where they sat at opposite ends of the couch. Francesca pulled out a copy of the *Los Angeles Times* and placed it on the table. It had today's date. Chiko saw the headline, "Attorney Found Slain." It was beneath the story, "Terrorism Suspects Found Dead in Prison." The reporters seemed oblivious to the connection between the two incidents, as if each were separate, random acts.

"Marielle's death was in the newspaper too," Chiko argued, as if to push away the reality of Reza's death, but her words were as weightless as paper in wind.

"I went to see Altovese's mother yesterday," Francesca said.

Altovese, Reza's receptionist. "How?"

"I looked her up in the phone book. At that fundraiser last year I met Altovese's mother—remember, she ran a women's shelter? I recalled that she had a really distinctive name—Gladiola Mahalia Mawbray. Luckily, she was listed.

"She didn't want to talk to me right away. Told me I wasn't the first person to call looking for her daughter. But I chatted her up about the shelter, told her I'd been to the event last year. I described the hat she was wearing that day—do you remember, it looked like a big orange sailing ship—and that seemed to break the ice. She told me her daughter and granddaughter had moved out of the country. She wouldn't tell me where, but she said before Reza quit her job she gave Altovese 'quite a nice severance' and told her to leave L.A. as soon as she could."

"Do you think somebody paid Reza to sell me out?"

"Or she realized she was in trouble and cashed out her savings to protect Altovese."

That was the kind of thing Reza would do. Chiko recalled suddenly that her truculent attorney had been the person she'd trusted second most in the world. Over the past weeks, that characterization had been replaced by the idea that Reza had set her up, had almost gotten her killed. But it was Reza who was dead; *she* was still here, and maybe Reza had died trying to ensure that. If she thought about that too much, she wouldn't be able to stand it.

"You can't blame yourself." As usual, Francesca knew exactly what was going through her mind.

Seeing that Chiko was on the verge of tears, Francesca took another tack. "Speaking of hats, this is quite a fashion statement."

Grateful for the diversion, Chiko rolled her eyes. "The other monk, Zenkei—he talked to you on the phone—thought I'd be less conspicuous."

Francesca pretended to study her. "Well, I don't know that you'd blend into a crowd, but I'd sure never recognize you as Marielle Wing. Though you do have a lovely shape to your skull." She traced a finger across the denuded scalp.

The easy banter was soothing to Chiko; the calm familiarity made her realize how many months she'd gone without a friend. Except for Dude—who was, she realized, still locked in the back bathroom. He wouldn't be happy.

She jumped up, nearly colliding with Koryo who was coming back with the tea. She flung open the door to the bathroom and her nose confirmed the worst. Her cat had strewn his feces as widely as the narrow space would allow.

"Dude, I'm sorry—" she began as he dashed past her. Rather than going to chase him, she found some rags and did her best to clean up. It wasn't easy, wearing the long robe; her feet kept tangling in the hem and the wide sleeves kept drooping into the mess.

When she returned to the living room, Dude was lolling on a cushion beside Francesca, offering his belly. His green eyes flicked briefly as she came into the room, as if to say, "Now *here* is someone who appreciates me," as he nuzzled closer to Fresh.

"I should have left him with you in the first place," she commented as she plopped into a chair.

"You know, I wondered about that after news of your death circulated. I couldn't imagine who else you'd give him to. I was a little hurt, although I was too sad about you dying to give it much energy. I thought maybe Liana, but when I asked her, she said no. Actually, she said you'd probably left all your money to Dude and set him up on the French Riviera."

"Good old Liana. Reza told me the first thing she asked about was the will." She'd asked Reza. Who was now dead.

"So what's it been like?"

"Which part?"

"I don't mean the scary parts. But what's it been like to not be Marielle? Have you still been working on your book?"

"I haven't been working on anything. I'm like a puppet once you pull your hand out and see it's only felt and yarn and glue."

"I don't know what I'd do if I couldn't paint."

"No need to do." Koryo had been so quiet in the corner they'd both forgotten he was there. "Just be."

"He's right," Chiko said, "but I suck at it."

"Me too," Francesca agreed.

A car door slammed outside, and she hurried to the window to look out. A silver Accord was parked on the street in front of the house. She took in the car's tinted windows and felt her heart drop. She didn't have time to consider whether or not she should run before the car door opened and Donald Watkins emerged.

He wasn't dressed in the gray suit he'd worn the last time she'd seen him. He wore a pair of pleated khakis and a pressed blue button-down shirt. Even his attempt at casual appeared stiff. His dark skin was set off against the blue of his shirt. As he came toward the door, she opened it. "Lorraine," he spoke quietly. If he had a response to her appearance, he did not voice it.

Lorraine? she wondered. *Who's that?* She was Chiko, the small bald tiger. How the fuck had he found her? Had Koryo turned her in? She turned to glance at the monk but he was pouring tea as if nothing out of the ordinary were happening. For a moment she calculated the odds of trying to make a break for it.

"Don't run," he cautioned as if he too could read her mind.

"Why? Are you going to shoot me?" She couldn't believe she was caught. All the effort of the last few days only to end up like this?

"I just want to talk to you. And I'm afraid we don't have much time." He turned to look behind him, a little nervously it seemed. "May I come inside?"

"What—I'm supposed to serve you tea before you take me to jail?"

"Please," he insisted in a tone she had never before heard from him; it was fearful. If Donald was afraid, things must have really gone haywire. She gestured for him to enter.

She introduced him to Koryo, then said, "I guess you already know Francesca."

He looked puzzled.

Francesca said, "That's not Donald Watkins."

"Yes," Chiko said, "it is." A curl of panic began making its way through her intestines.

Francesca explained that a man claiming to be him had visited her yesterday in Los Angeles. "He was African American, but not nearly as handsome as you."

That her friend could flirt in the midst of a potentially life-threatening situation astonished Chiko. It seemed natural, though, not designed to flatter. No wonder men always did whatever Francesca asked them.

Donald didn't seem to register the compliment. He asked a few questions about the other man's appearance, then asked, "Did he show you any identification?"

Francesca looked distressed. "It didn't occur to me to ask."

Donald took out his cell phone and typed something into it. He perched uneasily at one end of the couch and wasted no time in revealing the purpose of his visit.

He leaned forward. "Lorraine. It is my job to protect you. And for a long time, I believed I could do that job, even when it came to light that you were in communication with your attorney. As I told you on the phone yesterday, that contact turned out rather badly for Ms. Caldicott."

"How do I know you didn't just disappear her too, like you did me?" Her belligerence was reflexive, a holdover from Marielle. In her heart she knew it was true.

"I wish that were the case. At first, I thought your recklessness, and hers, had made things go awry, but in the last day or so I've come to realize that we've all been caught up in something far beyond what any of us understood."

"What are you talking about?"

"I can't tell you; I don't have all the pieces yet and I don't think it would help you to know. I will tell you this—members of the United States security apparatus have been working at cross purposes to the mission of our agency, and that has compromised the security of this operation."

Again, that maddening paternalism. "You don't think I have a right to know whatever it is you know? After all that's been taken from me? After someone who was trying to help me has been killed?"

As ever, Donald was unmoved by her protests. "I came today because I wanted to tell you this in person: If you happen to encounter anyone from the U.S. Marshals' office, or from Homeland Security, or if anyone contacts you claiming to be me, don't believe them."

Although she'd spent the last four days operating on this exact instinct, it was still terrifying to have it officially confirmed.

"Are you saying the government is out to kill me?"

"Of course not. But there may be people on the government payroll who have set up an operation of their own, who may perceive your continued existence as a threat. I am saying that you certainly can't rely on the government to protect you. Not even me."

"What about the JFK bombing? What about those young men killed in custody? Did they even do that bombing?"

"Lorraine, I'm not going to speculate with you. For the moment those deaths are being called suicide."

"Donald, you and I both know that's bullshit. Those guys were executed by someone, and who would want them dead more than the real bombers?"

"Lorraine, I'm sorry. There are channels and I have to proceed through them." He was a man who lived by his code of ethics, and although she found this infuriating, she had to respect it.

She changed tactics. "How did you find me?"

"I've been just a few steps behind you since Thursday night." The night her townhouse was firebombed. "I have to say, you're much smarter than the average person. You gave us quite a chase. But that VW kept showing up in too many places to be coincidental. I just hope you're smart enough to get out of this, somehow. You and your friends," he acknowledged Francesca and Koryo.

"How do we do that?"

"Go somewhere else, leave the country, start over. Reinvent your life."

"I don't suppose you brought me a passport that would make that possible?" She was not going to tell him about Minerva's documents.

"Anything official I could give you now would only hurt you. In fact, I need to go. The more distance between me and you, the safer you are." He stood to leave.

She had so many questions for him and no time. "So, are there any terrorists?"

He turned to face her. "Of course there are. I'm just not sure they're your problem right now."

As he walked out of the house, she noticed the bulge of what appeared to be a gun tucked behind his back under the drape of his shirttail. She wanted to stop him. She had the feeling she would never see him again and she felt inexplicably unwilling to let him go. For all their conflict, for all her mistrust, she realized she had thought of him as safe, one of the good guys. She supposed his visit here proved that. But if he could find her, who else could find her? *That VW kept showing up* and it was sitting right now in front of the garage behind the house.

She walked toward the still-open door just in time to see Donald's car make a U-turn in the street. Just in time to see a black Chevy van come speeding up behind the Accord. Two shots spit from the van into the back windshield of Donald's car. The silver car veered sharply to the right and crashed into a tall maple, wheels up on the curb.

"Oh my God," she heard Francesca say.

In a quiet voice Chiko replied, "Get upstairs *now*. Go to the attic and stay there."

Ducking low so as not to be seen through the front window, Francesca gathered Dude in her arms and made her way up the stairs.

She expected men to burst from the van, come running up to shoot her or snatch her, but it sped away in a squeal of tires. Instinct made her shrink back into the foyer, but Koryo burst through the door and ran in the direction of the Accord.

At first she didn't join him. The shooters in the van knew what they were doing; it would be a clean hit. Then she realized she had a different reason to join him. Koryo already had the door open, but neither could fail to see that the back of Donald's head had exploded into spatter on the front windshield. Koryo backed away and began chanting as he fingered his mala.

The driver's airbag had inflated, and gave off a chemical scent. It occurred to Chiko that she shouldn't touch anything, so she wrapped the long sash of her robe around her hands. Blood and gore were everywhere, and the smell of the body discharging its contents was overpowering. Still she summoned the strength from somewhere to slip her hand into his breast pocket and extract his cell phone. The skin of his chest was warm. The airbag had propelled his body backward, so it was more difficult for her to reach behind him and slowly pull out his weapon.

She felt the gun in her hand, its metal warm from Donald's body. It was heavy, heavier than the .38 she'd learned to shoot many years ago when she was researching *Rough Days Ahead*. That was her fourth novel, and it hadn't done that well. Marielle had gone to a shooting range and gotten trained. She'd been reasonably good at taking down the targets, cardboard cutouts shaped like men with concentric circles at their heart area, but she hadn't cared for it and never bought a gun for herself, even though the trainer had advised her, as a woman alone, to do so.

This gun must be a .44. It was a little too heavy for her, but it would be of more use to her than to Donald at this point. Now that Donald was dead, how would she ever find out what was really going on? Now that Donald was dead, how was she going to survive?

CHAPTER FOURTEEN

She was surprised to see the street had stayed empty. If the houses that remained standing had occupants, they had chosen to stay indoors in the aftermath of gunfire. Was it such a frequent occurrence in this neighborhood, or did people just feel they had enough trouble without involving themselves in someone else's?

If Koryo was surprised by her actions, he didn't indicate it. She remembered Zenkei telling her they'd both been in the war. The monk kept up his chanting as he ushered her back into the house. There was a telephone on the wall in the kitchen, and he used it to call 911. She recalled reading somewhere that police response time was slow in Detroit; still, it would be best if she were not here when the cops arrived.

She wondered if the black van was the same one that had chased her car last Thursday, another lifetime ago. This was a Chevy; that one had been—She tried to recall its appearance in her mind. This one had come so fast and seemingly from nowhere; it hadn't occurred to her to check the license plate.

Marielle would have definitely noted that detail, but where had all that careful observation gotten her?

She'd never told Donald about that van last Thursday. Would she understand things better if she had? Might she have prevented his execution?

She couldn't figure out why they would kill Donald and leave her alive. If they'd executed Donald because he had information, they couldn't know for sure what he had and hadn't told her. Or was it possible they didn't know whom he was visiting here in Brightmoor?

"It's a distinct possibility," she said to Koryo, "that those guys will come back for me. If you want to clear out of here, I don't blame you."

He shook his head. "I will die today or I will die some other day. It doesn't matter to me."

She wondered what it took to embrace this philosophy. She didn't feel at all ready to die today. Still, she was grateful he was in no hurry to leave.

"But perhaps you and your friend are better off to not be here when they return," he added.

She nodded, then rushed upstairs to retrieve Francesca. "We should go now," she told her friend.

"Is he dead?" Fresh wanted to know.

Chiko just closed her eyes.

"Oh my God!" her friend shrieked. "Do you think it was people from the government?"

"I think we should get in the car and get away from here. Now." She regretted the harsh tone. "Look, you don't have to go through with this," she told her friend. "There's no way to know how this might end. You can go back to L.A. and grieve your friend Marielle who died."

Fresh said, "You forget that you're talking to someone who's looked divorce in the face and laughed. It's gonna take more than bombings, murder, and government conspiracies to make me turn tail and run."

While she appreciated the loyalty, Chiko thought, *It's not real to her. It's a movie plot.* That's how Marielle had been at the beginning, too, and her denial had cost so much.

"Okay, then, let's go. Will you get Dude?"

Francesca began coaxing the cat as Chiko climbed back down the stairs and began to gather her meager belongings. When she grabbed the litter box and cat food Koryo stopped her. "The cat should stay with me until you get settled," he said.

This surprised her. For a moment she thought the monk must have developed a fondness for her orange-haired feline, but she then she realized how crazy it must seem to even think of bringing Dude with them on such an uncertain journey.

"Thank you," she said simply, and gave a little bow.

She started hauling Francesca's and her things to the red Cadillac, which had been left unlocked. Fresh's bags pretty much filled the large trunk, so she opened the back door and began loading her ragtag collection of paper sacks and the computer box onto the plush white leather upholstery.

Francesca joined her at the car a moment later.

"I've got blood on my robe," Chiko told her. "Should I put something down on this seat?"

"Don't worry about it," Fresh said. "I'll get the car detailed when I take it back to Armando. I told him I might need to keep it for a while."

"Are you okay to drive? I know you just drove here from Chicago."

"Sure. We'll need to find some gas, though. And are we going to Canada? Is that the plan?"

Plan? Chiko couldn't seem to summon the mental processes required to make a plan. Marielle would have already had a theory by now, would be spinning a story that would explicate events, fitting all the pieces together into something neat and cogent. She'd have plotted the next ten steps and be congratulating herself for doing so.

Marielle Wing was an idiot, she thought now, *privileged and comfortable living in her head, with no idea of how the world really works.* That was essentially how she'd been characterized in the manuscript of *Memory's Trail*. She'd been too arrogant to even read it. What might she know now that would have helped her if she'd only had the discipline to finish it and the presence of mind not to lose it?

It was one thing to deal in fiction, to move made-up characters through a made-up world, but what could she do now to bring about a resolution that was not calamitous? She didn't have a clue.

Francesca was settling into the driver's seat, checking the mirrors. When she started the engine, Chiko said, "Wait a minute!" Despite her urgency to leave, she was overcome by the urge to run back into the house to say goodbye to Dude. She didn't know when she'd see him again.

If.

As she rounded the trunk of the car, headed for the porch, she saw the same black Chevy turn the corner at a high speed.

"Fresh, get down!" she managed to scream, as she dropped to the ground and tried to climb under the car.

She heard the shot before the back windshield exploded.

She couldn't both shield herself and see what was going on. She didn't want to die on her belly in the driveway, assassinated by someone she couldn't even see. She felt inside the folds of her robe and found Donald's gun. Gripping the gun, she began to inch her body forward, staying as close to the car as she could, until she could see them. They wouldn't be expecting her to have a weapon.

Two white men were getting out of the van, both had guns drawn. She and Fresh were sitting ducks. "Fresh," she called quietly through the window. "Listen to me. I'm going to run and get them to follow me. I want you to gun it and get out of here. If they don't kill me, I'll meet you three blocks north of here. Don't argue, Fresh, it's our only chance."

She crouched then, ready to run, but not before she fired off a round. She had just one chance to surprise them and she had to make it count. At the shooting range you had all the time in the world to set up your shot, to get your stance, to aim, to breathe, to squeeze. In this moment she had no time, but she imagined the round going right into the man closest to her as she squeezed the trigger hard. She remembered not to let the blast knock her off balance and she saw the man go down before she broke into a run across the lawn. She headed through the weeds for the trash-filled lot, running clumsily in her robe and flip-flops. She heard the Cadillac back down the driveway and head in the other direction. The second man stopped for a moment to fire off a few rounds in the direction of the Cadillac, and that gave Chiko a hair's breadth lead on him.

She wished she were not dressed in orange, so visible amongst the trash where almost everything was blackened and burned. A few rusted corpses of cars, a boat, a structure that must have once been a roof, all surrounded by high weeds that obstructed as much as they concealed. She dove behind a pile of boards to plot her next move.

She had to keep her eyes on the man who stalked her, but she had to stay hidden. She understood he was not going to go away until she was dead, and that meant she had to kill him first. None of the people she had been—Marielle, Lorraine, Chiko—was someone who saw herself as capable of taking a life. Sure, Marielle had done it in fiction, but she'd believed that civilized, educated people did not kill one another, that there was always the possibility of dialogue, of negotiation. Now she had to recognize the animal in her—to keep her innocence she would have to surrender her life and, unlike Koryo, she was not willing. Not today.

Carefully lifting up her head above the pile, she could see the man circling through the lot. Of medium build, he was dressed in black jeans and a white tank top. He wore black wraparound sunglasses. He didn't look like anyone she'd seen before. His gun was drawn, and he methodically scanned from side to side. She hoped that meant he hadn't located her yet.

She needed him to get closer, but not too close. Her first shot had been lucky. She didn't know if that man was dead or just disabled but she had stopped him. She couldn't count on being lucky a second time. She was not a skilled marksman. She'd learned to shoot so she could write about it with some sense of verisimilitude. That was a long time ago. The humidity had her drenched in sweat, and the gun slipped in her palm. She set it carefully on the ground so she could wipe her hand on her robe.

Then she gripped the gun again. He knew she was armed but he couldn't see her yet. But she would have to kneel or stand to have a chance at wounding him significantly. A bad shot would reveal her location and likely would get her killed.

He moved closer. He did not seem to be trying to protect himself; maybe he didn't believe a woman could do him serious damage? His focus was on finding her. Something moved in the weeds, a rat or squirrel or something that darted across his field of vision and as he aimed his weapon in that direction, Chiko half crouched and fired. The first shot missed and he turned toward the sound, but she fired again immediately, and again and again. She watched him stagger and go down as her arm felt a burst of pain. It knocked her to the dirt. Her body understood before her mind processed it. She'd been hit. She watched the blood bloom up from her shoulder and thought she might vomit. She couldn't lie here; she had to get up, although she knew moving would make her lose more blood.

She didn't know the condition of her assailant. Was it possible that he too was only wounded, and might rise in a moment to finish the job?

Some sort of will made her rise and slowly move across the field, heading back toward the monks' house. She was unsteady on her feet and her vision clouded. Still, she clutched Donald's gun. The pain in her left arm was like fire, but adrenaline overrode it, kept her somehow moving forward.

She felt lightheaded—from fear, from blood loss, from not eating for too many hours. If she died here, no one would know who she was, who she'd been. She was surprised to find the idea didn't bother her as much as she might have expected.

From up the block she saw a figure coming toward her. Was it the first man, come to kill her, ready to finish the job? She could perceive the shape, the motion, but almost nothing about the details of the figure. Should she shoot? She lifted her right arm, but the effort of it caused her to stumble. The figure moved forward to catch her. It was not her vision but perhaps her sense of smell that let her know it was Koryo. He eased her down onto the sidewalk.

"The bullet went into your arm," he observed as he began to calmly examine her. "That's better than if he shot you in the chest or the stomach."

He unwrapped the sash from his own robe and began to tie it tautly above her wound, to slow the flow of blood from her heart. The tightness of the wrap was painful, but she found it a welcome pain as the spurt of blood began to slow. *Tourniquet.* She remembered the word for it.

"Can you lift this arm?" he asked her. It hurt like hell but she did it.

"That's good. Keep it up, as best you can, higher than your heart.

I know you are hurt," he continued in a low voice, "but you can't stay here. If these men work for the government, and you have shot them, the police are not likely to give you time to explain yourself."

He didn't sound censorious, just realistically assessing her situation. "Can you stand up?"

"I don't think so."

"Try," he insisted.

She rolled toward her right side, hoisting herself up onto her knees. He held her right arm and she leaned against him as she got first one foot, then the other under her.

"Can I take that?" He pointed toward the gun.

She didn't have the energy for words but slowly shook her head. He didn't insist, but began slowly moving them back up the street, one halting step at a time. The sound of her breath was so loud in her ears.

"Yes, that's good, keep breathing," the monk encouraged her.

The driveway was still blocked by the van. Its doors hung open and the engine was still running. The first man she had shot was lying face up on the sidewalk in front of the house. His face appeared surprised. His eyes were staring at the sky. His chest had a huge hole that was dark with blood. She gagged at the sight of him but there was nothing in her to vomit. She glanced down at her right hand, which still held the gun, as if it didn't belong to her. She was a Buddhist nun who killed people. It was so bizarre that she began to laugh. It was mirthless, hysterical, and it took energy she needed to remain upright. Koryo placed his palm on her back and that calmed her.

She heard the monk's soft intake of breath and looked up to see a young man running down the street toward them. He wore loose jeans that sagged below his waist and a gray T-shirt against coppery skin. An elaborate tattoo wound down his left arm, but she couldn't make out what it was. His head was covered in a blue bandanna. He had a gun tucked in his waistband.

He slowed as he approached them. He looked at the van, its engine still running, at the dead man sprawled on the sidewalk, then at her, the gun in her hand, and the monk beside her.

His hand reached for the gun in his waistband, but he didn't pull it out. "Did you cap this motherfucker?" he wanted to know.

Marielle had never liked to be questioned by a man. She looked him in the eye and said, "Who are you—a cop?"

He scoffed, "I ain't no cop. My grandmother lives around the corner. She heard shooting and got scared. She called me to come check it out."

He didn't look like an angel with that gun in his waistband, but there was no reason not to believe he was a caring grandson.

"He was trying to kill me," she explained.

He nodded. "And did he shoot you?"

"No. There was another one. He's over in the field by the burnt-out house."

The young man nodded again. He seemed to be trying to put it together. "And are you all monks 'n' shit? No offense," he added.

"He's a monk," she said. "I'm…Tell you the truth, I don't fucking know anymore."

"What about that?" He pointed toward Donald's car, still crashed into the tree.

"He was trying to help me. They killed him."

"And do you know who 'they' are?"

"Government."

The young man's eyes got big. "How come you're still here?"

Koryo spoke, "I was just getting ready to take her to the hospital."

The young man raised his eyebrows. "Look, it ain't none of my business, but if I had just shot two government dudes I wouldn't be goin' to no hospital."

"She's lost a lot of blood," Koryo countered.

"Well..." The young man seemed to be calculating in his head. "He's gonna kill me, but my brother was a medic in Iraq. I could take you to him, and he could fix you up."

"And why would you do that?" she asked him. She was having trouble forming the words in her mouth.

"Just seems like you could use some help," he said.

There was no reason to trust this young man, but she had no reason not to trust him either. There was something about how matter of fact he was in the face of everything that gave her confidence in him.

"Po-lice take their sweet time to get here, but you prob'ly don't wanna be around when they do."

She looked at Koryo and he nodded.

"Call me Chiko," she introduced herself.

"Lamar," the young man said. "Do you have wheels?"

"Let's take the van," she said. "There's gotta be something in there that will tell me what's going on."

Lamar looked at Koryo. "Is she always crazy like this or is she in shock?" To her he said, "There's prob'ly some kinda tracking device on it."

"If these two came then there are going to be more. I have to find out—" She broke free of Koryo's grip and staggered toward the van. She only made it a few steps before she stumbled and fell to her knees.

"Lady, you need to lie down!"

Koryo ran to the VW and backed it down the driveway. The two men did their best to load her into the back seat. They jumped in the front and were ready to go when Chiko said, "Dude! We can't leave him here."

"The hell we can't." Lamar thought she was talking about the dead man on the sidewalk, but Koryo put the car in park and ran into the house, returning moments later with the cat carrier, which he slid into the back seat beside her.

"Is that a mothafuckin' cat?" Lamar asked. Dude let out a loud yowl in response.

"We can't leave him here," she said again. "And we have to find Fresh!"

"I suppose that's your parakeet?"

"Three blocks north," she told Koryo, who backed out over the sidewalk and headed in that direction.

She had no idea what she'd find "three blocks north," no idea what she'd sent her friend into. She half believed Francesca wouldn't be there, either because she'd been menaced away from the area or because she'd decided to save herself and hightail it out of there. Dude's cries filled the vehicle, punctuated her anxiety.

Three blocks north turned out to be in slightly better shape than the street the monks' house was on. There were more houses standing, apparently intact, and one of the vacant lots had been turned into a community garden. The red Cadillac was parked on the street in front of that garden where, despite the heat of the late afternoon, a few people were tending to the abundant tomato and zucchini plants. The safety glass in the back window of the Cadillac was shattered, its shards spilling over the trunk.

When she saw the green VW in her review mirror, Francesca leaped out of the car before Koryo could pull up to the curb.

"Oh my God, I didn't know what I was going to do," she announced, leaning into Koryo's window, but she only stared when she saw Lamar, and saw Chiko's arm bathed in blood.

"Get in the back with me," Chiko said, without explanation. "But grab my purse, okay?"

"Why don't we take this car?" Fresh was, no doubt, concerned about leaving it on the street with all her things inside.

"Way too flashy," Lamar said. "And with that back window out, cops'll be all over it. You don' want that.

"Your friend's lost a lot of blood. We're trying to get her to my brother's to get her patched up."

Without another word, Francesca returned to the car, grabbed Chiko's large purse and her own, and set the alarm on the car before carefully climbing into the back seat of the Beetle.

"You've got Dude?" Francesca asked as she heard his loud meow. "Do you think I should give him a Valium?"

"Will it shut him up?" Lamar asked.

Francesca extracted the yellow pill from a bottle in her purse and broke it in half. She reached into the carrier and placed it in the cat's mouth.

Lamar used his cell to call his grandmother. "Nana," he said, "you're gonna hear some sirens once the cops come, but you don't have to worry. I have to take care of a coupla things right now, but I'll come check on you tomorrow. It's okay, Nana, I mean it. Whatever was happening is over."

Chiko could only hope that he was right.

CHAPTER FIFTEEN

Lamar lived with his brother in a neighborhood known as The Eye, but he didn't know how it got that name. The shaking of the old VW made Chiko's pain almost unendurable, but it wasn't long, maybe ten minutes, before they pulled up in front of a one-story brick home on a street where all the houses appeared to be occupied or at least standing. On the ride she'd leaned against Francesca and tried not to move the arm, which throbbed persistently.

She felt her energy collapsing; whatever she had been running on these last few days was at its end. She barely had the strength to extricate herself from the back seat. Lamar bounded up the walkway while she slowly followed, Koryo on her right and Francesca behind her, past a lawn that was weedy but neatly mowed. Fresh was toting both women's purses and the cat carrier with Dude.

From the open doorway they heard an angry voice. "Aw, hell no. No. You a muthafuckin' fool, Lamar."

Without a word, Koryo guided Chiko to sit on the top step. The three waited there. She knew the air was still hot, but her skin began to feel chilled.

They couldn't hear the words Lamar used in response, but they could hear him speaking fast, a dance of words designed to convince.

After some time he poked his head out the door and said, "Come in!"

Francesca gave him a skeptical look.

Lamar said, "Seriously, we're all gonna be safer if you all get off'a the street."

Koryo gently helped Chiko to rise and enter the house. From what she could see, it looked like a bachelor pad, not untidy but without the amenities—plants or curtains or decorative items—a woman's presence might add. They walked past a front room sporting a leather sofa, a big-screen TV, and a pile of free weights scattered over a scratched wooden floor. The walls were painted brown. It contained two doorways to the hall, at the front and back of the room.

Lamar motioned them down the hallway. Standing in the kitchen door was a scowling man with a bigger build and darker skin than Lamar. As he laid eyes on them, he said, "White folks, El? You got yourself tangled up in white folks' business?"

Pointing to Koryo, Lamar said, "He ain't white. He's Japanese."

"Vietnamese," Koryo correctly quietly, all the while holding onto Chiko's waist to keep her upright and moving.

Lamar led them to a back room and opened the door. The bed was a simple twin-size mattress on the floor, but it was neatly made. A straight-backed chair stood before a table being used as a desk; there were a few books stacked on it, but the shades were drawn and the light was too dim to read the titles. A folding chair leaned against the wall. A footlocker was pushed into one corner. A fan sat on the floor and barely stirred the thick air.

Koryo lowered her onto the chair, and propped her injured arm against its back.

He squatted on the floor. Francesca had not followed them into the back room, but waited in the living room.

A moment later Lamar entered with the angry man in tow. "Just take a look at her arm. Y'all, this is my brother Eddison."

Eddison gave his brother a hard look. "You're gonna owe me, brother. Big time. You are never gonna get out from under this. Now, go get my bag and a pan of warm water. Not *hot*," he specified.

Stepping into the room he said, "First thing, she's gotta lose the piece." He nodded at her right hand, which still clutched Donald Watkins's gun.

Although she moaned in protest, Koryo gently pried it out of her grasp; she had no strength to resist.

Eddison grabbed it, sniffed it. "It's been fired recently. Is this the gun that shot her?"

Koryo said it was not.

Eddison didn't pursue it further. He took her pulse; fingers encircled her right wrist and he counted. He said nothing but nodded as he registered the results.

"I need to look at the wound," he said and picked up her arm. As he bent closer, she could see the left side of his face was scarred, the skin stretched tighter and redder from chin to temple. His hands were warm and strong. He studied the tourniquet. "You do this?" he asked Koryo. "Nice job. Where'd you learn that?"

"In the war," was all Koryo said.

Lamar returned with a leather satchel and a large soup pot; he placed both at Eddison's feet. "Okay, now get outta here," Eddison ordered, as he slowly unwound the sash that was stiff with her blood. She had just enough Marielle left in her to be curious and want to see the damage.

He dipped a cloth in the water and wiped away the blood that crusted her shoulder. He gently fingered the hole in her arm. "You're lucky," he told her. "This is a through and through. Look like it went through muscle, not bone. Your friend did a good job stopping the bleeding."

"Lucky," she repeated, as if the word were foreign and she was just trying it on. She'd believed that once, but now the word seemed clumsy on her tongue.

"I'm going to clean this and bandage it. There's too much risk of infection to close it up right now. I'll give you antibiotics and Ibuprofen for pain. If you were in the hospital they could give you stronger meds."

She just shook her head. She felt like she was slipping under the surface of consciousness.

"Come on, now, stay with me here." He called out down the hall, "El! Make some tea and put a lot of sugar in it. Right now."

Then he asked Koryo, "Which war? Nam?"

The monk nodded. He'd begun chanting quietly, perched on the edge of the mattress, barely audible syllables that seemed to echo in the hot quiet room.

"Another fucked-up mess," Eddison commented.

Chiko focused on Koryo's soft sounds while Eddison applied a stinging solution to the hole in her. Painful as it was, it did bring her back to alertness; she bit down on her tongue to not cry out.

Eddison looked at her approvingly. "Well, you're tough."

She tried to shrug but it hurt too much. "Maybe just stubborn," she said.

To Koryo he said, "Women always tougher than men. They fool us with that shit."

Lamar came in the room with a mug of tea.

"That better not be too hot," Eddison scolded. "She's gotta drink it right now."

"It's not," Lamar whined slightly, like he was used to being on the defensive with his older brother.

"Drink some," Eddison said to Chiko. "Sip it slowly." He was a man used to giving orders. Marielle would have argued for sure, but right now that woman was nowhere to be found.

The tea wasn't too hot. It was way too sweet. Initially her taste buds recoiled, but then she felt herself start to come into focus as the sugar entered her bloodstream. The liquid felt good going down too; she must be dehydrated. She remembered a lifetime ago, Koryo had told her to drink a lot of water.

Francesca came hurrying down the hall. “Mar, it’s on the news. Three federal agents shot and Lorraine Kaminsky’s the suspect. There’s a picture of you with brown hair. They say you’re armed and dangerous.”

Chiko gaped at her. “They think I killed Donald?”

Eddison asked, “How the muthafuck you get mixed up with the Feds?”

As briefly as possible, she told him her story as he finished taping a gauze bandage on her arm. Including what Donald had told her before he was killed.

“Now we accessories.” Eddison narrowed his eyes and said to Lamar, “Get their car off the damn street. Drive it on into the garage.”

He pressed his temples as if the situation were going to make his head explode. Then knelt so he could look Chiko in the eyes. “You don’t have a chance in hell tryin’ to outrun them. And forget Canada; they’re gonna be watching the border.”

Chiko lay her cheek against the back of the chair. If she could have run out of the room she would have; she wanted to retreat from his words. She tried to wrap her arms around her torso, but moving her arm hurt so much. This time she could not contain her moan.

“Here, let’s get you started on these.” Eddison popped open a blister pack of tablets, then another. He placed them one at a time in her mouth and held the tea for her to drink. His face was a scowl and his tone had been harsh, but his touch was tender.

“Your only chance is to figure out who these guys are and expose them before they get to you.”

“I just want to disappear.”

“They’re not gonna let this go. You hide, you die. You got to make yourself visible. You say you’re famous? You got to go on TV and tell your story.”

The idea felt as impossible as a mouse wishing to be a horse. Marielle was dead and Chiko had none of her shine. She dimly remembered that she’d once had a fantasy of this, but now it seemed preposterous. Who would listen to her? She was no one, no one at all.

"That's it!" Francesca was already in action. "Marielle's got to come back. I know a woman who's a reporter for *The New York Times*. She'll know how to work this. I'll call her."

"Don't use your smart phone," Eddison warned. "If it's even on, they can track you."

"Shit, really?" She rummaged in her bag and pulled it out. "Oh, I did turn it off at the retreat house, to save battery." To Chiko she said, "You told me you bought a go-phone?"

"Yeah, use that," Eddison confirmed. Francesca went back to the living room.

Something was in motion now, but Chiko didn't feel part of it. The pain had dulled from the ibuprofen, but she had a hole in her arm. Francesca's animation was like a storm she was watching from a long way away, waiting for it to descend.

From down the hall, Chiko could hear her friend's voice, that tone she used when she wanted someone to do something for her. As she launched into Marielle's story, Chiko could only close her eyelids tight, as if to push it away. She tried to focus instead on the soft syllables Koryo was still emitting. They soothed her.

To Eddison she said, "You must want us to get out of here."

"You got somewhere to go?"

She shook her head.

"You been shot. You lost blood. You shouldn't be runnin' around out there with the Feds after you."

He left the room and came back a moment later with a cold bottle of Stroh's beer.

"I hate this government," he said. "They took my life and I ain't never gonna get it back."

He took a long drink. "Let's beat these muthafuckers."

CHAPTER SIXTEEN

"The last plane from JFK to Detroit is at eight p.m." Francesca swept back into the room, satisfied with what she had accomplished. "Araceli Vasconcellos will be on it. She's already investigating the story of the dead suspects in the bombing. She'll be here by eleven thirty."

Chiko felt a dim thud of recognition. "Who?"

"She's a *New York Times* reporter. She said she'd met you."

God. She wasn't a hundred percent certain, but she was pretty sure this was the name of the journalist Marielle had slept with at the PEN America conference back in February.

She wondered whether Araceli had told herself, or others, a story about being the last woman to sleep with Marielle Wing.

"El," Eddison yelled to his brother, "make us something to eat."

Lamar poked his head in the doorway to protest, "Why do I have to do that?"

"I told you, little brother, you owe me, and you've just begun to pay." He inclined his head toward Chiko. "This one needs some meat. This one"—he pointed in Koryo's direction—"probably doesn't eat meat. I don't know about her." He indicated Fresh. "Figure it out."

Koryo rose from his position on the mattress. "I will help," he offered and followed Lamar to the kitchen.

Eddison said to Chiko, "In the meantime, let's not wait around. You got to figure out who's after you and why."

Chiko said, "It's all connected to the JFK bombing. Those guys they arrested are dead now…"

"Maybe they're dead like Marielle Wing is dead?" Francesca said.

"No, man, they're trying to cover it all up now," Eddison insisted. "That's why they're trying to take your friend out." He stood up and flexed his shoulders. His skin had a fine sheen of sweat from the heat of the room. "Do y'all remember the Bay of Pigs?"

"I'm not *that* old," Francesca objected.

He cut his eyes at her. "I mean, *reading* about it. Castro makes revolution, grabs US businesses that had been ripping off the island for years. Corporations are none too happy; CIA decides to take Castro out. They fire up some exiles, promise to arm them, back them up, but really they don't know shit about what resources Castro has."

He took another long swallow of beer. "They send fifteen hundred guys to fight against a twenty-five thousand-man army. But Castro has air power, boats. US tries to pretend they don't know nothin' about it, like these guys just went down there on their own. They got their asses beat."

Fresh said, "What's your point?"

"This is a *conspiracy*. Why they gon' bomb the airport? And in such a chicken-shit way? People died, I know, but not *that* many people. No serious terrorist gon' risk all that to kill a few people. Not these days. This was theatre. This was a PR stunt." He gestured with the hand holding his beer, sending a small arc of it spilling onto the floor. He made no move to mop it up, but he did pull the folding chair away from the wall and sat down. "So who stands to gain from that?"

Although her main desire at this point was to not be conscious any longer, Chiko felt drawn into the puzzle of it. "When I was in Novi," she offered, "I tried to read a lot about the case. There was hardly any information about the bombing or the investigation, just a few things planted here and there and stated over and over again. But there were these two senators, Republicans, who right away introduced a bill to 'strengthen our national security.' They said we'd gotten lax about our vigilance, and that's why JFK was bombed."

Eddison said, "Plenty people in the government, and the corporate bastards they work for, lookin' to roll back the few rights they didn't already take away. You just got to make people afraid enough. After 9/11, a lotta people woulda given up all our rights, *just please keep us safe from the guys in the turbans*."

"You think those senators are behind the bombing?" Francesca asked, incredulous.

"Hell, no. But they make a coupla phone calls. They know some guys at the Pentagon or the NSA who aren't too happy with where the country is going, those guys talk to some other guys…Then they find two Muslim muthafuckers to take a payload to the airport; who knows what they promised them? Boom! *We got terrorists, and we told you so.*"

He continued, "But somethin' gets fucked up. Things don't go down like they're supposed to. The Muslims are supposed to die but they don't. And then there's you, takin' pictures."

Lamar came in with Koryo behind him. Each carried a couple of plates.

"Whadda we got?" Eddison wanted to know.

"We got spaghetti," Lamar said. "Some has sauce with meat, some don't."

"Okay," the older brother said, "but what about some vegetables? We got a salad, some broccoli, anything like that?"

"You said *meat* and *no meat*."

"Word. But how many times have I told you we need to be eatin' fresh vegetables. Shit, the way they eat, Black muthafuckers doin' genocide on themselves; white people can just sit back."

Lamar rolled his eyes. "Ever since you got outta the army, brother, you been whack."

"No, little brother. Ever since I got out of the military, I have been sane." He gesticulated with one big hand. "Now I know they want to annihilate us, and I am committed to not letting them."

"I'm just sayin', man, lighten up! No wonder Khadija booked."

"That's enough, Lamar." Although Eddison had been gruff throughout their visit, his tone had contained a mockery of its bad attitude. Only now was there was there real anger in his voice. "Fuck you, muthafucker." He struck the wall with one big open palm; the sound reverberated. He put down his plate and left the room. They could hear the back door open and slam shut.

He left behind a heavy silence. Only Koryo was slowly chewing his food, seemingly immune to the roil of emotions.

After a moment, Fresh asked, "Khadija?" Her voice broke the tension.

"His wife," Lamar answered. "He used to be all happy-go-lucky, always smilin' and jokin' around. Now…" His words trailed off; they'd all just witnessed the rest of the story. "I think he's got PTSD or something. Seem like he never sleeps; he's all paranoid all the time and then, he just goes off. She couldn't take it."

After she left, his brother had offered him a place to live while he was going to school. "But now I see how he musta treated her," he continued, "'cuz that's how he is with me."

When Chiko closed her eyes she could feel the heaviness of Eddison's mind, the tear in his spirit. Everything he had seen and done in Iraq, terrible as it was, had not damaged him the way his wife's leaving had. He had a hole in his heart, blown clear through. Through and through.

Liana used to complain that Marielle had no empathy for real people, only her characters. She wondered now whether it was being shot that had opened her.

"You should try to eat," Fresh said to her, putting a hand on her good arm. Chiko tried to twirl the strands of pasta onto her fork; they were overcooked and limp. The sauce was out of a jar, and the meat, which came in the jar with the sauce, was unidentifiable. Despite this, she took a bite and then another; she had been too numb to feel hunger but as soon as her salivary glands began to work, she was famished. She ate every morsel of the terrible food on her plate and scraped the last of the sauce with her fork.

"You probably woulda liked a vegetable, huh?" Lamar asked as he took her plate. She shrugged her good shoulder and thanked him for the meal.

"You wanna lie down?" Lamar said to Chiko. "You can use my bed. We got some time before that reporter gets here."

Although she felt as if a steamroller had flattened her, she didn't think she could rest. Maybe never again. It took a long time for her to get to her feet. She could feel the blood surge into her arm when she stood and it almost knocked her down again. She slowly made her way out of the room; no one tried to stop her.

She was barefoot. Her body recalled that she'd kicked off her flip-flops in the field but she hadn't been aware of it until now. Unsteadily, she made her way down the hall, through the kitchen and, with her right hand, carefully opened the back door. The backyard was plain but neatly tended. There was a maple tree at the far end of the lot and a picnic table underneath it. Shoulders hunched, Eddison sat on one of the wooden benches with his back to her.

She wanted to walk over and put her hand on his back, right in the spot where his heart was blown apart, but she couldn't risk it. Instead she walked to the other side of the table to sit down facing him.

He looked up, angry at first to be disturbed, but when he saw it was her, his face relaxed just a little. "You shouldn't be running around with that hole in your arm."

She didn't say anything. There was nothing to say. But she found herself moved to sit with him, to witness his consuming pain. She just nodded, and kept her eyes on him.

The sun was setting, charging the clouds above with swirls of purple and orange. It softened the shadows in his face.

"Those muthafuckers you shot?" he asked. "Did they call themselves federal agents?"

"They didn't say anything. They jumped out of a van and started shooting at us."

"You were in fear for your life," he coached her. "Michigan has a stand your ground law. If you do get the chance to talk to the police, just keep tellin' 'em that."

It happened to be the truth. He was trying to help her. She would tell them exactly that if she got the chance.

"Your friend said you write books. What kinda books do you write?"

She shrugged the one shoulder. "It used to be the most important thing in the world to me," she said. "But now it seems—I don't know—like it was somebody else who wrote them." Someone she'd known a long time ago.

Eddison looked at her, as if reading a deeper truth beyond her words. He nodded.

"They take it all away," he said. "The fuckin' government."

They were quiet. In the twilight she could hear the hum of mosquitos. It was that still.

"C'mon," he said. "You should get inside. I don't want you to get seen."

"Who's gonna see me?" She looked around at the backyard.

"Depends on who's lookin'; they could be usin' drones to find you." He pointed at the sky as if it were filled with unseen flying things.

She held her head in her hand. "How are we supposed to live in this world?"

"Just come on in now. If not, the skeeters are gonna eat us alive." He slapped his arm to illustrate.

She let him take her hand to help her off the bench, then followed him back into the house.

Inside the kitchen, Koryo was washing the dishes. Lamar had retreated to the living room; the TV was blasting its noise down the hall. Fresh was on the go-phone. She looked up to report, "Araceli made it to the airport. She's been calling around, trying to connect the dots between Donald and the two suspects and you. She wants to get you on *The Today Show* tomorrow morning, get you in front to the TV cameras first thing."

Chiko started to object that there was no way they would let her on an airplane, but Fresh said, "They'll patch you in from the affiliate in Detroit."

Fresh had a plan and all Chiko had to do was follow along. Everyone was going out of their way to help her, so why did she feel like she was about to be ground into dust? She'd once fantasized about Marielle Wing returning from the dead. She could no longer recall why. No matter that her body was still more or less alive, Marielle Wing no longer existed. You couldn't resurrect the dead.

Looking up from the phone again, Francesca asked, "Mar, what was the name of the marshal who was with you when you were first in Michigan?"

That was a lifetime ago. She'd been Marielle and then they made her be Lorraine and this man followed her wherever she went. She could see him, just a little taller than she was, with a wiry build and a neat mustache. *C'mon*, she urged herself. Marielle used to have an impeccable memory. Finally, a pocket opened in her brain and she said, "Eric." A second later she added, "Orellano."

Fresh repeated the name into the phone. Then turned again to ask, "And do you think he's trustworthy?"

Trust no one; that's what Donald had advised her. She had trusted Donald, mostly, but even he hadn't known everything. In the face of the question, she closed her eyes and withdrew. Chiko could almost picture herself falling through a dark tunnel inside her.

"You about ready for another ibuprofen?" Eddison was at her side, pulling her consciousness back into the room. He waved at Francesca to go back down the hall.

Chiko nodded and swallowed the tablets along with the water he gave her. Her mouth was so dry it felt like she'd held chunks of granite on her tongue; those rocks had sucked every drop of moisture from her.

"You wanna try to get some sleep?"

She shook her head.

"Okay, then. You said you had the Homeland Security dude's cell phone?"

She'd forgotten about that. Fresh had brought her purse into the bedroom; with her right arm Chiko rummaged in it and handed Donald's cell phone to Eddison.

"First thing we got to do," Eddison explained, "is disable the tracking software. We have to turn it on first, and if someone's paying attention, tracking it, we're fucked."

"Does my go-phone have tracking software too?" Francesca was using it to talk to Araceli, and was, Chiko imagined, telling her the whole story.

Eddison nodded. "It does but unless somebody knows you bought that phone they don't know who they're tracking. How'd you pay for it?"

"Cash," she said.

"It's all good, then." Indicating Donald's phone, he said, "Shall I turn this on?"

"Any chance the men I shot were the ones who would be paying attention to it?"

He shook his head. "They send nobodies to do the dirty work, but somebody higher up, he's in charge. But don't you wanna see what's in this phone?"

She nodded. He almost made her feel like there was something she could do.

He turned on the phone and began pressing buttons with his thumbs. He sure seemed to know what he was doing. "This is his personal phone; maybe he used it to keep from being monitored himself." A few seconds later he said, "Damn, this dude's a security guy but he doesn't use a password on his phone."

Eddison moved his chair next to hers so she could see the phone too. He opened the email first and it was blank. Recently deleted mail was also blank. "He must put everything in the trash and empty it."

"What about text messages?" she asked.

There were none.

"He doesn't keep anything," Eddison said. "He *is* a security dude, after all."

She remembered he'd written something in his phone when he was at the retreat house. They looked in Notes, and found it, but it was some kind of code, a series of letters and numbers.

They went next to voice mail. There were two new messages that Donald had never had the chance to delete. The most recent was from about an hour ago, from someone identified as Cynthia.

Eddison put the phone on speaker and pressed play.

The voice belonged to a woman; its pitch was low and sweet. "Donnie, I got your note. I know you're off somewhere on some top-secret business, but I hope you'll be able to come home soon. The bed is just too big when you're not in it. Call me if you can. Love you."

Chiko felt the stab of pain that shot through Eddison. Perhaps Khadija had once missed him that way. She felt her own sorrow that Cynthia didn't know what had happened to Donald. Was she his wife? His girlfriend?

She'd never imagined Donald having a love interest, but then, she hadn't really thought about him separate from his function. He'd been good at disappearing into his role and she'd been too absorbed in her own drama to consider his life.

"I wish we could let her know."

"No, you don't." He shook his big head. "You do not want to be the messenger that brings that news to anyone." Perhaps he spoke from experience.

He was right; Chiko didn't want to tell the unknown woman that her man was gone for good. She just wanted her to know.

"Do you think they'll inform her?" she asked.

"Depends on who she is and if anyone knows about her."

The other call was from a number with no name attached to it. It had come in at 15:40.

"Watkins, I'm just checking in to make sure we're still meeting in the morning to go over the evidence." That was all. The voice sounded oddly familiar, though she couldn't place it.

"What time did that come in? That was just a few minutes after Donald was shot." She had a very odd feeling about this message.

"Could be someone trying to establish his alibi," Eddison said.

"Check the calendar," she urged.

The calendar was not blank; there were entries but they too seemed to be in code: 9:00 a.m. XP3Y.

"Well, that's not much help." Eddison set the phone down in disgust.

"Wait, could we play that message again? I feel like I've heard that voice somewhere before."

He pressed play and she listened again. It was just outside the edges of her awareness. A trace of an accent. The sound so sharp it cut her. She listened again and again, but it eluded her.

"What about contacts?" she said, not wanting to give up.

"He's too careful. He's not gonna have contacts," Eddison insisted, but she picked up the phone with her right hand and set it on her lap so she could open the contacts function. Surprisingly, Donald did have contacts on his phone.

"I'll be damned," Eddison said when she turned the screen to him. "Looks like they're in code too."

"But is it the same code?" She tapped back to the calendar function at looked at tomorrow morning's appointment: XP3Y. Scrolling down the list of contacts, she did indeed find XP3Y. But what did that prove? Donald had an appointment tomorrow with someone in his contact list. She checked the number against the number of the incoming call; it was the same. That also proved nothing.

The man had called to confirm tomorrow's appointment. Nothing sinister, except she couldn't shake the feeling that this was significant. She wanted to call the number; if it belonged to the killer, he'd be surprised to get a call from Donald's phone. But maybe not. Maybe he expected the police to have confiscated the phone, or even the two guys who'd come after her. Maybe he'd been waiting for a call. Or did he know by now those two guys were dead?

She played the incoming message one more time; she was haunted by its familiarity but she still could not place it. She tucked the phone into her sash.

Eddison said, "As your medic, I'm going to insist you get some sleep. Nothing is better for healing than rest." He cleared the mattress of everything except the pillow and coverlet.

She wanted to tell him he should sleep too, but before she could get the words out he said, "I'll be right outside the door." He turned off the lamp as he left.

She had no inclination to argue. She carefully lowered her body to the mattress and curled onto her right side. She worried that she would leave dried blood on the sheets. She wondered where Fresh was, and Koryo, and Dude, but she could not hold onto these thoughts for long. Sleep came like an ocean wave and pulled her into the sea.

CHAPTER SEVENTEEN

In her dream she was on the bank of what might have been the L.A. River. It was dark and wild, yet the walls were concrete. The dream was in black and white, atmospheric with shadow, but up ahead of her on the path was a woman in red suit. She knew without seeing her face that it was Reza. She called to her but her words held no sound, or were carried away by the wind. She started trying to run but the more she labored to move her limbs, the farther away she was from the red-clad woman. Then she heard a boom and the woman fell.

The loud report seemed to come from her dream, but then Eddison was at her side, whispering, "Chiko! Wake up." He avoided touching her wounded shoulder but he made his voice insistent enough to penetrate her fog of sleep.

"What time is it?" She didn't know quite where she was or how long she'd been asleep.

"Shhh," he said. "Someone's outside. I don't think it's the cops."

She wasn't ready to come out of the dream, in which she might still save Reza, and wondered whether Eddison's words were true; Lamar had told them his brother was paranoid. But she knew it was all too likely she'd been found out. She attempted to roll onto her left side to escape his interruption, but her shoulder reminded her of its wound and pain shot down her arm. She gasped and Eddison said again, "Shhh."

In the dim light leaking from the hallway, she could see Eddison had an assault rifle over his shoulder. "Lamar and your friends are already in the basement," he said in that same quiet voice.

"Not the basement!" She was wide awake now, flashing back to the townhouse in Novi. "If they firebomb us, we'll never get out." She tried to keep her voice low but she was too agitated.

He did not argue. Instead he took hold of her right arm; his grip was strong and he easily lifted her from the bed. She was still dressed in the blood-crusted nun's robe and still barefoot. Half carrying her, he moved her into the hall. "This house has a bomb shelter," he explained.

There was no time for her questions as he hurried her through the kitchen and down the basement stairs. The lights were out and all she could do was trust the next step in front of her. The air was cooler in the basement; there was the scent of bleach. The floor was concrete beneath her feet. They moved all the way across the darkened room to a far wall. Eddison's fingers found a control panel, faintly lighted, and entered a code. This caused a heavy door to swing open. Beyond it was a room with concrete walls and floor; the ceiling was too low for Eddison's height and he had to stoop once he entered. It smelled musty; this room was not beneath the house but under the backyard. It was smaller than the bedroom she'd been sleeping in, but had a neat row of cots arrayed along its length, and shelves and cupboards built into the walls. A bare bulb hung from the ceiling and cast shadows onto the wall.

Koryo looked unruffled as he sat cross-legged on his narrow mattress; he was chanting again, working his mala beads between his fingers. Lamar and Francesca appeared more agitated. She clutched the carrier with Dude in it; the cat's loud howls echoed off the walls. Chiko walked over and sat beside Fresh on a cot, whispering to Dude to try to quiet him.

In a low voice, Francesca said, "I texted Araceli before we came down here. I told her to approach the house with extreme caution."

"Can we get a signal down here?"

Fresh shook her head.

Indicating the cat sounds, Lamar asked his brother, "Can somebody hear that?"

Eddison shook his head. "Soundproof," he said. He pointed to a corner. "Toilet's behind that curtain, water and food up on those shelves. This door is locked from the inside. Don't open it for anything. I've got the code to get in. Y'all just sit tight now." He stooped lower to go back through the doorway.

Chiko pleaded, "Don't go up there! They'll kill you."

His grin was without mirth. "They can't kill me. I'm already dead."

She knew the feeling. The metal door clanged as he pulled it shut behind him.

Lamar looked wild. He yelled at the closed, soundproof door, "He won't be happy until they do kill him."

Chiko took a look around the tiny room. She recalled that Fresh hated small, enclosed spaces.

"Are you okay?" she asked her friend.

"I'm hanging in." Fresh was doing some deep breathing.

"I'm sorry," Chiko said to all of them, although the words seemed ludicrous. She'd known how dangerous it was to involve others and yet she had done it anyway.

Fresh rubbed her back absentmindedly as she turned to ask Lamar, "Does every house in Detroit come with a bomb shelter?"

He managed a grin. "I never saw one till I stayed in this house. I guess a lotta white people put 'em in during the fifties. This used to be a white neighborhood. But Eddison got all excited when he found this house. I guess he used to make Khadija come down here and practice for some kinda emergency. She told me it gave her the creeps, and I don't blame her."

Dude was butting his head against the door of the carrier. Chiko fiddled with the clasp on the door. "Do we have the cat food down here?"

"No, it's in the trunk of the Cadillac," Francesca said.

Chiko used her good arm to rummage on the shelf until she pulled down a bottle of water, a plastic bowl, and a tin of sardines. Koryo left his cot to help her to pour the water and pull the metal lid off the tin. She placed these on the floor and Dude jumped out of his confinement. He was a little unsteady on his feet from the tranquilizer Francesca had given him earlier, but he lapped up all the water and devoured the sardines, then continued to push the tin across the floor with his nose. It was better than his howling, but the sound of metal on concrete began to grate against her nerves. She paced in the tiny room, but there was not much space to walk. A few minutes passed, then a few more. Her arm was throbbing, but she could not sit still.

Finally Koryo said, "I am chanting a mantra for the dead."

"For Donald?"

"Three men died today. We chant for all souls."

Three men died and two of them she had killed. Who would chant for her soul now? Or did she even any longer have a soul, and if she did, what was its name?

"All life is valuable," Koryo explained. "Would you like to join me?"

He spoke the question in a way that seemed to take for granted its answer, and although Chiko had no idea what she'd "like" at the moment, this made as much sense as anything. She sat cross-legged on the concrete floor. It was hard beneath her hips but she welcomed the physical discomfort; it was something to feel besides the pain in her shoulder, the shock that held her breath suspended and the fear streaming acid through her veins. Francesca sat down next to her and Dude settled his body into Chiko's lap. Lamar did not join them, but lay down on his cot.

Koryo did not bother to teach the mantra he was chanting; he simply closed his eyes and commenced. Rather than trying to replicate the syllables, she just allowed herself to fall into the sound. Listening, it felt as if the resonance arose from her own cells, a faint drone, a pattern of repetition that was oddly comforting. She could hear Francesca's voice repeating the words and eventually Lamar's light tenor joined in. For some moments, it was as if the sound current itself became the room and they were safe inside.

She wasn't sure how long they sat like that, her mind finally losing its usual restless tracking. It wasn't as if she'd fallen asleep but the normal chatter of her thoughts had been subdued. She wasn't sure where her mind had gone, what had become of her identity; she felt like she had been away and just now come back.

It felt good to do something for Donald, even something that seemed intangible. Donald, who had lost his life protecting her. And although Marielle had at one time thought herself very important, thought her life absolutely worthy of protecting, she understood now that she'd incurred a debt to Donald, to Reza, even to the other two, still nameless, whose lives she had taken—the Buddhists would call it *karma*—and she would have to make herself worthy of their sacrifice. If in fact she survived.

She had spent so much time in her life being concerned about what would be given to her, done for her. Even as Lorraine, she'd wanted Donald to protect her, Reza to get Marielle's life back. When Liana used to tell her she was selfish, she'd thought it was just because she wanted the attention that came to Marielle. She had not spent much, if any, of her life thinking about what she might do for others.

This thought dissolved her meditative peace and she spoke aloud. "What happened to the gun?"

"I have it." Koryo stopped chanting and answered. He showed her that it was tucked into the belt of his robes.

"Give it to me," she said.

Fresh said, "Don't even think of it," and tried to hold her in place, but Chiko was already on her feet and took the gun in her hand.

"He shouldn't be alone up there," she said.

"Come on, now, don't be crazy." Lamar was on his feet now too, trying to grab the gun away from her. It should have been easy with her injury, but she was a small tiger. The gun fit in her hand, a familiar grasp. She remembered holding it earlier, aiming and firing.

Fresh said, "What are you doing, Mar—"

But Chiko interrupted. "He shouldn't be alone. It's not his battle. There's a hole in his heart."

She turned the handle and threw her right shoulder against the metal door. It opened, spilling artificial light into the blackened basement, and she quickly shut it behind her. The exertion made her dizzy and nauseated; the left arm resumed its throbbing. It had its own little mantra that went *FuckFuckFuckFuckFuckFuckFuck*.

Fuck, what am I doing? she wondered as she realized she had no way to get back into the shelter.

But she could not let another person die because of her, not without trying to stop it. She hadn't known what would happen to Reza and Donald, though she'd been warned about breaking the rules. She'd broken all the fucking rules, and the consequences had been fatal. Even now, Eddison had said to stay put and here she was, doing the exact opposite. She couldn't seem to help it. But this was no time to second-guess herself.

The basement floor was cold under her bare feet. She made her way quietly to the bottom of the stairs and began to slowly climb, clutching the gun in her right hand, trying to be careful of her footfalls, careful of how to balance her weight so the old steps would not creak. She slipped off the safety and held the gun pressed against her thigh.

She tried to quiet her breathing. She wanted to give no advance signal to whoever might be in the house. As she reached the top of the steps she saw the door to the kitchen was ajar; peering in, she could see no one in that room and so carefully stepped in.

The air in the upstairs was much warmer. She began to perspire as she walked across the linoleum and peeked into the hallway. She heard voices from the front of the house and took a few steps into the hall. Staying close to the wall she craned her neck to see into the living room through the doorway nearest. The television was on with the sound turned down. She could see Eddison from the back, pointing his rifle at someone. She couldn't see that someone, but recognized the voice from the message on Donald's phone. From where did she know this voice?

Then she remembered. "We'll find you," the white man, cheeks blooming with rosacea, had said to her in the chaos of JFK after the bombing. "We'll find you." And he had.

To see that man, or to determine if it was just one other man, Chiko had to continue up the hallway to look into the front door to the living room. Every step increased the likelihood she would be seen or heard. Craning her neck she saw the man's scarlet face; he was pointing a pistol at Eddison. He seemed to be alone. But how would Eddison know who he was?

"You can't just break into my house, man," Eddison was saying. "You got no warrant, nothing. I have the right to defend myself."

"I'm an agent of the US government," the man said. "Whose word do you think they're going to take?"

"I don't expect to live to tell the story, but I'm gonna make sure you don't either," she heard Eddison say. There was no vantage from which she could see both of them without revealing herself.

"Why put yourself in the middle of this? Nobody wants to hurt you," the man said. *What was it Francesca used to say: How can you tell when a man is lying? When his lips move.* "I need to take Ms. Wing—or should I say Ms. Kaminsky?—into custody for her own protection; then I'll clear out of here and leave you alone."

Chiko considered that "I." It suggested he was here alone. Or was he lying about that too? If he was alone it was because his plan was falling apart. Perhaps he thought he could still get away with it; he would kill her and there would be no one who knew the full story, no one to testify against him.

With only one working arm, she had to stuff the gun in her sash before she could pull out Donald's phone. It was still turned on. She returned the call that had come in late in the afternoon.

The man's phone rang in the living room. He did not bother to look at it or silence it. It rang three times, then was silent. Would Eddison understand what she was trying to tell him? She pushed End, and switched the phone for the gun.

"Naw," Eddison responded. "You ain't takin' nobody nowhere. Michigan has a stand your ground law. It's like this: You broke into my house, pointed a gun at me. I did three tours in Iraq. I have PTSD. I was in fear for my life."

From her vantage, Chiko could see the red-faced man calculating; could he shoot Eddison before Eddison killed him? But now she noticed a blur of movement through the side window. Outside the window, she could make out a figure; he was pointing a rifle in Eddison's direction, just waiting for a signal from the man inside. How many more of them were out there?

She thought Eddison must not know the second shooter was there, or maybe he didn't care. *I'm already dead*, he'd said to her. Or did he think he could shoot them both?

She knew she was not a marksman. She was an author, or she used to be. She'd dabbled in experiences so she could write about them. She recalled the words from the fake novel, *Memory's Trail—It cost her writing career and it cost her fame and it cost her her belief that she was a good person.* Was it possible the red-faced man had written those words, that book, to communicate with her?

She was not a marksman. She had been extremely lucky today, but it had nothing to do with any skill. She'd just surprised them, or at least the first one. Although she didn't think the red-faced man or the man outside the window were aware of her presence in the hall, she didn't dare think she'd be lucky again. If she tried to take action she would just get Eddison killed along with her. *No.*

She could just surrender and go with the red-faced man. He might let the others go, but she knew better. He would want to make sure that no one was left to connect him to what had happened. She didn't have a choice.

She saw the man outside the window position himself for the shot. She had to get him first. She maneuvered her body to have the best possible angle without being seen. She remembered again her training...*One, two, three...*

She heard Eddison yell, "Chiko!" and she pulled the trigger at the same time he fired a barrage at the red-faced man, who collapsed. The window she was aiming at shattered and the man behind it fell away. She backed against the opposite wall, with barely the strength to remain standing.

"Stay there," Eddison ordered, and for once, she did not argue. They both waited to see what would follow, if more men would come through the front door. After a few moments, he stepped into the hall, the rifle down at his side. She asked, "How did you know I was here?" She took a step toward the living room.

"Don't come in here," he cautioned. "You don't wanna see this."

Then he answered her, "I'm trained to be aware of everything in the environment. I could smell the blood on you."

CHAPTER EIGHTEEN

The makeup artist in the WDIV studio in downtown Detroit was working from a photograph, the one from the cover of *Hard-Hearted Monday*. He was wielding half a dozen brushes against the planes of her face, trying to resculpt her into someone who looked like Marielle Wing.

Her scalp itched under the wig of blond curls he'd insisted upon. Though she'd wanted to, no one had thought she should go on *The Today Show* with her bald head. Not even Francesca, who'd argued, "It's going to be hard for people to believe that you're alive. The more you look like Marielle Wing, the better." Even Araceli had at first looked at her, incredulous, reluctant to believe the bald woman in the bloody nun's robe was the same woman she'd bedded six months earlier.

Araceli Vasconcellos had arrived about ten minutes after she and Eddison had shot the men who'd come to kill her. The reporter had had the presence of mind to bring with her a prominent criminal attorney from the Detroit area, Arthur McBride. Peering at him, Chiko felt embarrassed to be seen as she looked now. McBride had eyes so blue they must have been enhanced by contact lenses. He wore an Armani suit and a Rolex that looked like it cost more than Araceli's annual salary. McBride had insisted everyone depart the house before he called law enforcement. He had contacted the FBI and promised to personally deliver her and Eddison to meet with them at his offices later this afternoon. McBride was the reason they were sitting in this television studio instead of in a jail cell this morning.

Despite their concerns for his safety, Koryo had driven the battered VW back to the Zen Center last night, taking Dude with him. The Center was clearly the safest place for the orange cat to be at this time.

The makeup artist continued to poke and fluff at her face. Every few minutes he'd step back, regard the photo next to the live version, and shake his head. Then he would use another brush under her cheekbones, or down the bone of her nose, but clearly he could not transform her into who she had been.

"Ten minutes," a voice from the doorway warned. It belonged to a woman wearing black jeans and a headset. She'd introduced herself as simply the stage manager. "I need to get her back to the dressing room," she told the makeup artist.

Eddison stood in the corner of the room. McBride had insisted on hiring a security guard to watch her but she wanted no one but Eddison. The lack of sleep didn't appear to be affecting him, whereas she felt like a ghost. Perhaps that was only appropriate.

"There you go," the makeup artist purred with false enthusiasm. Like a bullfighter snapping a cape, he removed the cloth he'd draped over her. "Ready for your close-up!"

She mumbled a thank-you and was grateful he didn't ask her what she thought of his handiwork. She'd tried to avoid her image as she stepped back from the wall of mirrors.

The stage manager led her down the hall to the dressing room, Eddison shadowing close behind. A monitor perched high in the corner broadcast the program.

The face glumly reflected in the dressing room mirror looked like no one she recognized. How was she ever going to get through this interview when all she wanted to do was lie down? Her shoulder hurt even worse than it had last night; the pain made it difficult to think.

Francesca swept into the room and inspected her. "You never wear that shade of lipstick," she complained, "but maybe it will look better under the lights." She straightened the pearls around her neck and plucked a speck of lint from the lapel of the cobalt-blue dress Fresh had loaned her for this appearance, along with the pearls and the shoes that were a size too big. Fresh had run out to Meijer's at dawn to buy pantyhose, and helped Chiko to put them on, an otherwise impossible task with only one functioning arm.

"Five minutes." The stage manager returned, this time with a young man carrying a clip-on mic.

The man smelled of aftershave as he leaned in close to attach the body pack to the belt of her dress behind her back. He asked her to thread the wire underneath her skirt and feed it up toward her neckline, but Fresh had to help her do it. Then the man attached the mic to her lapel, accidently grazing her left arm, which caused her to moan involuntarily.

"Just breathe," Eddison advised her, "like that Zen dude taught you." He'd give her another dose of ibuprofen as soon as she was off the air.

"Do I really have to do this?" she protested to Francesca. "Can't it just be over?"

Fresh reminded her there had to be more people involved in the plot than the five who'd been killed yesterday. They too would want to make sure she couldn't testify against them. Fresh was kind enough not to add that they'd been over this about forty times already. Instead she shifted into reassurance. "You'll be great," she said, squeezing Chiko's hand. "And Araceli will do most of the heavy lifting."

Araceli had taken the scoop and run with it. *The Times* had held space on the front page, and she'd filed her report at one a.m., typing it as she juggled calls from various sources in New York and DC while Chiko relayed all that had happened to her. To Araceli, the story was much bigger—a government conspiracy, the battle over the need to protect against terrorism vs. the rights of citizens, the murder of a Homeland Security agent, of defendants awaiting trial—of which Marielle Wing was just a small and incidental part. Not insignificant, certainly, but not central.

Araceli would precede her on *The Today Show*, briefly relay Marielle's story and what she'd been able to piece together of the larger story, as well as the chaos erupting in Washington as the conspiracy came to light. At one time it would have infuriated her that someone else would get to speak for her; now she felt only relief. The last place she wanted to be was in the spotlight.

Fresh, Eddison, and Chiko watched Araceli on a monitor from the greenroom. She was explaining, "The defense team for Balian and Musafian—"

Anchor Darius Green interrupted, "The two men who were awaiting trial for the bombing of the American Airlines ticket counter at JFK?"

"Before they were found dead in their cells on Saturday," Araceli said, "their attorney told me that their clients were approached by individuals who claimed they were working for the US government and promised that if the defendants 'delivered this package' to a destination in the terminal, their citizenship applications would get fast-tracked. He says the two men had no idea their cargo was bombs."

"Are you suggesting the government planned the bombing?" The broadcaster registered indignation.

"Not the government per se, but evidence is pointing to a group of agents within National Security."

"That's a pretty serious charge," Green warned.

"I'm not making any charges; I'm just reporting a story. Ms. Wing had several attempts made on her life, both before and after being taken into the Witness Security Program. When the agent assigned to protect her was assassinated yesterday, Marielle Wing decided she might be safer in the public eye than she's been in hiding."

Darius Green looked into the monitor as the camera zoomed in. "When we come back, we'll talk to the woman claiming to be the celebrated author Marielle Wing—whose death was widely publicized last February—about her extraordinary story."

The woman in the black jeans came for her then. Francesca kissed her cheek and said again, "You're gonna be great." The stage manager walked her quickly down the long hallway. She passed Araceli coming back to the green room; the reporter looked at her in amazement. Perhaps for the first time she wholly believed she was Marielle.

The stage manager walked her onto the set, where she settled her into a chair in front of a video monitor. Except for the crew, she was alone on the set. The stage manager placed a mug of water on a table next to her. She double-checked the microphone clipped to the neckline of the cobalt-blue dress. Eddison posted himself in the wings, off camera but in Chiko's line of sight. She was grateful she could see him.

The lights were disorienting in their brightness. The wig made her feel like she had a blanket on her scalp. Marielle had once been accustomed to being interviewed, unfazed by microphones and questions, but now she couldn't remember how to do it. She wanted to flee the intrusive eye of the camera; she wanted to go back to the hotel and curl into a fetal position on the bed.

Before she came on-screen, there was a clip of recorded audio from Deputy Marshal Eric Orellano. He stated that he was present when Marielle Wing's death had been announced and knew her to be very much alive. He corroborated her entry into the Witness Security Program.

When the host introduced her, she could have sworn he was talking about someone else. She tried to replicate Marielle's smile, but the stretch of her lips felt tense, unnatural. He asked her to recount her story, and she began with being at JFK the night of the bombing.

"And what exactly did you see?" Green pressed.

"Since there is pending legal action, I've been advised by my attorney not to discuss this." Her attorney. That should have been Reza, but Reza was dead. Arthur McBride was certain this would be the case of his career.

The host summarized the conditions under which she'd been brought into the Witness Security Program. For a moment, he looked up from his teleprompter. "You're quite a well-known author, Marielle, weren't you concerned about your career?"

"Of course I was, but I didn't have any choice."

"And then you read your obituary. What was that like?"

This was an opportunity for a witty retort, but as she reached for it her brain seemed an empty sky. All she had was the hollow truth of it. "Really, there are no words to describe that experience."

Green seemed disappointed. "No words? That doesn't sound like the Marielle Wing we used to know."

All she could do was shrug. This was not going well.

The anchor pressed on. "So you lived a regular life. You've asked us not to disclose the location but it was not in California, is that right? You taught high school?"

"I was a substitute teacher, yes. I thought my biggest problem would be boredom; I wasn't used to a 'regular life.'" She recalled her restlessness during those months. Then she flashed on Garland Macpherson; she wondered whether he was listening, if he recognized her voice.

"And then the announcement of this book, your 'final work,'" Green prompted her.

"Donald Watkins warned me that someone was trying to coax me out of hiding. I guess they knew enough about me to know my ego wouldn't be able to just stand by and allow that."

"And when can we expect *your* book about this experience?"

She wanted to wipe the smarmy grin off his face, the one that suggested this was all a ploy to get attention, or at least a set of experiences she would be only too eager to exploit in the service of her career. Then she remembered that at the beginning, Marielle had been calculating this exact thing.

"I'm a novelist, Darius, not a journalist. I've never mined my personal life for my stories." She said it with utter conviction, with the old Marielle Wing panache. This was the performance she was expected to deliver. But although she might be able to dress up and portray her, she also knew that Marielle Wing was never coming back.

CHAPTER NINETEEN

On the advice of her attorney, she and Francesca were staying in a suite at the Marriott at the Renaissance Center in downtown Detroit. Arthur McBride wanted her to be in a hotel with professional security staff, in addition to her personal bodyguard, and his firm's office was also located in the RenCen. He was paying the bill for the time being, asserting that, "By the time we get through suing the government, you won't have to worry about money ever again."

He found it significant that no one was filing charges against her, despite the fact she had shot and killed three men. He praised her for "taking control of the story." But those deaths weighed on her; she found herself thinking about those men, wanting to find out about them.

She'd called the Zen Center and tried to talk to Koryo about it. He had said it was their karma to die, her karma to kill them. How would she have to pay for her karma, she'd wondered.

"Maybe you already paid," he said.

The man she had first seen at JFK was named Beyer. Peter Beyer. He was employed by the NSA in a role that was classified, and he was, if not the originator, at least central to the bombing plot and the cover-up. How convenient that he was dead, Eddison had remarked; they could pin the whole thing on him, and he wasn't around to contradict them. She wondered if he'd been the one to write that manuscript and claim it was hers, or if he'd hired someone to do it. Some writer so relieved to be paid to write anything that he or she was willing to not think too hard about the nature of the task.

The RenCen was a city within a city, seventy-three stories, seven towers and over five million square feet. It had been built during the 1970s, when Detroit was spinning into decline. The building was a fortress against its environs. An alternative city for white people, Eddison claimed, after Detroit became majority Black.

Staying on the sixty-third floor at the RenCen was not like being in Detroit; even she could tell that much. Her floor-to-ceiling windows did give her a lovely view of the Detroit River far below, but she might as well have been watching it on the flat screen TV. The RenCen itself had restaurants, stores, a hair salon, a post office; it had been designed so that one never needed to go outside.

Despite McBride's warnings, Chiko was curious to see the city. Accompanied by Eddison, she and Francesca had toured the River Walk, spent hours at the Detroit Institute of Arts, and explored sections of downtown that had been renovated. What she learned was that it was possible to see Detroit as a functional city, with wide streets and shiny buildings and cultural events, but if you ventured even a few blocks in any direction beyond these restored blocks, you would find open fields where structures had been razed, interrupted only occasionally by a boarded-up building or burnt-out house. So many parts of the city were like Brightmoor. In some way she identified with the city—once an industrial powerhouse, now broken, abandoned, but feisty still.

"So if people weren't trying to kill me," she asked Eddison on one excursion, "would I be at risk walking around here?" They were on Woodward Avenue near the art museum.

He shrugged. "Probably not. There's a lot of security down here." He pointed up at some cameras she never would have noticed. "Some of the businesses hire their own plainclothes." His forehead creased as he thought it over more. "But, you never know. Sometimes stuff happens, you know, wrong place, wrong time." Yes, she knew about that.

He'd grown up in the city and would have been the ideal tour guide were he not being paid to guard her life. Given his mission, he resisted her pleas to see "the real Detroit."

"It doesn't get any more real than what you've already seen," he insisted.

Real or not, nothing in the city reminded her of any place she'd been before, and that fact in itself was comforting to her. Marielle Wing did not belong in Detroit, but perhaps Chiko did.

When she'd asked Eddison if he would be her security guard, he agreed right away. "You saved my life," he said to her, as if he owed her. But of course, he'd saved her life too. What responsibilities did she have? She made sure McBride was paying him well.

Fresh had insisted on staying with her in Detroit. "No way am I leaving you by yourself until this thing is over." Chiko wondered if it would ever be over.

Francesca remained unfathomably upbeat, and her visual sensibility was wildly stimulated by their surroundings. "Look at the Pewabic design," she'd say, craning her neck to examine the architecture of a building that had not succumbed to the wrecking ball.

Almost immediately after *The Today Show* aired, Marielle had been deluged with phone and email messages. They didn't come to her, of course; where she was staying was a closely held secret. McBride had registered both her and Francesca under assumed names. She could barely keep track anymore of what appellation she was supposed to answer to.

The phone calls and emails came for the most part to Araceli at the paper. Many were from fans—they wanted her to know how glad they were she was alive; they wanted to know when her next book would appear. A few wanted to know if she would blurb their forthcoming book, or help them find an agent. For all these messages Francesca composed a stock email response:

"Marielle Wing is grateful for your good wishes and appreciates your taking the time to convey them. Thank you."

But not everyone could be so efficiently dispatched.

Liana had been one of the first to call, the same day as Marielle's appearance on *The Today Show*. Araceli had forwarded the message from the office phone to Marielle's cell phone.

Babe, it was awesome to see you on Today. *I never believed you were dead, cuz I knew you wouldn't do me like that, just leave me with no scratch at all. By the way, do you think Darius Green wants to do a follow-up? Cuz it might be interesting to have people from your life, y'know, like me, come on and talk about you. I'd be totally up for doing that for you, so let me know, okay? Peace!*

She and Francesca had burst out laughing as they listened. "Good ol' Liana," Fresh said. "She's a giver."

There were random calls from colleagues, other writers who expressed their gratitude that she was not dead. Dudley Harris from PEN was downright effusive, although this did not move her to want to call him back.

What she hadn't expected so soon were the calls from development staff of studios, directors, and stars, descending like vultures to roadkill, desperate to option the rights to her story. Some were straightforward requests; others came with elaborate pitches. She asked Araceli to direct these to Arthur McBride, and she advised her attorney to tell people that no action on these offers would be taken until her legal situation was resolved. McBride's specialty was criminal law, not entertainment, and her heart ached for the loss of Reza. She had to keep at arm's length the knowledge that her attorney had died trying to protect her.

Confident as he appeared to be, even McBride seemed a little dazzled by the offers that came in. "I just got off the phone with Spielberg's people," he called to report. "They're prepared to give you the first crack at writing the script. Are you sure you don't want to just take a meeting?" He'd picked up the jargon right away.

Aside from her occasional forays around Detroit, all she really wanted to do was sleep. Marielle Wing had never been one to feel sorry for herself. She'd believed this a great virtue, but now she realized that Marielle's capacity to feel anything had been limited. So where did that leave her?

The RenCen also had a movie theater and sometimes she and Fresh and Eddison would go there in the afternoon; it didn't much matter what they saw. It reminded her of those first days in Witness Security when she'd spent days in the multiplex at the mall in Michigan, with Deputy Orellano a few rows behind her. As she had been then, she was just as happy now to sit in the dark coolness and let somebody else's story wash over her. Afterward, Francesca would want to talk about the director's perspective or the star's acting choices, and Eddison would critique the story for its lack of realism; one of them would ask her opinion and she'd look blank and have to confess she hadn't really been paying attention.

For the first week, Araceli called with an update nearly every day. More NSA officials were under investigation. The families of the suspects had filed a wrongful death suit against the government. Francesca had been inspired to enlist Araceli's aid because the reporter spent her days tracking down sources, people within Homeland Security, in National Security, the U.S. Marshals and the FBI. She talked to people who were close to Reza and people who knew the two men accused of the JFK bombing. Marielle could see Araceli's ambition was kindled; she believed this story could be "as big as Watergate." She ruefully remarked to Francesca that it would be Araceli who'd end up getting the Pulitzer, but she couldn't begrudge it. Perhaps that was her karma.

It was Araceli who'd learned that right after Marielle's death was announced last February, two men claiming to be from the government had showed up to talk to Liana. They'd maintained they were charged with helping to settle Marielle's estate, so of course, Liana was eager to talk to them. Her ex had spent most of the interview bemoaning the fact that the only thing Marielle cared about was her writing career. Perhaps this had given them the idea to announce the publication of a posthumous book, as a way of flushing her out. It had succeeded all too well.

About a week after her television interview, she got word from Araceli that Caroline Kilhane, her editor at Knopf, wanted to talk to her. She was prepared to treat it as she had the other calls, ignore it, but Fresh said, "I think you should call her."

"Why? She was complicit in the near publication of a fraud in Marielle's name. Not just a fraud, not just a bad book, but a death threat." She was surprised by the fervor in her voice.

"Maybe there's an explanation. Mar, she was devastated at your memorial. You worked with her for so many years; I think you should at least give her a chance."

Fresh had risked her own life for their friendship, had in all likelihood saved her life. And all she asked in return was for her to take a walk in the morning, go to the movies now and again, and give Carolyn Kilhane a chance to explain herself. Didn't she at least owe her that?

Francesca arranged for them to talk at the end of the day; Caroline wanted to be out of the office so she'd be able to talk more freely.

At six p.m. Marielle placed the call. The phone rang twice before she heard Caroline's New England accent.

"Caroline Kilhane," she answered, as she always did, in place of hello.

"Caroline, it's me." She could not say Marielle.

There was a slight pause, followed by a dismissive laugh. "Marielle, I'm so glad to talk to you. I can't believe this incredible turn of events! I was absolutely heartsick when I read your obituary; everyone at Knopf was so upset. Everyone in literature was upset! I can't begin to tell you how relieved we are."

She didn't feel inclined to help Caroline with the conversation. She just held the receiver and waited.

Then Caroline got right to the point. "I'm guessing you read about your supposed posthumous work."

Again she said nothing.

"I want to assure you I had nothing to do with it. That press release was placed in the *Times* before I ever saw it. My boss came to me and said, 'We're doing this.' I said, 'We can't' and he said, 'We are.'"

"Did he tell you why or who asked him to do it?"

"He said he was getting pressure from corporate, but he didn't specify from whom. I knew right away that it couldn't be your work. I knew what you'd been working on and I said so, but he made it clear that it wasn't up to me."

"Did you ever see the manuscript?"

"No. I didn't really believe there *was* a manuscript." Caroline was sounding a little less sure of herself.

Chiko wondered if Caroline realized that Reza had been killed for getting her a copy of that manuscript.

Instead she asked, without rancor, "Did it occur to you to quit your job?"

"Excuse me?"

"Did it occur to you to quit your job when you were asked to be a party to something unethical?"

There was a long pause, followed by a sigh. Then Caroline said, "I didn't see how that would help anything."

They were both quiet again.

"I just wanted you to know I wasn't trying to exploit you," Caroline tried again. "We've had such a long working relationship and I hope you know how much I admire you and your work. I hoped you might still consider working with me on future projects…"

"Caroline, tell me you did not contact me at this time to solicit business!"

"No, of course not. I understand this is a terribly hard time for you. You don't even sound like yourself." Caroline paused, as if weighing whether to continue. She did.

"But as your editor, or former editor, I hope you won't mind if I offer a word of advice. This experience you've had represents an extraordinary opportunity for you professionally. You've had a strong career as a literary novelist, Marielle, one envied by many authors. But here is a chance for the kind of stratospheric success you've always said you wanted. Someone is going to take this story and run with it. Don't regret later that it wasn't you."

Marielle would no doubt have leaped at this carrot being dangled before her, but if Caroline believed this little pep talk would turn *her* around, she was in for a disappointment.

She said nothing at all.

After a long moment, the editor got the message. "Well, this conversation has gone badly and I supposed I might have expected that it would. I meant to reach out in friendship, Marielle, that's all, and to try to set the record straight. I hope this matter resolves for you in a safe and satisfactory way. Really, Marielle, I wish you all the best."

"Thank you," she responded simply, then hung up.

She blinked a few times, trying to figure out how she felt. Outside the window, she could see a few boats traveling north along the Detroit River. She breathed deeply, the way Koryo had taught her in meditation.

She had just closed the door on her most longstanding and important professional relationship. She might once have imagined they *were* friends, but she knew better now; her friends were Eddison, Zenkei, and Koryo. And Fresh. She waited for the floor beneath to drop precipitously, for regret to bloom in her chest. Instead she found that she felt a little wave of relief; she was one step further from who she had been.

CHAPTER TWENTY

Nearly every day, Araceli filed another story in *The New York Times*. Marielle wanted to avoid the news, but she felt obligated to read her byline. It was from Araceli she learned the names of the men she'd killed—Evans and McCauliff and Dunham. A total of fifteen individuals had been implicated in the actual plot, but as Eddison commented, this did not include the parties who had the most to gain from it.

"Do you think that's everyone?" she asked Araceli by phone.

"Probably not. I'm still working on some leads tying this to people higher up." Of course, she wouldn't implicate anyone until she had solid evidence.

Araceli reported that Balian and Musafian had been supposed to deliver ten suitcases to the terminal. The two unknowing conspirators had decided at the last minute to kick back and make it easier on themselves, not bring them all at once. They'd delivered the first four and planned to go back for the rest. The agent in charge of triggering the detonation—he was now in custody, Araceli said—had done so when he saw them put down the first load; his visual cue was the men, not the bags. Had all ten suitcases blown up at the same time, the explosion would have certainly created greater loss of life, including the two young men and, most likely, Marielle.

Lucky. She had been lucky.

"And what do you know about Reza's death?" Chiko asked her. She sat cross-legged on her unmade bed in the sterile hotel room.

"They were already watching Reza; they knew she'd been there the day you went into witness security," Araceli said. "They'd been putting the squeeze on her for a while but until you gave her your address, she had nothing to give them."

"But why did they have to kill her?"

"It was Reza who alerted Donald Watkins that other agents had been in touch with her about you. That's how he knew your security had been breached."

Of course, Reza would be heroic. She'd always moved through the world as if she were invincible. She'd taken care of Altovese. She'd tried to take care of Lorraine. But who had been looking out for her?

She could hear in Araceli's voice that she was ready to hang up. Congress was moving to impeach the president and calling for the resignation of the head of the NSA. This was her story now and she needed to stay ahead of it.

But there was one more thing she wanted to know. "What about Magda?"

"Musafian's girlfriend. She's eight months pregnant. In the country on an expired student visa. But given the legal proceedings, they're not moving too quickly to deport her."

So she was a person after all, not an acronym. Chiko recalled the day she'd been convinced that Tuna's grandmother might be the head of a terrorist ring. She tried now to imagine this young woman, far from her home, soon to give birth in world that had spun out of control. How scared she must be. How lonely. "Once there's a settlement maybe you could help me get in touch with her," she said to Araceli. "I'd like to see if I can help her out."

* * *

"So when will I have to testify?" she asked McBride a few days later. They were meeting in High Bar on the seventy-first floor of the RenCen. McBride did not like talking about the case outside her hotel room or his law office but she argued that she couldn't just spend all her time in her room. He was having a scotch; she was sipping grapefruit juice and soda. She didn't seem to want alcohol these days.

"Someone from the Justice Department will be here in a week or so to interview you. But they're trying to investigate this and manage a constitutional crisis at the same time, so I can't predict when it might go to trial."

"What am I supposed to do?"

"Just keep your head down and try to be patient."

"Easy for you to say," she snapped.

His shrug acknowledged the unfairness of it all. This terrible chain of events would likely take years to resolve. This was her life now.

She recalled something Koryo had said during his talk that first night she was at the meditation center. She was surprised to remember it; she'd been so out of her body that evening. But she heard his words again: *Peace within begins when we accept exactly how things are.*

This *was* her life now. She breathed that in.

"So who am I now?" she asked McBride. "Do I exist?"

"I've been talking to the Justice Department about it. There's plenty of precedent where an individual has been declared dead—in a war, say, or when they've gone missing—and then legally reinstated once it's confirmed they are still alive. We'll have to go through some court proceedings, but before too long you'll be able to reclaim all your assets and resume your life as Marielle Wing."

"What if I don't want to be her anymore? Can I change my name?"

"I wouldn't advise you to do that, Marielle. What about your career, your reputation?"

She didn't feel like confiding in her attorney that those things no longer meant to her what they once had.

Seeing that she wasn't convinced he continued, "And I certainly wouldn't want you to do anything to further complicate the matter of your identity until this case is resolved."

She felt no enthusiasm at the prospect of being Marielle Wing again. She had no heart for trying to crawl back inside that life. She didn't want to peddle her nightmare to the highest bidder or worry that some stupid prize committee had stiffed her. She didn't know if she even believed in writing books anymore. Rather than creating fictional characters, she thought her time would be better spent in figuring out who she really was.

* * *

Later that evening, she recounted her meeting with Arthur McBride to Fresh. "It sounds like it could be months if not years before this goes to trial. We're in limbo."

They were sprawled on the overstuffed loveseat in the suite, having demolished a plate of artichokes they had ordered from room service. The scent of garlic rose from the heap of discarded leaves.

Francesca gazed out the darkened windows as she processed this news. Her mouth was pursed as if she wanted to say something but was hesitant to do so.

Chiko had always been able to read her. "What?"

Francesca looked down at her lap. "I'm supposed to have an exhibition in October." Then she squared her shoulders as her eyes sought Chiko's. "Ordinarily I would just get Ernesto to handle the installation, but the truth is—" She paused before continuing, "I haven't finished making the work. I couldn't make myself paint when I thought you were dead and even after I got your card, when I didn't know where you were or what had happened."

Chiko felt as if the floor was giving way beneath her but stayed quiet.

"I can't bear to leave you," Fresh said, "but I don't know what good I'm doing you by being here."

"You're the reason I get up in the morning," Chiko protested, her voice tight. "You're the reason I'm still here." To her own ears she sounded pleading and desperate, something Marielle would never have allowed herself.

And while these sentiments were true, Chiko knew Fresh needed more in her life than to be somebody's reason for living. Although Marielle's ambition may have been extinguished, Fresh's had not. It wasn't fair to expect her to give up the career she had worked so hard for just to babysit a small tiger.

"You need to go home," Chiko said then. "You need to be in your life. And I need to figure out what my life is going to be now." As she said the words, she knew the absolute truth of them. Their veracity pulsed in the silence that followed.

Fresh regarded her for a long moment to see if she meant it. They had always been honest with each other. Finally, she nodded, comprehending and accepting Chiko's resolve.

"I'll come back," Fresh assured her. "The minute something happens in the case. Or if you need me—"

It was Chiko's turn to nod; she knew this was true. Why, then, did it feel like the end of something?

She reached over to wipe a fleck of butter from her friend's lip. It seemed natural to pop it into her own mouth. Then she cupped Fresh's cheek in her hand. It felt so familiar, so soft; her body grew warm at the touch. She had been an idiot to blow up their relationship all those years ago. Perhaps Fresh had offered the promise of more intimacy, more genuine connection, than Marielle was capable of then. So, she'd pursued Liana instead.

Staring deep into her friend's eyes, caressing her face, Chiko searched for a sign of opening to the connection they'd once shared. But some actions can never be undone. What she saw, reflected on her friend's face, was that although Fresh had been willing to risk her life for her, although their bond was profound and unshakeable, a romance between them would never again be an option. Koryo might say this was her karma.

* * *

The next afternoon, Fresh had made her flight reservations for the weekend. She would drive Armando's car, which she'd had repaired and detailed, back to Chicago and fly back to Los Angeles on Sunday night. Then she booked an appointment for a pedicure at the salon, and invited Chiko to join her. Chiko declined, saying she had a headache.

The truth was, Chiko was plotting to go out on her own. This was strictly against the rules McBride had set down. She told Francesca she was going to stay in the room and sleep. She told Eddison she was going to the salon with Fresh; they wouldn't leave the building, she promised.

She just needed to be out in the world on her own. She couldn't live in such narrow confines, not just the physical space, but the psychological restriction of always being accompanied by someone else. She was accustomed to spending a lot of time alone, navigating the world as her imagination guided her. She'd always craved a high degree of intellectual stimulation and her current circumstances were not providing it.

She wanted more than a mediated view of Detroit—sterile office towers, the cleaned-up parts, the affluent façade like a Potemkin village.

Being careful of the wound in her arm, which had not yet entirely closed, she slid into a pair of jeans, a Detroit Tigers T-shirt she'd asked Eddison to bring her, simple walking shoes. Her head was covered in stubble; her hair was growing in, but silver, not gold. Francesca kept pestering her to bleach it blond, but she kept protesting there wasn't enough hair to bother with yet. Surveying herself in the mirror, she looked like a not very well-off tourist from a not very fashion-conscious part of the country who was perhaps recovering from chemotherapy. *Works for me.*

She grabbed her purse, though it contained almost nothing. The bulk of her cash and papers were in the safe in her attorney's office, thirteen floors down and two towers over. She had a couple of twenties tucked inside, some Chapstick and her go-phone. She slid the key card to the hotel room into the back pocket of her jeans.

Chiko figured she had about an hour to go exploring and get back before either Fresh or Eddison knew what she'd been up to. If she didn't get caught she'd be able to do this again. She took the elevator down to the walkway that connected one building to another and exited the complex through one of the other towers, just in case the concierge had been alerted to keep an eye on her.

She didn't really have a plan about where she would go, but she decided to walk in a direction she hadn't seen yet. It was a rare—she was learning—cloudless day in Detroit and the sun was hot on her bare head. Maybe she'd get a hat.

She'd been driven past Campus Martius Park but decided today to see it on foot, heading up Woodward Avenue. This was one of those areas of Detroit into which resources had been invested to make it nice—green space, food stalls, tables and chairs to eat. Lots of private security, Eddison had told her. This part of downtown drew white workers who commuted in from the suburbs, along with African American residents and tourists. It was the tail end of lunchtime and the park still had lots of people in it. She stopped at a stall and bought a tall cup of lemonade packed with ice. Sucking on the straw she tasted a hint of ginger. She could have just stayed there and relaxed in the shade of a tree, watched people go by, but she felt a surge of energy and kept walking until she reached Grand River, then turned west.

Eddison had explained once that the city was laid out in a half circle, the Detroit River being its boundary. The major arteries in Detroit radiated out from the downtown like the spokes of a wheel. Woodward went to the north. Grand River Avenue to the west. On the other side of the river was Canada. Canada. Just a couple of weeks ago she'd thought that's where she should go, but when she and Fresh walked along the river in the mornings, Windsor did not call to her.

For a few blocks there were buildings, like a regular city, though only some of them appeared to be occupied. A few more blocks and the built environment rapidly began to thin out; over to her left an enormous casino dominated the landscape. As she crossed a freeway overpass the terrain that stretched before her grew more sparsely inhabited. Whole blocks along this major thoroughfare had only a single building, often boarded up. Everything else had been razed and either covered in concrete or allowed to return to prairie. The further she walked from the downtown center, the less tended were the streets and the scant structures that remained. It began to look more like Brightmoor.

A few cars drove by, but fewer than you'd expect on a weekday in Michigan's largest city. No one was walking or bicycling or waiting for a bus. She walked for a long time and didn't see any buses. It was eerie, as if some disaster had wiped out this area, just a short walk from downtown.

Squinting at her Timex, she realized it was past time to head back. She didn't want to worry Francesca, and she didn't want her friend to decide she couldn't be left alone. She liked being out by herself, free to discover and measure herself against this new environment.

But she'd also walked much longer than she ever did with Francesca, and perhaps longer than her still-recuperating body was ready for. She felt dizzy, a little overcome by heat and the glare that reflected off all the bare concrete. Her arm was starting to throb. In another city she would have hailed a cab to take her back to the hotel, but she was pretty sure she might wait for hours or days on this stretch and not see a cab go by. She could call Eddison and confess, ask him to come get her, but she was still hoping she might get away with this.

She turned around to head back east on Grand River; there was no compelling reason to walk on the other side of the street, no stores to peer into, nothing new to see. When two young men stepped onto the sidewalk from she wasn't sure where, she was at first glad to see them, other beings inhabiting this desolate landscape. They could have been in their late teens or early twenties; the taller one had a sprinkling of pimples on his nose and cheeks. It was the shorter one, his head covered in neat cornrows, who stepped too close to her. She could smell coconut oil on his hair as he poked something into her ribs.

"You're just gonna give us that purse," he said in a tone that almost sounded friendly.

She looked at him in disbelief. Her purse? Her purse with $35 and no wallet and no credit cards and no ID? He had no idea who she was, just some white lady where she didn't belong, easy pickings. But what could he take from her?

They must have thought she was thinking about resisting because the other one said, "You best hand it over now." Like he was giving her a useful piece of advice.

She glanced briefly at the deserted block. There was nowhere to run to, even if she could run. No one was going to stop for her. She recalled all she'd read about the understaffed police in Detroit, their slow response times.

The short one grabbed her wounded arm, and she bit her lip to keep from crying out. "Let's go, lady."

Willing her voice calm, she said, "Or what? You're gonna shoot me? Somebody already did." She pulled up the sleeve of her T-shirt, baring her shoulder, the bruise and the wound. "You're gonna kill me? Well, somebody already did that too. You shoot me, you're killing a dead woman."

With her good arm she threw the purse as far as she could. It landed perhaps ten feet from her, but it was enough that the two stepped away from her to scoop up her bag.

The taller guy said to her, "Bitch, you crazy," as the two men began to run past her, heading west into the desolation of Grand River Avenue.

She slumped to the pavement, feeling its heat against the thin denim of her jeans. Panting, she watched the two figures disappear into the wasted landscape, like dark birds swallowed by the sky.

She remembered that afternoon at JFK in February, when she'd seen two men running after the explosion in the American Airlines terminal. She realized now that nobody knew any longer where they were going or how their story was going to turn out. No matter how they ran, nor how she ran, none of them could elude the inevitable future waiting to devour them.

CHAPTER TWENTY-ONE

Some of the houses on the tree-lined block were decorated for Halloween—skeletons hung from tree limbs, construction-paper spiders and cats lurked behind glass panes, and of course pumpkins on porch steps sported toothy grins. This holiday had never seemed quite convincing in Los Angeles; it required a nip of frost in the air, the crunch of yellow leaves underfoot.

She'd needed a map to guide her car to back this neighborhood; the last time she'd been here it was summer. Now the leaves on the old maples were gold and red. Once she passed the small park, she had no trouble finding the red brick house with lavender trim, even though it was past dusk. Prayer flags, a little tattered now, still fluttered on the evening breeze.

She felt a stirring of excitement as she parked the car and started up the walk. Then she hesitated. She half wondered if she should go back and sit on the bench in the park, as she had done, soaking wet, four months ago. Should she wait on the bench for Zenkei to find her on his evening walk with Hakue? Or could the old dog even make that walk any longer, especially with the weather turning colder?

Before she could decide what to do, she heard an engine, and Koryo's VW bug pulled from the street into the driveway. He didn't wait to pull the car into the garage but stopped the instant he saw her.

The warmth of his smile took her by surprise as he stepped from the car to greet her. She'd once thought of him as "the stern monk," but there was nothing harsh in his demeanor now. Pressing his hands together at his chest, he bowed and said, "Chiko, you are here!"

She grinned at the reference to her "nun" name. Her hair was growing back; it was about an inch-and-a-half long now and, upon Francesca's advice, she'd been gelling it into little spikes. Its silver made her feel her age; Marielle would have bleached it back to blond, but she'd resisted. One thing the last nine months had cost her was her vanity.

Koryo gestured for her to follow him up the concrete steps and into the house. "Zenkei," he called, "come see who's here."

The second monk came through the kitchen door, guiding the yellow lab that moved toward her at a halting pace. Right beside the dog, as though herding her, was Dude.

She hardly knew which to embrace first. She dropped to her knees and scooped up her cat; she knew he was glad to see her because he tolerated her hold for about ten seconds before kicking away with his back legs to signal he wanted to be put down.

As she let him go, she reached for Hakue's large head and planted a kiss on the top of it. She marveled anew at how comforting she found this animal's presence.

Zenkei came toward her then and, without regard for protocol, she threw her arms around him, almost pulling the slight man off his feet. He laughed and patted her back.

Then Koryo shooed them into the kitchen, where he poured cups of tea and served them around the table. She sat on the chair beside the dog's bed—strange how she thought of it as *her* chair at this table—and Hakue flopped down beside her with a contented sigh. Dude jumped up and curled his body into her lap; paws began to knead the fleece of her terra-cotta sweatshirt as he stared into her face. In the past Marielle would have stopped him, but she didn't now. Instead she cupped her hand over his face, and he rubbed and rubbed his nose against her fingers.

Koryo then set a sea-green platter arrayed with delicate cookies in the middle of the table.

"I can see he's happy you're here," Zenkei teased him, "because he only bring out cookies on special occasion."

She nodded her thanks to the tall monk. The first time she'd been in this kitchen, months ago, she'd been numb with anxiety. Now she felt at home, as comfortable as she'd felt anywhere in a long time.

After her robbery experience downtown, she'd put her foot down with McBride. "I don't want to live in a hotel or an armed fortress," she told him. "I don't want to feel like I can't go outside. I don't have it in me to be afraid anymore." Using the cash she had on hand, she'd bought a once-grand, now falling-down house in Midtown. McBride had been opposed to the whole idea but relented when Eddison agreed to move into an apartment in the attic; his uncles were helping with the renovations. Fresh called every few days to see how she was doing and periodically checked in with Eddison to get his take on her.

Chiko occupied her days working on the house, sitting with the carpenters and masonry experts and getting them to tell her stories as they worked. She went to physical therapy to rehabilitate her shoulder. She went to the library. And she'd been doing some volunteer work, planting trees with The Greening of Detroit and teaching writing to teens through a program called InsideOut. The people she met now didn't know her story, or if they did, it wasn't important to them.

She felt no pressure from them to talk about the Justice Department investigation or the progress of the lawsuit. She found that the more she focused on those events, the worse she felt. She'd stopped reading Araceli's articles in *The New York Times*; in fact, she'd stopped following the news altogether, something she would have once found unimaginable. Still, she could not escape the car radio, or the flat-screen TV in a restaurant. The president had not resigned, although his party was expected to be resoundingly defeated in the next election. The head of the NSA had resigned, only to be replaced by another of his ilk.

Arthur McBride had succeeded in restoring her identity; in her purse she carried a driver's license and a passport with Marielle's name and Social Security number. She would have to keep this name until the legal proceedings were finished. After that she would petition to change her name; she didn't yet know to what. Maybe she would keep Chiko and find a suitable last name.

Occasionally she would talk to people she used to know, people whom Marielle would have considered friends. They pressed her to tell them what she was going to do, and assumed it had to be something important, but when she tried to look into her future the picture remained blank. She knew she did not want to return to the life she'd lived before. She didn't think she would return to live in Los Angeles. Detroit suited her for now, the sense of horror at its decay alongside optimism about its possibilities. Pronounced dead yet refusing to surrender.

So far she hadn't been moved to write; the space where her imagination had once resided felt hollow to her now, even though Fresh believed she might feel differently after more time had passed.

It was odd to be in her fifties and have no sense of what she wanted to do. But she no longer wanted to invent a life, a persona, a plot for herself. If it turned out that there was any blessing in what had happened to her, it would be that she now wanted to meet each day as the thing she had once dreaded, an empty page.

This was the first time she'd been back to Ann Arbor since the summer, though she'd talked to the monks a few times. They did not ask her how she was or what she intended to do; they just sat with her in a grinning silence that seemed to strip away the clatter of everyday concerns. She sank into it as into a warm bath, lulled by the vibration of Dude's purring against her chest, the soft snores arising from Hakue's deep slumber, the steam of the tea rising from her cup.

Tonight she would stay in Ann Arbor, not at the Twin Pines nor the truck stop motel, but at a little inn not far from where the monks lived. Tomorrow she would go to Farmington to visit Garland Macpherson. She wanted to apologize for the chaos she'd brought into his life, and let him know how much his companionship had meant to her during those lonely days when she'd been Lorraine. She was looking forward to seeing him again.

A clock chime alerted them it was time to set up for the evening meditation service. She told the monks she would clear away the dishes while they set up the room. As she rinsed each cup, she grew more nervous. She contemplated staying in the kitchen for the rest of the evening, but Zenkei returned and shooed her out.

Walking the length of the hallway, she entered the meditation room from the back. Almost immediately she saw the bloom of dreadlocks above Tuna's tall frame. Her back was to her, and she had one arm draped loosely around her grandmother, who wore a lavender caftan.

The little explosion of feeling that went off in her solar plexus made her feel foolish. Heat rose on her cheeks. She was fifty-four; Tuna was twenty-nine. She was torn between the impulse to hide from her and wanting nothing more than to see her face. But Tuna would not want to see *her*, she was certain. As Lorraine, she had used her, lied to her, and abandoned her to the Feds. She didn't expect Tuna to forgive her, but she'd deserved better, and she hoped she'd give her the chance to tell her that.

Koryo chimed the bells that called everyone to order. She took a chair in the back. Tuna sank to a cushion up front, while her grandmother sat a few rows in front of her. Tuna never turned around. Chiko tried to calm her ragged breath.

Tonight it was Zenkei who gave the talk. This surprised her; when she'd been here this summer she thought she understood that Koryo had a position of superiority. Zenkei's talk was about the blessings that could come from even the most terrible hardship.

"In the war," he was saying, "so many die. My sisters die, my parents. Aunts and uncles. Neighbors. So much death. I pray to die too, to be with my family again. I didn't know then that I would come to United States. That I would meet Koryo, and Hakue, and all of you good people. That I would live in this house and have the chance to keep improving myself."

She wondered if he was saying all this because she was there. But Francesca had told her it was like that whenever she went to meditate, that the words seemed to be chosen specifically because she needed to hear them.

"It's not enough to 'get over' those hardships. It's not enough to 'forgive' the people who seem to bring them. Better we should go to our knees and give thanks for them, bless them, for the obstacle always contains the path, and destruction always carries the seeds of rebuilding."

He transitioned the group into meditation then, and although she followed the breath pattern well enough, tears washed down her cheeks. She made no effort to wipe them away. Something in her believed Zenkei's words, believed that everything was now possible.

When the meditation was over and the closing chants had been performed, she made herself remain in her chair. She used the breathing technique the monks had taught her and just sat, as everyone else got up and begin to converse with one another in the room.

She felt it when Tuna's gaze fell on her and lifted her eyes to meet hers. From across the room Tuna smiled, a little cautiously, and she returned the smile with a rueful grin.

Bella Books, Inc.

Women. Books. Even Better Together.

P.O. Box 10543

Tallahassee, FL 32302

Phone: (800) 729-4992

www.BellaBooks.com

More Titles from Bella Books

Hunter's Revenge – Gerri Hill
978-1-64247-447-3 | 276 pgs | paperback: $18.95 | eBook: $9.99
Tori Hunter is back! Don't miss this final chapter in the acclaimed Tori Hunter series.

Integrity – E. J. Noyes
978-1-64247-465-7 | 28 pgs | paperback: $19.95 | eBook: $9.99
It was supposed to be an ordinary workday...

The Order – TJ O'Shea
978-1-64247-378-0 | 396 pgs | paperback: $19.95 | eBook: $9.99
For two women the battle between new love and old loyalty may prove more dangerous than the war they're trying to survive.

Under the Stars with You – Jaime Clevenger
978-1-64247-439-8 | 302 pgs | paperback: $19.95 | eBook: $9.99
Sometimes believing in love is the first step. And sometimes it's all about trusting the stars.

The Missing Piece – Kat Jackson
978-1-64247-445-9 | 250 pgs | paperback: $18.95 | eBook: $9.99
Renee's world collides with possibility and the past, setting off a tidal wave of changes she could have never predicted.

An Acquired Taste – Cheri Ritz
978-1-64247-462-6 | 206 pgs | paperback: $17.95 | eBook: $9.99
Can Elle and Ashley stand the heat in the *Celebrity Cook Off* kitchen?

Printed in the USA
CPSIA information can be obtained
at www.ICGtesting.com
JSHW022317080424
60844JS00001B/2

9 781642 475142